# BLACK SWAN AFFAIR

K.L. KREIG

Black Swan Affair

Copyright © 2016 by K. L. Kreig

Published by K. L. Kreig

Print (alternate cover) ISBN-13: 978-1-943443-38-3

Cover Art by Veronica Larsen

Editing by Nikki Busch Editing

Published in the United States of America.

*To everyone who has loved and lost then loved again. It's there. You just need to be open to it.*

# PREFACE

The **Black Swan Theory** is a metaphor describing an event that comes as a surprise, results in major impact to the environment or our personal lives, and tends to be rationalized after the fact with the benefit of hindsight. Because we're humans, we try to invent explanations for an occurrence that doesn't necessarily have one, so it makes sense to our small brains. We try to use that event and those explanations to predict future events like it. To learn from them. Deal with them better, maybe. Stop them from happening again, I suppose.

In the sixteenth century, when the phrase itself was coined, the black swan was presumed an impossibility, assumed not to exist. Therefore the *Black Swan Theory* in and of itself has no merit.

But impossibilities *do* exist. I am living proof of the **Black Swan Theory** and that sometimes there is no rationalizing events away. There is no simplifying the complex. Some things happen simply because they happen. And in the end knowing why doesn't change a damn thing anyway. The damage is already done.

~ Maverick DeSoto Shepard, 2016

**M**y gown sells false truths. Makeup covers the lies. Fake smiles and soft words divert and deceive. Three carats on my left hand blind all, except me.

I know the truth.

I take myself in, from the perfectly coifed hair to the French-manicured toes peeking out from my sling-back shoes. I stare at myself in the full-length mirror, not recognizing the superficial woman staring back.

A frown turns down the corner of her mouth. Condemnation clouds her unusual green eyes. Sorrow plays in the thin lines on her face and in the slight slump of her bare shoulders.

She's judging me.

She should.

I'm a horrible, awful person.

In less than ten minutes, I will let my father walk me down an aisle lined with fresh flowers and silk bows tacked onto the corners of every other pew.

I will reach the end, let Daddy kiss my cheek with tears blurring his vision, and give me away to another man.

I will take my fiancé's hand in mine, gaze into his puppy dog eyes overflowing with joy, and betroth myself for life to someone who is noble and loyal and kind.

I will promise to love, honor, and cherish him all the days of my life.

I will exchange in-sickness-and-in-health-forever vows in front of

God, our family, and friends to a great man out of spite and revenge. A ploy. As a giant fuck-you to the man I really love but can't have.

I will marry a man I genuinely respect the hell out of and love... but just as my very best friend.

Who does that?

A destructive, selfish bitch. That's who.

I let my gaze fall down the length of my body, trailing over the hand-beaded lace wedding dress that hugs my rounded curves. The same dress my best friend sobbed over the second I walked out of the dressing room, telling me *"that's the one."*

I didn't pick blush or ivory or cream or even something unconventional like gray.

Oh no. I went with stark white.

The symbol of purity.

A satirical laugh escapes my scarlet-painted lips.

I'm anything but innocent. My soul is lost. My heart cold. I'm a devil in angel's skin, trapping a man for life who could have any woman he wants but for some reason wants me.

And why?

Because I'm a masochist, I guess. Though I should be running as far away as possible, I can't seem to do anything but run in the direction of the one man I've loved my entire life: his brother.

The only man I truly want even though he betrayed me in the worst possible way.

*There's still time, Maverick. Do the right thing.*

I should call it off. Tell Kael this was all just a big mistake. Confess I'm not in love with him the way a wife should be. Tell him the entire time I'll be saying my vows, I'll be picturing his brother standing in front of me instead. Let him find true love because he'll never be that for me.

Fuck me.

I might as well write my own ticket to hell. If I go through with this, that's exactly where I'll burn for eternity. I already feel the flames of deceit licking the soles of my feet.

*Do the right thing for once in your godforsaken life, Mavs.*

I find my eyes in the mirror once again. I already know I won't listen to that small part of me that begs to be righteous. I can't. The bigger part of me is contaminated with retribution and anger and the need to hurt *him* just a little. The only way I'd call this off is if—

A knock on the door startles me and I jump.

It's time.

Fuck. *It's time.*

I take a calming breath in. Blow it out slowly. Turning away from my deceitful eyes, I make my way to the door and open it after only a brief hesitation, expecting to find my father on the other side.

But instead of graying hair and deep laugh lines framing a soft smile, I'm greeted with a melted dark chocolate stare and thin, angry lips.

He's here.

My "if" has arrived.

"Killian?" I breathe, hope rising in me like a tidal wave. I discreetly pinch my arm to make sure this isn't a dream. Nope. I look both ways down the hall to find we're alone. "What are you doing here?"

He steps inside and closes the door. Then he gets right in my space, grabbing my face between his monstrous hands. My soul sighs, and I close my eyes to focus on the touch I've been paralyzed without.

This is happening.

It's *really* happening.

He's come for me at last. It's almost too late, but that doesn't even matter.

He's here.

*Kiss me, kiss me, kiss me,* I silently scream.

When I don't feel his lips on mine, I pry my lids open. Killian's staring at me with turmoil on his face. My heart sinks. He's standing here, touching me, yet a whole gulf still separates us.

"I love you," I vomit.

It's the same words I spoke to him on his own wedding day two years ago. To my sister.

I begged him to choose *me*. Love *me*. Marry *me*.

But he butchered me, marrying her instead.

"Don't do this, Small Fry," he pleads, his voice strained. "I'm begging you not to do this."

I used to love that endearment...now I fucking *hate* it. Every time he says it, it reminds me exactly what he thinks of me.

"Leave her," I demand. "Tell me you'll leave her and I won't."

His face screws up. His eyes close. His head drops heavy on his neck. It's the same response he always gives me.

*He's not here for you, Maverick. He never is.*

I yank out of his hold, pushing him away. The half sandwich I ate an hour ago threatens to make a reappearance. "Get out," I choke, stabbing my finger toward the door.

He squares his broad shoulders, standing to every inch of his six feet. "You're being reckless and immature. You're not in love with him."

"Fuck you. You don't know shit." He hates it when I curse. Says it's "unladylike." Well, fuck him and the fucking gentlemanly horse he fucking rode in on. Fuck has now become my favorite fucking word.

"Maverick..."

"Don't," I whisper, close to breaking, which I swore I would never do in front of him again. "Unless you're here to finally admit you married the wrong sister then just get the fuck out."

"Just wait. That's all I'm asking."

"*Wait?* Wait for what, Killian? Wait for you to grow back the balls Jilly cut off and tucked under her pillow? Wait for you to tell her that you know what my pussy tastes like or how you can't forget that I made you come harder than you have in your life when I deep throated you? Wait for you to confess that all you can think about is fucking me and you can't stand the very sight of her in your bed? Wait until she gets hit by a car so you're free to be with me? Tell me...what *exactly* is it I'm supposed to wait for?"

"You're being crude and petulant." My eyes track the crossing of his arms. I hate that I throb in my very center, knowing what every muscle and ridge under that tux feels like. *Tastes* like.

"Well...bleeding out on the inside tends to make me snarky and bitter."

His clean-shaven jaw clenches and his stare turns flinty. He's here begging me not to marry his brother, but that's all I'll get. Sorrys, empty promises, no commitment. Nothing. Always nothing.

A wave of incredible—almost debilitating—sadness washes over and through me, threatening to drown me in a lifetime of permanent sorrow at the prospect of being without him in the way we both want.

I don't get it. I don't understand how we got here...to *this* very moment. I don't know where the wheels fell off, changing our course or why he won't just admit he made a mistake marrying someone who treats him like a worthless pile of shit.

Killian Shepard loves *me*. He always has, and that's not the neurotic projection of a psychotic woman feeding into her own mental illness. It's true. It's *always* been true. Which makes his own farce of a marriage to my sister all the more confusing. She must have a golden fucking vagina and mind-altering powers. Could be. I haven't met a bigger witch than my sister, Jillian.

"You need to leave." *Before I drop to my knees and make a bigger fool out of myself than I already have.*

He opens his mouth to no doubt try some other tactic to get me to change my mind, but the voice of my father bellows from behind him.

"Shep, there you are. You need to get back up with the guys."

Neither of us moves. I feel frozen, dead. Empty.

"Ready, Tenderheart?"

I cringe inwardly at my father's childhood nickname for me. How ironic that he gave me a boy's name but tries constantly to turn me into a lady. It's a lost cause I wish he'd just give up on.

"Yes, Daddy," I answer evenly, my eyes never leaving Killian's.

*Don't let this happen*, they beg.

*Don't make me choose*, I assume he replies.

*Fuck you*, I say. *Fuck you and your misplaced honor.*

I see Daddy's head peek around Killian's broad frame. "Come on, sweetie, almost showtime." *How apt.* I couldn't put on a bigger fucking sad play than if I'd scripted it myself. I catch his joyous eyes lined deeply with wrinkles and adoration and smile as brightly as I can while I let myself mourn inside.

Then, I skirt around Killian Shepard, take my father's hand, and leave him behind, wondering how you go about falling *out* of love with one man and *in* love with another. I've tried for years and still haven't mastered it.

I can't breathe.

Literally.

There is no air.

I suck gulps.

It's pointless. All I hear is pathetic wheezing and my future breaking into pieces.

Black edges my vision, the inky rings drawing me under.

My head falls between my splayed legs in an attempt to get closer to the floor, where I pray the blessed darkness takes me at long last. I want her to. If he dies, I don't want to live.

Oh, God.

This can't be happening. *Why* is this happening? Why aren't the doctors coming out? It's been six hours.

*That can't be good, can it?*

Distant buzzing fills my head, getting louder by the second.

*You deserve this, Mavs,* she whispers sweetly in my ear.

Karma, that ruthless bitch. Her saccharine tenor cuts through the incessant ringing with clarity.

*You caused this. You deserve this.*

Do I?

I don't know. Maybe. Maybe this is the only way to atone for past indiscretions and sins. Losing the one person in this world I hold most dear. I start sobbing uncontrollably, my cries muffled by my position.

"Maverick, calm down," he says sternly beside me. He reaches for my hand, but his touch burns. I jerk away, hissing like an infected animal ready to attack.

"Hey," he says softer this time. The gentle, calming tone I've heard my entire life echoes loudly off these four bland white walls that hold chaos, suffering, and shattered lives. It sounds like nails being driven into my ears. "It's going to be okay. *He's* going to be okay."

*Okay?*

*O-fucking-kay?*

He was shot! Gunned down by a fucking lunatic at work, and he's telling me everything is going to be okay in that eerily calm voice like I'm ten years old and my gerbil just died.

I hate him. I hate that *he's* here, talking, breathing, *living*, and the man I want more than anything is fighting to come back to me.

"Just breathe. Nice and slow. You're going to pass out."

His hand lands on my shoulder and squeezes lovingly, reassuringly.

I snap.

I jump up and lose it. "I don't want you here." My voice is strangely even but poisonous. "This is your fault."

My behavior is irrational, but how does one react when the love of her life is fighting for his? I need to transfer the bone-crushing agony and debilitating fear that's threatening to overtake me. I'm suffocating. Drowning slowly in heart-wrenching torment and a lifetime of regrets and wrong decisions.

We haven't had enough time. Not nearly enough.

His mouth drops open then closes. Without a word he stands, grabs my shoulders, and forces me back down into the hard plastic chair I've been occupying for hours and hours. I don't even feel it anymore. My body is as numb as my soul. Kneeling in front of me, he takes my hands, grips tight, and just breathes with me.

My shoulders shake with silent terror and morbid thoughts. Tiny stings of misery run in droves down my face. They hurt. *I* hurt. Every part of me hurts. I take it back. I'm not numb. I'm nothing but a distorted ball of pain.

The past pelts me as I struggle to remember every touch, every word, every memory. There are so many. So many.

Our lives are eternally interwoven. Our futures together already penned. They have been since the day of my birth.

*He can't die.*

We were just starting our lives together. The way it was meant to be.

I can't go on without my soul mate.

I bore my watery gaze into the man in front of me, the one who loves me so much, and spit venomous, hateful words. Words I don't mean but can't call back now that they're out. "I wish it was you," I say heartlessly, callously.

I ignore the hurt in his eyes. Hurt my words inflicted. He's already devastated enough after how things ended between us weeks ago, and here I am...adding to it with my heartless tantrum.

I wish I could make myself care.

I am destroyed. I will never survive this if he's taken from me.

"If it would save you even a moment of pain, Maverick, then so do I," is his quiet, sincere reply.

He doesn't move. He doesn't release his grasp, even the tiniest bit. He's holding me here, tethering me to a place I'm not sure I want to be a part of anymore.

He doesn't move, so neither do I.

We both sit just like this, leaning on each other, praying like we've never prayed before.

I park my car in the desolate, dim parking lot, turn the key to the off position, and sit there for a few moments, gathering my wits for the day ahead. The glint of my wedding set catches in the streetlight, drawing my eye. I hold my hand out and study it, ignoring the French manicure that's now grown out.

It's stunning. A near flawless three-carat cushion cut surrounded by a carat of pavé diamonds, all set in platinum. The wedding band boasts another two carats of round diamonds that span the entire length of the circle.

It was bought with love. It was given with trust. Neither of which I deserve.

I stare at the expensive piece still in disbelief that I did this.

I'm married.

*Married.*

To Kael Shepard.

My best friend since I could walk.

Brother to the man I really want.

I am now Mrs. Shepard. Ironic. It's the name I've always wanted. This just isn't exactly how I pictured getting it.

I can't recall a single second of my wedding day after I walked out on Killian. I don't remember Daddy giving me away. I don't remember the vows I recited or the cheer of the crowd as Kael and I walked out man and wife. The taste of our wedding cake eludes me, even two weeks later. The chords of our first song are just white noise. The feel of him moving inside me on our wedding night was as if it was happening to someone else while I watched, detached, from above.

This situation is so messed up, I struggle to get my head around it most days. I'm self-destructing. And I don't know how to fucking stop it.

I haven't stopped riding an emotional rollercoaster for over two years. Since the day Killian Shepard married my older sister. One second, I'm still in shock and the next, I want to die. Outwardly, I'm portraying the perfect, happy newlywed, but inside all I feel is desperate, lonely isolation. I think that's probably called despair.

And I'm angry. So fucking angry.

All the time.

With Killian. With Jilly.

With Kael for marrying me, refusing to see what was right in front of his fucking face.

With this godforsaken town and life to which I feel chained.

But mostly I'm angry with me. Why can't I cut a man loose who spouted his love through cryptic words but showed his true colors through real actions? Why can't I return the love of a man who treasures me more than air or life or his precious restored 1969 Camaro? If I could, I'd go back in time and change so many things. The first being: I would never let myself fall hopelessly in love with Killian Shepard. Liar. Betrayer. Saboteur.

And guilt? God...the *guilt*. That emotion has this entire despicable scenario wrapped up in a nice, neat little bastardized package, tied up tight with a bright shiny bow of infamy.

Pining after someone's husband is one thing. Pining after someone's husband when you're now married—to his *brother*—is taking immorality to an entirely new level. But that's me. I always manage to find fresh and juicy ways to skirt around the edges of acceptable social behavior.

Sadness and regret envelop me. Completely. Thoroughly.

This ring represents my own betrayal. My own duplicity. My

self-destruction. It should belong to someone else. Anyone else but me.

I love Kael. I *do*. I can't imagine a day in my life without him. The last thing I want to do is hurt him, but I don't know if I can ever love another person the way I do Killian. I have made a grave, life-altering mistake that will do nothing but bring pain to people I love. This time, I've gone too far, and I don't know how to fix it.

I breathe out a long sigh, knowing there aren't any answers to be found. None that I want to face anyway.

I glance at the clock. It's just past 4:30 a.m. Shit, I need to get inside. Putting on my game face is tough sometimes, and after the last two weeks, today will be a true test of how well I've perfected my acting skills, because I'm back in bumfuck, Iowa.

Dusty Falls.

Population 5,339 according to the last census. We're not quite like *Cheers* but pretty damn close. Everyone knows your name. It's especially true for me, given who my father is.

Looking in my rearview mirror, I paste on a fake smile and test it out.

"Did you have a good time?" I mock play, watching my own reaction.

"So good!" I reply.

Ouch. That was terrible. I sound flat, like an out-of-tune piano.

One more time.

"Did you have a good time?" I try again.

"Oh my God, it was so fantastic!" I say to my reflection, injecting myself with faux enthusiasm.

Eh. Tone down the Valley Girl accent and I'll give myself a pass. Barely.

Exiting my car, I head down the sidewalk toward the bay with a single light glowing from inside. The one that's mine. I let myself dawdle in the quiet for just a moment. Taking a giant whiff of the sugary confections, I already smell baking. Pride swells for at least one thing in my life I've done right. I gaze up at the neon sign I designed, not yet lit for the day, and smile.

*Cygne Noir Patisserie.*

Black Swan Bakery. My brainchild. My baby. The one piece of solace I can completely immerse myself in. "I've missed you," I whisper, holding the key to my business tightly in my fist.

Opening a business, a French bakery at that, in a small town that caters to modest people, was a huge gamble, but it's doing well. Much better than anyone expected. Well, except Kael, that is. He always thought it was exactly what this stuffy town needed.

He was right.

I see movement inside and shake my head. MaryLou's screeching voice grates—I mean *greets*—me the second I walk through the glass door. "How was it?"

I would say the turn of the lock or the sound of chimes bouncing against the steel frame gave me away, but that would be a lie. I bet MaryLou's been here since before 4:00 a.m.—a panther waiting in the bushes for her chance to pounce.

I've been dreading this interaction the most. The twenty questions, the scrutiny, the knowing, hawk-like stare. She'll watch every twist of my fingers, listen to every inflection in my tone, or track my hand as I tuck a piece of unruly hair behind my ear. She'll read something into everything I do.

She's too damn perceptive, but of course...she knows the truth. She's always known the truth. She's been my best friend since the first grade when I saved her life.

Well...that's the way she looks at it. All I did was save her waist-length hair from being chopped off when Petie Marshall stuck not one, not two, but *three* giant wads of bubblegum in it, right in the roots. She was in the bathroom trying to rip it out, along with fistfuls of her strawberry-blond hair when I led her to the lunchroom instead, asking the lunch lady for some peanut butter. Half an hour and a few hundred strands lighter, she was gum free. She stunk of peanuts for days, no matter how much washing she did, but at least she held on to her beautiful locks. Ones she still has to this day. *Exactly* the way it was in first grade. Girl needs a makeover.

"Wow, a girl can't even get a cup of coffee before the interrogation starts?" I say, throwing my keys onto the counter with a flourish. I guess I'm not quite ready to paste on my fake smile yet.

"Here." She offers me a steaming black cup of life and manners.

"Kissing the boss's ass?" I watch her over the rim of my mug as I take a nice long swallow of the hot, sweet brew. It tastes like a cup of sugar with a little coffee thrown in. Just the way I like it. Wow, I've missed this place.

She huffs. "I don't like the taste of ass."

I laugh. I've missed bantering with MaryLou James for the past fourteen days. "That's why we're friends."

"So...how was it?"

"What exactly do you mean by 'it'?" I ask, stalling for time. Kael and I returned two days ago from our two-week honeymoon on the exclusive Calivigny Island, just off the coast of Grenada. It was paradise. I should have enjoyed our private, luxurious, fully staffed home, fine sandy beach, and unmatched sunsets more than I did.

My chest clenches hard. *It's the exact honeymoon I imagined taking with Killian.*

"Well, I'm not talking about the view from your private balcony."

"Why not? It was spectacular." I take another sip and wait for her to take the bait.

"Was your husband's tight naked ass framed in it?" she asks, her arched brows wagging.

"Maybe," I tease.

"Do you have a picture?" Her voice pitches an octave higher. I laugh harder.

"Possibly." I do.

"Oh fuck." MaryLou fans herself with both hands and my entire body shakes. She's had some unholy fascination with Kael's behind since the ninth grade when she swears we were mooned by three seniors driving the loop on a Friday night. I keep telling her it wasn't

Kael. It was David Brandt. Kael was the one driving, but no matter what I say, she won't listen.

"I think I just had a mini orgasm. For real."

"Oh. My. God," I squeal. I wad up a paper napkin and throw it at her. "That's my *husband* you're ogling over."

"Hey, I can't help that you married a ridiculously good-looking man. And that's the most protective I've ever heard you get about Kael. Guess the sex was more than good, huh?"

"Hasius Crepes, bitch." I may use fuck like punctuation, but if I so much as utter JC's name in vain, I kid you not, the taste of Lava soap magically appears in my mouth. A bad side effect from my childhood.

"I hate it when you say that. You're a grown-ass woman now."

"Well...I hate your face."

She grins widely, showing off her slightly crooked two front teeth. "That's lame, Mavs. You can do better than that."

I flop onto the wooden stool behind the counter. "I know. I'm tired. I haven't been up this early in two weeks."

"Yeah, you've been in a sex coma for a straight fourteen days."

That's not *exactly* true, but I don't correct her. I feel guilty enough as it is. Believe it or not, while Kael and I had done plenty of fooling around, we hadn't slept together before we were married. It's not that I'm old-fashioned or was saving myself because I certainly wasn't a virgin. It's just that a large part of me wasn't willing to cross that line with him, hurt him even more if I didn't walk down that aisle. And it was just so...*weird* to have sex with my very best friend, a boy who used to sneak toads through my open bedroom window at night to scare the shit out of me. But thankfully, Kael was understanding, the way he always is. He assured me that we'd have a lifetime to get to know each other "that way."

Besides, we threw the wedding together on a wing and a prayer, married only six weeks after we got engaged. I didn't want anything fancy and I certainly didn't want a long, drawn-out engagement.

Although if I had, maybe I'd have come to my senses before it was too late.

"Is that all you think about? Sex?" I ask.

"Says the woman who's probably been banged day and night since she left. I know if it were me I wouldn't let that hot piece of ass out of bed even to eat. Well...except if he wanted to eat—"

"Okie dokie, then." I stop her before she digs herself any further into a hole. Then I shift subjects, not wanting to dive into my lame honeymoon, sexwise anyway. "What happened to Fifty Shades night?" I ask, genuinely wondering if she actually went through with letting her husband, Larry the plumber, flog her with the cat-o'-nines she bought from an online sex toy store.

And by the blush I see, even in the dim lighting, I'd say she not only went through with it, she *enjoyed* it. "You slut."

"Hey, don't knock it 'til you try it." She laughs, throwing the napkin back at me, which I successfully dodge.

"What else did you do?"

MaryLou's shoulders rise and fall quickly. Too quickly.

"Come on," I whine. "Don't leave me to my imagination." When she bites her lip and looks away, I can't resist. "Nipple clamps? Some anal beads, maybe?" Her eyes snap back when I mention the anal beads. "Anal beads?" I practically scream in disbelief.

MaryLou James is about as tight-laced as they come, and up until I plied her with enough alcohol so she'd watch *Fifty Shades of Grey* with me last month, she'd never been exposed to anything other than vanilla.

"You go from missionary sex and sweet nothings to floggers and anal beads in the span of two weeks? What the fuck, MaryLou? Next, you're going to tell me you ordered a sex swing." Her eyes shift. It was slight, but I saw it. "Oh, hell. Just stop. I don't want to know any more."

I may have forgotten to mention that Larry the plumber is also my cousin and is like a brother to me. In retrospect, I should have never gone down this line of questioning.

I push myself up and head through the swinging doors into the kitchen. In short order, I have all the supplies I need to start the chocolate croissants, one of our best sellers. MaryLou has already made two batches of brioches and I smell the baguettes baking that we'll use for lunchtime paninis.

"Napoleons and apple tarts are done. The apricots didn't come in, so I tried that organic farm in Greenwood and they sold me twelve flats of gooseberries at a steal."

"Really? We've been trying to negotiate with them for decent prices for the last three months. They wouldn't budge."

"Well, turns out Larry's boss's sister, Patty O'Shea, is married to the owner's girlfriend's son, Burt Leeland. She didn't take his last name, though, so we never connected the dots."

I chuckle. That's rural Iowa for you.

"Well then. Glad we got all that worked out. I'd love to buy more ingredients locally if we can. How are they?"

She stops filling the coffee filter with our flavor of the day, which smells like Snicker Roo, and stares at me. "I'll tell you if you tell me how your honeymoon went. And no bullshit this time. Don't think I didn't know what the hell you were doing out there with your little diversion tactic."

I let a curl turn a corner of my mouth. "I can just try it, you know. Answer my own question."

"Mavs." That's all she needs to say. My name in that tone of hers.

I flip off the industrial KitchenAid and take a deep breath before I say, "It was...nice."

"Nice?" Her voice positively drips with incredulity.

"Yeah. Nice."

"Sex with the hottest guy on the planet was just...*nice*?"

I know why she's acting like this. Kael Shepard is stunning. Tall. Lean but buff. Soulful eyes the color of well-aged Scotch, thick lashes, cut cheekbones. An ass you could bounce a quarter off of. Big hands and thick fingers, which I'm a total sucker for. But his devastatingly good looks don't change the fact that he's still my best friend and that my entire sexual appetite has been elsewhere. Namely his brother.

I shrug one shoulder. "It was strange, you know." She blinks, so I elaborate. "I guess it's what I imagined sex with my best friend would be like. It was pleasant, but I don't know..."

*...he's not Killian,* I leave unsaid.

Her sigh says it all. She's disappointed in me. Well, the fuckup club is accepting new members. One is an awfully lonely number. "So, pleasant and nice, huh?" she injects with sarcasm.

"I'm trying, ML," I tell her quietly. "I'm just not sure how to fix this mess I've made." My eyes sting. I blink the feeling away. If I let one tear go, a whole waterfall will gush. It might not stop.

"Maybe it doesn't need *fixing* at all, Mavricky," she replies just as softly. "Maybe it just needs nurturing."

*If only it were that easy.*

I don't respond and we both fall quiet, prepping for the day ahead. But I can't seem to get her words out of my head.

It can't be that easy...*can it?*

Small towns. They're incestuous, some say. Lives intertwined, pasts linked, destinies already determined.

In some regards "they" are right. Not the incestuous part, of course, but there is no such thing as anonymity, even if you want it. Everybody knows everybody. People are up in your business. They gossip. Judge. They formulate opinions of who they think you are simply because they sent flowers on the day of your birth and heard "rumors" of when you lost your virginity in Harbor Park (untrue, by the way).

You can't drive a mile down the road without waving at a dozen people you know. You can't make a quick run for milk or eggs without bumping into a distant cousin or someone from your graduating high school class you never even liked but who will talk your ear off for thirty minutes about shit you couldn't care less about. Your Auntie Marge has a big-ass hemorrhoid? Nice. A visual I didn't need, but thanks for sharing.

You learn secrets and shames about your friends, neighbors, and community you never wanted to know.

And *they* learn *yours*.

My first day back in a place that generally fills me with pleasure and accomplishment was anything but comfortable today. I felt like a bug being studied under a microscope. Spread apart. Pinned down. I was sure I was the topic of gossip on every single street corner and in Big Stan's Diner two blocks over.

But the more I recited my lies, the easier it got. With each story I told about romantic moonlit dinners or the best rum cocktail I've ever tasted or even the spider bites I woke with one morning, the more I began to believe that I *had* had the honeymoon of my dreams. With the man I'd dreamed about having it with.

That is until Samantha Humphries strolled in.

Sam, or Hamhock as she's known in certain circles due to the shape of her nose, has always had the hots for Kael. The feeling was not mutual, but that didn't stop Hamhock from living pretty in her little delusional world.

I've known Hamhock, as well as most of my fifty-nine Catholic-school classmates, since before kindergarten. But we were the furthest thing from friends. Her envy of my family's wealth has always been a sore subject. Grants, funded by people like my father, paid for her parochial education. Her family struggled to make ends meet while mine went on exotic vacations every summer. She shopped at the Pretty Nickel, a local thrift store; I had designer clothes (which I rarely wore, for the record). In fact, she was so poor that people in town renamed pennies "Humphries" and when they drove by her house, they'd throw the copper coins in her yard. I did it once. Couldn't sleep that night, I felt so bad.

But all of that paled in comparison to what I had that she truly wanted.

The affection and attention of Kael Shepard.

Sam's never gotten over her feelings for Kael, and the fact that I'm now married to him probably burns her like I imagine it burns me that Killian's married to my sister. Except in my case, Killian really does love me. So when she saw the blinding jewelry adorning my left hand, it didn't just bring out claws, it brought out the rabid. The second her eyes fell to my hand, they hardened and I knew shit was about to get ugly.

*"I'd heard you'd gone through with it, but then I told my mom it must be one of those small-town rumors. There's no way the Maverick DeSoto I know would marry a good, honest man like Kael Shepard when she's still in love with her sister's husband. But I guess you did."*

*I hear a gasp behind me at the same time the chatter in the bakery dies. Instantly, like a needle being pulled from a record.*

*"Get the fuck out," MaryLou growls angrily. After not so gently ushering Hamhock to the door, MaryLou yells after her, "And swines aren't welcome unless you want to be on the menu."*

*When she mumbles, "Pig-nosed fat ass," under her breath, a snicker of laughter runs through the small bistro.*

*"She's just a jealous cow," Elda Hansen, an eighty-year-old regular announces. Several others join in agreement. Elda smiles sympathetically when my eyes swing her way. I muster a weak smile back, trying to hold my head up while shame threatens to drag me down.*

MaryLou then insisted she take over in the front while I remained in the back until we closed at 2:00 p.m. She has a better eye in the kitchen and I'm better with customers, but after that run-in, I was so shaken up there was no way I could muster up any more happy lies.

All I kept thinking for the next several hours was how right Elda was. Sam was jealous. But sadly, Sam was right, too. I married a good, honest man while I'm still in love with another. She just had enough balls to call me out on it. As much as I don't like her, I have a whole different respect for her now. And at least I know what half the town actually thinks.

After we closed for the day, MaryLou pulled out her emergency stash of Jim Beam, practically forcing two shots of that swill down my throat. Jim, Jack, or Johnny may not solve the world's problems, but they do a fine fucking job burying the ugly truth for a while.

Two hours and a bottle of wine later, we now sit at my kitchen table, and MaryLou says the harshest, most candid words she's said to me yet. Her bluntness is both what I adore and loathe about her.

"You're a married woman now, Mavs. You made the choice to be Kael Shepard's wife."

"I know."

"He's crazy about you. That man has been by your side your entire life, not Killian. Killian is a dickless, gutless prick."

"Once again, I know this," I say, my tone holding a slight bite. *Could she make me feel any worse about myself?*

She stares at me for a few beats. "If you didn't think you could fall in love with Kael, you shouldn't have married him. If you don't think you have that ability now, you should do the right thing and end this before you do any more damage."

"Ouch." *Apparently so.*

"Truth hurts like a bedsore, doesn't it?"

I nod my agreement because my throat is too clogged with emotion. My teeth dig into my cheek so hard I'll probably have a canker sore tomorrow.

She reaches across the table, gripping my hand in hers. It's hard to see her through the water now glassing over my pupils.

"It's not such a bad thing to fall in love with your husband, Maverick."

"How do you do that when you're in love with someone else?" I whisper, desperately wanting someone—anyone—to give me that answer. If I was handed the key to falling out of love with a man who's nothing but destruction, I'd use it. In a heartbeat. Then I'd throw that fucker in the Keg River so I wouldn't be tempted to undo it.

"Simple. You have to let him go first."

"It's not that simple, ML. If it was, I would have done it already." Only a woman who isn't hopelessly pining away for a man she can't have would think in such naïve terms.

"It *is* that simple, Mavricky. Know what I think?"

"No. But that won't stop you from telling me anyway."

My snarky comment doesn't slow her stride in the slightest. "I think up until the second you walked down that aisle you were hoping for a miracle."

I look away, embarrassed at my transparency.

"But what I think you're failing to see is that you've got one. He's right in front of your face and if you don't pull your shit together and realize the gift God has handed you in Kael Shepard, you'll end up losing him, too."

I don't respond. Once again, she's right. Kael is an amazing man. He wanted me. He married me. He loves me. *Him.* Whatever Killian's excuses are for giving up on us, they aren't enough. He's lost to me forever. The truth is he's been lost to me for years now. It's time I begin the grieving process and start accepting it. But the pain of that thought weighs me down until I feel I can't take a full breath.

"I'm not sure there's room for anyone else, MaryLou," I say honestly.

"That's because you haven't tried making room for anyone else. You need to kick him out. He's taking up space that's not his to take anymore. Now, come on. Let's try out that religieuse recipe you've been babbling about."

"Yeah. Okay."

Two hours of baking and drinking fly by. Well, more drinking than baking. By the time MaryLou left shy of an hour ago, we'd managed to kill almost another entire bottle of wine. Larry came to pick her up while his brother followed behind with my car. One benefit to living in a small town, I guess. Folks think nothing of doing small favors like that for others.

Losing myself in whiskey, wine, and laughter, I'm now sufficiently tipsy and my rough day feels like a distant memory. Of course, it's not. And come tomorrow, I'll have yet another regret to add to my growing mound: a bitch of a hangover.

I'm just pulling out a fresh batch of choux from the oven when the garage door opens indicating Kael is home.

*Home.*

Kael is home.

To *our* home: a modest two-story, shafty, old Victorian house that was once mine, which we now share together. As man and wife, not a couple of roomies.

Wow. It will take me a while to get used to that.

Growing up, Kael and I spent so much time together it was as if we practically lived with each other anyway. *This is no different, Mavs.* Except it is. He's now sleeping in my bed, *naked*, not camped out on the floor in a pile of blankets and pillows, watching reruns on TV Land until we fall asleep.

When I hear his footsteps, I keep focused on the double cream I started to whip, calling over my shoulder, "Hey, how was your first day back at work?"

I feel the warmth of his body heat right before he molds his front to my back. Heavy hands land on my hips at the same time his lips land on my exposed throat. "Long. I missed you."

"I missed you, too," I tell him softly, knowing it's what I'm supposed to say.

"Whatcha making?" he breathes in my ear. "My mouth is watering."

I try to forget how much he sounds like Killian when I answer, "Religieuse. I'm thinking of putting it on the menu, but I need to perfect the crème pâtissière first."

I'm on my third batch of the custard. The first one curdled. The second one didn't set quite right, but this time, I think I've finally perfected it. Too bad I did it half-cocked.

"God, I love it when you go all French on me, Mavs."

I laugh, but it comes out more like a huff when he places another hot, openmouthed kiss on the very back of my neck. My stomach flutters a little when his teeth clamp my skin. When he runs his tongue along the line of my throat to my ear, I can't suppress a light moan.

"You smell incredible. Like sugar and nutmeg. And maybe a little wine."

"MaryLou came over."

"Mmm. That explains everything."

"Want a glass?" I sound breathy and needy and apparently it's all the encouraging Kael needs.

"No. I want something else entirely."

He reaches around and scoops up a finger full of custard. The gooey-ness disappears out of view and I think he's going to taste it, but I jump when he begins to paint the cool crème along the length of my shoulder.

It's hot today. And so damn humid. August in Iowa can be intol-erable. Temps are nearing a hundred degrees. The heat index just an hour ago was one hundred ten. It's so hot the air conditioner is working round the clock and it's still not keeping up.

So I have my frizzy hair thrown in a messy tangle on top of my head and a short, strapless sundress on trying my best to keep cool, but now my internal temp just shot up ten notches. Not only is Kael nibbling his way along my collarbone, his right hand snakes under-neath my dress and tunnels into my panties.

"This is so fucking good," he murmurs hungrily. I'm not sure if he's talking about the filling or the finger he's pushing north.

"Kael, what are you doing?" I squirm, responding to his touch. My mind may understand I'm sleeping with my best friend, but my body...she's not confused in the slightest. She's drunk. Thanks to said drunkness, now she's horny. And she wants the devastating pleasure he's offering. Even if it is weird, I'll admit Kael is a very talented lover.

"You know...I know you so well, Maverick." Hot breaths fan my cheek and fall down my neck, doing nothing to quell the goose bumps now blanketing me. "I know you can't sit still longer than five minutes. You bite your nails when you're bored. You're a tomboy who's strangely addicted to lip gloss and carries around thirty-two varieties in your oversized purse."

"Oh, shit," I gasp when he joins another finger with the first. I'm starting to get very wet and very pliable.

"But for as much as I know about you," he husks, "I don't know what makes you drip with desire. I don't know what makes you so fucking hot you'll combust in my hands."

His fingers leisurely move in and out as he talks. It's as if he's trying to learn every bumpy ridge inside me. Or drive me wild. When his thumb starts lightly grazing my clit, my head falls back against his shoulder. Wild. Definitely wild.

I should stop this. Stop him. I shouldn't want this...*should I?*

"I want those secrets, Maverick. And your body will tell me everything I need to know."

His caress is whisper soft as he traces a line across the top of my dress, over the slight swell of my breasts. It's slow and languid and makes my skin tingle. I hold a breath when he dips shallowly in to tease a puckered areola before tugging one side down, freeing a breast, which now feels swollen and achy.

His overly light circles around and around my sensitive nipple make my back arch and my breath catch.

*Sweet Lord.* I need more.

"Mmm, a soft touch makes you quiver. Let's see what else does."

*Stop. Tell him to stop.* But God, I can't. I don't want to tell him no like I have the last three times he's tried making the moves on me. And let's face facts: the way I'm undulating under his ministrations doesn't exactly scream back off.

The hand between my legs still working its magic, I silently watch on as he leans forward to dip a finger into the ganache I planned on icing the choux pastry cases with. He brings a chocolate-covered digit up and circles it around my peaked bud. I gasp loudly when he pinches and tugs.

Hot, dirty words trickle into my ear. "Oh fuck, yes. This makes your pussy pulse, Swan."

There's no denying it. I felt the clamp around the fingers inside me as much as he did.

"You like a little pain with your pleasure?"

I like it. I like it a lot. When I don't answer, he tweaks again and I choke out a *yes.*

"You know how sexy it is that you're this wet for me?" he groans. "Fuck. I want to bend you over this counter, Maverick. I want to rip off your soaked panties, hike up this dress over your bare ass, and adorn your cheeks red with my handprints. I want to wind your gorgeous hair in between my fingers and pull your head back so I can watch your eyes as I slide into you and mark my wife as mine. So you never forget."

Gulp.

Holy shit.

My head is spinning. My bones are liquid.

Did someone just drop a dirty-talking Kael look-alike in my house? What the hell happened at work today? In all the months we've been an official "couple," he's never spoken to me like this. He's treated me like glass...or as a bride who might flee any second. Even on our honeymoon, he was tender and gentle.

"I want to do such sinful things to your body, Swan."

And God, who knew his childhood pet name for me could be so damn sexy when purred like satin in my ear?

Kael expertly brings me up, higher and hotter. I'm burning. Already throbbing for release, but he demands an answer. "Tell me you want that, Mavs."

I nod.

I want to tell him the more sinful the better but I don't have a chance. With a strong hand, he pushes my face toward him so he can capture my lips in a heated kiss. It's forceful, a clear stamp of owner-ship, but it's so damn sensual at the same time it makes my toes curl. I feel gooey chocolate smear on my face, but I'm too gone in an alco-holic sex haze to care.

I want this.

I need this.

*You can have this...stop thinking so damn much.*

My breath kicks up and my sex spasms as he picks up the pace, shifting into high gear. Playtime is over. He means business.

"Yes, Mavs," he pants against my lips, encouraging me.

*Yes, Mavs. So fucking tight and hot and soft. Come for me, Small Fry. I want to feel your pussy clench my fingers hard.*

Fuck, Maverick. Stop.

Stay with Kael.

His thick erection twitches at the small of my back. A sting on my clit, now hostage between two fingers, makes my knees tremble. I beg for more.

"Yes, so good, baby," he croons softly.

*Jesus Christ, so fucking good, Maverick. He grips my hip so hard, I'll bruise. I want bruises.*

No. Please. *No.*

I squeeze my eyes shut, completely disoriented. My body moves in time with fingers pumping in and out, in and out. Fingers that demand everything from me, while the past and present cruelly play tug-of-war.

"Come for me."

*Come for me.*

"So fucking close. Give it to me. I've got you."

*Give it to me. It's mine.*

His pace increases, supplicates, and I already feel an orgasm barreling down on me. The other side of my dress is tugged down, my nipple rolling between deft fingers. I'm adrift in that space between yesterday and today. Invisible. Confused. Wanting.

"You're right there."

*Fuck yes, you're there.*

I'm there. "I'm coming," I announce on a short, ragged breath. *God, I'm coming.* My hands fly to his forearms and my fingers dig into his flesh.

*I'm coming, Killian. Oh, God...I'm coming, I tell him as I let myself soar, riding out the intense wave of ecstasy crashing through my body like a tsunami.*

I'm falling, tumbling, starting my downward descent into the rabbit hole of bliss and obscurity when his body tenses and he releases me like a hot ember. I'm suspended midair, desperately trying to reach that pleasure now rapidly slipping away.

Then I'm being whipped around. I glance up, blinking rapidly, to find hard eyes and a ticking jaw.

*Oh no. Shit. Oh, crap. Did I say Killian's name?*

Kael yanks my dress back in place, not bothering to wipe me off first. The sugary substance sticks to the inside of the thin fabric like paste, molding it around my still stiff peaks like cellophane.

"What's wrong?" I ask, completely breathless. Scared shitless.

*Oh shit. Oh no no no. Please tell me I didn't...*

"Company."

*Huh?* "Company?"

"Company," he repeats, clearly irritated.

*Oh, merciful God. Thank you, Lord. Thank you. Thank you.*

"Who's here?"

"Who do you think?" he grates.

Who do I think? *Who do I think?* It's hard to think about anything except the fact that I was on the precipice of one hell of an orgasm that I genuinely wanted. I needed that orgasm, dammit. I don't give a crap who is here; I'm about two seconds away from grabbing his hand and putting it back down my underwear, forcing him to finish what he started.

Kael snags a dish towel hanging from the oven handle and vigorously wipes the mess from my face. He's rough. It hurts. I know I'll have a red streak against my skin when he's finished.

His entire demeanor has shifted from sexy and playful to downright angry. My brain is still trying to catch up to what's going on when it hits me. Only one person would make him react like this.

Killian.

Oh fuck.

*Killian.*

I hold my breath as the sound of knuckles raps on the front door. Kael and I exchange a look, probably both thinking the same thing.

Welcome back to the real fucking world.

*Kael*

I watch her from across the playground, wondering if she needs my help. She's one of the scrappiest girls I know and I don't think she'll be too happy if I run to her rescue, but I can see she's getting more upset by the minute. I've seen firsthand what she's capable of when someone riles her. It ain't pretty.

Tommy Johns and his sidekick, Mark Flinn, have her cornered over by the giant snow pile in the corner of the yard. Their backs are to me, but I'd know that stance anywhere. Legs spread, arms crossed, shoulders set, heads cocked. Bully mode, locked and loaded.

They're assholes. My dad would wash my mouth out if he heard me use that word. I'm not allowed to swear, but he does it all the time...so I figure what the hell. What he doesn't know won't hurt him.

Another thirty seconds pass. I tick them off in my head, one by one, praying for their sake they'll get bored and walk away. Though Mavs is trying to ignore them, it's clear they aren't leaving without getting some sort of reaction out of her. The third-grade bullies generally pick on those younger and weaker than them. Like kindergartners who cry for their mommies during recess. Today, though, kindergarten and first grade are on a field trip to the Art Center in Des Moines, so their prey is limited and they've turned their sights on her.

I know she can take care of herself, but I still don't like it. Not a bit. It sets my protective instincts to red. At age ten, I don't know where these feelings come from when it comes to Maverick DeSoto, but they've always been there, from the time she was born. They won't go away. In fact, they seem to grow stronger every year.

Telling myself that I'm doing this more to protect them than her, I decide to wander over that way even if it means I'll have to listen to her bellyache about it on the walk home from school for the rest of the week. She doesn't know it yet but she's mine and I protect what's mine. It's how my father taught my brother and me.

As I get closer and closer, what I hear makes my blood boil hot. My fists clench tightly. "Heifer, heifer. Your name means heifer," Tommy Johns sings in an off-key voice.

*They're calling her a cow?*

Oh, hell no.

"Shut up," she says in a flat voice as if what they're saying doesn't bother her. Except I know it does because those green eyes I dream about are narrow slits and her chunky cheeks are a dark pink.

To anyone else looking on, they may think she's just cold. I know better. When she's just cold, the pink is brighter, almost like candied apples on the fattest part of her face. When she's embarrassed, it's more of a light blush that starts at the line of her hair and disappears underneath the neck of her shirt. It's the shade of her ballet slippers. But when she's getting ready to slug someone in the face, which she's done to me before, it's more the color of chewed bubblegum before all the sugar is gone. The very tips of her ears get just a shade darker, like raspberry flavor.

Her color now tells me these two jerks better watch it—she's ready to punch someone's lights out.

"Do you even know what a heifer is, heifer?" Mark Flinn taunts, following "the hole's" lead.

We call Tommy Johns "the hole" behind his back because he got stuck in an abandoned well when he was five. Dumbass thought he could shimmy down there with a coil of rope tied around a tree trunk. Only he was five. He couldn't tie off a knot to save his soul. Was in that dark, dank dungeon for darn near two days. Almost died. I'm not a mean person, and I hope God doesn't strike me down for thinking this, but I don't think the world would be a worse place without "the hole" in it.

"Nah...she's too dumb to know what a heifer is," "the hole" jabs.

In slow motion Maverick looks up from the tunnel she's been digging. Standing leisurely, her burning eyes not leaving Tommy's face, she brushes the snow stuck to her mittens off on her jeans. I watch tiny bits of frozen water float to the ground, knowing "the hole" is about to join them, probably face-first.

Which means that Mavs will be sent to the principal's office. *Again.* And she'll get grounded. *Again.* Maybe even get kicked out of school, which she's come close to before. This will probably get her suspended because there's no way this is ending without blood now. At only seven and in the second grade, she is already trouble, the whole damn word capitalized, not just the "T."

"Why don't you slink off in a corner and lick the *heifer* manure from your stinky-ass shoes, hole," Mavs smarts back, taking one step forward.

Shitballs.

She's really going to do this.

It doesn't matter that she's right. "The hole" lives on a cattle farm five miles outside of town. And his shoes do stink. I've smelled them before in the lunchroom. I usually hold my breath when I'm near him.

I now have about two point five seconds to make a decision here: let this scene play out or take matters into my own hands, saving Mavs from herself. She needs to be saved a lot. At least she has me. She needs me more than she will ever know.

So I do the only thing I can—the same thing I've done my whole with life with this reckless, fly-by-the-seat-of-her-pants, infuriating girl. *My* girl.

I reach out, grab the back of "the hole's" winter coat, and throw the first punch.

*Maverick*

When I was eleven I almost died.

It was New Year's Day.

Jilly and I had each received the most perfect pair of white leather ice skates for Christmas. In typical stuck-up Jilly fashion, she thumbed her nose at the gift and threw the skates in the corner of her closet.

*"Oh my gosh, Jilly, don't you love the skates? They're my favorite present!" I squeal.*

*"Love them? I hate the cold. It makes my skin dry," she says in her snotty-ass voice.*

She never took them out of the box. Once.

I, on the other hand, loved mine. As usual, we each had a giant pile of presents we didn't need and most I probably wouldn't use. The skates were the least expensive of my gifts that year, but I treasured them as though they'd been dipped in gold.

I remember that year as if it were just yesterday.

Both Killian and Kael had been distant. Killian turned sixteen in September and had gotten his driver's license. He was never around. He'd dropped out of our homegrown band, which we thought we'd smartly named DeSheps, a combo of our last names. And since he was the drummer and none of the rest of us could play drums, DeSheps fizzled shortly thereafter.

Kael had started high school that year, ninth grade, and was starting to change. He was in football, which took up a lot of his time. When that ended, he immediately picked up basketball. He didn't get home from school regularly until at least seven and then he had homework. I was lucky if I saw him once a week.

I terribly missed not only the boy I crushed on but my best friend, too. I specifically recall feeling as if I was the little kid being left behind while they grew up. And my sister was a raving bitch, as usual, never giving me the time of day.

I was lonely inside. I think that's what prompted me to go out that day even when I knew I shouldn't. I was smart enough to know better.

It had been cold and snowy early in the season, bitterly so, and the ponds and streams had frozen up ahead of normal. But we'd had a warm streak for the two weeks leading up to Christmas. Temps soared into the forties and even fifties on a few days. In that atmosphere, thin ice melts rapidly.

I was dying to try out my new skates, begging every single day. Both my parents had told me no. *"It's not safe, Tenderheart,"* Daddy said. He'd even gone so far as to hide mine because he knew me. He knew I'd do what I wanted when I wanted. But I knew all their hiding places. It took me all of three minutes to locate the box in the shed on the top shelf behind a box of Halloween decorations.

So that morning, while Daddy went deer hunting and my mother rode out a New Year's Eve hangover, I tied the strings of the skates together, threw them over my shoulder, and headed out.

When I was a kid, I loved the isolation of rural Iowa, especially because we lived on twenty acres on the outskirts of town. Right next door to the Shepards.

I loved the silence. The peace. The freedom. The centering I felt going on inside me when I just sat, listened, and took in the fresh, clean air. I loved the color of the sky, the sound of crickets chirping, the crackling of bonfires at night. Everything about living in the country made me feel whole and present. It was a balance I couldn't find anywhere else.

And that day, the second I'd crossed our open lot and set foot into the dense woods behind our house, obscuring me from the real world, I felt better. Calm. Like I'd stepped into a dream.

Yeah, ice-skating was exactly what I *thought* I needed.

The memories of what happened next are fuzzy.

I do remember the excitement as I stepped from the trees and gazed upon my private paradise. I recall the thrill that ran through me as I laced up my skates tight around my ankles. I can still feel the air that was warm but held a bite of ice on my cheeks, reminding me it was still very much winter. The texture of the smooth ice as I set my first footfall down still reverberates through me sometimes.

Then the rest is relatively blank. I remember shivering. I was wet. Freezing. Rigid. My lungs hurt. My fingers and toes were heavy and numb. My mind full of cotton. And I was being carried in a pair of strong arms.

*"Hang on, Maverick DeSoto. I've got you. I have plans for you, and they don't include you dying."*

*That voice.* I couldn't open my eyes. They seemed glued shut by thick icicles layering my lashes, but I'd know that voice anywhere.

I was in Killian's arms. And I was safe. I leaned into his warmth, let his life leach slowly into me, and let darkness take me before waking to the steady beep of machines.

I spent three days in the hospital. Hypothermia had dropped my core temp to 89.9 and they hooked me up to a hemodialysis machine to rewarm my blood. No one knows for sure how long I was in the water, but long enough that my organs showed signs of early shut-down, so it must have been a while.

I was lucky that day. Lucky I didn't drown and even luckier I was found on such a remote part of land where no one was supposed to be.

Turns out Killian, Kael, and some of their friends were snowmo-biling and rode past at just the right time. Someone spotted my bright orange knit cap sticking up from the middle of the water.

Jilly always gave me shit about that hat. She said I could be spotted from the space station in it. That I should wear something more feminine and stop acting like a boy. But I loved that hat. It was a gift from Killian on my birthday the year before. He bought it from a lady in town who knit and sold them dirt cheap. He said I looked good in orange.

That's the day I was given another chance at life.

That cap saved me. *Killian* saved me.

And when I heard silent promises in that voice pleading with me to live, that's also the day I knew I was hopelessly in love with Killian Shepard.

I never looked back.

---

The tension in our booth is palpable. It's almost as if you can reach out and touch its mercurial pulse. When Killian and Jillian, or the "Illians" as everyone now refers to them, walked into our kitchen half an hour ago, Killian's gaze immediately fell to my chest.

*"Did we interrupt something?"* he'd asked in a tight voice.

I thought he was talking about the state of my protruding nipples that were still throbbing, but upon dropping my own gaze, I noticed I had ganache smeared above the line of my dress. It was obvious where the trail led. And for the first time, I felt something cool at the base of my neck. When I reached up and wiped, I came back with a glob of custard.

My face had flamed before Kael interjected that yes, in fact, they had interrupted something and told them we'd meet them at The Red Rooster (aka The Bloody Cock) in half an hour for dinner.

When they walked out the door, I was left with the beginnings of a headache, an unfulfilled ache a little farther south, and a pissy husband. I knew facing Killian was inevitable, but I'd hoped to stave it off for a few more days at least. Or months, even. Give me enough time to start the slow process of carving Killian Shepard from my heart like I should have done the second he said "I do" to someone else.

"What are you getting?" Kael leans over and asks me, his voice strained.

My stomach churns as I keep my face planted behind the menu. The wine I drank earlier has turned sour. I feel Killian's assessing stare on us, watching. I can actually sense his anger seep slowly across the table. It's tarry and stifling. And his jaw hasn't stopped clenching since we sat down. It makes me angry that *he's* angry. He has no right. He is the one who set this entire thing into motion. But what's done is done and it can't be undone as much as I wish it could. For all our sakes.

"I don't know yet," I reply. All I see is one big blob of black in front of me. Never mind I don't need to look at the menu. There are all of two decent restaurants in Dusty Falls. We're regulars at both. Which means we know the menu very well.

"So, how was the honeymoon? Do tell," Jilly's sultry timbre rings. Maybe that's how she lured Killian. Maybe that voice bewitched him like a sea nymph and once caught, he couldn't get out of her titanium vise without the Jaws of Life.

Kael plucks my menu from my hands and places it on the table. He throws an arm over my shoulder, tugging on me until I'm practically sitting on his lap. I don't have to look at him to know he's directing his answer to his brother, not Jilly. I choose to keep my gaze anywhere but on the two people sitting across from us.

A cross between a gasp and a laugh escapes me when Kael smugly replies, "It was...adventurous."

It was no such thing. When my eyes snap to Killian's on instinct, he's not looking at me. He's pinning his brother with a hard, almost hateful glare. But there's something else floating behind the flint of his eyes. It looks like grief. I have to look away before I break into tears.

"Sounds like it was sexy," Jilly adds, completely clueless. Or maybe she's not. Maybe she just acts like it. Maybe Killian's type isn't a strong, feisty woman who can handle a four-wheeler, fillet a fresh-caught fish, or open her own business. Maybe it's a weak, dependent, whiny one with catlike claws, a cutting tongue, and an eye for Louis Vuitton.

"It was," I pipe up, suddenly furious that Killian thinks he has a right to act all high and mighty that I got married and actually had the audacity to have sex. *With. My. Husband.* "In fact, we hardly left the bedroom."

That part is somewhat true. I think for the first three days I was so distraught at what I'd done I made myself sick. It was either that or the sushi we ate on the plane. I blamed it on the sushi, of course.

I glance up at Kael, very much aware he's now staring at me along with the "Illians." When I see a broad smile and a twinkle in his eyes, I immediately match it. Then I melt a little when he leans in and kisses me on the lips. It's sweet and genuine, not a *fuck off* to his brother, but an *I love you so very much* one instead.

My nose burns a little. I do not deserve this man. In any way, shape, or form.

MaryLou's words play around in my head. *That's because you haven't tried making room for anyone else.* I think maybe she's right. I haven't. It's time I try with the man who's currently looking at me as if I'm the single match that lights his entire world.

"Well, if it isn't the Shepard brothers. What brings y'all out on a Wednesday night?"

Thank God...a life raft in the way of one Patsy Leddy. With a wink and peck to my cheek, Kael faces our waitress. "We're celebrating, of course. Mavs and I just got back from our honeymoon. We were giving my brother and his lovely wife here the lowdown."

"Yeah, congratulations. 'Bout time you two finally tied the knot. I always thought you were meant to be together."

I bite my lip, forcing my eyes to stay on Patsy instead of straying to Killian. She was in Kael's grade but went to the public school. She is a total sweetheart, not a malicious bone in her body. If she's saying this, it's not because she's heard rumors and is trying to be spiteful like Hamhock; it's because she truly believes it.

"Thanks, Pat. How's Tommy? He staying away from abandoned wells?" Kael turns back to me and grins like a kid in a candy store.

Patsy laughs, taking the joke in good humor. She may not have gone to Saint Bernadette's, but everyone knows the story of how Kael Shepard knocked Tommy Johns out with a single punch to the jaw and was not only suspended for three days but was grounded for a month. I was furious with Kael. I should have been the one grounded. *I* wanted to be the one to knock "the hole" on his ass that day. Teach him a lesson. To this day, I still don't care for Tommy Johns, but Kael and Tommy get along great. Then again, Kael is magnetic. He gets along with anyone.

And now, Patsy is engaged to Tommy "the hole" Johns. They're to be married the day after Christmas. "Not many abandoned wells on the corner of Main and Lake. And you know he goes by just Tom now."

"Yeah, yeah. He'll always be "the hole" to me, though."

She giggles again then asks, "Now, what can I get the newlyweds to eat?"

Kael looks to me first. I give him a soft smile. "Did Hank make his kick-ass meatloaf tonight?" I ask her.

"You know it."

"Then I'll take that."

Kael orders the same thing. Killian orders a burger, medium rare. And Jillian orders a salad.

"No dressing. No olives. No onions. No croutons. No cheese. Banana peppers if they have them. If they don't have banana peppers, tell them not to just throw a yellow pepper on because it's not the same thing. Oh, and make sure the tomatoes are on the side of the plate. The side. If they're not on the side, I'm sending the entire thing back."

Killian's face gets stormier with every curt demand. "So...you're just getting a plate of Gucci food then," he says to his wife. Gucci was the Shepard boys' pet bearded dragon that died just last year. He lived primarily on lettuce.

"Shep, stop." She throws him her signature ugly face. "You know I'm trying to lose a couple of pounds." Jillian is about a size two. On the first day of her period. The rest of the time she's a size zero.

Kael clears his throat and my lips are pressed together tightly. We're both biting back a laugh, which will totally set Jilly off.

"Oh, and bring us a pitcher of Miller Light, too," Kael adds before Patsy smartly decides to slink away.

"You don't have any extra weight to lose, Jillian," Killian growls.

"You don't know anything about being a woman, Shep. I'll feel better if I lose five pounds."

"So now, a couple of pounds has turned into five?"

"Well, everyone knows the first two are just water weight."

"Apparently not everyone," Killian mumbles while tearing the edges of his paper napkin to shreds. I hate that I know it's a sign of his building anger and that his own wife has no fucking clue.

"Tell him, Maverick," she says.

"Tell him what?" I shoot back, pissed she's trying to drag me into this stupid conversation. And this is yet another difference between my sister and me. I'm a curvy size ten and though every once in a while, when I glimpse a pocket of cellulite on the backs of my thighs, I wish I was smaller, my weight has never once been an issue for me.

"You know. Tell him how good it feels when you lose a few pounds."

Bitch.

I let my mouth curve into a sugary smile. "Well, I wouldn't know, Jilly. I'm perfectly comfortable in my own skin."

Both Kael and Killian start snickering. Jilly just huffs and turns her attention to the booth behind us. When her gaze cuts back to mine, I can already see the blather winding up. Instead of doing anything productive with her life, my sister lives off her trust fund and has deemed herself Dusty Falls' own Gossip Girl as her full-time job.

"Did you hear that Sally Jameson hooked up with that Isaac Newton?"

Yes. We have an Isaac Newton. His mother is a science teacher at the public high school and apparently wrote her PhD thesis on Sir Isaac Newton's views on space, time, and motion. She obviously became a big fan.

"What's wrong with Isaac?" My jaw now hurts because of all the retorts I'm biting back.

"Jillian," Killian warns her.

"Well, he's totally beneath her, of course. I mean...he's a *mechanic* for God's sake," she says in a whisper that's more of a yell. I think half the restaurant probably heard what she just said. I'm so embarrassed I wish the floor would swallow me. *Her*. Make that her instead.

"Wow," Kael mutters beside me. Killian looks like he's ready to blow, his napkin all but destroyed.

Have I mentioned my sister is a classless, unfiltered, egotistical bitch who is nothing like me? No? *#Truth*.

"Yes, a talented one who owns his own business. It's not easy to own your own business, you know," I challenge loud enough to avenge Sir Isaac.

"I know." She shrugs as if she didn't indirectly put down what I do. I'm just a lowly baker, after all. Her words. Not mine. "I'm just saying he works with his hands all day."

Oh, how I hate her. I can't believe we share a single cell of the same DNA. More and more, I'm convinced I'm adopted.

Suddenly I can't take any more. Of her. Of Killian's not-so-sly examination of every touch Kael's giving me. Of this godforsaken tension. It's making it hard to catch my breath. I have no idea why the "Illians" just showed up unannounced, but I'd bet my half of the DeSoto inheritance on the fact it was Jilly pushing Killian into it. She thrives on rubbing it in that she's married to not only the man she knows I loved all my life but one of the hottest men to ever be bred in Dusty Falls. She parades around with Killian Shepard like he's some goddamn prized quarter horse. I'm surprised she hasn't leashed him yet. Maybe that also happens in the bedroom. I can't even go there.

"I need to use the restroom," I say, pushing Kael so he'll scoot over and let me out. I pray as I weave through the tables half-filled with patrons that no one follows me. I don't need Kael's soothing or Jilly's catty digs or Killian's sorrys. I need five minutes to myself to slow down the boil raging inside.

Taking my time in the stall, I close my eyes. I take long, deep inhales and try to exhale all the angst I feel building. I think of my lake. An immediate peace settles over me. You would think after a near-death experience in water, I'd avoid it like the plague, but I don't. I still go there sometimes, even as an adult.

By the time I'm washing my hands, I feel slightly better. At least I think I can make it through the rest of dinner. Evidently, I didn't think this whole marriage thing through to the end. I've done a good job avoiding time spent with the Illians for the last two years, but now it will be an impossible task since I'm married to Kael.

When I hear the door squeak open behind me, my heart drops. I'm sure it's Jilly but catch the reflection of none other than Sally Jameson in the mirror.

"Hey," she greets me.

"Hey, Sal." I grab three paper towels because they're so damn thin, even doubling up won't work, then turn to face the woman my sister just heartlessly put down. By the look on her face she heard it, too.

"I'm sor—"

"Oh no you don't. Don't even apologize for that cow."

Sally Jameson is five years younger than me and is the daughter of the district county attorney. She's bright, bubbly, and she's been through one shit relationship after another. Isaac may be a bit quirky, but he's a kind man with a good heart. I, for one, hope it works out for them.

"I don't know how you put up with her."

I snort. "It's a challenge."

"You're more of a saint than I would be. I think I may have set her on fire by now."

"Wow." I laugh. "Harsh." My sister and I may be polar opposites and she may have gutted me by marrying Killian, but she's still my flesh and blood. No matter what, there will always be a part of me that can never completely cut her loose because of that tangible bond. Family is family is family. Always. There is a decent human being underneath her thick layers of entitlement and haughtiness. I have to believe that. I *try* to believe that, anyway.

"Just honest. Say, congrats on your wedding. Kael's good peeps. You guys look great together."

A twinge coils in my stomach. Can wine curdle? The smile I force on my lips hurts. I try hard for lighthearted when I say, "Speaking of, I guess I'd better get back. Kael may call a search party in a minute."

It must work. She giggles. It's cute. I scoot around her and start opening the door.

"Hey, Maverick."

"Yeah?" I turn around, the chatter of conversation now flowing through the partially open door.

"I may be completely out of line saying this, but anyone who marries that woman can't be worthy of you."

Oh.

Fucking.

Hell.

Small freaking towns.

"Thanks," I croak. I try to force the corners of my mouth up again, but they feel heavy as lead and won't move. When I hear the snick of the latch behind me, I lean against the hallway wall surprised to find a tear running down my face. I wipe it away, along with the one that follows it.

The only thing I want to do right now is climb into my car and drive. No destination. No thinking. No guilt. No nothing. I want to run away, but the only person I really want to run away from is me. I wish that was possible. If it was, I'd have lost me long ago.

A few deep breaths later, I'm sliding back into the booth beside

Kael. His big brown eyes run over my face, concern scrunching his forehead.

"You all right, Swan?" he whispers sweetly.

I nod, focusing all my attention on the unappetizing lump of meat waiting in front of me along with a beer I won't drink. I feel the heat of his palm on my thigh before he gives me a comforting squeeze. I force a brief smile, which seems to appease him...for now.

The four of us eat in silence for a few minutes. Blessed silence I needed. I'm just beginning to think I can make it out of here without tearing the roots out of a certain someone's bleached-blond hair when Jilly's abrupt—and very unexpected—announcement throws up on my world once again.

Her silverware clangs against her plate before she pushes it away, her half-eaten salad mocking me for the fat-laden forkful of mashed potatoes I just shoved in my mouth. She makes a production out of grabbing Killian's hand and looking up at him lovingly before she turns to me and says, "I wanted you guys to be the first to know it's time."

"Time for what?" I reply evenly, not liking the cat-that-got-the-canary gleam on my sister's face. I set my fork down on the table, tucking it under my plate for fear I may reach for it and stab her eyes out at what she's going to say.

With a broad smirk on her face, she tells me something that makes my heart sick.

"That Killian and I are finally ready for a family. We've officially started trying to get pregnant."

I stop breathing. I'm sure I do. I blink, blink, blink. I keep blinking. Maybe if I blink long enough and fast enough I'll magically transport myself to another place and time where this doesn't hurt so fucking much.

Killian's trying to catch my attention. I see him in my peripheral crooking his head, silently begging for me to look into his cheating, Judas-kissed, dream-swallowing chocolate orbs.

I don't.

Fuck. I can't. I can't possibly stomach the silent conversation we'll have if I do.

*I'm sorry, Small Fry.*

*I don't give ten fucks.*

*You do and I hate it when you swear.*

*I hate you.*

*I love you. Please forgive me.*

*I can't.*

*You will.*

No. I can't possibly hear more unspoken apologies and platitudes.

After I find my runaway voice, half-hearted congratulations are exchanged. On my part anyway. Kael sounds genuinely—maybe too genuinely—happy. Then I'm forced to pick through the rest of my dinner with Jillian babbling on about nursery colors, baby names, and private schools.

That night, after a round of trying-to-forget-my-fucked-up-life-and-one-Killian-Shepard sex, I go to bed wrapped up in Kael's arms, warm on the outside, but dead cold in the place it matters most.

"When are you coming back?" I try hard to keep the disappointment from my voice, but it's tough. I miss him.

"Soon."

"Define soon," I push. He's been saying that for weeks. He took a job in Pensacola, Florida three months ago, leaving my father's construction business, taking us all by surprise. DeSoto Construction Industries is the largest, most successful, most powerful transportation infrastructure construction company within the entire Midwest. Killian was a top salesman with the political savvy necessary to reel in the large clients and keep them happy.

All of the Shepard men work for DeSoto Construction, actually. Arnie Shepard, Killian's father, is the CFO and also sits on the board. Kael just recently started as a corporate lawyer and Killian is in sales. Hell, three-quarters of Dusty Falls is employed by Richard DeSoto. Even I work for my father as a project director.

"Mavs, you need to be patient."

Patient? I've spent my entire life drowning in patience, waiting for this man. He moved away to attend college. Then he moved back, but I was still "too young." Then it was my turn at college, and though I came home from the University of Iowa to intern for my father in the summers, Killian still wouldn't touch me. Until one night behind the grain bins early this summer when everything changed.

"Two months after I move back from college you leave me here by myself. I've been patient for almost twenty-three years, Killian. I'm tired of being patient. I'm tired of waiting. I'm tired of hiding. I don't understand why you had to move away."

"We've talked about this, Small Fry. I need to prove that I'm successful because of me, not your father's name. I don't want to be under his thumb my entire life like my pops. I don't want that for us." Killian's entire family's livelihood is dependent on Richard DeSoto and he's not willing to cross my father. Although it makes me angry, in a way, I can't blame him.

"I know." I sigh, knowing he's right. "I'm sorry. I just—"

"Don't apologize. And besides, you know he can't find out about us just yet. He was starting to get suspicious."

Killian and I aren't technically "together, together." We don't date like other couples. We hook up in the dark. Sneak around like a couple of married people having an affair. It's ridiculous. It pisses me off, in fact. But my father is not supportive of anything other than a friendship between Killian and me. And what my father wants, he gets. I hate displeasing my father but there's a big part of me that just doesn't care anymore. It's not his choice who I love. It's mine.

"So when are you coming back to see me?"

"I'll try to make it back next weekend."

"Try?"

His exhale is heavy and long. "Maverick, you know what's going to happen the second I set foot in that town. Pops is already all over my ass to come back to DSC."

"Fine. Then I'll come to you. I can't wait any longer."

"That's not smart. Someone's going to figure it out."

"Someone" meaning my father.

"You don't want me to come?" I ask, my voice a little shaky.

"Baby," he coaxes, "it's not that and you know it. I want to be together. It's just not the right time yet. It will be soon. Just not now."

My eyes wander to my bedroom window, the blinds pulled all the way up. I watch the rain fall. It's nourishing and cleansing. It usually feeds my soul to listen to the soft pitter-patter of the drops hitting the metal gutters and to know it's soaking into the roots of corn and soybeans that grow along the windy roads of our rural town. But today my mood matches the weather. Dreary and stormy. I have this impending sense of doom I just can't shake, and it happened the very second Killian stepped on that plane in Des Moines.

"I miss you so much."

His voice drops low and smoky. "I miss you, too, Small Fry."

"I want to marry you."

"I want you pregnant with my babies."

I turn giddy when we have this conversation. Our romantic relationship may be new, but I've known Killian Shepard my entire life. I know what he wants, how he thinks. "How many?" I prod, already knowing the answer.

"Five. All boys. I'm going to keep you pregnant for six years solid."

I'm now beaming ear to ear, my dreariness all but forgotten. "You have to marry me first."

"Patience is a virtue."

"Virtue is overrated."

"No. Virtue is what makes you who you are, Maverick. God, don't ever lose that. That's one of the things that drew me to you in the first place."

My throat clogs. "I love you, Killian."

"I love it when you say my name like that." I can practically hear the smile in his tone.

"Like what?"

"Breathy and wanting."

"I am. I'll show you just how much next weekend if you come home."

"How about you show me now instead? Let me listen," he challenges on a soft groan.

I like me a good challenge. "M'kay."

I tunnel my fingers down, down, down...

I'm jolted from the best part of my memory when MaryLou quips, "You know...maybe this is exactly what you need." No...what I *need* is to relive my fantasy in peace.

"What are you fucking on about?"

I lift my eyes from my task to watch her meticulously place a single raspberry just perfectly on each of the mini cheesecakes on the tray in front of her.

Mrs. Kenner is having an early luncheon at the lodge today for the Federation of Women's Club and ordered thirty-three of these, along with an equal amount of individual ham-and-cheese quiches. We also have two smaller catering orders to fulfill, so I admit...I snipped. Snapped, whatever. And I'm pissier than I have any right to be over news that knocked me into yesterday. *I* was the one who was supposed to have kids with Killian...not *her*.

MaryLou stops what she's doing and looks up. She stares at me for a full two seconds before she starts laughing. "Been a few days, has it?"

Yes. But what I'm referring to and what she's referring to are two different things. "Fuck off, MaryLou." I grab my pastry bag and a macaroon, but I pinch the delicate pastry too hard, causing it to crumble in my hand. She snags my wrist and pushes it down on the counter, but because I fight her I crush about a dozen more cookies in the process. "What the hell, bitch?" I screech.

That makes her laugh louder. "You can make more. It's just eggs and sugar."

"That's not the point."

"I think that's exactly the point," she says matter-of-factly. Picking up a handful of the now-destroyed multicolored disks, she lets them fall slowly through her spread fingers, back down to the workstation. We both zero in on the mess in front of us as if the pattern will now mystically deliver answers to all the world's unsolved problems...like what happens to all those people who disappear in the Bermuda Triangle and was there actually a government cover-up of a UFO crash in Area 51? Or maybe, just maybe, why I am now Mrs. *Kael* Shepard and not Mrs. *Killian* Shepard.

"You need to blow apart everything you thought you knew and start back at ground zero."

*What?* Start over? Pretend I was never in love with Killian Shepard?

Is *that* what she's suggesting?

There's no way that answer lies in the crumbs before us.

And how do I do that? How is that even possible after all this time? He's in me so far and deep, he's actually woven throughout my every cell.

No. There's no pretending. There's no forgetting. There's only compartmentalizing. There's then and now. Past and present. Killian versus Kael.

I have so many bitchy things just sitting on the edge of my tongue, waiting to be flung at the one person I feel I can take everything out on and she'll still love me unconditionally. But that's not fair to her. Especially when she's only trying to help.

"I just can't believe he's actually doing it."

"Why?" she chucks back.

"Why? He doesn't love her. He can barely stand to look at her. Why would he have a kid with her?"

"I didn't mean why is he having a kid. I meant why do you *care*, Maverick? Whatever you had with Killian ended the day he came back to Dusty Falls and stood in front of you at your father's house with your sister on his arm and announced his engagement. You deserved the courtesy of not only some advance fucking notice, but an explanation. You got neither. And even if you did get those things, it wouldn't have been good enough. *Nothing* he said would have been good enough to justify what he did. Cut the fucking cord, babe. He's not worth it. If he wants to procreate with that witch and create a gaggle of little witches, that's his business, not yours."

My lips want to curl so I let them. So do MaryLou's. When a noise that sounds strangely like a giggle escapes from my throat, she matches it. Then in ten seconds flat, we're both doubled over laughing so hard tears stream down our faces.

"A gaggle?" I ask on broken breaths.

"Yeah...a gaggle," she responds in such a high, wailing pitch my rubbery legs won't hold me anymore and I slide to the floor in a giggling heap. Pretty soon, she's sitting next to me and we're gasping for air.

"I think you mean a coven," I correct when I can finally suck oxygen again.

"Coven, brood, gaggle. Makes no difference. All I envision are a bunch of little broomsticks lined up against the mudroom wall rather than shoes."

That restarts our cackling. "Oh my God, you're terrible."

"Maybe." She wipes away tears that have gathered under her eyes. "But don't tell me you can't envision the same thing."

"I can," I tell her. Sadly, I can.

The last of my fit subsides and the last of my smile fades. The only sound left in the room is our labored breathing, along with my wild thoughts. MaryLou snakes her hand around mine, holding tight. Neither of us makes a move to look at the other.

"I love you, Maverick. I'll always love you. I'll always have your back. But I gotta be honest. I'm tired of seeing you put yourself through this. One of the things I admire most about you is the fact you never let anyone keep you down. I miss that girl. The one who walks around with her head high and her middle finger higher. The same one who drove to Des Moines to get a small business loan for this place because she wanted to be evaluated on *her* merits and not because of her father's name. You could have easily used his money or your trust fund, but you didn't. It makes me sad—no, *angry*—it makes me angry to see you wallow in memories like some fucking jilted lover. You *were* jilted. Get the fuck over it. Plenty of people have been in your shoes before and not only survived but thrived. Remember Penny Lane?"

"By the Beatles?" I ask, confused.

"Jesus, no. You and your old music. Penny Lane, the girl that lived in Honeybrook?"

In my head, I'm rolling my eyes. "No."

She waves her hand like she's swatting a fly. "It's not important. Anyway, what's important is that Penny Lane was engaged to Ludwig Vandenberg. They'd reserved the church. She had her wedding dress picked out. They'd even bought the plane tickets for Grandma Lane to come in from Louisiana for the ceremony. Then Penny went over to London for a semester of study abroad and by the time she came back, Ludwig had not only cheated on her, he'd *married* the adulteress. And do you know who he married, Mavs?"

I could give two shits who Penny Lane's Ludwig married, but I play the game because if I don't, MaryLou will sit mute until I do. "Who?"

"Her sister, of course."

I rotate my head her way. "You're making this shit up."

"I'm not," she deadpans. "Larry knows the brother of Penny's now girlfriend."

An unknown force yanks my eyebrows up. "Girlfriend? Didn't you just get done telling me she was engaged to a dude?"

"Yup." She smacks her "p" so loud it hurts my eardrum. "When life hands you lemons, you don't make lemonade. That's for panty-waisters. No. You pucker up, suck them dry, then throw the used rinds back in life's face with a giant fuck-you and a gesture for more."

I snort before I realize she's serious. Sobering, I confess, "I think I may have already done that."

"No. You haven't. You think marrying Kael was a middle finger to Killian, but you're wrong. You could have married *anyone,* but you married Kael. And you married Kael because you love him, Maverick. If you actually take a long, hard look at what's in your heart, yes, you're hurt, but underneath the hurt and betrayal is where true love lies, Mavs. You just have to unearth it. And gift it to the *right* man this time. One worthy of *you.* And that's not the older Shepard brother. It never has been."

My eyes water. She tugs on me until my head falls to her shoulder. We used to sit like this on the playground sometimes when we were little. Backs up against the brick wall. All the other girls wanted to do was cause drama, but MaryLou and I...we couldn't stomach it, even then. We plotted how we were going to conquer the world when we grew up. We would ban dresses and bubble gum and any shoes except tennies. We'd burn every pair of tights. We'd extend recess by two hours and cut out social studies because social studies was stupid. And we'd make outdoor survival a mandatory class. Everyone should know how to thread a fishhook and load the barrel of a gun.

When my best friend talks again, the vibration of her voice runs through me, along with her words. "There will always be a part of you that's sad over Killian, Mavricky, and that's okay. But this kind of sadness is like a slow-growing cancer. Pretty soon it will consume you entirely and smother all the good out of you. Don't let Killian Shepard snuff out your soul. He's not worth it."

After a bit of silence, I acknowledge her. "I know." And I *do* know this. Everything she says is spot-on. Continuing to love Killian is the equivalent of eating a whole pint of Ben & Jerry's in one sitting. You know all the reasons you should put that shit away after one spoonful, but you can't stop shoveling in bite after bite because it's so damn sinful. Then when you're staring at the empty container, you hate yourself even more, wishing you could rewind time for a do-over. *That's* exactly how I feel. I hate myself for still loving him but for some reason can't stop.

"Uh...anyone in here?" a disembodied voice calls. MaryLou and I look at each other. She gives me a flat smile and mops up my tears with her thumbs before we both pop up at the same time.

"Yeah, whatcha need, Carol?" I ask, proud my voice didn't crack or wobble.

Carol's gaze bounces back and forth between us before she announces, "There's someone here to see you, Maverick. Should I say you're busy?" The last thing I feel like doing is pasting on a smiley face and pretending that I care, but business is business. I can't let my personal problems drag down everything I've busted my ass for.

"No. I'll be right there."

"I'll finish up in here," MaryLou says as I start toward the front.

"Thanks."

As I push through the doors, however, I freeze midstep when I catch the russet hues of one Killian Shepard, drumming his fingers methodically on the countertop while he waits. With a couple days of growth smattering his jaw and droopy bags under his eyes, he looks tired. But still so damn good at the same time. He's so gorgeous, it makes me short of breath—and apparently brain cells—every time I set eyes on this stunning man.

Rocks spin around in the pit of my stomach as we quietly take each other in. It's been two weeks since the little homecoming dinner we had at The Red Rooster. I haven't seen or heard from him since. It's been both a blessing and a curse.

Mindful of where we are, I glance behind him to see he's alone, no wife in tow.

"What are you doing here?" I demand tersely, letting the swinging door close behind me.

It's Monday, midmorning. The crowd is thin as breakfast is over and it's too early for lunch, but I'm well aware of all eyes in my establishment burning into me. Including Carol's. I slide my gaze over to her. When I thin my lips, she knows she's made a critical error. She should have told me the "someone" here to see me was my brother-in-law.

*Yes...brother-in-law. Remember that.*

*Brother-in-law.*

*Brother.*

*In.*

*Law.*

He's just a plain ol' brother-in-law. *Yeah...one you've had your mouth all over.*

Fuck.

When he doesn't respond right away, I ask again, "Killian, what did you need? Is everything okay with Jilly?" I made the last question sound so damn sincere I could win an Academy Award. That makes him snap to attention. I wish I could stop the self-satisfied smile that is turning my lips at this very moment, but even gravity loses.

"She's fine."

"That's good to hear." Yup. Katharine Hepburn, right here. I can almost feel my fingers curling around that weighty statuette now. "Then how can I help you?"

For a second, he looks taken aback at my aloofness. He quickly recovers, though. "I, ah...I wanted to talk to you about a catering job."

Liar.

Killian has set foot into Cygne Noir Patisserie exactly three times. Once when we had the ribbon cutting on opening day. The day after Kael and I announced our engagement. You can imagine what that was about. And now.

He's here for a reason, but as usual, it's about him.

Red starts to seep around the edges of my vision. How dare he have the audacity to show his face in here, making up a bullshit catering excuse. Even if he does have one, he's the fucking president of sales at DeSoto Construction. He has not only one assistant but two.

"Okay." I play along. "Let me just grab my pad." I have one right in the pocket of my apron, but I put my back to him mostly to gain my composure. My movements are jerky and irate as I open a drawer and grab a pen and pad of paper. When I turn back around, I don't look at him as I make my way over to a table in the corner by the front window. I need to keep this fake order as public as possible.

"Is there someplace we can talk that's maybe more...private?" he asks lowly as he slips into the chair across from me. Eyeing the table of Q-tips three over who have taken a very keen interest in us, he throws them a megawatt smile before landing his gaze back on me. I roll my eyes when I hear them swoon. Traitors.

"Why? I didn't realize ordering croissants or quiches was top-secret fodder?"

His only reply is to sigh. Heavily.

I poise my pen right over the paper, stare at him hoping I pull off the blank look I'm trying for and wait. If it's games he wants to play, fucking bring it. I decide right then and there I'm done with him. I'm done with his lies. Dragging me along while I hang on to his shoe-strings, muddying myself and flaying my pride in the process.

I deserve more. From him. From me. *For* me.

"I wanted to talk to you about the other night."

Well, I don't.

"So you don't have a catering order, then?" I ask blandly.

He hedges. It's momentary, but that's all I need. I knew he was lying. "I do, yeah, but..." He lets his sentence drift, seems confused at the way I'm treating him.

My eyes flick to the sidewalk when I feel hairs prickle on my neck. Fucking great. Staring me down is none other than Hamhock and a friend of hers. They stand outside Mitzi's Nails and Tanning while Hamhock not so subtly points our way as she blabs a mile a minute.

I see the contempt on their faces from here.

It doesn't matter that I'm doing nothing wrong. It doesn't matter that he came to me and not the other way around. It doesn't even matter that we're in public for all to see, not caught slinking around behind the rosebushes out back. Rumors don't need truth; they just need a single drop of juice to power them.

I turn my attention back to Killian, forgetting about our judgy audience. The sooner I get this over with, the better. "Then why don't we get to that?"

"Mavs—"

"This isn't the time, Killian," I whisper in a growly voice. "And it certainly isn't the place." Raising my tone a couple notches, I finish all businesslike. "Now...if you can tell me the type of event and number of people, I can give you some ideas on options."

The resigned expression creeping over his face almost makes me feel bad.

Almost.

MaryLou is so right. There is no reason good enough for what he did to me. I trusted him and he didn't just break that...he blew it the fuck up. For good. Even if he left Jilly today, was on his knees in front of me begging for forgiveness, I'm not sure I could give it. Or that I want to anymore.

I have spent most of my life pining away for this man. And look where it's gotten me. I'm a solid, soiled mass of rage and bitterness. I am no better than he is, marrying someone I wasn't in love with, no matter the reasons. In fact, in many ways, I'm worse, because I genuinely love Kael, and Killian only ever tolerated Jilly, even as kids.

It may take a while. Years even. But I vow right here and now to whittle Killian Shepard from my soul. It will hurt like a mother-fucker. I'll stumble. I'll fall. I'll skin my hands and knees when I do. Then I'll pick myself back up, dust myself off, and try again. I've never been more determined to sever this invisible hold Killian has on me once and for all.

I'll do it for me, but mostly, I'll do it for my new husband.

Kael deserves all of me—not half a woman.

After two months, I have finally discovered Maverick DeSoto's little secret hiding place. She's been avoiding me more and more lately. Disappears for hours at a time without so much as a word.

When she resurfaces, I'll ask her where she went. She dodges. I get angry. She stomps off. I yell after her. A day later, she'll forgive me and we'll be back to normal. Until it happens all over again.

I'm sick and tired of it.

Of her ditching me.

The secrecy.

The fighting. That's not us.

So today I'm following her. She's developed somewhat of a pattern. I don't think she's even aware of it. But I am. Every Tuesday morning she'll just up and vanish. Fridays, too. And sometimes, on Saturdays, I won't see her until the afternoon. That's the one that really makes me mad.

Tastie's is open exactly three months out of the year. June, July, and August. They're closed on Sundays because the owner doesn't work on "God's day." And they're only open until noon on Saturdays. For the past three summers, every Saturday morning, Mavs and I walk the half mile into town, wait in a long line outside the booth that's no bigger than a porta potty, and watch the old, intricate machine make fresh donut holes right before our eyes. When it's our turn, we each hand Mr. Higgins two quarters. He smiles that toothy smile of his then shakes the fried dough balls in cinnamon and sugar before filling our bags extra full.

We stuff our faces on the walk home, always promising Killian and Jilly that we'll save some for them. We never do. We both figure if they want some, they can walk their asses with us. They don't.

Tastie's is a summertime staple in Dusty Falls. Tradition. And Mavs is breaking it without so much as even an explanation. I've now gone the past two Saturdays without a Tastie's donut hole and I'm getting cranky. I need to find out what's so important that she's ditching our weekly ritual. And in truth, it kinda hurts my feelings she won't share whatever she's hiding. We share everything.

So this morning, at the crack of dawn, I parked myself behind the DeSoto's shed and waited. The dew still sticking to the blades of grass soaked the tops of my running socks, but it felt good as the heat and humidity had already set in.

I'm not sure how long I waited. An hour maybe. Then I saw her slink out the side door of the garage. Her long, dark hair was pulled back into a sleek ponytail and she sported her usual cut-off jean shorts and one of the DeSheps tees we had made. She had a backpack strapped on and I wondered what was in it.

I watched her look around to make sure she was alone. When she was satisfied she was, she sprinted across the open plain of her back-yard until the trees that ran the length of the property between our two lots swallowed up her small body.

The second her foot hits that forest floor I go after her. I keep my distance, of course. Don't want to spook her. More like I don't want to piss her off. It doesn't take much to set her off like a firecracker. It's fun to watch and I do it plenty of times on purpose, but if she spots me now, I may never find out what she's trying to hide. Every once in a while, she'll look behind her, but the trees are so dense, it's easy to duck behind one before she spots me.

For what seems like hours, we wind our way over fallen, rotted logs and around two hundred year oaks, forging deeper and deeper into the muggy, still, lush grove. We've been in this forest plenty of times. Exploring. Building stick forts. Watching the wildlife. Playing Ghost in the Graveyard or just plain hide-and-seek. Just being kids, I guess. I love it as much as she does. Know it almost as well as Maverick. But we only ever go so far because there is an invisible line in these parts you do *not* cross.

The DeSoto and Shepard properties butt against Old Man Riley's, a recluse who owns more land than our two families combined. He's a legend here in southern Iowa. Kinda like the Greek gods, only Old Man Riley is nowhere near a mythical man of beauty. I saw him once in town when he came out of Markell Sundry. Scary as hell. He looked like a mountain man with shaggy, unkempt hair and a thick graying beard down to his belly button. His flannel shirt was ragged and the T-shirt he wore underneath was supposed to be white. I think. His jeans had holes and not the fashionable kind. I was sure I could smell his foul stench from across the street. My mom scolded me, saying it was just my imagination.

But as with any folklore, the stories multiply and grow until they're completely far-fetched. Like he's supposedly richer than that guy who owns that big computer company that has an apple as their logo. Or that every piece of furniture he owns is stuffed with fives and tens because he doesn't trust the government. He reportedly shoots stray cats and dogs for sport and buries them under a dirt pile where he adds a new rock for every corpse hidden underneath. I guess there are thousands of rocks on that pile. I've never seen it firsthand. I also heard he makes necklaces from the teeth of rats and he regularly practices voodoo. There are a hundred even more ridiculous tall tales.

But the most rampant rumor is that he has his entire border lined with traps buried underneath the brush and dirt so they can't be detected. Some say they are explosives that would blow your leg clean off. Others say they are homemade snares with teeth so razor sharp, it'd bite your ankle in two before you felt a thing. Yet others say he's put voodoo hexes around his entire lot line.

Maybe they were just rumors. Maybe they weren't. But the one thing *everyone* knew was if you slipped even a toenail onto Old Man Riley's land, he'd know and you were as good as dead.

In all the times we've been in our little sanctuary, Mavs and I have not once crossed that imaginary line. We've toyed with the idea, but we each end up chickening out.

So the fact we are now traipsing into unknown territory—on Old Man Riley's property—scares the ever-living shit out of me. Not gonna lie. The deeper we travel into the woods, the more my stomach bubbles and the more worried I become. With every step I take, I am sure agony will rip through me a second later. I want to turn around more than anything, but I'm not about to lose Maverick so I forge ahead.

This is what she's been doing? Risking her very life? If Old Man Riley catches us, who knows what the hell he may do. All I know is I don't want to end up on the other side of a shotgun barrel with half my face blown off, in an unmarked grave beneath an evergreen. Nor do I want Mavs to either. The second we get to our destination, I am going to give Maverick DeSoto a piece of my mind.

Once again, she proves she needs someone to look after her. Careless, reckless girl. I'd bet my entire baseball card collection and even my prized, officially signed Ken Griffey, Jr. card her parents have no idea where she escapes to. Her dad would have a shit fit. He's very protective of his daughters, which is why he pulled me aside when I was eight and asked me to keep one eye open around Mavs at all times. He knew she needed it. Just like he knew he could count on me.

Wondering when this torture will end, I try to drag in a breath. It burns my lungs, which now feel wet with moisture. With no breeze, it's absolutely suffocating in these woods. My mouth is dry and my stomach is rumbling. If I knew we'd be hiking this long, I would have brought a bottle of water and something to eat. I wonder if she has any food in that bag of hers.

Up ahead, I see the trees spit her out. I pick up my pace so I don't lose her because I have no idea what's on the other side of this wooden prison I've now found myself locked in. It takes me another couple of minutes to catch up, though. I practice the words in my head the entire time, my speech now perfected. First, she's going to get an earful; then I'm going to throw her over my shoulder, if necessary. And we'll hightail it outta here as fast as possible before we're found out.

I'm so furious with her I'm shaking. My mouth is open; my angry words ready to fly. But now...

Now, with my sweat-soaked T-shirt sticking to me like paint and my mouth puckering from lack of saliva, I stand in the shroud of the trees and just watch, the words dead on my tongue.

I gawk in awe.

Right in the center of a grassy, overgrown field is the most spectacular, crystal-clear blue lake I have ever seen. It's not that big. I could swim across it in the time it takes me to make a couple of laps in our local swimming pool. Pussy willows and tall, billowy grasses shoot up around the edges, giving it this sort of peaceful, secluded vibe. Hearing the croak of toads, I spot dozens of lily pads in the far corner. This paradise seems out of place in the middle of nowhere, but yet it...it doesn't.

I spot the backpack Mavs wore, now open, carelessly thrown on the ground. The straps dangle in the water, causing small ripples against the edge. But what has me fascinated more than the impressive sight of this undiscovered haven is Mavs herself.

She's kneeling on a giant, flat boulder that juts up from the center of the water, just two feet in from the grassy banks. She giggles and coos as she leans over the water precariously, throwing haphazardly torn up pieces of bread to two beautiful white swans. They gobble them up greedily.

The smile she has literally splits her face in two. It's blinding. Breathtaking.

*She's* breathtaking.

The swans—clearly mates—circle her, waiting for more. Her laughter draws them in close. I don't think it's the food. I think it's her. She's a magnet. She has no idea the power she exudes and holds over people. Over me. The swans seem comfortable around her. Like they know her. The *real* her. Like I do.

For long minutes, I simply stare. She sings. Talks to them. She's even named them. I've never seen her so happy or relaxed. I'm all of fourteen years old, and she's only eleven. I know I have my whole life ahead of me with adventures I can't possibly comprehend. But as I stand here with stars in my eyes and wonder in my heart, I know without a shadow of a doubt it doesn't matter how many people I meet or how many girls capture my attention...

I will always come back to her. I will always be drawn to her.

My swan.

Now I get it.

Mavs has always felt like an outsider. She's not a girly girl like her sister or her parents want her to be. She'd rather fish and hunt than ever touch a doll. Hell, she ripped the heads off of every single one of Jilly's Barbies when she was just six—after she sheared their hair clean to their heads. Got in big-ass trouble for that one. She's more comfortable in torn jeans and baggy vintage T-shirts than the expensive ones her mom buys her. She'd spend every single minute outdoors if she could. Camps under the stars in just a sleeping bag—no tent necessary.

Now, here, by the gleam in her eye I see even fifty feet away, she's willing to risk the wrath of Old Man Riley because, without her even saying so, I can tell she's in her element. She's finally found the one place where she feels she can just be herself without judgment.

But the thing she doesn't understand yet is she's always had that place.

She always will.

With me.

"Hey, babe."

"Hi," I call over my shoulder.

The screen door slams before his voice whispers over my cheek. "Aren't you getting eaten alive out here?" His lips land softly on my skin. He lets them linger like he's breathing me in after a long, hard day and I'm the only balm that can soothe away the grit. I allow myself to concentrate only on that feeling and nothing else until he takes them away. When he does, I feel a little sad. I want them back.

"A little," I reply, slapping one that just took a vial full of blood from my thigh.

The mosquitos are horrible this year. We had more than double the rain we normally get in the spring. The fields had standing water for weeks, which not only caused delays getting the crops planted, but was the perfect breeding ground for mosquitos the size of fists. The county wanted to crop dust some of the worst spots with an organophosphate insecticide to try to control them, but they were met with huge opposition by not only farmers but a band of mothers who "don't want their kids getting cancer in five years from the chemicals that will end up in our drinking water."

My opinion is we're all going to die of something, so just spray the fuckers so we can all enjoy the outdoors with the little time we have left. But in the end, they didn't. I've now been outside all of ten minutes and have half a dozen bites.

"I tried that new organic repellent MaryLou was going on about." She wouldn't shut up about it until I did.

"Yeah?" He chuckles as I shoo another flying, bloodsucking fiend away. "How's that working out for you?"

I crane my neck to look at my husband and practically melt with the adoration I see shining down at me. It makes my eyes burn a little. Kael grabs my hand, bringing it to his smiling lips as I say, "I'm going back to cancer-inducing deet."

He full-on laughs before kissing my cheek, announcing, "Your mom stopped by my office today."

I groan. Of course she did. When she doesn't get her way from me, she goes straight to Kael. I've been avoiding her for the past two weeks. I know what she wants and I can't stomach the thought.

Three weeks have passed since Killian visited me at the bakery. Jilly ignores me, as usual, except if she needs something. And my mother? Well, either she can't sense the tension between the four of us when we're together or she just plain doesn't care. I would vote for the latter. So a family dinner to celebrate Jilly's little declaration is the last thing I want to do.

"Let me guess. I've been trying to reach Maverick. She's ignoring me, as usual. I thought perhaps you could talk some sense into her. You always can," I mock my mother in her superior-sounding voice.

He slides into the seat beside me with ease. He's still all dressed from work in his pants and button down, tie dangling undone. He must be dying of heat.

"Pretty much sums up our conversation."

I stay quiet. A quick flash of yellow from the yard draws my attention. By the time I look, it's gone. Then it appears again slightly to the left.

Fireflies. I love fireflies. Used to catch jarfuls of them when I was a kid. Then I would release them the next day because I felt bad living while they slowly died.

"You can't ignore her forever, Mavs. We need to go."

"I don't want to." *Dammit,* I want to add, but don't. I will sound like a spoiled brat if I do.

"It's important to your mom, Swan," he says.

I watch more fireflies wave their mating calls to the others for a while before I answer. Vivian DeSoto has accomplished her goal. I give. She has Kael on her side and I don't want to disappoint Kael. Things have been good between us for the past few weeks. I feel like for the first time I'm *really* trying. "When?"

"Sunday."

Swiveling my head his way, I smile softly. Inside, though, I'm anxious. I don't think I'm ready to see Killian again yet. I need more time. That fucking cord is so thick I need an oil drill to chew through it. Maybe we should move to Texas. "Okay. If that's what you want."

"I think it will be nice."

"Nice?" A brow crooks. Dinner with my family is the opposite of nice. I will have to listen to my daddy drone on about how I could run DSC someday if I just come back. He'll be subtler than my mother, though, who will just put it out there that I'm better than baking loaves of bread all day. And then I'll have to pretend to be happy for my sister when I'm anything but.

"Fine. Tolerable. They want to invite my parents, too."

"Really." I make it a statement, but it's more of a question. The DeSotos and the Shepards were once an inseparable duo. They worked together. Vacationed together. Spent weekends together. Both of our mothers were active in the church and so many committees I lost count.

Then when Arnie Shepard retired a couple of years ago, they sort of drifted apart. Arnie and Eilish Shepard started spending half the year in Florida at their retirement home and when they were home, it seemed they always had something else to do. I feel bad for my parents. It's almost as if they lost their best friends of thirty years. "I didn't know they were back yet."

"They get back Saturday." He looks happy.

Every family has its issues. The Shepards are no different. His relationship with his father has been strained for the last few years, although he won't talk much about it. But Kael loves his mother like no man I've ever seen. He hates it when she's gone for so long.

"Good. I'm looking forward to seeing them." I always felt more comfortable around Kael's parents than my own, anyway. Eilish, a sassy Irish redhead, loves me like a daughter. She accepts me for who I am and what I want to do. Next week, I know I'll get a call from her. She will insist I bring her an entire box of éclairs and croissants. Then she'll make her famous slow-roasted corned beef, a mound of boxty, which is a fancy Irish potato cake, and we'll sit in the gazebo and gorge ourselves on carbs. My mother hasn't touched a carb in twelve years.

"Do you want to call her or should I?"

I take a breath in until my stomach bulges. Then I blow it out, taking my time. "I will. I'll get the ass-ripping over with before Sunday."

Kael chuckles. When I slap another mosquito, he asks, "Want me to grab that bug spray and a couple of beers?"

"Sure. Sounds great."

Five minutes later he returns to our back porch, sporting nothing but a pair of baggy black gym shorts. Two bottles of Michelob Ultra hang in one hand, bug spray in the other.

He sets the beers down on the whitewashed wooden table between our two Adirondack chairs but doesn't open them yet. Then he goes about spraying himself with the repellent, slowly running the mist over one arm before switching hands and doing the next. I sit back and watch him as he generously covers his torso before working his way down one thigh.

He's like Killian in so many ways, but I realize those ways are only superficial. They both share the same square jawline and chiseled cheekbones. Their eye color is only a shade or two different, with Kael's being lighter, but their hair color is exact. Kael's a couple inches taller than Killian. He's leaner, though, whereas Killian is a little more brawny.

But where Killian is ruthless, Kael is compassionate. Kael is outgoing and chatty, Killian more reserved. He's serious to Kael's fun-loving personality. And where Killian would apparently do anything for himself, Kael would do anything for me.

I think back to the day he followed me to my lake. Well, Old Man Riley's lake, but I quickly thought of it as mine. We had an understanding, Old Man Riley and I. He wasn't nearly the monster everyone created. He was just a lonely old man whose wife had died ten years earlier.

So when I stumbled across him in the woods one day, I couldn't breathe. He was hunched over a mewling animal and for a split second I thought all of the rumors around town about him were true. I thought for sure I was dead along with the animal he was butchering. But then our eyes connected and I knew none of the rumors were to be believed. He motioned me over to help him free a baby red fox who had been caught in an illegal hunting snare.

It turned out Old Man Riley, or William as he asked me to call him, was a quirky, misunderstood, loveable man who revered animals as much as I did. He took that fox back to his home and nursed it back to health before letting it loose again. Then he showed me his lake. Said besides his Lilly, his dead wife, I was the only one who knew about it, although that wasn't entirely true.

Kael thought he was doing a good job of being stealthy that day— the day he followed me. I'd already spotted him behind the shed, waiting for me. I thought about trying to lose him. I could have, but I didn't. I knew it was only a matter of time before he found out anyway.

I laughed to myself the entire way. It sounded like a herd of elephants was pounding behind me. I don't think the deaf could have missed him. When we got to the lake, I knew he stood behind the safety of the leaves and brush, watching me. He never came out. He was patient until I was ready to leave and followed me back out. He never brought that day up. But every time I went to that spot, I sensed him there...following...protecting me, I guess. It was as if he knew I wasn't ready to share. He was okay with that, something I appreciated greatly.

Then the next summer, I broke my leg when I wiped out on my bike. I wasn't bedridden, but I certainly couldn't trudge the mile it took to get to my private paradise. I cried and cried and everyone thought it was because I was in pain. I was, but the pain wasn't in my leg, it was in my heart. Only Kael knew the real reason.

Charlotte had laid eggs. Nine of them. And they were just about to hatch when I had my accident.

Kael never said a word. But two days later he came back with pictures. Then, without my even asking, he went to my lake every single day that summer to check on the eggs, reporting back when they'd hatched. And along with Old Man Riley, they built protective fencing around the nest, trying to guard the cygnets when they were at their most vulnerable to predators. In the end, only two of the nine made it. But I'm not sure any would have had it not been for Kael watching over them.

Over the years, there were countless acts of selfless kindness just like this one. And I think maybe I've taken them for granted. Kael Shepard loves me—*has* loved me—like no other man ever has. Even Killian. *Especially* Killian.

I just never saw it because someone else's aura was blinding me.

Now, as I watch him struggle to get the backs of his legs, I know I should offer to help, but I don't. I'm frozen to my seat, gaping at his raw masculinity. I marvel as he moves with beauty and grace, his taut muscles fluid underneath tanned skin. My mouth waters a bit. I don't think it's for beer.

Then I do something I should have done a long time ago. From the very first time I said yes to a real "date" with Kael Shepard only a mere eight months ago.

I take my friend hat off and put on one of a woman instead.

And when I do that...when I open that door I've had sealed shut by another man for twenty-six years and view him through an entirely new lens, what I see astounds me. Floors me, actually.

My body suddenly feels weak and needy.

My core is starting to sizzle, and it's not because it's almost ninety degrees today.

It's because of Kael.

It's almost as if I'm seeing my husband for the very first time as the unparalleled male specimen he truly is.

He's beautiful. Knee-weakening beautiful, if I'm totally honest. He's not ripped like those guys you see in muscle magazines. His thighs are powerful, but lean. His skin holds the healthy glow of summer's rays. He doesn't have six-pack abs like romance novelists write about. He is defined, though, and I easily see the outline of muscles that lie just beneath his taut flesh.

His stomach flexes and his bicep bulges when he brings his arm overhead and tries to get his back. I must make a noise because all of a sudden he's looking at me, and his grin gets bigger and wider the longer he stares.

"What?" I ask him all breathless like.

That earns me a chuckle. It sounds more like the sexy rumble of a motorcycle revving in the distance. "I like that way you're looking at me, Swan."

That nickname. Hot damn it gets sexier every time he says it in the way that means he wants me naked.

"Yeah? How is that?" I lean my head all the way back and rest it against my chair. I bring my legs up, crossing them Indian style. As I'm wearing another sundress, the way I'm now sitting gives Kael a clear view of my panties. They're nude and benign everyday under-wear, but you'd think I was wearing a crotchless pair of lacies by the way storm clouds have swept into his eyes. I feel the burn of them making me hotter, wetter. I think he sees it, too, because he lets his gaze leisurely travel back up my body as if he's out for a Sunday drive.

It stops. Lingers on my breasts. One...two...three beats. Now they ache, too. Throb. My nipples feel ultrasensitive pressing against the thin cotton material. I swear I feel each individual thread. My tongue pushes out to moisten my now-dry lips. He zeroes in on that and swallows hard. His Adam's apple bobs up and down a couple of times.

How did I never notice how tingly that makes me?

When our eyes finally reconnect, something different—*new*—sparks between us. And if I didn't feel the heat of his want from the ten feet that separate us, I'd certainly see it from the six-person tent now pitched in his shorts.

"What way am I looking at you?" I prompt again, letting my eyes fall purposefully to the hardness which now seems to strain for me.

The sound of the metal can meeting the wood beneath his feet doesn't even faze me. He strides—no, *ambles*—with the grace of a jaguar to where I'm waiting for his answer. Desperately wanting it. Spreading his legs wide, he bends, props his knees against my chair. Then his palms meet the armrests and he leans down until his nose is a whisper away from mine. My eyes have to strain to keep him in focus, that's how close he is.

"It's the way I've imagined you looking at me my entire life, Maverick."

God in heaven. Chills just spread over the entire length of me.

"How...how is that?" I rasp, squirming wildly underneath the pin of his stare. I'm so unbelievably turned on right now.

The mint of his breath washes me in desire before his croaked words sink in. "With hungry eyes."

Holy merciful Mary.

I am nowhere near hungry. I'm famished. Ravenous. I could eat a horse, I'm so starved for him right now. It's an unfamiliar, yet heady feeling.

I don't want to let it end.

Reaching out, I let my nail scrape over his stiffness. Just once. Slow. Root to tip. The sharp breath he sucks in makes me shudder, scalp to pinky toe. His half-lidded gaze burns me with equal parts love and lust. I haven't done this for him yet. He's too much of a gentleman to ask and I've still had my head buried firmly in the murky sea of denial that we would, in fact, end up here.

Silently, he encourages me, but also gives me an out if that's what I want. As always, he's leaving the decision about how far we go squarely in my hands.

And tonight, I want to give him what he's always given freely of.

Myself.

Eyes screwed firmly to his, I grip his upper thigh, my thumb right on the inside of his groin. When I move it a half inch, teasing his arousal, his lips part and my name falls out on a hoarse whisper. Feeling 100 percent in control, I drag the meat of his leg through my hand as I make my way down until I feel the stickiness of his flesh. He's sweating. So am I. I don't even notice the bugs feasting on me anymore. I have my own meal I'm after.

I work my way back up, now under his shorts, until the prize I'm chasing comes just into reach. Then I falter.

Sweet Lord of Lords.

*Commando.*

Kael's mouth parts and the gravel in his voice stirs when he says, "Don't stop now." It sounds like a command, but it's not. He's begging. He never begs. I love it.

"What about the neighbors?" I tease. Our house is in the city limits. The lot is bigger than most and the old maple and ash trees that line either side give us immense privacy. But if Helena Winters, the eighty-one-year-old widow to our right, decides she needs to prune the flower bed butting up against our adjoining fence, there's a broken board where she could possibly get an eyeful. It wouldn't be the first time she's tried to spy.

A devious expression now plays on my husband's lips. "I think Helena could use a lesson or two in snooping around, don't you?"

I laugh at the same time he gasps when I close my fist around his massive erection and squeeze. "I couldn't agree more."

He's now standing tall. My face is nearly level with his groin. Instead of pulling his shorts down, I move the black fabric of one leg up toward his waist. His cock springs free. His thick fingers wrap around the loose material, keeping it from interfering with us.

I slide my hand down the steel rod encased in velvet and squeeze the base.

Time decelerates. Just a bit.

I draw in a short breath. For some reason I'm nervous.

The look in his eyes says it all. *Fucking do it. Please.*

It's all I need.

I let my attention drop and whimper a little when I take him in. He's like crack for the visual senses. Intoxicating. Heavy. Weeping. Pulsing madly in my hand already. When I swipe a thumb over the creamy drops already collecting on the tip and massage it around, his head falls back on a loud, long, pleading groan.

Then my head dips forward. Earthy man and chemicals assault my nose. My mouth opens then closes around him. His eyes roll. My tongue swirls. A hand finds my hair and weaves inside my haphazard bun. I suck and pull him to the back of my throat. He curses over and over.

I do it all again, this time cupping his balls ever so slightly. I roll them gently between my fingers...then make sure my lips securely cover my teeth as I drag them back up his long length.

I run the tip of my tongue through his slit, moaning when more salty flavor gushes onto it. I feel the vibration of it all the way to the hand gripping the base of his shaft. I twist that hand. Then the one in my scalp does the same. It stings but feels unbelievable.

I'm so wet right now, I'll leave a stain on the chair. My jaw is sore already from his thick breadth. And the throbbing between my own legs feels like a drum beating in time with my own heartbeat.

He slips a finger under my chin and gently tugs up so my eyes lift. They lock tight to his. He wants this connection. Needs it, maybe.

Okay. Fine by me.

I watch him watch me.

I like it more than I remember ever liking it before.

*Go on*, he silently urges.

*Nothing will stop me*, I quietly convey.

"You look so fucking incredible with my cock sunk in your mouth, Swan. So good. I feel like I'm dreaming." The last part is so wistful, I want to cry. More than ever I want him to feel good. Feel loved.

My head bobs faster. I suck until my cheeks hollow. Until I feel him swell. Until I know he's close. He takes over, then. Picks up the pace and I let him. He fucks my mouth as if he owns me. In that moment, he does. I'm all his.

"Oh, fuck, yes. Like that."

He's there, pulsating inside my mouth. He tries to pull away. I won't let him. I run my free hand up his backside, grip, and hold him to me. He reads my intentions, telling him it's okay to let go.

With one more uncontrolled thrust in so far I nearly gag, he does.

On a low rumble, he comes. Empties himself on my tongue, down my throat. I swallow. And swallow again. Until every drop of him has been consumed and his soft chanting stops.

After his last shudder, I release him from my mouth with a soft pop, wishing it wasn't over already. His shorts fall all the way back down, but still tent because he's not all the way soft yet.

I work my jaw back and forth a bit to ease the slight ache. Wanting to reach down and relieve the one lurking in my very center, too, but I don't. This was all about Kael, who is currently hunched over me. Panting, leaning his forehead against his forearm, which is propped against the brand new siding we had installed two weeks before the wedding. I lay my head all the way back and gaze up at him, a small smile on my face. One that he immediately mirrors.

He reaches down to stroke my cheek. It's tender. Pure idolization. The fact his hand trembles slightly makes my grin all that much bigger. My heart feels soft and squishy.

"I think I heard rustling in the bushes over there," I tell him. I'm not sure if I did or not, but I feel positively giddy right now. I feel like twirling outside with my arms out and my head flung back during a thunderstorm. I just worshiped my husband with everything in me, but more than that...I didn't think about Killian one time. For the first time in the last six months that I've been intimate with Kael, not one thought strayed to him. It feels good to see a pinprick of light through the shroud of darkness I've been sunk in. To finally take a real breath that doesn't feel completely tainted by him.

"You did, huh?" His chuckle is still breathy. It makes my blood hum. I feel powerful.

"I think we gave her a show."

His eyes flutter over to the fence then back to me. That smirk kills me. "I think it's a show I'd like to experience again."

"Yeah?"

"Yeah," he tells me softly, sobering a little.

"Then we will," I promise, my mood matching his.

Taking a step back, he holds out a hand, palm up. "Come."

"Where?" I ask, setting mine in it.

He easily hauls me up into his arms. "Shower. Then a healthy dose of calamine lotion for those welts you have all over you."

"Oh." Why does that make me feel slightly disappointed?

"And then," he whispers against my stretched, swollen lips, "I'm going to spend the entire evening making love to my incredibly sexy wife."

My smile returns. "Aren't you hungry?" Kael still works for my father. A couple years ago he was promoted to cocounsel. He puts in long, grueling hours sometimes. It's now almost eight thirty and he's only been home about half an hour. I doubt he's eaten.

"Absolutely starved, Swan." He wags his eyebrows up and down, making me giggle. He scoops me up in his arms and I squeal all the way inside knowing this is a new beginning for us.

"Here." I ignore the cup of coffee being extended to me. "Maverick, you need something in your stomach," Arnie Shepard pleads. He's as out of sorts as the rest of us, but I wonder if he has a right to be. I don't think so.

"I can't handle anything in my stomach right now."

"He's going to be all right."

His confident tone irritates me. Infuriates me. I'm tired of hearing the same fucking thing. It sounds trite and banal. The truth is...we don't know what's going on behind those secured doors that separate us from him. We don't know the skill of the doctors working to save his life. We don't know shit. And the longer we wait, the more bad stuff we get to make up in our heads.

Mine can't possibly get worse.

"So everyone says." I keep my stare firmly on the matted carpet beneath me. I wonder how many oceans the tears stuck in it would fill if we could separate them from the fibers of pain they're now wound around.

A lot, I bet.

The entire world would probably be flooded.

My gaze drifts past Arnie to the mocking face of the clock on the wall.

7:03.

I watch the seconds tick off, leaving crushed hope in their wake and uncertainty in their future.

Eight hours.

It's been eight long, torturous hours.

Four hundred eighty unbearable minutes.

We've had one update. An hour ago.

*He's still in surgery. As soon as we know anything else, I'll let you know.* The heavyset nurse gave us news that was no news at all in a tone that attempted at sympathetic but bordered on preparedness. She looked as if she'd seen her fair share of grieving families and was numb to the pain.

I asked her if surgery would normally take this long. *I'm sorry. I don't know anything else.*

Lying bitch.

She knows something. She just won't say. Delaying pain doesn't make it better. It just keeps you balanced on a knife's edge, the razor sharp tip digging in farther with each new breath you breathe. Either way, the end result is the same. You're sliced in two. One is just a slower process than the other.

"You have to keep the faith, dear," Arnie preaches in a resigned voice. I'm unsure if he's trying to convince himself or me. I hear him sigh above me. See his body slide out of my line of sight, leaving me alone once again.

Good.

It's what I want.

I don't want comfort.

I don't deserve it any more than anyone else here does. We all have our crosses to bear, our share in the events that unfolded. Every one of us played a part, some bigger than others.

Why I ever considered giving up on us is a guilt so suffocating I can't bear the massive weight of it. It's absolutely crushing. I stare down the hallway where the nurse disappeared and wonder: is he alive? Is he fighting? Maybe he's already dead and they're leaving us on that fucking edge a little bit longer as they try to figure out the string of words they think will comfort but won't. Can't. Never will. Why even try?

I stand and look at no one as I walk out of the place that feels like a coffin whose lid is slowly closing. I leave everyone behind, ignoring my name being called over and over. I need air. I need something. Anything but desperate despair.

I stop at the coffee machine. Look over at my choices. Stand there so long someone taps on my shoulder.

"Excuse me, miss. Can I get you something?" a kind female voice asks.

*A miracle?* "I don't know," I reply blandly without looking at her.

"Here," she says, plunking a few coins into the slot. She pushes some buttons and opens the dispenser a few seconds later. Hands me a paper cup. It's hot. I look down. The liquid is tan and smells sugary. It reminds me of him. I lumber away, not even sure I said thanks. I hope I did. I take one sip. It's bitter and feels like ash on my tongue. It congeals in my stomach. It ends up in the next garbage can I pass.

I aimlessly walk the sterile halls. For how long, I'm not sure. But the farther I burrow into the belly of the hospital, the more unwanted hang-ons I collect. Antiseptic sticks to the hairs inside my nose. Moans of agony wallow in my ears. Finality squishes underneath my feet. It soaks into my shoes, staining my socks black. The energy in this entire place is sad and deathly still, even though there's frenetic activity everywhere.

Somehow, I end up in the chapel. I'm not even sure where it is. What floor it's on. How I got here. Oddly, it's empty. I'm glad. I slump into a hard pew in the dimly lit room where countless others before me have prayed, begged, tried trading their lives for someone else's.

I don't do any of those things. I've already prayed my mind empty. I've begged until my soul is bled dry. And God already knows I'd trade anything for his life, including mine.

So instead, I watch the candles flicker and reminisce.

In my mind, I wind back time and remember when I was once happy. It all started with him. And it will end with him if he goes. I smile as I let tears flow once again when I picture his loving brown eyes.

The bass of AC/DC's "Back in Black" thumps, the beat setting a new rhythm for my heart. I let it thrum through me. Enjoy getting lost in it. Tonight, at Peppy's, it's karaoke night. It's supposed to be a once-a-month event on Friday nights, but somehow it's turned into more of an every-other-week event. I think somehow Kael popularized that a few months back.

"Beer or Captain tonight?" Kael's question whispered in my ear makes me shiver with lust. I feel his knowing smile against my cheek. One hand skates up my side. He rests his thumb right underneath the mound of my breast. Now, I'm practically trembling. He starts chuckling, muted and sexy.

We turned the corner last week. Granted, we haven't had a lot of it, but we had the best sex we've ever had after I blew him on the back porch. It was rough and dirty in the shower before turning sweet and sensual in the bedroom. He fulfilled his promise of making love all night long. Four o'clock came around pretty damn early the next morning. And it turns out Helena may very well have caught our little show because she hasn't looked me in the eye since. She moved faster than any eighty-one-year-old with a bad hip should have when we met at the mailbox. She was clearly trying to dodge me.

"Barley pop," I tell him on a grin. I want to keep my head clear tonight, hoping for a repeat. Some people swear drinking improves their performance, but I think it dulls the senses too much. I want to feel every slow stroke into me. Ride that glorious wave to the top and let it crash over me, reveling in the too-swift rush of euphoria that's harder to reach and even shorter when too much alcohol flows through you. I want to actually enjoy making love to my husband, not just get through it like I have been since we've been married.

"Barley pop it is, Swan." The corner of his mouth lifts at our inside joke as he walks away.

"You guys and your weird sayings."

I just shrug, eyes glued to Kael's backside.

When I was six, he stole a Bud heavy from his father's garage fridge and tricked me into drinking it. He told me it was "barley pop" and see...I loved pop. My parents didn't buy it because "it will rot your teeth," they said. I wasn't generally naïve, even at six, but he knew I'd be a sucker for this prank. But the joke was on him. He got a face full of foamy beer and the rest of the "barley pop" ended up soaked into the mulch of the forest floor.

"You look happy, Mavs. So does Kael for that matter. And I mean newlywed, I'm-getting-the-shit-banged-out-of-me happy."

I tear my stare away from my husband's fine ass, which is molded perfectly in his dark-wash jeans, I might add, when MaryLou's slides a finger under my mouth and closes it. She grins. So do I. I feel it reach my eyes and dive into my soul.

"I am." I shift toward MaryLou, tucking my right foot under the thigh of my left leg, and take the few minutes we'll have by ourselves all night to dump out my soul. I keep an eye out for Kael and Larry just in case. "Some days are harder than others, though."

The edges of MaryLou's mouth fall into a sad smile. "Like Monday?"

"Yeah, like Monday." This past Monday was Killian's thirty-first birthday. I didn't call. Didn't text. Didn't even send an impersonal Facebook post. I pretended it was a regular ol' day in Dusty Falls. I patted myself on the back, but stewed in that decision all night, wondering if I'd hurt his feelings. Would he think I was acting child-ish? Did I care if he did? I hated that the answer was yes.

"There will be days like those, I guess."

"I suppose. But I can honestly say I feel I'm finally taking baby steps forward instead of standing still. So there's that, at least. It feels good."

"An inch is an inch, Maverick. As long as it's forward it's movement in the right direction."

"I feel like this lifelong shell Killian has around me is finally cracking. And the more cracks I get, the more room for Kael I seem to have. He's seeping in, little by little." *In the way a husband already should have*, I don't add.

I look over to catch Kael watching me. He's intense. Almost as if he knows what we're talking about. I want to reach up and rub the ache in my chest. I don't, though. I let my lips turn up reassuringly. Kael does the same.

"I'm glad," MaryLou says.

"Me, too," I mumble to her, meaning it with every fiber in me.

Our conversation shifts to the bakery menu as the guys return with a drink in each hand. They set them down and I notice that MaryLou's looks clear. And not bubbly like a 7 and 7 would. Then I notice she's found something extremely fascinating with the tabletop.

"Hey," I prod as Kael slides into the booth beside me and throws an arm around my shoulder. I lean into the possessive kiss he plants on my cheek. "Hey," I say again, a little louder this time. MaryLou doesn't look up so I kick her under the table.

"Ouch." She reaches down to rub her shin. Angry eyes find mine. Good. At least I have her attention.

"What's that?" I point to her glass.

"What's what?"

I reach for it, but she's faster. She grabs the cup and yanks her arm back, spilling liquid in the process. She thinks she has the upper hand on me now. I see it in her smug grin. She should know me better.

I dip my finger through the liquid now on the table and stick it in my mouth. It's gross. I know. I'm not sure how well these tables are cleaned and there's some unsavory stuff that can happen in this more secluded corner of the bar. But hey...I've had worse things in my mouth.

"You're sick," she chastises. "Do you have any idea whose ass germs you may have just shoved into your mouth? I heard Andrew Bolger was banging Holly Brummer on this exact table last weekend. She came all over it and everything."

Both Kael and Larry chuckle. I ignore her diversion. If that were true, she would have picked another spot. Still, I plan to use the complimentary mouthwash in the bathroom in a minute.

"And you're drinking water. Why?"

It's not that I care she's drinking water. I'm not about to get rip-roaring drunk tonight, even if a two-day hangover would be a good excuse to get out of Sunday's family brunch. So I don't need a drinking buddy. But MaryLou can drink any man here under the table. And the girl like's her Seagram's, so the fact she's drinking water is highly suspicious.

"Are you pregnant?" I ask. I'm dumbfounded. That's the only reason she would be drinking water. Why would she not tell me she's pregnant? I notice Larry glance away. That stabs me.

"No," she responds fast. "But we're trying again." Reaching across the table she links our fingers. I let her, even if I do want to pull away just to hurt her the way I'm now hurting. That my best friend kept something this big from me stings more than I can articulate.

Wow.

First Jilly. Now MaryLou.

I've felt as if I've been left behind my entire life. With men. With love. Now with babies. Everyone's happiness crowds around me until I feel smothered.

Kael squeezes my shoulder. He knows I'm upset. "Hey, Larry, how about a round of darts?" Larry, the clueless fuck, says no. Kael slips out, scoops up Larry's drink, and takes off. He knows Larry will follow like a bloodhound when alcohol is involved.

When they're gone, I ask, "Why didn't you tell me?" I can't keep hurt from double coating my words. I try. Really I do.

She just stares at me until my dense brain works through it.

*Ah.*

I get it.

"You could have told me," I tell her firmly. "We share everything." And I mean everything. From learning to use tampons together to practicing French kissing on each other when we were ten to crushing on the same boy. There's not a female in all of Adel County who hasn't crushed on Killian Shepard.

"I'm sorry. I should have. You've just been going through a lot. I didn't want to add to it."

"You could have added to it. You *should* have, MaryLou. We're best friends. I don't want you to feel you don't think I can be happy for you just because I'm going through my own shit. I am. Happy for you, I mean."

"I know." She's contrite. "But the bigger part of me is just scared. It's like if I start telling people, it becomes this real pressure and..."

She doesn't need to say any more. MaryLou was pregnant when she got married. At five months she lost the baby. They were both devastated. I was devastated for them. But they tried again. Twice more. Unsuccessful, they gave up. My heart has bled over and over for her.

"Hey," I say. I see her glassy blues peak through her lashes. "I guess you'll get good use of that sex swing then." When she laughs a tiny tear rolls down her cheek. "And then when you're done, he can just tip you upside down and let you ferment a while."

She fake slaps me. "You're terrible."

"Yeah. But I can tell by the sparkle in your eye you think it's a good idea."

She fights a smile for all of five seconds before whispering conspiratorially, "I never thought about that."

"Well, see...that's what best friends are for."

"Thanks, Mavricky." Her relief is palpable. The weight of secrets is a heaviness MaryLou can't handle. I wish I was like that.

"No problem, babe."

Our attention turns briefly to our men. Kael looks smug and cocky. Larry a bit more pissy. Guess we know who's winning.

"Hey, karaoke's going to start in a few. Let's hit the bathroom before we miss Paulie singing 'Walk Like an Egyptian.'"

Paulie, our forty-five-year-old town pharmacist, not only sings a good rendition of The Bangles' most famous song, he's choreographed a pretty fancy little routine. He even brings his own tambourine and does that side eye roll better than Susanna Hoffs. And since he hasn't lost his eighties mullet yet, he's very entertaining to watch. He usually gets the first spot to start karaoke night off with a bang, pun intended.

"Good idea," I say.

I follow her into the ladies' room. We chat through the stall walls as we always do. After we wash our hands and I've sufficiently rinsed my mouth with the generic version of Scope, I watch MaryLou primp her hair, vowing to be a better friend. I want to be there for her as she is for me. I can understand why she didn't tell me. I've been pretty self-absorbed lately.

"We good?" she asks, eyeing me behind her.

"Of course. Why wouldn't we be?"

She launches herself into my arms and hugs me tight as a boa constrictor. She takes a breath and I know she's going to apologize again. I cut her off. "Don't. It's okay. I'm not mad."

She breaks away. Plants a sticky kiss on my lips. "I have all the feels for you, you know that right?"

"Right back at ya."

When we walk out of the bathroom, my head is tweaked to the back. I'm hysterical as MaryLou hops on one foot, trying to pull off a long string of toilet paper that's stuck to the bottom of the other. I'm so focused on her I'm almost knocked backward when I run smack into a solid, massive wall. Warm hands grip my waist to prevent my ass from meeting the gummy floor.

"I'm sor—" I start. But when I crane my neck forward and up, my apology drops off a cliff of confusion. I find it's not a wall at all I ran into.

It's Killian.

The scent of Burberry Brit mixed with expensive leather blitzes through me two seconds too late. It makes my knees weak. It makes my heart race. It makes me want things I know I shouldn't.

Fuck.

Damn him. I was doing so well, too.

Mostly.

"What are you doing here?" I demand. I'm angry he's here. Furious, actually.

One of the unspoken reasons Kael and I come here together is that Jillian refuses to lower herself to Peppy's. And because Jillian refuses to come, Killian's not allowed to either. If he were with me, I would never control him like that. He knows it.

"It's a public place, Small Fry."

And why doesn't he look surprised to see me in the least? Asshole knew we were here. "Don't call me that," I spit.

I realize that MaryLou is quietly observing behind me, the bathroom door now blocked by the three of us. Then she moves into action faster than the dazzle of a lightning bug.

"Come on, Maverick." Swooping past me, she snakes her arm through mine. She has me halfway down the hall when Killian grabs the hand swinging behind me. His hold is firm. Unyielding. It burns in the most hatefully delicious of ways. A memory flashes of that palm curved perfectly around my ass as he drove into me from below. By the hungry look drawn over his face, he's remembering the same thing.

Shit. I need to get the hell out of Dodge. Pedal to the metal.

Except Killian has no intention of letting me.

He tugs one way, MaryLou the other. They're both pulling so hard, I feel like Gumby.

"Killian, please," I beg. We simply can't be caught in the darkened hallway alone. Especially by Kael. I can't believe he would have missed Killian walking in.

"Two minutes. That's all I ask. Please, Maverick."

My gaze cascades between MaryLou and Killian. The looks on both their faces are the same, yet so different. He's begging me to sin. She's begging me to choose salvation. "Two minutes," I tell him. "Starting now."

A sinner I am, then. *Put it on my tab.*

MaryLou sighs audibly but drops my hand. I can tell the second she's gone because the energy left in this small, enclosed space just charged up a thousand kilowatts. My armpits start to sweat.

"One minute fifty seconds," I announce, crossing my arms, hoping to keep Killian from seeing how he's affecting me. Damn him to hell. Five beats in his presence and all the progress I've made is evaporating like dew. How can one person have this much power, this much control over me?

"I must have missed your call on Monday." He says it with a quirk to his mouth, only his nonchalance is meant to hide the hurt. It's plain as day in his dark eyes. And just like that, I feel contrite and small. I hate that he can make me feel that way with a simple statement or a look. I hate that he still has this effect on me. I hate that Killian is my puppeteer, holding strings to parts of me I can't figure out how to slash...no matter how hard I try.

"My phone's broke." His quirk falters. My repentance deepens. "Is that all you wanted? A little ego boost?" My question is full of vinegar. It's pungent on my taste buds.

He ignores it. And with the next intentional stab of his words, makes me feel even worse than I already do. As if that's possible. "I was looking forward to my chocolate. I think this is the first year I've gone without one of your infamous concoctions."

My heavy head drops. I breathe deeply. Run my tongue over my teeth while taking in the dark, spongy speckled floor.

Even when we were away from each other, I made Killian something for his birthday every year. I never failed. It started out as a runny mud pie when I was four. And by mud, I don't mean fancy chocolate pudding with crumbled cookies on top.

I remember the light in his eyes and his throaty laugh as he pretended to eat it. Pretty soon, it was gone and he'd convinced me he'd swallowed every bite, but he managed to drop them all on the ground behind him. He may have just been placating a four-year-old, but I did the same thing the following year. And then each year after until I learned how to bake. Then I made him real treats. They were always chocolate. His favorite.

Last year, I spent hours perfecting a molten chocolate cake dusted in a mixture of powdered sugar, cinnamon, and fresh nutmeg shavings. I delivered it to his office myself. I knew it was wrong then. He was married. No longer available. No longer mine. I should have stopped a tradition that had become just ours because it wasn't just us anymore. There was no "us" anymore, period.

That's why I knew I couldn't do it again this year.

Cutting the cord sucks ass.

"Mavs, please. I—" His head falls to the wall with a dull thud. His gaze floats to the ceiling then back to me. He looks as sad and lost as I feel most days. "I miss you. So much."

I feel so confused. I've replayed every moment, wondering where we went wrong. What did I do? What didn't I do? Why wasn't I enough? I gave him everything and he gave me away.

*Be strong, Mavs.* Be brave. Be anything but putty in his oh-so-skillful hands. I think of Kael. If he's wondering where I am. If he knows I'm back here—alone—with his brother.

"You're down to less than a minute now." I have to get the fuck out of here before I let us do something we shouldn't. My lips haven't been on Killian's in over two and a half years. Since he announced his engagement. I physically ache for him right now. More than I ever have.

He straightens tall and takes a step toward me. I take one back, shaking my head. Inhaling deeply, he asks, "Can we find some time to get together? Just the two of us? I'd like to talk."

Since he married Jillian, I try to limit my time with him alone. *Especially* alone. Neither of us seems to be able to keep our wants or thoughts from straying. I think we both know if we're confined in any space by ourselves for any length of time, we will become adulterers on top of everything else. And that's one hard line I just won't cross.

"I don't think that's a good idea."

"Why?" He edges toward me. I stay still this time. I loathe me right now.

"You know why, Killian."

"You still love me," he whispers. It's hoarse and warm and inviting. And so fucking true. "I see it every time you look into my soul. No one has ever looked at me the way you do, Maverick."

His eyes skate between mine and my lips, which I've now just wet. I feel a hand graze my hip and know it's not a passerby. This hallway seems to be deserted at the worst possible time.

Then he bends down and runs his mouth over my jaw. It's light. Barely a touch...the skip of a rock on top of the water. When I hear him inhale and moan, I almost turn my head and place my mouth on his, ending the torture we've both been living through. Jumping over a line I just said I refused to.

I swallow. Hard. It hurts forcing saliva past the twisted, confused ball of emotion sitting in the middle of my throat.

*Lord, if you're listening...please give me strength. I need Your help.*

"I belong to Kael now," I manage to push out on a rush of nearly nonexistent air.

He leans back. Too far, yet not far enough. I still don't move when the heat of his anger drizzles over my forehead and down my cheeks. "You belong to me. You've always belonged to me."

*Then why did you marry someone else?* I want to scream. *Why did you treat me like I didn't even matter? Why did you break every single promise you ever made? Why won't you just tell me why the fuck you did it?*

How can you love someone so much yet hate them with equal passion at the same time? He is such an insensitive, conceited, hypocritical bastard. He can't have me but no one else can either? Well, fuck that. Fuck *him*.

"This says different," I smart back, shoving the finger between us that holds my vow of monogamy and forever to his brother. I grab his hand and point to the titanium band circling his fourth finger. "And so does this."

"This doesn't lie," he retorts hotly, flattening his other palm between my breasts. Right over my heart, which thumps erratically beneath the warmth of his hand.

What kind of twisted fucking head games is he playing? Has been playing for years now? I'm sick of it. I'm sick of him. It's like he makes a sport of keeping me tied to him. *How long can I dangle her before she breaks?* Little does he know his selfish actions are helping him to eradicate himself from my heart. I hope the door bruises his ass on the way out.

I bring my arm up from beneath us in one swift move and knock his away. "Time's up." I spin, practically sprint away, mentally trying to saw through that knot he has embedded deep within me. I wonder when it will get easier. If ever.

———

I don't head back to the booth. I keep my eyes focused ahead, not even glancing in that direction, afraid my flushed face will give me away.

Peppy's is now packed. Anticipation for the night ahead hums in the air. I weave and shoulder through the crowd. Apologize as I knock people out of the way, heading straight for the bar. I realize as I wait to be noticed that Paulie has started his set. Damn. That means Kael and Larry will be back at the booth, waiting for me.

My ribs heave. My mind spins. My heart is thumping against my breastbone so damn hard I think I may have internal bruising. I wish I had a switch so I could flip it all off. Every hurt. Every want. Every thing. I'm so lost in what just happened...what *almost* happened that I nearly don't hear Cathy calling my name, asking what I need.

"Jose silver and Sprite. Make it a double. Short glass," I bark over the commotion. Her brows pinch. She knows my usual order. This isn't it. But, like a dutiful bartender, she goes off and does as I ask, no questions asked. A minute later, I have a cold glass enclosed in my hand and half the contents down my throat. I signal for another, wishing my buzz would be instant instead of twenty minutes from now.

I jump when a hand gently grips my neck a second before scruff tickles my cheek. My earlobe is then between the gentle bite of teeth. "What's wrong, Swan?"

"Nothing," I rasp back just as Cathy sets another clear-tinged drink in front of me. She scoots her attention briefly to Kael before moving along to the next customer.

"Really? Why the switch to the hard stuff?"

"I—" I freeze. I don't want to lie to Kael. That's no way to start off a marriage. But I don't want him to know I was just hobnobbing with Killian in the dark in the back of the bar if he doesn't already know. That I almost kissed him. That I'm still thinking about kissing him. And I can't tell by his tone if he does or not.

"It's MaryLou, isn't it?"

The lids on my eyes fall shut. Out of relief or guilt, I can't be sure. *You're sure*, my inner self quietly chastises. He's giving me an out, so what do I do? Do I do the right thing? Oh fuck, no. That would be too hard. Right now, I just can't deal with any more hard.

Black-hearted sinner. That's me.

So I take the gift he's handing me.

I take it and sprint.

"Yes." I'm not sure he hears me, but he does feel the nod of my head.

Kael takes the glass I'm currently clinging to like a buoy. Pries my fingers off. Sets it down before gently spinning me around. Patrons are elbowing on either side to get their next mind-numbing fix, but

Kael shelters me. Protects me. As always. When he takes my face in his hands and tips up, the movement causes a stray drop of water to slip from the corner of my eye. He wipes it away with his thumb.

"Baby, don't cry."

"I'm not. I'm just..."

"Hurt?" he prods.

"Yeah." It's not *technically* a lie. I *was* hurt. I *am* hurting. Just not for the reasons he thinks.

"This is a big step for them. I'm sure she just doesn't want to get her hopes up and then have everyone know about it if it doesn't happen for them again."

"I know," I manage to muster.

I should be thinking about MaryLou. About Kael. About anything except what I am. Instead, I want to look around. See if Killian is still here. Watching. Waiting for another opportunity to strike.

In some ways, I wish Kael did know he was here. Maybe then Killian would just leave us in peace. Maybe I should just tell him? Be courageous. Do the right thing. I stare into his guileless, loving eyes and I know I need to vomit it all. Tell him everything. I want to *deserve* the way he's looking at me right now. I open my mouth to do just that when J Ton—aka Johnny Littleton—announces Kael's name.

The crowd goes wild. And I mean, on their feet, clapping, screaming, cheering wild. The place is nuts. The grin that comes over my husband's face is absolutely boyish. Glorious. I fall into it, forgetting everything that happened just minutes ago.

"What's going on?" I laugh as he drags us through the crowd toward the tiny half-moon stage. When we reach the front, someone sets a chair right smack in the meager open space. Kael gestures for me to sit then proceeds to lean down and kiss me hard, slow, and very, very thoroughly. The catcalls spur him on and he comes back for one more. I'm panting. Damp, in all places one can be damp.

He hops up on the stage where J Ton has placed a stool. He

hands Kael a guitar. Kael's mischievous eyes snap to mine the second he's taken a seat and has perched the guitar just so in his lap.

This is exactly what he did the night he asked me to marry him. Not only can he play the guitar like a pro, he has a voice like melted butter. He got up on that stage and turned me into a blubbering mess when he sang Lenny Kravitz's "I'll Be Waiting."

If you've ever listened to that song, it starts out with him singing about how he knows someone else broke the girl's heart. Says he'll give her time. Says he's the one who truly loves her. How he'll be waiting until she's ready. Kael never took his eyes from me the entire time. Every perfectly tuned note, every haunting word was sung just for me. When he was done, he hopped down, dropped to both knees in front of me, dug a three-carat diamond from his pocket, and nearly wept himself as he bared his soul to me.

*"I know it's soon, Swan. But at the same time, it isn't. I've been by your side our entire lives. No one knows you better than me. You breathe, so do I. You hurt, I ache. When you smile...fuck, Mavs, it's hard to see through the stars blinding me. Every time you laugh, I fall a little more in love with you, if that's possible. I want to be with you until we're gray and wrinkled and don't give a shit if what we say offends people. No one will love you like I do, Swan. Your soul belongs to me. Everything you need is here, staring right at you. If you're not ready, I understand. But know that I'll be waiting. I'll wait as long as it takes. As long as you need. But if you are...then put me out of my misery and be my wife. I promise you won't regret a single second of our life together."*

I laughed and sobbed through his heartfelt, heart-melting proposal. How could a girl say no to that? No one in their right mind would. Every single woman and half the men in the bar that night were misty-eyed. I couldn't have the man I really wanted and here was a man who genuinely wanted me. Loved me so much I could actually feel the warmth of it surround me. I was wrapped up in the moment; I said yes.

Kael was already a household name, but after that night, people from surrounding towns started coming out on Friday karaoke nights just to see if there would be a repeat performance.

Guess he chose tonight to do it. I half wonder if it's coincidence or more?

With a wink and a smirk, Kael strums the strings, dragging me back from then to now. He clears his throat and announces, "This song is for my new crazy-hot wife, Maverick Shepard. There's no one I'd rather waste time with than you, Swan." The last part is said low and sultry with promises to come later.

All the females swoon. Including me.

Then he starts singing.

"Oh fuck," I mutter before covering my mouth with my hand. I'm welling up as the raspy words of Saint Asonia's ballad "Waste My Time" filter into a room that's now humming quietly with anticipation.

The lyrics are soft and beautiful. Once again, our world narrows. Me and him. He's telling me I'm that one person he just wants to lay back in the cool grass under a moonlit sky with and simply do nothing. The nothing that is perfect. The nothing that isn't wasting time at all, but becomes moments that live inside you always, no matter what else is going on around you. You know you're with the right person when you can do that. Just be. I've always, *always* felt that way with Kael. There's a sense of peaceful comfort and tranquility with him I don't have with anyone else. Even Killian.

At that realization, suddenly those cracks I told MaryLou about widen and spread. I practically feel them snaking around me, splitting me open. So much of Kael floods into me in a single second it makes my breath catch hard. I sink into the words he's singing. Live in his joy. Break apart a bit more.

The song ends way too soon. The room is still. Not even a sniffle or a cough. We stare at each other until he professes, "I'll love you 'til the day I die, Mavs." I whisper it back, my voice gone. My face streaked. My heart crammed full and beating out of my chest.

Our thrall breaks when a deep male voice yells, "Thanks for

making the rest of us look bad, man," and the entire bar erupts in laughter and whistles and deafening chatter. Then someone starts chanting, "Encore, encore," and everyone else joins in.

Kael glances at me and raises a brow. Silently asks for permission. At this second, the only thing I want to do is take my husband outside, unzip his denims, and suck him off until he's dry and spent. But he's a showman, too, and I can tell he's itching to do this. So I shrug and smirk. Hold my index finger up indicating one more.

J Ton comes over, and he and Kael confer quietly. Kael hands him the guitar. A few seconds later, the familiar notes of eighties hair band Steelheart's "I'll Never Let You Go" blare loudly through the speakers. Kael grabs the mic once again and proceeds to not only put on one heck of a show, he continues to melt me in the process with a song he used to teasingly sing me when we were teenagers. He even falls to his knees during the crescendo, like he always used to.

Everyone is on their feet. Fists pumping. Lighters and cell phones in the air. Singing every word. It's like falling back in time ten years. The only thing he's missing is the long, permed hair and a red-checkered headband.

I laugh.

He laughs.

We take more baby steps forward.

And I never do look around to see if Killian is still there.

I no longer care.

*Maverick*

"I heard you put on quite the performance Friday night," Jilly says in a catty tone she has down to a science.

Fuck her.

Fuck *me*. This is the last place I want to be. Kael and I have barely left the bedroom since we arrived home Friday night. In fact, we didn't even make it to bed for the first round. I jumped him the second we were in the car. My hand was down his pants before the door closed. I had his already-stiff cock trapped between my lips before we pulled out of the parking space. I thought for sure I'd make him blow before we got home. But the guy has the stamina of a prize bull. Instead, he had me riding him the second we pulled into the driveway, both of us too impatient to make it inside. I came on a cry that I'm sure carried over to Helena's open windows. Whoops. Oh well.

Kael takes Jilly's goading in good stride, though. "Oh, I'm sure it was blown out of proportion. It was just a couple of songs." He brushes his lips against my temple. I smile.

"Oh, it wasn't blown out of proportion, babe," I say smugly, eyeing my sister with glee. I wonder who she heard this story from? Killian? Did he stay and watch, then? Was he witness to what I felt was an obvious change in Kael's and my relationship? If he was, I can't read his face. He's been avoiding me since we got here and disappeared ten minutes ago with his cell pressed to his ear. He always works. Twenty-four seven. He's driven, I'll give him that, but I surmise it's to get away from his wife.

"He was almost as brilliant as the night he asked me to marry him," I add. A night I never stopped to appreciate. That makes me sad because I'll never get it back.

"Thanks, Swan," Kael whispers against the shell of my ear.

Jilly looks away, angry. Jealous, more likely.

I've never been able to work it out, but my sister has always had something against me. If I'm happy, she tries to snuff it out. She took the man I loved; yet that still doesn't seem to have satisfied her.

The story she tells about how Killian asked her to marry him has to be embellished or simply made up. It's so cheesy. Killian would have never done anything like that. Hire a mariachi band? He hates mariachi bands. Mexican food gives him heartburn. And he's not a grandstander in any sense of the word. But he always stays silent when she tells her tall tale. He never validates or refutes. Just stays mute and grimaces.

"So, Kael, how is the Mills County contract coming along?" my father asks. "We need to secure that project, son. The potential bonus on that one is huge."

Kael stiffens slightly beside me. He never talks about work with me. Never. It's like this big black hole he doesn't want me sunk in with him. My daddy is demanding, driven, and ruthless. I sometimes wonder if everything he does is aboveboard. When I worked for him for two years, I didn't see outright unscrupulous behavior, but it was questionable at times. Government contracts are tricky. You're talking about millions and millions of taxpayer dollars at play. It's all too easy to shuffle that money around with a simple sleight of the hand that would take auditors years, if ever, to find.

"There are a couple of snags with completion requirements, but we're working through it, Richard. No worries. I always get it done." I did not mistake the fact he bit out the last part as if telling my father to butt out.

"And the Frigid Airways lawsuit? Did you get the deposition pushed out?"

Now, this one I'm familiar with. A small airline is suing my father's company because a piece of the runway was damaged during landing, causing an eight-passenger Cessna Crusader to lose control and crash. Luckily no one was severely hurt, but since DeSoto Construction was responsible for laying that particular part of the landing strip, they are named in the lawsuit.

When Kael removes his arm from around me and leans forward, proceeding to launch into a bunch of legalese I couldn't care less about my attention shifts to my mother.

She's anxious. It's so obvious. I want to ask her why she let us in her hallowed little space in the first place if she's going to need an entire bottle of Xanax to get through it. Her gaze keeps flitting to the plush, pure-white carpet now matted with dozens of footprints. I hope when Kael's parents arrive that lessens the tension somewhat but since it will multiply the rug mashing by two more souls, though, I doubt it.

The posh "sitting" room we're currently occupying is a sanctuary we were under no circumstances allowed to enter as kids. I never understood why. It's just a room. I always wondered if this was a shrine of some sort. Did this space hold someone's sacred ashes? Precious artifacts? Family secrets? Jilly and I both got busted several times sneaking in here. We attempted to cover our tracks. Every time, we failed. Somehow, someway my mother could always tell. She has a carpet rake, for God's sake. A. Carpet. Rake. Who rakes their fucking carpet? It's *carpet*.

As the boring discussion drones on, I take the opportunity to escape my family for a few moments. Making sure to squish my toes extra hard into the fibers below, I mosey into the kitchen to get a glass of iced tea. For all my mother's faults, she makes a mean sweet tea. It's only 10:00 a.m., but it's shaping up to be a real scorcher today, a little unusual for late September. A cold glass of tea is the perfect antidote to the heat.

I'm halfway across the kitchen when I falter. Killian is standing off to the left, by the fridge. Not even two feet away. Staring at me. His eyes burn. I know it's for me. I want to turn around and flee back to the safety of Kael's arms, but dammit...I want that tea more. I'm so thirsty my mouth hurts. And I'm not going to let the way Killian is scoping me up and down stop me. As much as I wish I could, avoiding him for the rest of our lives is simply impossible. I just need to develop enough calluses that he can no longer penetrate me.

*Yikes. Bad word choice.*

"You look stunning."

"Thanks," I reply tightly trying to skirt around him. But he gently wraps his fingers around the crook of my arm as I brush by, stopping me.

"Don't..." he chokes softly. "Don't go yet. Please."

*Don't do it*, I coach myself. *Don't look at him. Don't give him that satisfaction.* Unfortunately whenever he touches me, any resolve I've built up melts like a sugar cube in water.

My head turns, even though I command it to stay forward. When my gaze lands on him, his pierces me so far I should feel violated. I stand there for seconds, minutes. I don't know because time now seems irrelevant.

I take him in. *Really* look at him, deep and long.

Friday night it was dark, but in the light of day, he looks...defeated.

He has more worry lines circling his eyes and forehead. The grooves framing his mouth look thicker, cutting into his otherwise youthful face. His eyes...they're hiding ghosts, secrets. He looks as if he's aged ten years since he got married. *He deserves it, Mavs. Sometimes, the bed you lie on is filled with shards of glass and duplicity and it fucking hurts to sleep on it night after night. I should know.*

"I'm not on board with the baby thing. That's what I've been trying to talk to you about. I just wanted you to know," he proceeds to whisper.

I push back against the hope stirring within me. It doesn't belong there anymore, and if I keep letting it gasp another goddamn breath I'll never snuff it out. "Maybe you and your wife should get on the same page then," I retort sharply.

"You know your sister once she gets something in her head."

Boy, do I ever.

"What do you want, Shep?" I finally make myself ask.

"I don't like it when you call me that," he bites on a low growl.

What the fuck? Even his *wife* calls him Shep.

"Why? Everyone else does."

"You're not everyone else. You're like *no one* else, Maverick."

Our eyes remain glued on each other. They bounce back and forth, gauging. Once upon a time, when he said something like that, it would stir flutters deep in my belly. I would replay the words for days, always finding new, poetic meanings. Now all it does is blend confusion and anger and regret until it's runny brown and stinks of shit.

I sigh heavily, tired of his fucked-up head trip. "Back to my original question, what do you want, *Shep*?"

His eyes harden at the punctuation of his nickname that "everyone" uses. He leans toward me until I think he's going to kiss me. My entire body tenses, unsure if I want his face wearing my lipstick or my handprint.

"I want every fucking thing I can't have," he tells me hotly.

Handprint, without question.

"Whose fault is that?" I prod evenly, proud of myself for holding it together this long. "*You* gave me up. *You* walked away from everything we had. No answers. No explanations. No second thoughts. No nothing. Even now. I get nothing from you except...nope, nothing. You don't deserve me."

"You don't know shit," he practically thunders. "Everything I do is for you. With you in mind."

What. The. Actual. Fucking...*fuck?*

"That sounds like a line from a song. Or a really bad Kevin Costner movie," I snap.

His half smirk is self-deprecating. Good luck trying to convince me sleeping with my sister and then marrying her was for me. It wasn't. It wasn't for him, either. I'm convinced of that. But it sure as hell wasn't for me.

Yanking out of his grip, I back away a good foot. "Stop fucking jerking me around. You're married to my sister. I'm married to your brother. You need to let this go. I have." I tack on the lie with surprising ease.

"Let what go?" he asks in a dark voice, stepping right into the empty space I'd just made between us.

Goddamn him. Why does he continue to do this? I'm trying my damnedest to erase that soul-deep love for him and the dreams he shattered. I'm trying my level best to give 100 percent of me to my marriage and love Kael the way I should. Yet he's determined to interfere with that every chance he gets.

Why? Why now when I would have given up everything for him just weeks ago...on my wedding day to boot?

Now, it's just too late. I've accepted it. He needs to do the same.

My vision blurs. I fight to hold on to every salty drop threatening to escape. If anyone is undeserving of my tears, it's him. "Us," I whisper, my voice pleading. "You need to let *us* go. Please. I'm begging you."

*Let me get over you*, I want to scream at the top of my constricted lungs.

"Never. I'm too close, now."

*Too close? Too close to what?*

"Don't ask me to give you up. I'd do *anything* for you but that, Maverick..."

That sweet, softly spoken, ragged way he whispers my name drags an unwelcome memory I've tried to bury back up to the surface. His arms banding me tight, groaning my name against my neck as he slips inside me the first time. I'm drowning in yesterdays, not even realizing Killian's hand is halfway to my face when Kael's solid, rigid voice bellows from behind me, "Shep, your *wife* is looking for you."

Killian's arm flops unceremoniously to his side as his eyes flit over my shoulder then back to me. He doesn't look shocked or contrite. He looks pissed. "Yeah. I was just grabbing her a bottle of water from the fridge." I shuffle back and look down to see he does, in fact, have a glass bottle of 90H2O in his opposite hand.

Kael snorts, noticing it, too. "Evian not good enough anymore? She need designer water, too now?"

"You know Jilly," he retorts bitterly. He doesn't even try to mask his disdain for his own wife much anymore.

The warm, strong arm of my husband snakes around my waist, tugging me into his chest. His lips land on my temple before he pokes the bear. Cruelly, right smack between the eyes. "Lucky for me I married the right sister. Mavs doesn't have a pretentious bone in her body."

Oh. *Snap*.

Killian's face turns stone hard. Dilated chocolate pools now flood with orange flames, boring into his younger brother. Punches are about to be thrown and I'm about to be collateral damage.

When I feel Kael stiffen beside me, readying for a throwdown, I step in to defuse the situation before it gets out of control. I hate that I'm the wedge between these two brothers who were once close. At least, I can say the animosity between my sister and me wasn't the result of her stealing my future husband. Our war started way before that.

"Hey," I say, lightly turning fully in to my husband, blocking any body shots from Killian. I grab his face between my hands, forcing his stiff head down to meet my gaze. When his eyes land on me, they soften somewhat but are still packed with vitriol. "I need to talk to you about something." His jaw just clenches and I quickly add softly, "In private."

I don't let him answer. Without a look back at Killian, I grab his hand and pull him along behind me. We make our way to the laundry room right off the kitchen and I close the door behind me. I lean against the thick wood while Kael stalks to the opposite side, pausing at the window overlooking the thick forest behind my parents' palatial estate. His muscles are tense. His breathing is fast if the quick rise and fall of his shoulder blades is any indication.

I hate the awkwardness now hovering heavily between us.

"What did you want to talk about?" he asks absently, running his hand through his hair, making it stand on end. Traces of anger make his already husky voice even huskier.

Would it always be like this when our family was together? Awkward? Uncomfortable? Tension so thick you could carve out the center with a spoon, leaving the rest intact?

*Yes, as long as you're in love with his brother and he's in love with you. You caused this, Maverick. If you had done the right thing from the beginning...*

When we're alone, just the two of us, we can almost pretend that we both entered into this marriage with honorable intentions, when we both know we didn't. I wanted someone else. He wanted me, regardless.

But when we're with our families, feigning to be this solid, madly in love newlywed couple—or maybe it's just I who pretend—we unravel. We let others tug on our stray threads; try to rip us apart at the seams. If we let them, they will ruin us. And I don't want to end up broken, sad, and filled with loathing for someone I've loved since the day I was born.

I will not let Killian or my sister or even *me* destroy this marriage.

"Nothing," I eventually answer. His head swivels, his intense, fiery, toffee gaze gluing fast to mine. The whirling combination of conflict I see—*feel*—nearly buckles my knees. This hurts him. *I'm* hurting him. So damn much.

We've never once spoken of the feelings between his brother and me. Not one time. And I have to wonder why he's never confronted me about that dirty shame, especially before he asked me to marry him. I used to think it was either blind stupidity or irrational denial, but now I think it's because Kael is a good man. Possibly a better man than I ever gave him credit for.

He loves me unconditionally. No matter what. It's a constant I can count on.

Emotions slam into me. I am suddenly overcome with an insatiable need to soothe his ache, prove my worthiness as his chosen life mate. Be what he needs, wants, and more importantly, deserves.

I vow to work harder on what needs fixing inside me. As much as you want to or should, you can't stop loving someone just because you tell yourself to. I wish it worked that way.

In the meantime, he needs reassurance that I'm bound to him and him alone. That I'm in this for the long haul. That he made the right decision marrying me. And he needs it now, not later.

Reaching behind me, I undo the zipper holding my dress together, letting it pool on the floor. His eyes track my every move, turning molten as I unclasp my bra and let it fall down my arms, leaving myself standing before him in mint-green panties and four-inch red spiky heels that scream "do me now."

"What are you doing?" he asks, his voice husky.

I let my eyes drop to his package, happy to see the heavy outline of it now prominent in his tan dress pants. "I think that's pretty obvious," I reply saucily, not moving an inch...waiting to see what he'll do next.

"You want me to fuck you in your parents' laundry room?" he asks in disbelief, his forehead scrunched.

God help me, I do. I didn't realize until this very second how much I *want* this. Want him. And I want him to want me regardless of any of the shit outside of this moment.

I try to inject confidence in my answer when I don't feel an ounce of it. I'm terrified he's going to refuse me. "Yes."

"Anyone could be right outside that door, listening," he adds on a dare, cocking his head. We both know who he means.

"And?" I smugly kick back the challenge into his court.

His eyes flare right before they hood. I watch his throat work to swallow. He has to try twice. When his voracious gaze kisses its way down my practically nude curves, stopping for long seconds on my tight, straining nipples, my stomach trembles. My entire being vibrates with hunger for my husband.

"Slip your hand under those panties and stroke a finger through that pussy, Mavs. If you're wet enough, then I'll fuck you. Right here and now."

Uhhh...okay? That made me gush.

Knowing if I do this, I'm about to get what I want, I obey, sliding my middle finger through my thick arousal before bringing it out to show him that I am, in fact, desperate for him.

"Suck it off."

Wait. *What?* I blink rapidly, trying to make sure I've heard him right. Kael's talked dirty to me before, plenty of times, but he's never been so dominating or authoritative. And the fact that he's chosen this place and time to turn that side of him on is not lost on me.

He spreads his sinewy legs wide, leans his backside against the window ledge, and crosses his arms. "If you want me to bend you over this counter and fuck you until you can't walk straight, stick that finger in your mouth, Maverick. Now."

"Shit," I breathe. I'm so damn turned on right now.

It takes a third silent prodding—his brow quirking—before I finally comply. Lifting my glistening finger to my mouth, I actually groan when the muskiness touches my tongue. My mouth waters, but only because the primal rumble that leaves the back of his throat is just about the sexiest thing I've ever heard.

"So fucking hot," he mutters. Palm up, he commands, "Come here."

I practically run, leaving my clearance Gap dress in a puddle by the door. Not having to worry about wrinkles or dust on a two-thou-sand-dollar garment is why I shop at places like the Gap, unlike my sister.

"You are so beautiful." The second he has me ensconced in his arms, he rains kisses over my jaw, my throat, and my collarbone before working his way downward. "So fucking perfect and beautiful, Mavs. I can't get over the fact you're really mine."

"I am," I admit on a long rush of air when his lips close around a pert bud, sucking so hard I have to stifle a gasp.

"I will never get enough of these. They're perfection." A cool trail is left behind as he makes his way to my other aching breast. My hands fly to the back of his head, holding him to me as he feasts.

Throbbing everywhere, I writhe and shift, trying to get closer to him. My entire body feels liquid, weightless. The energy surrounding us thrums with potent electricity. So much so I'm sure everyone outside these four walls will have to sense what's going on in here. I've never felt so uninhibited and wanton in my life.

He tugs on the lace around my hips. "I'm going to ruin these and eat my fill of my wife first."

"God, yes," I beg, wanting that more than oxygen.

Cool air hits my heated core at the same time Kael drops to his knees and spreads first my legs then my lips wide. With no warning, he dives in headfirst.

At the first swipe of his tongue from back to front, I moan loudly, "Oh shit, Kael." My knees buckle under the weight of pleasure pushing down on me as the feel of his mouth works me up. The contrasting feelings are confusing and thrilling. I chase them, needing to feel this high more than anything.

When he slips a finger inside, I claw at his short strands, trying to hold on to anything for purchase. He's doing diabolical things to my clit with this tongue right in the center of the room and I have nothing else to hold me up but him.

As if sensing my predicament, he tightens his grip on my hips with his other arm and mumbles against me, "I've got you, Maverick. I always do. Let go," before jumping back in to finish the job.

I gasp. I squirm. I cry out softly as he pushes me to places I want him to take me. When he plunges a second finger inside and hooks them forward, I cry out. Sharp and loud.

I'm almost there when Kael reaches behind him and fumbles for a few seconds before the whir of the dryer comes on. "What are you doing?" I pant, completely breathless, pissed my orgasm is now running in the opposite direction.

He stops everything and looks up at me. Lips wet. Eyes wild. Fuck, he's sexy. "I don't care if they know what we're doing, but I don't want them to hear it. The sound of you coming undone belongs to me. *Only* me."

"Oh." I heard his unspoken meaning. "Okay."

"Now be a good girl and come all over my face, Mavs, so I can fuck you hard."

I let a smile slowly curve my lips, loving this foul-mouthed, dirty side of my husband. "Your face has to be buried in my pussy for that to happen, Kael."

I laugh. But it's short-lived because my taunt did its job. Kael's mouth is back on me and if I thought he was focused before, he is absolutely ferocious now. With single-minded intent, he devours me. There's no other way to describe it.

And then I'm coming. Crazy hard. Long. Probably so loud I could wake the dead if the dryer wasn't humming in the background. White-hot heat rushes from my middle up the length of my spine, down the expanse of my arms and legs. I chase it while it spreads and radiates through every cell until I'm nothing but a liquefied mass of utter, glutted bliss.

"Holy God," I heave, trying to gulp fresh air into my lungs. I'm now sitting on the marble countertop, the cold rock trying to steal the warmth still flowing through my blood. Kael is furiously stripping out of his clothes, also uncaring about wrinkles or dirt as he throws them to the ground.

My muscles are strung tight and I would think it's because of the viciously beautiful climax that just ripped through me. It's not. It's the raw hunger Kael has on his face. It's so brutal, it's unnerving.

"I thought you were going to bend me over," I jibe, trying to lighten the heavy mood. He steps into me, grabs my hips, and drags me so I'm perched right on the edge. I have to tighten my stomach muscles to hold myself there.

"I'd rather watch your face bliss out when I make you come again, instead."

"Yeah?" I gasp when he runs the crown of his dick through the wetness between my legs, pushing in ever so slightly. Kael is mighty and thick. Each time he's inside me, he stretches me to the breaking point.

"Oh fuck, yeah," he responds smugly, pressing in another teasing inch.

*Hasius Crepes, he feels good.*

I run my fingers down the slight trail of hair on his bare, buff chest. His abs ripple as I descend past them to grip the base of his cock. "That's a pretty lofty goal, husband, but I'm not sure..."

His nostrils flare. I'm not sure if it's at my use of the word husband or if it's a challenge he's seen laid before him that he'll pick up and run with. I'm not generally a multiple-orgasm type of girl, no matter how hard he tries. It's not him. He probably thinks it is. It's how I'm wired. But Kael loves a good challenge. And he's taking this as one. Leaning in, his lips a hair from mine, he whispers, "I *am* sure. And I'm nothing if not generous, *wife.*"

On that promise, with his mouth fastened to mine, Kael enters me. Harsh and abrupt. I'm so damn wet and ready for him he slides in with ease. He fucks me with swift, sure strokes before switching to long, languid ones. He alternates smoothly, balancing me on a knife's edge no matter which way he's taking me. Over this past couple of months, I've come to appreciate how amazing Kael is, not only as a friend but as a lover. The more he's inside me, the more it feels as if I've been missing out all along.

As much real estate as Killian is still taking up, Kael's quickly buying him out. I do believe I'm actually falling in love with my husband, slowly but surely.

"You feel phenomenal," he praises quietly. "So slippery, so hot, so fucking unreal. So mine."

"Don't stop," I beg. *Don't ever freaking stop.*

He's just hit his stride, well on his way to showing me he means to give me that second orgasm when we hear footsteps approaching the door. He stops mid-drive and throws a hand over my mouth before I can protest.

A light rap accompanies a deep boom. "Tenderheart, everything okay in there?"

Oh shit. I feel like a sixteen-year-old getting busted making out with J. C. Ferrera on the back porch swing. Except instead of J. C.'s hand halfway up my blouse, this time, I'm buck-ass naked with my husband's dick buried inside me and only a flimsy, *unlocked* door between us and authority. I'm not doing anything immoral, but it's probably considered uncouth to fuck in the middle of the day in your parents' house with them home. Even for married people.

"Get rid of him or he's gonna get an eyeful," Kael drawls with a chuckle.

Kael removes his hand and smirks, resuming his thrusts, but this time they're agonizingly slow and deep and feel so mind-blowingly good, I almost moan my reply to my father.

"You can't be serious," I hiss, wishing I had modesty within my reach. His grin only widens and he does some swivel thing with his hips he's not done before, making me whimper. "Stop." Grabbing two ass cheeks, I try to halt his movements, but all he does is shackle my wrists between his fingers and drag them behind my back not giving me a second to catch my breath.

"Maverick, everything all right?" my father's concerned voice resounds.

Crap. I know that tone. He's about two seconds away from opening the door. Growing up in a house with three women, my daddy learned pretty quickly not to just barge in. My two minutes are just about up.

"Yes, Daddy. Fine," I manage to choke out.

"You sure? You sound...upset."

*Upset?* I'm so far from upset it's ridiculous.

"Please stop. Just for a second," I beg Kael. Blessedly he gives me a reprieve. But only a slight one. I wonder where this wicked man who's now pumping his hips back and forth lazily has been all this time.

Racking my brain for a white lie, the sound of the dryer gives me the excuse I need. "Kael spilled water on his shirt. We just threw it in the dryer," I yell, hoping I sound convincing.

I must. "Oh. Well, Arnie and Eilish just arrived and your mother has called the fifteen-minute warning, so..."

I roll my eyes at her stupid ritual. Within the next fifteen minutes we'd all better be sitting around the table in our assigned spots, palms clasped, eyes closed, ready to recite the mealtime prayer.

I hold in a moan when Kael's finger lands on my oversensitive clit and starts rubbing small circles. I can't do a damn thing to stop him because my own hands are still imprisoned, so I try my best to ignore the heat building in me once again, but *fuck, that feels so good.* "Uh, no problem. We're almost done."

"Okay, then. Hurry up."

Kael chuckles softly in my ear. "You heard the man. We best hurry up."

We can still hear my father's footfalls when Kael slams his mouth to mine and starts fucking me ruthlessly, taking me like he owns me. And he does. I feel like I'm becoming his, piece by broken piece. My mind isn't anywhere else but on him and the sinful things he's doing to me, making me feel.

"My dirty girl," he mutters. "Letting me eat you, fuck you right under our families' noses. That makes you hot, doesn't it?"

Yes. God, yes. A million fucking times *yes.*

I nod, unable to find my vocal cords at the moment, let alone use them.

Kael's breaths pick up; his grip tightens. He's close. I know the signs. I feel the swell of his cock. Hear the hitch in his exhales. "You like it when I talk like this to you, Swan."

Not a question, but I answer, "Yes," anyway.

"I know," he breathes in my ear. "Your hot little pussy tightens deliciously around me."

My inner walls react and he groans, low and wolflike. *God almighty that sound is hot.*

Seconds later, we're both at the top looking down. Kael's grip is bruising. His thumb works that bundle of nerves furiously, relent-lessly. Expertly. All while he fucks me like there's only us in this big house.

"You're getting close, Swan." So close. So fucking close I can taste it. "Come for me. Come *with* me, Mavs. Right fucking now."

His intense gaze coaxes. But his cock, his touch, sells it. Scorching fire builds until it bursts. Then I'm falling. Tipping over first with him right behind. It's all I can do to keep my eyes open and on him as wave after sharp wave of euphoria races through me.

With a chiseled jawbone and full lips, my husband is more than handsome. He's magnificent. I'm the envy of most of the single—and some of the married—women in Dusty Falls, but at this singular moment when he throws his head back and groans his blissful release, he is absolutely breathtaking.

And he belongs to me.

And when he opens his hooded eyes, pinning me with a sated, wicked, joyful grin that tells me wordlessly I'm his everything, I see an entirely different man.

One I've always known but never let in all the way.

One who gives me all of him while I hold back.

One I can't bear the thought of losing. Ever.

He's the one who has always walked beside me. Selflessly. Silently. Steadfastly. Without exception. Without expectations.

Still catching his breath, he confesses, "I love you, Swan." He presses red, full lips to my forehead, wrapping me up tight in his embrace. "I don't think you comprehend how deep my love for you runs."

"I think I do," I whisper into his sweaty chest, finally under-standing.

There was no mistaking what he walked in on in the kitchen. Two people who still care far too much for each other, given the fact they're both married to others. This coupling was my offering to him. My selflessness. Yet once again, I wasn't. It was as much for me as for him. Maybe more so. It was another way I was trying to eradicate this poison infecting our relationship, our future. To make space for our own love. He gave me what I had no right to ask of him. He gave it freely. And I love him so damn much for it.

"I love you, Kael."

I mean it. I really do love him. And while I have said these words to him countless times over the years, the way I just said them now is unlike how I've ever uttered them before.

By Kael's reaction, he knows it.

"Christ, Maverick." His voice breaks. His arms squeeze me until it's hard to draw air. I swear his body is trembling.

"I—" I want to say I'm sorry. For everything. For all these years wasted. For hurting him. For loving Killian. For all my failures and shortcomings as a friend, as a wife. But I don't want to ruin a tender moment we've not yet experienced as a true couple, so I settle for another "I love you" and hope he hears the lame implicit apology I'm giving him instead.

As Kael draws back, cups my face, and lowers his mouth to mine, I see everything he wants me to see.

Understanding.

Devotion.

Forgiveness.

Us: Forever.

The way it's always been.

With his lips melded to mine, there is little doubt in my mind what's beating wildly in the center of my chest. In the depth of my belly.

I am falling for my husband.

*Maverick*

At any one point in my life, I have been infatuated, in lust, in love, or just plain obsessed with Killian Shepard. It's hard to explain how difficult it is to shut off feelings you've had for the same person for twenty-some years. It's not like a spigot you can flip closed. And even if you try, there's still that slow trickle you can't seem to shut off. It's there, constantly in the background. Eventually I guess you just learn to tune out the slow, annoying drip. For the most part, at least. But sometimes that drip is all you hear. All you can concentrate on. It's all consuming until it makes you neurotic.

Like now.

Kael is out of town on business for the night and I'm left alone to stew and reminisce. And for some reason, I find myself drifting back to the time Killian found me in the bed of Robbie Reams' truck. As far as I know Kael never found out and for that, I'm grateful. Wasn't my finest hour.

It was my seventeenth birthday. Kael was away at college, but Killian was working for my father as a sales assistant. Two weeks before school started my friends, in their infinite wisdom, decided they were going to throw me a kegger to celebrate not only my birthday but the start of our senior year.

As her father was a farmer, Kimmy Reams had access to not only a few rural abandoned grain bins but also an older brother, Robbie, who was all too happy to get a bunch of underagers set up with thirteen gallons of the cheapest beer known to man. Especially since he had a crush on me.

"What are you majoring in next year?" Robbie asks innocently enough, handing me a bottle of water. I open it and take a swig before answering.

"Dual major. Business and finance."

He wipes off a few stray droplets that fell on my leg. His thumb lingers. I let it, parting my lips to grab some air. It creeps up toward my short line and traces the flesh just under the hem. I shiver when it edges toward my inner thigh.

Eyes lidded, he takes my water, caps it, and sets it aside. We lie back in the grass. The sky is dark. The stars are starting to pop, one by one. And Robbie Reams just tucked his hand in mine. My head is buzzing. My mind fuzzy and bland from all the beer I've drank. I hear his head turn toward mine. I do the same. His eyes glitter in the moonlight. They're pretty.

"I always knew you were smart, Maverick."

I let a smile out. "Thanks, Robbie."

Time passes. We drink more. Talk. Flirt. Couples start pairing off, disappearing. The crowd thins. My stomach feels woozy. My ears ring. Then Robbie's lips are grazing mine and I'm kissing him back. His hand cups my breast and I let him. Next thing I know I'm in Robbie's truck. Shorts unbuttoned. Bra unclasped and pushed up. His hungry mouth indulging in my breasts as eager fingers move between my legs.

I'm not sure what the fuck I'm doing, but I know it shouldn't be this. Why does it feel as if I'm headed down a one-way street with no exits for miles?

I'm on the precipice of indecision but hesitate only seconds before my brain fogs over with the incredible pleasure Robbie's making me feel. I'm sinking into it when one minute Robbie's there, driving my body to new heights, and the next he's gone.

Then I'm being lifted into a pair of strong arms. I notice Robbie Reams is on the ground, blood trickling from his nose and mouth. Stunned. Angry. But he doesn't make a move to get me. Shithead.

*I swear a voice mutters, "I've got you."*

*I'm dumped gently into a car. Leather and testosterone drift up to meet me. I feel my shorts being rebuttoned, my blouse yanked back down. A seatbelt buckles across my lap. It takes me a couple more seconds to shake off the haze of lust and alcohol, but the minute we're driving down the dark, dusty road, I know.*

"What the fuck, Killian."

"Do. Not. Talk. Right. Now." *His command is level, deliberate. Uncompromising and full of turmoil. I open my mouth to say something else, but when he whips his head toward me and pins me with a glare that's nothing short of rage, I clamp it shut. Now is not the time, I guess.*

*Twenty minutes later, we slow and turn into the elementary school parking lot. It's dark. Deserted. Eerie.*

"What are we doing here?"

"I'm asking the questions," *he grits.*

"How did you find me?" *He ignores me all day—my birthday of all days—but conveniently shows up when I'm with another guy? What the hell?*

"I said"—*he turns in his seat*—"I am asking the questions."

"You're not my fucking father, Killian. I can take care of myself."

"By getting pregnant?" *he roars. His eyes are wild. His jaw set hard. I have never seen him so angry. Ever. About anything.*

*Shame assaults me and my buzz starts to wane. A headache sets in. My stomach roils. I can't possibly tell him why I let Robbie Reams go to no-man's-land. That I was hurt, acting out because he hadn't called me yet today. That the whole time I was picturing it was him instead.*

*I reach for the door handle, done with him. Done with this conversation. I'll walk the half mile home, even if it is dark and scary and animals may rush me from the ditch. Half of me is outside the car, half still inside when I'm propelled backward and being yanked over the console of his interior. My hip smarts where it jams the gearshift. Then I'm on his lap, straddling him, his erection prodding my center.*

"Tell me what the fuck you think you were doing," he demands, chest heaving, tone hard, eyes...I don't know. Wanting, maybe?

We're so close, we're breathing each other's air. Maybe thinking the same thoughts. Killian has held me before, but never like this. Never possessively, like I'm his.

I can't help myself. I don't know if it's the alcohol or the pheromones coming off him, but I shift my pelvis back and forth, rubbing it against what I know is thick and long. He groans. His eyes close as if in pain. He takes a deep breath and holds it before blowing it back out. When his palms land on my hips, they're firm, but they don't stop me so I keep on going.

Then his eyes open, snag mine. And when they do, I know I've not imagined anything. He wants me. Hasius Crepes, Killian Shepard wants me. And when he breathes my name, like he's offering up a prayer during Sunday mass, I come completely undone. All my teenage hormones come out to play.

I slam my mouth to his. He lets me. Moaning, he lets his tongue get to know mine. Intimately. Thoroughly. He tastes sweet. Like my daddy's brandy. A warm hand cups my cheek and I'm lost. I think he's lost with me because I'm not mistaken his pelvis is moving with mine. I'm zooming toward an orgasm already, the real so much better than the imagined. But then his mouth slows. And he's pulling away. He looks torn. Wrecked. Remorseful, maybe. The hand burning my hip squeezes, signaling for me to stop.

I'm panting. So is he.

"What's wrong?" I ask. More like squeak.

His arms go around me and pull tight so I'm forced to either put my face in the crook of his neck or suffocate it in the headrest. It's an obvious choice. "What's wrong?" I mumble again, confused at why my clothes aren't halfway off already.

Without saying a word, he opens the door and swings his legs out. He stands and I cling to him, not ready for this to end. He walks around the car, opens the door, and slides me into the passenger seat. After he buckles me in and closes the door, he stands there for probably *a whole minute before he slams his fist into the steel above me, making me jump.*

*Then he's back inside. He starts the car while I sit there, dumb-founded. He drives slow, careful. In complete contrast to the tension I now feel crashing over me from his side of the car. When he pulls into my driveway, he leaves the engine running and says evenly, "Take some aspirin and drink a glass of water before bed. Gatorade in the morning. I already talked to your dad. He'll cover—"*

*"You did what?" I breathe. It tastes of beer and fire.*

*"Maverick," he chastises. "You have no fucking idea..."*

*"You had no right, Killian."*

*"I have every right!" His roar scares me and I shrink to the corner of my seat, terrified of him for the first time in my life. "You almost let that motherfucker..." He stops, composes himself before rasping, "You're seven-fucking-teen years old, Maverick. You're emotionally immature and you have no idea what you want."*

*He's breathing fast. His knuckles are white, wrapped around the steering wheel like wax melted in the sun.*

*"You're wrong," I tell him softly. "I know exactly what I want." When he doesn't say anything, I add, "It's you, Killian. I want you."*

*He doesn't look at me. For the longest time, he stares straight ahead, blinking slowly as if his lids are on a timer. His chest expands and collapses, but his breathing has changed. It's still fast, though it's no longer from anger. It's from desire. I may be only seven-fucking-teen years old, but even I know the difference. That's what he sounded like just minutes ago with his tongue down my throat.*

*Finally he faces me. We just stare at each other. I wait for him to do something, say anything, but he just swallows. When he opens his mouth, it's to crush me. "You're too young, Maverick."*

*I flick my challenging gaze to his jeans, which are still straining. "You want me."*

*He moves a hand from the wheel to his lap, covering up the evidence. "Go to bed," he replies plainly as if only his opinion matters.*

*Our face-off lasts so many beats I lose count. And I know I've lost him before I even had him.*

*"You should have left me with Robbie Reams. At least he had the balls to take what he wanted."*

*Then I open the door and don't look back, even when he calls, "Robbie Reams lays another fucking finger on you, he's dead. Remember that next time you get drunk and want to act out like a child."*

———

I almost made the worst decision of my life that night, letting Robbie take something from me I desperately wanted to gift to Killian instead. But I was drunk. Robbie wanted me. Killian didn't. At least that's what I thought at the time.

But I realized the next morning as I nursed my hangover that as mad, humiliated, and confused as I was that night, Killian saved me from making a huge mistake.

Killian was supposed to be my first. My only. Instead, after that night he refused to barely even acknowledge I existed—until we became too big to ignore years later.

The goddamned drip that's his constant echo gets louder and more annoying and before I know what I'm doing, I'm kneeling in my closet, the carpet fibers digging into my bare knees. The box I swore never to touch again is in my hand. The lid is off. The contents of yesterdays stare up at me.

Birthday cards. A get-well drawing when I broke my leg. A lone drumstick from our DeSheps days, signed by all four of us.

Peeking out from under a Hallmark moment is a plain, smooth black rock he gave me after my gerbil died. He told me he didn't want to see me cry over another lost pet. He made me name it Wilson, after that stupid volleyball in *Cast Away*. I kept it by my bedside until the day he announced his engagement to Jilly.

I lightly finger the dandelion crown lying on top, all withered and brittle. Dried, blackened stems, roots, and leaves break off, scattering everywhere. Killian's voice echoes from across the years, as if the moment were happening all over again in real time.

*"For you, Small Fry." His deep voice slicks over me, making my tummy feel weird.*

*"What's this?" I turn over the woven crown in my hands. It leaves that pungent weed smell behind on my fingers that most people hate. Not me. I love it.*

*"Your birthday present, of course."*

That was my thirteenth birthday. I remember initially being upset he made me a dandelion crown. It was a child's gift, not one for a now teenager, but somehow the fact he made it with his own hands, with me in mind because he knew how much I loved dandelions, took that sting away.

A yellowing, curled slip of paper catches my eye. I gingerly move aside the contents to snag the tip of a fortune Killian gave me right before he left for college: *"The one you love is closer than you think."*

At the time, I thought that was a sign we were meant to be, he and I. That he loved me as much as I loved him but he just couldn't tell me yet. Now, I wonder if it was prophetic in an entirely weird way. That the one I was truly meant to love was always hiding in plain sight. *Closer than you think.*

Kael.

I look down at the square box holding ancient history of another man. Memories fall around me like black rain. Part of me mourns the many plans lost now in this minuscule six-by-twelve-by-three-inch cardboard resting place. The rest of me is almost apathetic, finally accepting that future was never really ours for the taking.

The chime of my cell drags me kicking and screaming from past to present. It's my husband. The man I *should* be thinking about instead of the one who continues to torment me.

*Drip.*

*Drip.*

*Fucking drip.*

On the second ring, I shove the top back on, wondering why I can't just let these painful memories go. I know I need to. Doing so will dissolve another thread that binds Killian and me together. But the thought of permanently letting go of remnants of our history— times that were good—hurts my heart to the point of actual pain. So I stash my ghosts back in the wall, wedge the board back into place, and rush to grab my phone in the nick of time.

"You sound out of breath," Kael's gravelly voice rings from the other end.

"Yeah, ah, I was in the bathroom. Sorry." My conscience chews me out for the white lie. One of the reasons I wasn't keen on Kael going out of town is because too much alone time is not a good place for me to be right now. It leaves me to think too much...to remember things I should be forgetting instead.

"No problem. How was your day?"

I settle back onto the bed, laying my head on my Tempur-Pedic pillow. "You sure you want to know?"

"Wouldn't ask if I didn't, babe."

Little by little, I let my muscles relax, willing my mind to return to the here and now. I take a deep breath before I start. "Well, Wesley Harvey's cows got loose somehow. Shut down Highway 28 for three hours until they managed to round them all up again."

He chuckles. It's soothing and missed. Just hearing his voice seems to right the wrongs inside me. "Too bad I missed that. What else."

"I heard they moved Abigail LeMonte to hospice." Abigail is a single mother of three who was diagnosed with pancreatic cancer a mere three months ago. She's going to die, leaving three teenagers without a parent. It's tragic.

"Oh, I'm sorry to hear that, Swan. I know how much you like her."

"I hate it when bad things happen to good people."

"Which is why we need to live in the moment, right?"

"Yeah," I agree quietly. *I'm trying*, I want to tell him. *It's hard and sometimes I slide backward, but I am trying. Please don't give up on me.*

"So, how can I cheer you up? Anything good happen today?"

God, I love this man so very much. He works tirelessly to make sure I'm nothing but happy. I wish I deserved him. Twisting a stray thread around the tip of my finger, I answer, "Hmmm...I won five dollars on a scratch-off ticket."

I hear the smile on his face when he teases, "You gambler, you. Don't spend it all in one place."

And just like that he makes me feel better. "Too bad Tastie's isn't open. We could blow it all on donut holes. Eat ourselves sick." Being as it's mid-October, our favorite childhood haunt is now closed for the year.

"You're making my mouth water," he says, groaning.

"Really?" I lower my voice, hoping it sounds sultry. "What else can I do to make your mouth water?"

"Fuck, Swan. You have no idea how hard you just made me."

I laugh, sinking my head farther into the pillow. "Tell me."

"Why? You want me to get myself off while you listen?"

*Whew. Is it suddenly hot in here?* I pluck at my tee to get some air moving.

"No. I'd like to watch instead," I shoot back. It sounds a little breathy. Okay, a *lot* breathy.

"You want me to switch this to a Facetime call, then?"

"Would you?"

He lets loose a long, deep growl that would have me stripping if he were home. "You are a very naughty girl, you know that?"

*Yeah, it's definitely hot.* My skin feels flushed and I'm very damp between my thighs.

"I thought you liked me that way," I tease.

"I don't." I'm getting ready to challenge him when he adds, "I fucking *love* it." There's a slight pause before he says, "Christ, I miss you, Mavs."

The softness around those last words sobers me. "I miss you, too, Kael," I whisper, genuinely meaning it.

It took weeks to get used to having him here, day in and day out. Now he's gone just one night and this old house feels drafty and cold and lonely. He only left this morning, yet I miss him already. More than I expected to. "What time do you think you'll be home tomorrow?"

"I'll come right home after my meeting. I'll be there by the time you get done at the bakery. How does that sound?"

"You don't have to go into the office first?"

"Fuck the office."

"I'd rather you fuck me instead," I counter.

His chuckle is dark. A little wicked, even. "I think that can be arranged."

"Will you be naked and ready and waiting for me to ride you when I walk through the front door?"

"Damn, Mavs," he breathes hard. "If that's what my lady wants, it wouldn't be very chivalrous of me to deny her, now would it?"

I smile. Teeth and all. "My knight in shining armor?"

"Spit shined and everything."

We laugh and talk for a few more minutes before he tells me, "As much as I don't want to, I gotta run, babe. I have a business dinner in thirty minutes and I still need to take a quick shower."

The doorbell rings just as I reluctantly say, "Okay."

"I'll text you later, 'kay?"

"Will you make it dirty?" I quip.

He barks a laugh. "Oh yeah. It will be so filthy you'll need a shower afterward."

That sexy promise sets a small fire between my thighs. Later can't get here soon enough. "I can't wait. I love you, Kael."

Instead of saying it back, he says, "And I'll never take that gift for granted, Maverick. Not ever. You know you've given me everything I've always wanted, don't you?"

Guilt pricks me. I've accepted that it always may. "I know," I reply quietly.

I feel a light-year away from where I was just a while ago. I'm happy and warm all over and I don't want that feeling to end. I want to beg him to wave off dinner and spend the rest of the night on the phone like we used to so I stay grounded in today, not lost in the past. But he has obligations and I need to respect that.

"See you tomorrow."

"Counting down the seconds, Swan."

"Me, too."

I hit the end button as the impatient peal of the doorbell echoes through the house a second time. Sitting up, I take in my ratty gold Hawkeye tee and black cotton shorts that have seen better days. I contemplate not answering. I'm not feeling very social. All I want to do is curl up with a glass of wine and a good book and let this feeling of contentment stay put. I lie there for a few more seconds, thinking my uninvited visitor must have gotten the hint when the bell rings a third time.

"Dammit," I mutter, popping off the bed and heading toward the stairs. Twenty seconds later, feeling a little surly, I throw open the door not even bothering to check who's on the other side. A grave mistake, I find out when my eyes land on all too familiar ones. Ones Kael expertly made me forget over the last thirty minutes.

"Hi," Killian says. His smile is light and genuine. My belly flutters. I fall back in time to when I was thirteen again and he gave me those stupid weeds.

Fuck.

Shit.

One tiny step forward, five giant ones back.

Goddammit...why is he here?

"Hi," I say back evenly. I don't move. I don't offer to let him in. I just stand there, waiting. He looks past me, then back.

"Can I come in? I have something for Kael." A manila envelope enters my sight when he holds it up and shakes it as if to prove he's not lying.

"He's out of town."

His brows furrow momentarily before smoothing back out. I study him. Is it actually possible he doesn't know Kael is away on business? They work at the same place, just doors down from each other.

No. Surely he knows. This is yet another one of his mindfucks. Sabotage Maverick while Kael is gone. My temper flares. Selfish, selfish bastard.

"Where is he?" he asks, scooting by me without waiting for an invitation.

"Help yourself," I mutter under my breath.

Looking over his shoulder, he kicks a side of his lip up. He heard me. Whatever.

I follow him around the corner into the kitchen. Reluctantly. Truly wishing he wasn't here. And just slightly worried that he is. And that we're alone. And could be...all...night...long if that's what we wanted.

Holy Mary Mother...he needs to go.

"Here," I say tartly with my hand out. "I'll put it in his office. Anything else?"

His eyes flit between mine and my open palm. He clutches the envelope, maybe thinking if he gives it up he loses his bargaining chip. So he doesn't. Then he makes no bones about the fact he's checking over every inch of me. It's a slow, deliberate perusal. Messy hair to pale pink painted toenails. When his gaze—now hot and longing—lands on mine again, his voice is pure gravel. "You didn't answer my question."

I cross my arms, trying to hide my beading nipples and tamp down the flush spreading over me. I start chewing on my lip, tapping my foot anxiously. "He's in Minneapolis. Why?"

"Minneapolis," he repeats, more of a question to himself than anything. His eyes lose focus for a few seconds before he shakes his head.

"What's wrong?" I ask, instantly worried.

"Nothing." He answers quickly, but his inflection gives him away.

He really didn't know.

"You didn't know about this trip?"

Shaking his head, he answers, "No. Must be something your father sent him to do, I guess." He's confused and he's doing a shit job of hiding it.

Now, all I want to do is call Kael back and drill him about what he's really doing. He told me he was going to work through details on a contract for the Minnesota National Guard Armory. Said something about government funding to tear down a few old buildings in disrepair and rebuild infrastructure. I found the trip odd, as he rarely travels for work, but he said there were intricacies they needed to deal with in person versus a conference call. But if that were the case, Killian would know. Killian is involved in *every* single deal at DSC as is Kael.

And he clearly does not know.

I decide to deal with Kael separately, not letting Killian know Kael's obviously kept a secret from both of us. The last thing I need is for Killian to latch on to that and use that as a wedge between us, making a big deal out of something that surely has a valid explanation.

"I guess. So do you still want to drop that off then?" I gesture to the papers he's holding hostage.

That damn smirk returns. "You trying to rush me out of here, Small Fry?"

My shoulders, eyebrows, and the corners of my mouth all lift at the same time. "Busted."

When he laughs, I can't help but join in. The tension that was mounting fizzles. Mostly. I've decided there will always be that little bit of uncomfortable between us. Because of what once was and no longer is or ever can be again.

"Got a beer?"

I tense. He notices.

"It's just a beer, Maverick. Just a beer."

I stand in indecision. Having him here when Kael isn't, is not a good idea. Not now. Probably not ever. But on the other hand, it's asinine to think we'll never have times in our life when we aren't alone. We need to start dealing with it. Maturely. Without temptation to sin.

So this is a test—one I plan to pass.

"Okay." I retrieve two Michelob Ultras from the fridge and hand him one, careful to let go of the bottle before his fingers have a chance to graze mine. In my haste, it almost falls to the floor, but Killian catches it in time. He grins, knowing exactly what I did. Again, I shrug and grin back.

"Can I sit down, or do I need to chug and go?" he asks teasingly.

"Depends on how thirsty you are," I banter smoothly.

He doesn't sit. Instead, he pops the top and tips the bottle to his lips, taking a nice long pull. He watches me as he does it and I try to force myself not to notice how his throat works when he swallows. Or how hot I'm getting all of a sudden. I take my own drink, just a sip, breaking eye contact before I can't.

"Those what I think they are?" His gaze has strayed to the counter where a plate of macadamia nut cookies sits. It's Kael's favorite. Killian's, too.

"Yes, sir."

His eyes flare. *Shit*. Bad word choice. Clearly I suck at tests.

Steeling myself, I make a mental note as I turn to grab the plate to refrain from saying that again to him. Keeping my eyes glued to his beer bottle, I hand over the cookies, which he silently takes. He sets the plate on the kitchen table before snagging one.

Neither of us speaks. It seems like minutes but is probably only a few seconds. Killian breaks the quiet with, "Will it always be this awkward between us?"

Resignation.

I hear it. It's faint, but there. It's the first time he's acknowledged that we're over and while I know this, even want it most days, it hurts worse than I thought it would.

"I hope not," I manage to choke.

"I hate it."

"So do I."

Killian clamps the cookie between his teeth then walks out of the kitchen. I think maybe he's leaving without saying good-bye, but he makes his way through the family room to the large bay of windows that overlook the backyard and wraparound porch.

As he stands there enjoying his treat, I can't stop myself from remembering that I fantasized about this exact moment when I bought this house. When I saw that window seat where the early morning sun streams in and provides nearly complete privacy to our neighbors, I imagined Killian reading to me there. Making love to me there. Creating our first baby on top of those thick cushions.

That won't happen, though. Deep in my soul, I knew it wouldn't happen when I bought this house to begin with. Killian was already married to Jilly then. I feel like I've aged a lifetime in the year and a half since I first walked through that front door. And seeing Killian there now makes me realize how far I really have come in the past few months, because instead of wishing he was the one to fulfill my fantasies, I now think I want Kael to.

I make another mental note. Get Kael to fuck me in that exact spot Killian is now standing. I need to erase him from every part of me, including my fading dreams.

"Do you remember the night I found you with Robbie Reams?"

*What the hell?* "How could I forget?" In fact, I didn't. I haven't. I was *just* thinking of that less than an hour ago.

"I wanted to kill him," he goes on, still staring out the window. "For having his fucking mouth on you. For touching what was mine."

"I wasn't yours." I hate the fact that my voice breaks. "You even said so that night. I was 'too young,' remember?"

He looks at me then. Looks *in* me. Deep inside where I can't hide the feelings for him that I've tried in vain to tuck away. "You *were* too young. Always too fucking young."

My mouth turns down. "Guess we are a classic romantic tragedy." It sounds as if I'm belittling what we had. I'm not, but I don't know what else to say. Every word was true. I lick my lips. His gaze follows. "Killian," I breathe, suddenly uncomfortable that we're alone. "This is pointless. What's done is done."

He turns his body toward me but doesn't move closer. The cookie is gone. So is the beer. As if preparing for battle, he stands to his full height and asks me, "What if it *wasn't* done, Maverick? What if all of this"—he waves a hand around the room—"could be undone?"

I'm tired. So goddamned tired of this round and round. It's making me dizzy and nauseous. My knees give and I rest my butt against the back of the couch. I look to the floor, studying the worn hardwood under my bare feet. It's original. Almost a hundred years old. Worn, but in good shape. It needs to be revarnished, though. I'll talk to Kael about that when he gets home. I should have done it before I moved in, but I was too anxious to get out from under my father's thumb.

"Maverick, look at me."

I refuse to obey. Not this time. I should have refused to let him in. Refused the beer. Told him to shove the fucking cookie. Dammit. "What if I don't want it to be undone?" I ask without looking at him. If, right this very instant, I was given one wish, would I use it on that? Would I go back and make Killian mine, erasing all the suffering we've both been through? Would I choose to leave what I've built with Kael to be his? Three months ago, I would have said yes. Unequivocally. Now, though? That answer's a little murky.

"You don't mean that."

My eyes snap to his. "Why did you marry Jillian? And no bullshit this time. All you've ever given me are bullshit answers. I want a real one. The truth. Do you love her? Have you always loved her? Was what we had even real?"

A derisive look overtakes his face. Whenever I've asked him this before, he remained completely impassive. Like a fucking carved piece of marble. Now, though, he's actually letting emotion bleed through.

"I've never had anything more real than what I had with you. You're as real as it gets, Maverick."

"Then why?" I plead. "Why did you leave me? For *her*, of all people?" It would kill me to see him walking around with someone else—anyone else—but I would rather have chewed off my own arm than have him be with *her*.

He moves to sit. "Don't," I bark. "Don't sit. Don't make yourself comfortable. Don't do anything except answer. The fucking. Question."

"Which one?" His mouth twitches.

He wants an out. Well, he's not gonna get it. He's had over two and a half years of outs. "All of them." He won't answer. Just like every time before. I already see it in his eyes.

He picks up the packet he dropped onto the mantel. It crumples a bit when he tightens his fist. "Not everything is as it seems, Maverick."

More stinking shit of the bull. I push to stand, done with him. "You need to go, Shep."

Flinty eyes burn into me. "I mean it. You think you want answers, but sometimes it's the truth that destroys, Small Fry, not the lies. I have tried protecting you my entire life and this...I'm sorry I couldn't protect you from this."

"That's a lie. You've led me on my entire life. Kept me dangling on your hook while you fucked other women, including my sister. You said you were done with my father, yet you came back from Florida an engaged man and two rungs higher on the ladder. Jesus, how naïve was I not to know exactly what you were doing? You couldn't get what you wanted with me because my father wouldn't approve of it, so you moved on to the daughter who could."

His jaw tightens, along with every muscle in his body. "You are dead wrong."

"Tell me you weren't fucking Jilly and me at the same time?"

"Maverick..."

Yeah...that's what I thought.

"Tell me I'm wrong," I demand, feeling my face flush with humiliation. "Tell. Me. I. Am. Wrong."

His head falls. He's breathing hard now. My chest hurts. I want to cry.

"Go. Please. And don't do this again. I can't do this anymore. If I am your real, as you claim I am, then you will let me go." *Just as I'm doing with you.*

Our eyes lock and my knees weaken at the heartbreak I'm witnessing right before me, but I can't...I just can't. I am beyond my breaking point. Truth be told, I'm already broken. I need someone to put me back together again, not tear me to unrecognizable shreds.

"Please," I beg, my eyes filling. His do, too. "For me, Killian."

He swallows, long and hard. If the lump in his throat is anything like the one in mine, I understand. When he walks past, he grabs my hand, telling me softly against my cheek, "He will never love you like I do."

His lips pucker against my skin. They're warm, soft. They linger. A tear races down my face. I feel another one and think it may be his. He lets me go and continues toward the front door.

"You're wrong," I say achingly to his retreating back. "He loves me more than himself. I wish I could say the same thing for you."

It was hurtful. It was meant to be. I hurt. He needs to hurt, too.

He stops. Remains frozen for several long moments. His shoulders slump, but he doesn't turn around. He doesn't dispute or deny. I'm not sure how I feel about that. Then he's gone. The door clicks softly behind him and it doesn't matter that it's only eight thirty. I head upstairs, peel out of my clothes, and crawl into bed, tears streaking my face, snot clogging my nose.

The rope he has tethered to me is unraveling, thread after fraying thread. I hear them snapping, faster and faster now. Feel the stinging bite of each one against my tender flesh as they break apart.

Tomorrow, I'll sever another one. Tomorrow, I'm burning that fucking box. Tomorrow, I'll ash even more memories, pretending they don't exist. Tomorrow, I'll let another precious piece of him go.

Tonight, though...tonight I'm letting myself mourn tomorrow.

*Maverick*

I feel greedy eyes on me from across the crowded room. His gaze burns into me, making me hot and needy. I position myself against the closest wall, cross my heeled feet, and take in my husband. The blatant manner in which he's eating his way up my curves is heady. My blood already buzzes thickly with alcohol. Now it buzzes for nothing but him. His mouth kicks up on both sides, the knowing smile making his golden eyes glisten.

"I want you," he mouths.

"You can have me," I mouth back.

"Jesus Christ, why aren't you fucking his brains out somewhere?" MaryLou drawls as she eases in beside me. "He's making *me* horny looking at you like that."

I tip my cocktail to my lips, taking a generous gulp. "Had it been up to me, we would have stayed in and watched the Halloween marathon on TNT like we always do. But Kael wanted to come."

Tonight is the annual Halloween bash thrown by Jared and Marta McQueen. Kael is one of Jared's closest friends as well as his personal attorney. And Jared is one of the few people in town not owned lock, stock, and barrel by Richard DeSoto. That's because at twenty-nine, the McQueens are also one of the few who don't need his money.

Jared owns just over ten thousand acres of farmland, which he inherited at the young age of nineteen after both his parents perished in a two-seater plane crash. He owns it outright. No loans. No liens. No corporate conglomerates. And at the current value of $13,000 per acre, that makes him the richest independent farmer in all of Iowa. Probably the Midwest.

But other than the brand new 7,000-square-foot home we're celebrating in this year, the McQueens are down-to-earth people. Jared still drives his father's farm truck: a 1979 spearmint-green American beauty he named after his sister Gayle, who also died too young at age eleven. She drowned in only a foot of water when she dove into a shallow lake and broke her neck. It was horrific. Gayle was only two years younger than me at the time she died.

"Thanks for last week," I say, knowing she gets what I'm talking about.

MaryLou reaches over and takes my hand in hers. She gives it a comforting squeeze. "Welcome."

She stood by my side, nonjudgmental as usual, as I stared at the burning barrel in her backyard and chickened out. Each time I tried to shred the past, I was struck with an anxiety attack. My relationship with Killian may have gone south, but I just couldn't do it. Not yet. There are still too many good memories I'm not quite ready to let go of. I have to believe one day those will outweigh the bad ones.

Was it another wrong decision? I don't know. I can't even tell anymore.

"Did you ask Kael about Minneapolis?"

"No," I say distractedly. Kael's attention has been diverted away from me by Vanessa Hammer, who is outfitted tonight in a clichéd Playboy bunny costume. Ears, tail, and plunging neckline that display her goods to the nines all scream *I'm a fucking tramp.* I'd heard stories about her and Kael hooking up. When I brought it up to Kael, his brow quirked and he asked if we were really opening that discussion. *"Turnabout is fair play, Swan,"* he'd said darkly. I promptly changed the subject.

In all these years, I've never been jealous over another woman when it comes to Kael. I may not have liked them all, but it's never been jealousy.

Until this very second.

Huh.

As if sensing what I'm thinking, MaryLou announces loudly so anyone nearby can overhear, "I heard she had a botched boob job last month. Look at the right versus the left."

"MaryLou," I chastise, turning away from Vanessa Hammer for fear she's now staring us down.

"Oh stop it."

She pushes my face back toward Kael and Vanessa, holding it there. Vanessa's attention is still entirely focused on Kael. I bite back the need to stalk over there and stake my claim, although I'm not sure why.

"Do you see it?" she whispers in my ear. Pushing down the jealousy, I focus on her chest. I feel weird drinking in another woman's boobs, but the more my eyes bounce back and forth, the clearer it becomes.

"Oh my God. I do."

"Okay, now that we've got that over with, why haven't you asked him?"

"Asked who what?" I ask absently, totally preoccupied by the misshapen left sphere my eyes are now glued to. I tilt my head, trying to get a better look. Poor Vanessa Hammer. Now I totally understand her dilemma. Divert from the obvious. Her cleavage is fantastic, but look a little farther down and...damn. Even the padded bra she's wearing can't smooth that shit out.

"Kael," she answers impatiently. "And stop staring. Jesus."

"You're the one who told me to look." My voice is a low whisper.

"I said look, not rubberneck. Now, for the third time...why didn't you ask Kael about Minneapolis?"

I finally rip my attention away from Vanessa's breasts, which look like a science experiment gone horribly wrong, and give it to MaryLou.

When I arrived home the other day, I intended to ask Kael about his trip, but he distracted me by being sprawled out on our wooden staircase. He was casually leaning back on his elbows. Feet perched two steps below. Legs relaxed to the sides.

And he was Buck. Ass. Naked. Every girl's fantasy come to life, right there.

A cocky grin split his lips as he motioned me over with his index finger. What's a girl to do but take advantage of that situation? My knees still bear faint bruises from how hard I rode him right there in that exact spot. Then he whipped us up scrambled eggs and bacon and fed me in bed. Everything was so perfect, I didn't want to upset the applecart. Mentioning Killian would have blown it the fuck up.

"I decided not to."

"What? Why not?"

I breathe deeply. *How to answer this?* MaryLou knows how upset I was about this. "Because. Then I'll have to tell him that Killian came over and I don't know how he'll react."

"But nothing happened." She pins me hard, squinting her eyes. "Did it?"

"No," I answer quickly. "Nothing happened." I didn't tell her about Killian's ambiguous remarks. "Besides, I trust Kael. If he said he had a business meeting, he did. If I start asking twenty questions like some paranoid wife, it will make it seem as if I don't trust him and he's the only person I do trust one hundred percent."

"Ouch," she kids, knocking her shoulder against mine.

"You know what I mean, ML."

"I do. I'm glad. You guys have come pretty far in a short period of time. You're really falling in love with him, aren't you?"

I find Kael again. He's now surrounded by three guys, laughing with his head thrown back, a half-full beer in his hand. He looks magnificent, even wearing those ridiculous whitewashed jeans and gold chains. The plain white tee that's two sizes too small stretches across his sinewy muscles just the right way to exploit his tone and definition. He pulls off the eighties look well. My mouth waters.

With every day that passes I realize what I've always had right in front of me, and despite the confusing feelings for Killian still rattling around, I fall in love with Kael more and more.

"I am," I tell her in a low voice.

"You know, I remember when he came tearing into Peppy's that night. I knew then that you were in big trouble."

I laugh. "You mean the night he grabbed me and kissed me in front of everyone?" The same night he demanded I go on a date with him.

"That's the one," she says, her voice light.

I fall back into that memory and smile.

---

*Ian strokes a finger down my arm. His face is so close to mine, I can see each black fleck in his crystalline eyes. Whenever he talks, the smell of his whiskey sour floats between us.*

*"So...maybe you and I could—"*

*A loud crashing noise in front of the bar interrupts Ian's proposition. Over his shoulder, I note a fiery Kael scanning the place. My shoulders square when he zeroes in on me. His perturbed glare keeps flipping over to Ian Summerfield, who's been flirting with me all night.*

*Kael hates Ian. Ian feels the same. I don't really like Ian. Not in that way, anyway. I kissed him once when I was fifteen. It was sloppy and he used his teeth in ways that were the opposite of sexy. But I was hopeful I'd get to test whether time and experience had changed that. It's been nice to have some attention by a man who clearly wants me. One who's available. One not married to my sister.*

*I watch Kael watch me, his pace picking up. The closer he gets, the more I see it. Barely checked fury. Then he's in front of me, chest heaving in rapid fire. His usually full lips are pressed into a skinny, ropelike line. Eyes that normally remind me of an inviting glass of whiskey look more like caramels that have hardened after being microwaved too long.*

"Get lost." He pitches his command to Ian without so much as a courteous glance.

Ooohhh...he's mad.

Who the hell called him anyway? I knew I should have sulked ten miles down the road in Hudson.

Ian mumbles something but apparently decides I'm not worth getting the snot beaten out of him by a livid bear nearly twice his size. Whatever. I can find someone else to stroke my bruised ego. It needs a lot of stroking right now. Preferably between the legs.

"What are you doing here, Kael?" I try to yell over the boom of 50 Cent's "Just A Little Bit," but I think my words slur together. Just "a little bit." I laugh at my own joke, which only I heard. I laugh so hard I start to slide off my barstool. It's a slippery fucker.

"You make my name sound like a dirty word," he snaps, grabbing my elbow in his unyielding grip to steady me. I have no idea why he's so pissed. A girl's allowed to get hammered and laid in peace, isn't she?

"Who called you?" I try to break Kael's hold, intent on ordering another Jack and Coke. I pull back so hard I almost fall again, but his catlike reflexes reappear and he steadies me once again.

I look up to see him glowering down at me. "Why are you here?" I demand, gripping the sticky bar top like a lifeline. "I'm not ready to go."

"I'm here because you need me. And, yes"—he pries my kung fu grip from the beat-up wood—"you are ready."

"I think I know when I'm ready and I'm not—"

It happens so fast I don't see it coming. In retrospect, that was probably his intent. I'm stunned silent when, right there in the middle of the bar, in the middle of town, in front of dozens of people we both know, he palms the back of my head and slams his mouth to mine.

This is not the kiss of a best friend. It's not calm and sweet. It doesn't remotely suggest platonic. It's a kiss of possession and want. It's raw, unadulterated need. And I want to be wanted. I need to be the air someone breathes. Even if it is tainted with all kinds of wrong.

When I gasp, Kael dips his tongue inside. It's seeking and sure. He *duels it with mine. I fight back to see what he'll do. He responds by tightening his fist in my hair and groaning. It's unexpected but so damn sexy that my fingers sink into his jacket and I yank him closer, greedily gulping down his erotic noises. His hand travels to the small of my back and when he presses me to him, I feel the hardness between his thighs swell.*

*Too soon, his lips are gone, but I feel the heaviness of his breath fanning over my face with each hard exhale. Just as mine is doing. "You ready now, Swan?" he rasps against my trembling lips. Or maybe his are the ones trembling. It's hard to tell. My eyes are shut when I nod a yes. "Good."*

*He shoves my arms into my winter coat and zips it up to my chin. Looping our fingers together, he leads me outside. The cold January night sucks away my oxygen, but Kael doesn't notice my lack of breath, nor does he slow down as he drags me behind him to his black Ford F-150.*

*After he settles me in, gravel spins as he leaves Peppy's behind in his angry, irrational dust. He keeps his eyes on the road. His jaw flexes and releases. Is he mad? Remorseful? God...is he turned on?*

*I sit there, quiet. My drunk mind reeling. I want to say something. About the kiss. About the way he's acting as if I've stepped out on him or something. I know Kael has feelings for me. I know they extend beyond friendship. But in all the years I've known him, he's never once crossed the line into intimating that we be something other than we are—not after I shut him down at my senior prom, telling him we'd never be anything but friends because I was in love with someone else.*

*On the interminable ten-minute drive, the tension is taut. So I fidget. I clean the garbage from my purse. I coat my mouth with cherry ChapStick. I count my change. I organize my cash, making sure the presidents all face the same way and the bills go from ones to twenties.*

*I do everything in my power not to look at my best friend who was just playing tonsil hockey with me. But I also can't stop thinking about the way his lips felt on mine. They still tingle a bit. I set my elbow against the window and nonchalantly rest a finger against them, trying to get the feeling to stop.*

*Finally we pull up outside the house I bought last summer. The same one Kael came over to help me fix. He painted. He tore up flooring and put a new one down. He replaced all the hardware in the kitchen to make it look more modern. Then, after a long day of sweat and sometimes a little blood (his) and tears (mine), we'd veg in front of the TV, order Chinese, and fall asleep in a sea of blankets and pillows, just like old times.*

*Without a word, Kael leaves the vehicle running, but I hear the silent demand to stay put while he gets out and runs around the front. He opens the door, holds out his hand, which I take, and helps me to the ground.*

*He still won't look at me. Do I want him to?*

*I don't like this awkwardness now hanging here. I don't want anything to change between us. I plan to tell him to forget what happened and that I will, too.*

*He walks me the few steps to my front door, takes my bag, and digs out the keys. He shoves the one for the house in the lock and turns. It disengages, but he doesn't open the door. Instead, he swivels to me.*

*"Kael..."* Stop. Whatever this is, please stop it.

*He looks me straight in the eye. "I want you, Maverick DeSoto."*

*"Kael," I try to say more forcefully this time. "What just happened was—"*

*"Not a mistake. And if you fucking say that, I'm gonna lose it. Just listen." When he sees I'm going to remain quiet, he continues. "I want you. I'm sick and fucking tired of pretending I don't. And I felt it back from you. Just now. With our breaths mingling and your moan on my lips. I felt it." He pounds his chest with his index finger three times to punctuate the last three words.*

*I felt something, too. I'm not sure what it was, but I know what it can never be. No matter if I shouldn't be or not, I'm still in love with his brother.*

*"I'm drunk," I announce as if he doesn't know.*

*Half of his mouth lifts up. It's adorable. And a whole lot of sexy. Stop it, Mavs. He's your best friend.* "Yes. You are. But even drunk you can't fake what we just felt."

"Kael," *I draw out. As if saying just his name enough times will be sufficient to get my message across. Or keep my thoughts from dangerously straying.*

*Grabbing my face between his freezing hands, the space between us vanishes in an instant. Now we're touching, knees to chest. He thumbs my lower lip. It's moist from the lip balm I just applied minutes ago. His eyes track his movements, which are now almost hypnotic. His next statement is gruff and gravelly and sends the flutters of a thousand butterflies zinging through my belly.*

"I want to kiss these fucking lips, Maverick. And not a kiss of a boy who has been friends with a girl for almost thirty years. But as a lover. I want to bite and suck and own and devour. Whenever I want. However I want."

*I don't want that...do I? What would it feel like to be completely owned by my very best friend? My head is so full of fuzz at the moment, I'm not sure, but the word* inviting *creeps around the edges.*

*Kael's lips drop to my forehead like they've done countless times before. Only this time, I feel the mania of his hunger unleashed. As a man for a woman.*

*I groan. He groans, too.*

"Oh fuck, Mavs. The things I want to do to you."

"What are they?" *I ask, dying to know. Knowing I shouldn't.*

"They're wicked. And dirty. And sinful. Fuck, they're so bad, you'll be begging for more."

"Kael." *This time, his name is a plea. For what, yet, I'm not sure. Stop? Go? Slow down? I don't know. If I say yes, if I even give a hint of a yes, everything between us will change. Everything. I can't handle losing him, too. I wouldn't survive losing both Shepard men.*

*A shiver racks my entire body. His arms tighten.* "Go out with me," *he demands in my ear.*

*I tunnel my hands under his coat. My body melts into his warmth.*

"We go out all the time." My nose is running now. I sniff, unladylike.

"Not like this. I want to woo you."

I laugh. That sounds so funny coming from the mouth of the boy I knew had chicken pox on his tongue and his privates. But when he presses a thick indication of truth into my lower belly, I stop. This time I stifle that moan.

"I...I don't think we should," I counter back.

"One date." I don't say anything and he demands again, "One date, Swan. That's all I'm asking."

"Why? Why now? After all this time?" It hurts when I swallow. It hurts to think. It kind of hurts to hope.

"You weren't ready."

"What if I'm not ready now?"

"You are, Mavs."

His reply is so sure, so confident, he's even managed to convince me. He winds his own hands underneath my jacket. His touch feels good. Too good. So wrong.

"Okay," I say at last.

His muscles stiffen. "Yeah?"

I nod, my nose rubbing against the shell of his coat. I leave some snot behind. Then my face is once again in his hands. His lips just ghost mine this time. There's restrained passion, but unreserved promise in it. It feels good. Maybe more than good. I want more, I think.

"Saturday night," he calls over his shoulder as he bounds to his car like a teenager.

"That's a whole week," I moan, kinda just wanting to get this date over with. I'm sure it will be like every other time we've gone out and he'll see his feelings for me aren't really what he thinks they are. And I'll convince myself the swirls in my stomach are from the five cocktails I had and not unfurling desire. Then we can get back to being just us.

"I need time to plan, Swan."

*"Plan what?" I yell. He's now in his car and his grin is infectious.
"You'll see," he mouths.*

---

We went on that date. Then another after that. And another and another until we barely spent any time apart, which wasn't a whole lot different than before except that Kael Shepard "wooed" me unlike anything I've ever experienced before. And I fell for it. Maybe I've always felt more for him than I realized. It was just buried underneath the impenetrable cloak of another man.

Suddenly I remember something about that first night our friendship shifted. Something I'd completely forgotten. I thought I'd glimpsed MaryLou over Ian's shoulder once, but when I looked again, she wasn't there. I thought it was a figment of my hazed imagination, but now...

"It was you, wasn't it?"

"What was me?"

"Don't play dumb with me, MaryLou Colinda James." She loathes her middle name. Spits fire when I use it. "It was you who called Kael that night I was at Peppy's with Ian, wasn't it?"

She straightens up and leans close until our noses kiss. Smoke and fire tango in her green gaze. The flames lash out at me when she spits unrepentantly, "You're fucking right it was."

Putting a hand between us, I set it against her chest and push. "Why would you do that?"

"Are you kidding me, Maverick? You were self-destructing. Pining away for a man who threw you away like trash when Kael has always stood on the sidelines admiring you for the treasure you are."

I'm stunned. I feel duped. And maybe a tiny bit grateful. I'm still sorting through those clashing emotions, deciding which one I'm going to go with when I spot *them* over her shoulder.

"Oh fuck," I mumble, taking a step back.

Her gaze follows mine and MaryLou lets loose a string of expletives that would embarrass a nun. "What are they doing here?"

And this was another reason I didn't want to come tonight. Once upon a time, Jilly and Marta McQueen were besties. Then they had a falling out. No one will say why, but rumor was Marta didn't approve of what she did under my nose with Killian. I've seen them around town a few times lately, though, so I was wondering if they'd mended fences. Guess the fact she's here answers that.

Jilly stops to talk to Marta, kissing her on both cheeks like she grew up European or something while Killian beelines over to grab a beer from the fridge. He stands off to the side, alone, checking out the partygoers.

I see the minute he spots Kael because everything about him changes. His posture. His demeanor. His face. He starts searching the place for me. When his gaze finally catches mine, he looks... momentarily happy. But then his mouth turns down and he leans back against the post he was holding. He brings the can to his lips but never looks away from me.

"Fuck this shit," MaryLou sputters, before yelling, "Hey Larry, Kael!" Our husbands hear her booming voice, even over the drone of the melee, and when their heads turn our way she follows up with, "Glowing tombstone time!"

"Oh boy," I mutter under my breath. The glowing tombstone is a tradition in Dusty Falls. There's a small town fifteen point three miles away on Highway 169 that you'd miss if you blinked your eyes driving through it called Saint Peters. Saint Pete's houses four old homes and a small Catholic church—called, you guessed it, Saint Peter's—where I attended kindergarten through second grade. And on the hill behind Saint Peter's is an old cemetery that has about a hundred plots. On a cloudless night, with the moon hitting it just right, one of the tombstones actually glows from the road. It's eerie and beautiful.

I know exactly what MaryLou's doing...and I love her for it.

For a second, I think Kael's going to protest. He hates drunken glowing tombstone trips, but then he spots Jilly. Two beats later he eyeballs Killian. Watching us.

"Oh, hell yeah. We're in," he shouts. Before I know it, he's at my side, palming my nape, lips taking mine in a hunger-filled, possessive kiss. Larry grabs two other couples, which is all that can fit in their minivan, and soon we're heading out, each fisting two beers. Kael catches Jared as we pass. We say our good-byes. Kael says we may be back, but we both know we won't.

"I'm not sticking my naked ass on that tombstone," Larry announces as we make our way to the back door.

"Your fucking pansy-ass is so spanking Leila tonight," Kael smoothly replies. *Leila Goulding. Age 29. Died 1849.*

"I bet Leila's seen more ass than my gynecologist," MaryLou says, snaking her arm around her husband.

"She's seen more balls, that's for damn sure." Larry palms Mary-Lou's ass. "I swear mine tingle for days after they touch that crumbling sandstone."

"Maybe it will fire up those swimmers." Kael huffs a laugh when Larry shoves him playfully in the chest.

Laughing and bantering, we all file out, leaving the McQueen party in full swing behind us. And though I don't look back, I don't have to. I know the weight of Killian's stare. It's laden and searing.

And still all too welcome.

"Go away," she demands tersely through gritted teeth.

"No." I could give a shit if she wants me here or not. I'm ditching classes for her. She needs me. And as usual, she won't admit it. Stubborn, stubborn girl. Jesus Christ, she just plain pisses me off sometimes.

"I'm tired, Kael."

"Then I'll lie down with you. Scoot over."

She doesn't move. Crosses her arms and turns her swollen little mouth down. Like that's going to do anything but fire me up more. So I stoop low, lift her up against feeble protests, and gently lay her a foot or so over, careful not to jostle her. I then settle myself in, tugging her into my empty arms.

*Oh fuck.* My soul sighs long and loud. I'm surprised she doesn't hear it. I am absolutely whipped for this tiny but mighty thing I'm finally holding close again. This last year in college, away from her, has been excruciating. The parties. The girls. The games. I don't need any of it. Or want it. The only thing I want is currently acting like a spoiled-ass brat as she grabs a fistful of my shirt and yanks.

"Hey," I cry, prying open fingers she now has firmly twisted in my chest hair.

"Hey, what? You're such a baby."

I rub the smarting over my nipple first and lace our fingers together so she can't do it again. "Let me reach downtown and give your rug a couple quick tugs. See if your eyes don't water."

"Kael." She swats me. It stings, but I laugh. "That's gross."

Jesus. If she thinks that's gross, she wouldn't want a glimpse into the inner workings of my filthy mind. With her perky tits pressed into my chest and the heat of her pussy currently burning a hole through my jeans, she's the very epitome of clueless.

Me and my cock? Yeah...been having a little heart-to-heart with him ever since I walked into this room, saw her spread out on her bed in terrycloth short-short-shorts and a barely-there tank. White. Sans bra. Even now I'm talking him down.

She wriggles against me. I groan.

"Stay still," I chastise, reaching down to still the leg that's creeping way too close to my inflating woody. *Fuck, dude. Work with me here.*

"Why?" She tips her head up, this sweet innocence written all over her. She has no idea.

Clueless.

So fucking clueless.

"I thought you were tired."

"I am," she shoots back before promptly closing her eyes.

She relaxes her hand over my heart and pretends to sleep while I pretend I'm not staring straight down her gaping tee. *Fuck. Me.* I see a hint of pebbled brown. My mouth waters. I make myself look anywhere but *there* when all I really want to do is strip her from this shirt, tongue my way down her neck, and suck that perfect nipple until she's writhing underneath me.

There are so many depraved things I want to do to her almost sixteen-year-old killer body. But I run the words that would end me and my budding legal aspirations on repeat: *jailbait, jailbait, jailbait.*

In the state of Iowa, at nineteen, I could technically be charged with statutory rape if I so much as lay a fucking inappropriate finger on her before her sixteenth birthday, which is in three weeks.

Even then, she won't let me touch her, though. She doesn't think of me *that way*. Never has. She's got a teenage "crush" on my brother while I have officially been "friend-zoned." And that smarts more than any hair being pulled on my body. Hell, I'd pluck them out myself, one by one, if she looked at *me* the way she looks at Killian.

The shit of it is...Killian returns some of her feelings. I see the way he looks at her out of the corner of his eye when he doesn't think anyone is watching. I am in for a lifetime of torture if these two hook up. It will fucking end me.

But I will never give up fighting for her. Ever. Killian doesn't know Mavs the way I do. He never will. He doesn't know she leaps into her bed from a foot away after she's shut off the light. Or that she eats green beans right out of the can, cold, not because she's impatient, but because she likes them that way. Or that she has the tiniest little twitch in her right eye when she's getting ready to spew her personal brand of sarcasm.

No. She's mine. Period. He can't have her.

Trying my level best to ignore that black rock from him she keeps on her nightstand, I take in the muted show on TV Land. *Gilligan's Island.* God, how I love this girl's quirks. Old shows. Old movies. Old music. Old clothes. She's a classic through and through. So very opposite from her snobby family.

"How's the mouth, Swan?"

"How do you think?" she snaps, eyes still screwed shut.

"I think you need some more painkillers to curb that sass. That's what I think."

Brilliant eyes the color of blades of grass after a heavy rain snap open and latch on to me. "You're not supposed to be mean to a patient after surgery. That's against the rules," she sasses back. I can tell it's hard for her to talk.

"You didn't have surgery, Mavs. You had two wisdom teeth pulled."

"Well, they gave me anesthesia and anytime you get anesthesia it's technically considered surgery."

I don't argue. It's pointless.

"What can I do?"

"Nothing," she says lowly. I push a piece of that thick, shiny chocolate hair I love so much back behind her ear. Her eyes flutter shut this time. She looks happy and peaceful. She looks so right next to me. *My God, I love her.* She is maturing into an exquisite woman.

"Hungry?"

The shoulder she's not lying on lifts. That means yes.

"I can't eat any solid food for another three days," she mumbles.

My girl's jaw is swollen and starting to yellow on one side where she clearly bruised. If I could carry all her pain, I would. In the span of a heartbeat.

"Good thing I brought your favorite nonsolid treat then."

She pops up like a jack-in-the-box, using my gut as leverage. Practically pushes all the air out of my lungs. "You did not!"

Her eyes glitter. Literally. Like stardust or laser beams. And her smile? Jesus. It would make any sane man do stupid, stupid things to keep it there. She looks so damn excited I want to kiss her, slam my mouth to hers, taking everything I've held back from taking all these years. Instead, I slide a hand under my head and grin. "I did."

She bounds to her knees, her "tiredness" and "surgery" all but forgotten. Right now she looks every ounce the fifteen-year-old she is, affirming I can't push her for anything. She's not ready.

Mavs jumps on top of me, throwing her hands down on either side of my head. She's now nicely placed her scorching center mere inches from my rapidly hardening junk.

Oh...fuck.

*Breathe, perv. Just breathe.*

Then she dips, her nose touching mine. "Where is it?" she prods playfully. She starts wiggling again. I can't take it. She scoots back even the tiniest fraction and she's not going to be clueless much longer. I clamp my hands around her waist, trying not to picture her naked...riding me...those amazing tits bouncing...head thrown back in ecstasy...tight pussy sucking me in...

Holy living God, I want her.

"Freezer," I choke.

I don't even have the word all the way out before her door flies open and she's running down the hall, bounding down the steps to the kitchen. I have about forty-five seconds before she's back. I use that time to scold the unruly adolescent in my jeans who refuses to obey. I'm hard as a fucking two-by-four. Two strokes is all it would take and I'll be shooting all over her pristine white sheets.

Slowly, I inhale. Exhale. Repeat. Repeat again. A third time.

It's no use. With every breath I take in, I smell her. She's all around me. Honeysuckle. Roses. Tulips. I have no fucking idea what kind of flower she smells like, but I forever associate it with her.

I prop myself against the headboard and throw a pillow in my lap at the very second Mavs walks back in. Blissfully unaware, she settles in beside me, hands me a spoon, and unmutes the TV.

We eat her favorite ice cream—strawberry explosion, a creamy concoction that boasts chocolate-covered Pop Rocks—in silence. Pretty soon, we're both laughing at Mary Ann, who is currently trying to sing "I Wanna Be Loved by You," but keeps forgetting the words. I love this episode. It's the one where Mary Ann hits her head and thinks she's Ginger.

After a while, Mavs sets the bowl of melting ice cream on her nightstand and lays her head on my shoulder. "Thanks, Kael."

"For what, Swan?" I throw my arm around her and hold in my moan when she snuggles.

"For coming. I know you should be at school."

"If it's a choice between you and Statistics, you win every time."

She cranes her neck, looking up at me. Smiles. Moves a few inches to kiss me innocently on the cheek. Her lips are soft. Supple. Cool from the ice cream, but they feel so damn good. My free hand involuntarily snakes in her hair. I tip her head back. Her eyes bulge a little.

I want to taste her. God almighty, how I want my mouth on hers.

"I have another surprise for you."

Her grin wrenches me under. Bewitches me.

"It can't be better than strawberry explosion."

"Oh, but it is," I tease, bopping her on the nose.

That smile widens. I'm gone to it. To her.

"What could be better than that?" Is it my imagination or did she sound breathy? Did her eyes dilate just a tad? Did her muscles relax into me a bit more?

*"North by Northwest."*

"Get out!" she squeals, throwing her arms around my neck, burying her face in the crook.

*Please don't mount me again. I'm not sure I can take it without going to jail.*

"Where is it?"

"On the seat of my car," I tell her. Like an idiot—or maybe it was a blessing—I forgot the DVD when I came in. I was more worried about the ice cream melting. "How about we watch another episode of *Gilligan's Island* and I'll go get it. That is...if you're not too tired."

"I'm not too tired." But she is. She sounds like she's fading.

My lips find their way to her forehead. They linger too long. "Time for a pain pill?"

She hesitates. Finally, "Maybe."

"Okay. Stay here and rest. I'll get you some water."

I've just slid from the bed when she grabs my hand and tugs until I look back at her. Time is suspended as she just looks at me and breathes. It seems as if she wants to say something but can't.

"What's wrong?" I ask, unsure what to do. My heart is beating out of my chest.

"Nothing. I just..." She stops. Licks her pink lips. My dick starts to grow again. "How long are you staying?"

I'd stay as long as she asked. "Is the weekend okay?"

I'm lit from the inside when she beams. Her smile isn't normal, all broad and mesmerizing because of the swelling but it still takes over her entire being. She lights up like Venus. Her eyes sparkle and I swear she glows like the full moon on a clear night when she looks at me like that. It's what I need. What I've been missing.

She blinks slow and languid. "That's perfect. Love you, Kael."

My eyes shut briefly, wanting her words to mean more than they do. "Love you, too, Swan." *More than you comprehend.*

I want to kiss her. Feel her lips moving against mine for the first time. Make sure she knows she's meant to be mine. When I do, though...when I finally have my lips fused to hers...it will be the last first kiss I ever have. I plan to kiss one woman for the rest of my life. Only one. Maverick DeSoto.

Gazing into innocent eyes, I remind myself she's nowhere near ready for that.

I smile gently and give her hand a squeeze, get the water, and hold her as she drifts in my arms.

We watch Cary Grant in *North by Northwest* four times that weekend.

It's blissful perfection.

"Where are we going?" I ask for the eighth time.

And for the eighth time, Kael patiently answers in the exact same way he has the previous seven, "It's a surprise, Swan."

But I already know. Once we got on I-35, I had it figured out. There's not much between Canada and us except ten thousand lakes.

Kael's taking me away for a "long weekend." Today marks our four-and-three-quarter-month wedding anniversary. He does things off the beaten path. It's one of the most endearing qualities about him. So he took the day off. Arranged for coverage at the bakery all weekend. He even packed for me, saying he knew exactly what I needed.

He picks up my hand, kisses my palm, and places our laced fingers in his lap. On his upper thigh. Close to his dick. A dick that's more talented than I ever imagined.

Well...*maybe* I imagined. Once or twice.

I'll never forget the first time I felt it pressed against me. I was young, immature, inexperienced. Had no idea what a girl could possibly do to turn a boy on so much his cock would swell from flaccid to rock hard in under five seconds.

I was four days into wisdom teeth recovery. I remember waking up from a drug-induced sleep. Kael was snuggled up behind me. We were in my bedroom with the door shut, a rerun of *Gilligan's Island* on in the background. My parents trusted Kael implicitly and while no other boy could get away with slipping so much as a toenail into my room without a chaperone, Kael always could.

Kael's arm had me anchored to his torso. His leg was slung over mine. Our bodies were pressed together from shoulder to shin. His measured, even breaths tickled my ear. Lying in his arms then felt different than it ever had before. I began to get warm. Flush. His body heat had me on fire from head to toe. I squirmed, trying to get comfortable when I felt *it*. It was hard. So damn hard and thick and long. When I wriggled to assure my inexperienced almost sixteen-year-old brain I wasn't feeling what I thought I was, he groaned my name, still fast asleep.

I lay still as an injured animal, unsure what to do next. That warmth spreading through me was raging hotter with every second that passed. Especially between my legs, where I began to ache and long for something I'd never longed for before. I was still in love with Killian, but for the first time, I imagined what it would be like to kiss my best friend. *Really* kiss him. Not a peck on the cheek or like that time he tried to kiss me when I was ten. But a real kiss with tongue and heavy breathing and passion.

"You awake, Swan?" he whispered in my ear just seconds later. I pretended I wasn't. Then he got up, went into the bathroom, and stayed there for a good ten minutes. The door did nothing to disguise what was happening on the other side. His rapid breathing and low grunts quickly gave it away.

That was my first inkling. Kael had feelings for me. Real ones beyond eating strawberry explosion and watching old movies together. Lust was obvious, but when I remember the way he held me, I think I always knew it ran deeper than rampant teenage hormones.

He spent every minute with me for four solid days. I hadn't realized how much I'd missed him that year until he was lying in my bed, watching TV, and doting on me as if it was the only thing he wanted to do. We built a blanket fort and spent all day Saturday underneath it, playing silly games, talking, napping when I had to take a pain pill. He made me grape Jell-O: my favorite. He made sure I had Kitty McGoo, the ratty stuffed cat he'd given me when I had my tonsils out at age seven. And we ate two whole quarts of strawberry explosion in four days. He cared for me like I was already his.

Maybe I was.

"You're awfully quiet over there. Whatcha thinking about, baby?"

I let my eyes run over his profile. Strong, angled jaw. Aristocratic nose. Plump, kissable lips. Wavy hair that's soft and thick. *Stunning.* My face matches his when he breaks into a grin. He knows I'm staring.

"Remember when I got my wisdom teeth out?"

He laughs. I really like making him laugh. "It was utterly unforgettable, Swan."

"Why do you say it like that?" I ask, swiveling to face him. I draw a foot up to the seat and rest my chin on my bent knee.

"Like what?"

"I don't know. With that smirk?"

"What smirk?" he asks, the corner of his mouth tilting way up.

"What aren't you telling me?" I giggle, poking him in the arm. When I see him adjust his package, I really let loose.

"Do you know how many times I jacked off that weekend, Swan?" He grabs my wrist and drags my palm to his cock. It's stiff. Eight inches of utter glory. And so thick, I couldn't fully circle it even if I wanted to. I clamp my fingers around him, the nails scratching the denim. My girly parts start to throb.

His own palm warms the top of my hand as he begins to guide me up and down. "Oh fuck, Maverick. You have no idea." *I think I have some idea.* When he looks at me, his pupils are larger. Darker. The brown of his irises a little murkier. The skin on his face seems tighter. "I lost count after ten."

"You did?" I ask on a breathless laugh. I lean over and nibble his neck. He moans. My fingers tighten. "You're right. I had no idea." Well, no idea he'd taken care of himself so many times.

"Why...*oh fuck*," he breathes hoarsely when my thumb caresses around his mushroom tip. "Why do you think I wore a pillow like a diaper the entire time?"

I remember that very well. Chuckling in his ear, I take the lobe between my teeth. The metal of his zipper is between my fingers. I start to tug down, but he stops me. "What's the matter, babe?" I whisper. "Not up for a little road trip adventure today?"

The hand holding mine steady whips up, threads through my hair, and yanks me back so he can take my mouth in a punishing kiss, all while keeping his eyes on the road. His tongue dives inside, sweeping in long, drugging strokes. I feel the car shift, pull to the right. We start to slow before he lets me catch a breath again.

We turn right. Right again. I have no idea what we're doing as my mouth is working its way up and down his neck, over his jaw. Our fingers are again dueling against his jeans. Mine south, his fighting north. He's winning, dammit. Then he's releasing me while he shifts the car into park. I blink a few times to clear my haze, realizing we're at a convenience store off the interstate.

Kael hops out and opens my door. I smile up at him as he takes my hand in his. "Thirsty?" I tease laughingly. When he drove us to school we always had to leave in time to stop at the local gas station for his sixty-four-ounce Biggie filled with half Coke half Dr. Pepper.

"Fucking parched," he mumbles. Very seriously, I might add. With our fingers locked, he drags me behind him inside, weaving between aisles until we reach the restrooms in the back. He tries the men's door first. Locked. He curses. He tries the women's next. It easily swings open.

He ushers me inside the one-person unit and closes us in. When he twists the lock, I ask, "What are you doing?"

"Being adventurous," he replies simply.

"Oh," is all I can think of to say.

Then he's all over me. Lips fused to mine. Hands sweeping my curves. Wrenching my jeans open. Tugging them down, along with my underwear. I'm being lifted in the air and my ass hits cold ceramic, but it does nothing to cool down the blaze now burning out of control inside me.

After wrapping my hands around the sink, Kael spreads me wide, drops to his haunches, and with mischief written all over his face, never breaks his eyes from mine as he proceeds to eat me out right there in the women's restroom at Casey's. Within seconds, he has me writhing. Within minutes, I'm coming undone.

Scorching fire bursts through my veins, heats my muscles. Makes me nothing but boneless satisfaction. I'm still chanting his name when he invades and conquers. The growl in the back of his throat when he first pushes inside me is so fucking sexy, I detonate again almost immediately.

"I will never get enough of this, Swan. Fucking ever," he grits against my ear. "So long I've waited for you."

"Oh, God," I pant when his thumb snakes between us. His fingers make my body hum and my blood sing. His teeth scrape along the length of the straining tendon in my neck and when he sucks that spot right below my ear, I feel myself clench around him.

"Yeah, that's it. Come again, Mavs."

For a girl who wasn't able to orgasm more than once, if ever, Kael has turned me into a nymph. He expertly works me now. Every. Single. Time. It's like he's opened some floodgate—a sexual Pandora's box—and I can't stop them now. That's not a complaint, by the way. Just an observation. I've come to appreciate the way he subtly controls both my desires and my reactions to them.

My nails curl, now digging into his shoulders. I hang on for dear life, perched on the tip of a sink and the edge of sanity at what he does to me.

"Oh, yes," he praises when I finally free-fall. He's right behind me, releasing into me on punishing drives. I love it when Kael lets go —another thing I've come to appreciate over the last few months. His body seizes up. His grunts are growly and sexy. He grips me with just the right amount of hardness. It borders on bruising but isn't. It's enough to stamp me with his subtle ownership, though not enough to mark me.

He stills and his hands come up to meet my cheeks. Breath still harsh, he kisses me sweetly, but senseless, then draws back and stares into my eyes. He doesn't make an attempt to break us apart yet even though we both just heard the knock on the door and an urgent plea to "hurry."

"What?" I ask.

His smile is tender. I shiver a little when he brushes stray hairs behind my ears. "Sorry."

Sorry? What the hell for? That was hot. "For?"

"For having no control when it comes to you. I've had enough of both of our palms to last me a lifetime. I needed to be inside you."

God. The things he says sometimes are ridiculously romantic.

I wrap my arms around his waist, pulling him closer. He's softening and slips out at the sudden movement. Now, cool air mixes with the mess between my legs, but I don't care in the slightest. "I'm not sorry. You shouldn't be either." I close the two inches between us, taking his lips lightly between mine. "I loved it."

"Yeah? Even in"—he takes in our less than sanitary conditions —"here?"

"Are you kidding? I bet this sink has seen more action than Sylvester Stallone."

His laugh warms me. "I bet you're right. We should leave our notch somewhere."

"Let's do!" I clap my hands together in excitement.

The pounding is getting more urgent, so I push him back slightly as I slip off the edge of the sink. My ass is now numb and my upper thighs are tingling. Kael doesn't just reach over to grab some paper towels, which would be the handiest route. No...he rushes to get me a big wad of toilet paper instead.

"Softer," he says with a wink.

And that right there is why I should have loved this man all along instead of Killian. It's not grand gestures but the small things that seem so mundane and inconsequential that slot themselves inside our memories forever. When everything else fades with time, *those* are what shine bright, undying. This is the core of who Kael is. My needs come first. My comfort. My pleasure. He wants the best for me. Always has. Why did I not see that before?

"Kael?"

He abandons his own cleaning up, eyes sweeping to mine "Swan?" The look on his face is pure, utter bliss. Feeling a burn start in my eyes, I band my arms around him. Tight. Strong. Unbreakable. *We're* unbreakable.

"I love you."

He gently runs his hands down my hair, smoothing it back in place. His touch is slow and purposeful. Reverent is the word that comes to mind. With lips against my temple, he whispers on a sigh, "I love you more."

*I don't doubt that.* That should make me feel bad, but all it does is make me feel drunk on him instead.

We rush to put ourselves back together and Kael scratches a crude marking in the peach-tinged paint of the wall with his keys. He insists on a selfie first to mark this memory then swings open the door and leads us out, hand in hand, uncaring that a middle-aged woman is standing right there with a young girl who is holding her hand between her legs. She looks absolutely stricken we had the audacity to be seen together in broad daylight fresh off an—well, let's just call it what it is—afternoon fuck in the Casey's bathroom.

"Men's room is out of order," Kael announces smoothly as we pass. Not two seconds later—kid you not—the men's door flies open. Out bounds a man who has clearly enjoyed his alone time, although the next person won't so much. The woman's mouth turns down even farther before she pushes the girl into the bathroom and commands her not to touch anything. We giggle like teenagers, rushing away from her condemning glare.

Hand still tucked in mine, he says, "Let's get some snacks while we're here."

Another road trip must. Junk food. "Oh hell yeah."

A few minutes later, our arms full of sodas, candy bars, nuts, and crackers, we dump them on the counter and wait for the attendant to ring them up. I laugh when I see what Kael has picked out. Several flat strips of taffy. The exact kind they used to sell at our pool in the summertime. Banana flavored. He was more of a strawberry lover, but he's picked banana. *My* favorite. Then I almost double over when I see them. Pop Rocks. Three packets of them.

"Pop Rocks?" I tease. I haven't had Pop Rocks since I was seventeen.

He winds his arm around my waist, drawing me to his side. "I thought you loved those."

"I do. In strawberry explosion."

Leaning down so far I think he's going to plant one on me right in front of the cashier and the patrons behind us, he whispers salaciously, "We can make our own explosion with them."

My eyes flick to the big man standing behind us. He's snickering, not even bothering to look away. "Okay," I reply lamely, not understanding what he means.

Kael does kiss me then. And he makes a big production of it. Tongue. Moans. Even a little backward dip. I hear a few gasps and whispers but keep my eyes tightly shut. When he releases me, my face is flaming. Kael is grinning. The cashier is gaping. The guy behind us is full-on laughing.

"Newlyweds," Kael offers loudly. Out of the corner of my eye, I spot the woman who was outside the bathroom, eyeing us with disdain as she skirts her daughter outside.

"Congratulations. Lucky guy," hefty behind us says with appreciation.

Kael's grip tightens. "Don't I know it." But he didn't say it to him. He said it to me. Soft and sexy and with so much love it makes me liquefy. My lips turn up so high my face feels as though it may split in two.

God, who knew I could be this happy after being crushed a few short months earlier? But I am. The more time I spend as Kael Shepard's wife, the lighter and happier I feel. The more I think maybe it was meant to turn out this way all along.

We collect our goodies and head back on the road. Two hours later we're pulling into the driveway of a quaint, all-brick Victorian B and B just a few blocks from downtown Saint Paul, Minnesota. The wraparound porch is enviable with wrought iron drop lights every few feet and large cushy furniture you could get lost in.

Kael turns off the engine and slides his gaze to me, that smile firmly intact. "I know how much you love these."

I do. I love the intimacy of such a small setting. That one-on-one attention you get from the owners. The fabulous, over-the-top breakfast they make. The comforts of home while away from your own bed.

I lean across the interior and kiss his cheek. "Thank you. This is perfect."

In this moment, there's absolutely nothing that could top this. Getting away from Dusty Falls and the shit we left there is exactly what both of us needed.

"What do you want to do today?" The soft stroke of Kael's fingers lightly on my bare arm gives me goose bumps. I shiver and he chuckles, holding me closer.

"Don't stop," I tell him quietly when he wraps that hand around my waist instead.

"Your wish is my command, Swan," he replies saucily, already sweeping his fingers over my flesh once again.

I sigh, utterly replete. We're curled up in bed. Naked. Blissful. Momentarily sated.

After arriving yesterday afternoon, we were greeted by Sheila, the plump innkeeper, who told us all about her five grown children (all girls) and six grandchildren (all boys). She also informed us if we heard any unusual noises, it was just Pierre LeMars, the original homeowner—who hung himself in the attic after his wife and daughter drowned in a boating accident. He is apparently their resident ghost and friendly, she assured us. Kael just shrugged but I was a little unnerved as she ushered us up a wide, grand, two-tiered staircase. The energy changed. Unseen eyes were on me. I was convinced I walked through a pocket of cold air.

I squeezed Kael's hand so hard he winced. All of that nervousness evaporated, though, the second she opened the door to the King's Suite—one of four bedrooms in the old mansion—and settled us in a very stately, spacious room.

An enormous, antique-looking sleigh bed sat in the middle, covered in an ivory eyelet comforter and a mound of neutral throw pillows. The bathroom boasted a walk-in, all-glass shower and a sunken whirlpool tub that could fit four. There was an expansive turret with a cathedral-like ceiling off to our left. A small table and two chairs sat in the center of the glassed-in area. It would be lovely for a cozy cup of coffee in the morning or cocktail in the evening. And the views from the tower were spectacular.

But what drew me like a magnet were the walls. Above the white-washed wainscoting was the most unique wallpaper I'd ever seen. Secrets whispered from it. They echoed softly in my ear. I could feel haunting pain radiating from the foreign words even before Sheila spoke. My breath caught when she told me it was a replica of a love letter written by a young Italian woman who had fallen in love with an American soldier during WWII.

---

*"This letter was supposedly found in the young soldier's pocket by his brother. The soldier died in his brother's arms from several gunshot wounds to the chest. And rumor has it in a strange twist of events, the young lady ended up marrying the brother," Sheila whispers to me as Kael checks out the bathroom.*

*She married his brother? My heart pounds. Is this some sort of strange coincidence or was I meant to be here hearing her story? Seeing her words? Feeling her pain?*

*"Was she happy?" I ask absently, tracing my fingers over softly muted print. Did she love the second as much as the first?*

*"I like to think we all end up in the place we're supposed to be eventually," Sheila answers wistfully. "The sum total of our choices carries us to our destiny."*

*Is that true, I wonder? Or do those choices really change our future instead? I want to believe her. I want to believe that I'm standing here in this room for a reason other than the stacks of bad decisions I've made.*

*"Do you think so?" I turn then and look at this woman I don't know at all but who radiates this innate purity that's enviable. Maybe*

*it can wash away all my sins. Maybe that's why I'm here. She stares into my eyes as if she knows exactly what I'm thinking. What I've done. Can she see inside my guilt and free me?*

*She reaches out to gently wrap her fingers around my arm and smiles warmly. "I do."*

---

I'd never wished I could speak another language until right then. I wondered about her. That woman. Although I couldn't read the words, they looked forlorn, wistful. Were the rumors true? Did they go on to live a long and fulfilling life together? Or did she look at him and always think of the one she lost? Is it possible to lose the love of your life then find it again in the most unexpected of places?

Four months ago I would have said no. But now, I think the answer is maybe.

Even at this moment, as I lie in Kael's arms, I'm still thinking of her. Hoping she got her happily ever after. Feeling like I actually might get mine when not that long ago, I felt hopeless. I imagine that's how she felt when she discovered her American lover had died.

"Earth to Maverick."

"Hmmm," I hum absently against his chest. I twirl the few hairs he has smattering between his pecs around my index finger.

"Care to don some clothes and do something or do you want to lounge in bed, naked, all day?"

*Naked sounds like a good plan to me.*

I tilt my head up. "You mean you don't have the entire weekend planned, minute by minute?"

He laughs. Kael may do things off the beaten path, but he's a planner while I'm more comfortable winging it. As much as it makes him itch to do it my way, it makes me equally itchy to plan every single second of life. That leaves no room for spontaneity. I'm not sure if I'm like this to spite my mother, who is spontaneity's death-blow or if I was born this way. And although my impulsive tendencies have gotten me into more than one mess, I feel like they also may have led me to my true destiny.

Kael.

"I'm free-balling this weekend," he tells me.

*Yep...naked it is.*

"Mmm. I like the sound of that," I quip. My hand snakes down beneath the sheets but doesn't reach its intended target.

"As much as I want your hand wrapped around my cock, Swan, don't you want to get out and see the historic city of Saint Paul?"

I run my tongue along his throat, whispering in his ear, "I was kind of digging the naked and lounging suggestion." I try to break his hold, to no avail.

"We could have just done this at home," he says. "Come on, baby. I want to show you the city. You'll love it."

As many times as I've been to Minneapolis, I've never spent time in its redheaded stepchild. But right now, I don't care to get out of bed. I want to live in this bubble we've created for as long as possible before we have to head back home and face our real lives. As much progress as I'm making eradicating Killian from my soul, it's a laborious process. Somehow not being in the same vicinity, knowing he's not just ten minutes away, makes it easier to forget about him.

"It's cold," I whine, snuggling closer. It's December in Minnesota. It hasn't snowed yet, but the temps are about ten degrees cooler here than in Dusty Falls.

"That's why I brought your favorite sweater. I hear the Cathedral of Saint Paul is supposed to be one of the most elaborate in the entire country. I know how much you love old churches."

I push up on my elbow, resting my head on my palm. I run my other hand, which he's now freed, over my breast, down my torso, and sweep the globe of my ass before I use my finger and thumb to pinch my nipple to a pointed peak.

He groans, long and needy.

"You really want to leave this?"

Then I'm on my back, my hands stretched above my head. He's

wedged perfectly between my legs. I already feel how fast he's thickening. His breathing has picked up and his eyes have gone dark.

Yes.

I win.

Only he doesn't make a move to use the impressive equipment he's been blessed with. It's mere inches from home plate and twitching like mad. "As much as I'd like to say otherwise and as much as your romance novels contradict me, I can't physically fuck you all day. You know this, right?"

We've had sex three times already since we left Dusty Falls less than twenty-four hours ago. A quickie in a dirty public bathroom. Languid lovemaking last night after an intimate Italian dinner at a hole-in-the-wall down the street. And a rough and dirty round this morning when Kael whispered all the sinful things he's been dreaming of doing to my body as he made me come repeatedly with his mouth first, following that up with his talented cock. I'm pretty sure I screamed his name more than once. I bet I screamed so loud even Pierre LeMars heard me.

Just thinking about it makes me all hot and bothered again. I wiggle, trying to align him the way I need. "Care to test that theory out?" I taunt, my breaths now coming in short pants. I move my hips down and tilt my pelvis up. Almost...there...

Kael dips until his mouth brushes mine when he says, "No. I care to show off my sexy as fuck wife around town, then come back here and fuck her all night long on every surface of this room instead."

I stop moving. "Oh? All night, you say?"

He laughs even though his lips now cover mine. I wriggle my hands free so I can wind them around his neck. I bury them in his hair. Scrape my nails along his scalp as he kisses me slow and sure.

"Now, come on," he tells me, drawing back all too soon. "If I have to lie here any longer and smell fresh cinnamon rolls and hazelnut coffee, I'm going to start eating my limbs."

I grin. "You can eat me instead," I offer. Selflessly, of course.

Chuckling, he shakes his head and pushes himself off me. He's hard as stone. I bite my lower lip, letting my eyes drink in the erotic sight of my husband stark naked. "You are a wicked temptress, you know that?"

"I do." I lever up to my elbows, acutely aware of my tight nipples pointing in his direction. "But apparently not tempting or wicked enough."

"Oh, trust me, Swan. You are," he rasps. "I just happen to have tremendous self-control." After a quick, hard peck, I watch his fine, tight-as-a-running-back ass saunter away. I sigh when he disappears into the bathroom, flopping back. My entire body is throbbing with unfulfilled need.

"Shower, Mavs," Kael yells from the other room.

"Shower, Mavs," I mock quietly.

"I heard that, snotty girl." He pokes his head around the corner and holds out his hand. "How about I offer to wash your back?"

That perks me right up. "Just my back?" I ask, sliding off the soft sheets and making my way toward him. The subway tiles are cold on my feet the second I step from the carpet into the bathroom.

When he presses me against his manly nakedness, he whispers, "Be a good girl and you can get me to do anything for you."

My skin tingles as chills break out.

"Anything?" I look up into his brilliant brown eyes, a big smile on my face.

"Yeah," he replies softly, tucking wild hairs behind my ears. It's a gentle move. One he's probably done more than a hundred times before, but it feels so different now. At least for me. I'm getting that it's always meant something more to him. "Anything."

The way he says that one word is ominous. Foreboding, even. Like he would kill, lie, cheat, and steal for me. "I think you mean that."

His lips turn slightly before flattening back out. The moment turns from playful to serious in an instant. "I've never meant anything more." Then, the moment passes before I can blink again and he brightens up, all good-natured again.

Less than forty-five minutes and two more orgasms (mine) later, we're heading down the theatrical stairs. I'm relieved that I don't feel any cold air or that sense of being invisibly stalked. We wind our way through the grand parlor where two guests sit reading the paper and enjoying their coffee. We politely say good morning, but keep walking.

"Is breakfast over?" I whisper to Kael, noting it's almost 10:00 a.m. already.

"Got it covered, Swan," he whispers back.

"Ah, the newlyweds." Sheila beams when we walk into the luxurious dining room. The dark damask walls are beautiful, along with the ornate maple ten-person dining room table, which only holds two place settings.

"I hope we didn't cause too much trouble for you by being late," I apologize as I take a seat.

"Oh, *pffft*. No trouble at all dear. I may be old, but I remember what it's like to be a newlywed." She winks conspiratorially before heading through a swinging door, presumably into the kitchen.

"Why didn't you tell me we had to be down here at a certain time?" I chastise Kael, knowing very well breakfast must have been served quite a while ago.

He leans over, taking my chin between his finger and thumb. "Because we don't. I want this weekend to be fun and relaxing and not on anyone's timetable but our own. Okay?"

"Okay," I say, a bit breathless. He places his lips chastely to mine right as Sheila returns holding a tray stuffed with quiche, breakfast sausage, fried potatoes, fruit, a stack of powdered-sugar-dusted French toast a mile high, and the cinnamon rolls Kael was going on about earlier.

"This looks incredible. Thank you, Sheila," Kael tells our hostess.

"My pleasure. And I took care of everything for you just as you asked." With a wink, she wanders back into the kitchen. Wordlessly, Kael takes my plate and starts filling it with bits of everything. He picks the pineapple chunks from the fruit bowl because he knows I don't like them.

I just watch him, waiting. When he hands me my plate and picks up his own without offering an explanation, I laugh. "Free-balling, huh?"

He eyes me, his mouth and brows quirking up simultaneously. "Is commando close enough?"

The corners of my mouth stretch into a giant grin. "No woman in her right mind would complain about her man going commando."

"Good." He winks playfully then sits with such grace I sigh.

We eat in silence for a few minutes before something hits me. I should keep my mouth shut. I tell my vocal cords not to press any air through. It doesn't work. I vomit the question I've been wanting the answer to for almost a month now. "So, how's everything going with that National Guard contract?" I ask, trying for nonchalant. I pass. I think.

Kael eyes me shrewdly.

Nope.

Missed the boat there.

"Why do you ask? You never ask me about work."

Busted.

"No reason. I guess just coming here made me think of it is all." Quick thinking, Mavs. Way to go.

He holds my gaze steady and answers me straight-faced, no inflection. Nothing to make me think he'd be lying. "It's delayed." But there's something in the *way* he says his spiel—as if it's been smoothly practiced—that has my red flags flapping in the wind.

"What happened?" I press, wanting to see what he'll say.

His shoulder rises and falls at the same time his mouth turns down. "You know the government," is his only reply. He goes back to his breakfast, indicating our conversation is over.

I don't want it to be. I want to ask more questions. Ferret out what he's hiding because now I'm convinced it's something. Under any normal circumstances, I would end it with that. Federal contracts are the worst. They're competitive and drawn-out and we lose far more than we win. We both know this.

But I can't ignore that feeling in my gut. The one that screams he's keeping something from me. Something major. Opening my mouth to push the issue, a single word spills out instead when Kael starts grinning into his plate. "What?"

"What, what?" he asks, eyeing me from underneath those ridiculously long lashes I envy more with each year.

"Why are you smiling like that?"

He sets his fork down, lavishing all of his attention on me. "Like what, Swan?"

His grin is an epidemic infecting the air. With a single breath, I catch it, too. "Like that." I wave two fingers at him. When he quirks one brow, I add, "Like...like you just swallowed sunbeams." He looks...jubilant, almost.

"I know you like the palm of my hand."

I lean back and cross my arms. A little grumpily. "Spend a lot of time in the palm of your hand, do you?" I throw back. *Very* grumpily.

He barks a laugh, followed by a headshake. "Oh yeah. My hand knows every single ridge and vein in my cock very, very well. We became almost inseparable when I was milking myself to fantasies of you all these years."

My mouth falls open. I sputter when I hear Sheila's sharp "oh my" from behind me. Kael isn't fazed in the least. He keeps that Cheshire grin planted firmly on his lips. The sudden sound of the swinging door brushing the doorframe back and forth indicates Sheila's quick exit as our conversation has taken a deliciously salacious turn.

"You did that on purpose," I chastise. "You saw her there." He has a direct line of sight to that kitchen.

"I have no idea what you're talking about." Kael pushes his chair back and comes to pull mine out. He grabs my hands and helps me stand, enfolding me into his embrace. "Now, I want to take my wife out and have every man we meet envy me."

I grin ridiculously, everything else forgotten.

He grabs my coat, which I'd hung on the back of the chair and slips it on. He zips me up. Reaching into my pocket, he removes my fluffy white gloves and slides them on my hands, one of by one. His tender care of me is sweet and endearing. After he's done, he efficiently eases into his own winter gear.

Cupping my cheeks with his now leather-clad hands, he presses a kiss to my lips. "Ready?"

"Ready."

It's not until we're striding out the front door, hand in hand into the cold winter day, that I realize he stealthily redirected our entire conversation.

We spend the morning walking around Saint Paul's bustling downtown. We have the most divine coffee at a locally owned pastry shop. I get caught up talking to the owner about how her partner is moving to London and she's debating whether to buy him out or sell. Kael eventually drags me away but not before I get her recipe for the best cheese-and-grape turnover I've ever had. We exchange e-mail addresses, promising to keep in touch.

Next, we hit a quaint used bookstore where Kael allows me time to meander through overpacked shelves and pick through everything from thrillers that came out last year to first editions of classics from the eighteen hundreds. Those were under lock and key, of course. Yet another place he has to drag me from.

Finally after an unconventional lunch of award-winning ice cream from a place called Greenery Creamery, we arrive at the Cathedral of Saint Paul. When we pull into the parking lot I note all the cars and navy and ivory ribbons hanging from the gorgeous tall red doors.

Shit. Saturday afternoon at a Catholic church. Of course. "There's a wedding going on. We can't go in."

Kael scoffs, cutting the engine. "Of course we can, Swan. A wedding is a celebration."

"Yes, one it's customary to be invited to," I shout as he exits the car and shuts the door. Then he forces me from the vehicle by grabbing right behind my knees where he proceeds to tickle until I'm putty in his hands. A few minutes later, Kael has one arm snug around my shoulders, his other hand tucked securely in mine.

We're officially wedding crashers, sitting in our jeans and sweaters a few pews back from the dapperly dressed invited guests in this breathtaking church, watching a heart-wrenching ceremony.

Tears balance on my lashes. The groom is an utter mess. The bride is a breath away from losing her shit. And I'm barely holding it together when the first drop of water trickles down my cheek.

I don't know this couple. I don't know their lives, their story, or how hard they had to work to get to this moment. But what I do know is—as I sit here and watch two people clearly in love twine their lives together forever—I am filled with hot regret.

I squandered my day.

I stood in front of Kael, repeating the same vows this couple is now saying, and wished wishes I should never have wished.

Now I wish for entirely different things. I wish I had a chance to look deep into Kael's soul when speaking true words of love and devotion. I wish I could make him understand how he's painstakingly pieced my broken parts back together. I wish he knew that I will be eternally grateful for the unexpected gift he's given me. Given *us*. I wish for a redo of it all. Our courtship, our wedding day, our honeymoon, our first time. Our entire life together.

I quickly wipe remorse from my face as the crowd stands and cheers for Mr. and Mrs. Stanley Needlemeyer. *Eck.* Poor girl. When the happy couple glides by us, they're so lost in their own bubble we could be four-headed aliens and they wouldn't even notice. We stay put as the wedding party passes us next, followed by the cutest little girl in the most adorable navy-blue dress and matching patent leather shoes. Petals from the small bouquet she's winging back and forth sail to the ground behind her. She squeals and takes off down the long aisle as a boy a few years old in a smart navy suit chases after her. Following on their heels is a crazed woman, presumably the mother.

"Cassie, Aiden!" she yells. "Stop this instant."

Cassie starts nimbly weaving between the pews, Aiden hot on her heels. Neither of them slows a stitch.

Kael squeezes my hand and when my eyes find his, they're alight with...anticipation? For our own? That thought would have petrified me just months ago. And not because I didn't want kids. I've always wanted a family of my own. But because I always pictured them with Killian instead. Now...now, though, my picture is starting to slowly morph and twist.

When Kael drops his lips to my temple, I exhale in utter contentment. God, how could I not know I had these crazy feelings for him before? So many years wasted. "Good idea I had, huh?"

"I will have to concede you that point, yes," I agree with a smile.

"Come on. We can slink out the back, undetected." He tugs on my hand. I stop him, though.

"No. Let's go give our congratulations to the happy couple."

He blinks a couple of times before a wide grin takes over his face. He nods. "I like the way you think."

Wagging my brows, I say excitedly, "Maybe we can finagle an invite to the reception? I can put on that sexy little black number you brought and let you make all the men envious."

He tucks me into his arms. "Ah yes, but then you'd show up the bride. And every bride deserves to be the center of attention on her special day." Dropping a fast kiss to my lips, the celebration fades away as he continues in a low, promising timbre, "Besides, I have something planned for tonight with you in that sexy little black number."

"Sheila's surprise?"

"No. It's *my* surprise. Sheila just helped me with a few loose ends."

This man. He's so good to me. Too good.

I wrap my arms all the way around Kael's waist and cinch them hard. Burying my head in his chest, I inhale a lungful of his masculine scent and spicy cologne, wondering how in the hell I got so lucky.

"Kael?"

"Mavs?"

"Would you maybe, ah, want to renew our vows someday?" It won't make up for what I took from us the first time, but maybe it gives me a second chance to do it right.

He stills. Most of the guests have exited the church or are milling around the entrance. So there's no one around when he pulls back a short breadth and cups my cheeks with his big hands. When I see the fat drops of water in his eyes, my own blur.

"You want to renew our vows?" The surprise in his voice slays me.

Suddenly I feel flush. My stomach flips like a net full of fish is in it. I can't speak, so I nod instead, spilling all the drops that have built up in my lids.

"Mavs." His voice cracks. He stops and swallows. Shuts his eyes for a brief moment. "I would renew my vows with you every single day for the rest of my life if that's what you wanted. My life has *always* been pledged to you."

I bite my lip, trying like hell to hold in a sob. "I want," I whisper hoarsely. I want more than anything.

Kael places his forehead gently to mine. His lids fall shut. He breathes in deep. "Just name the date and time, Swan."

It's easier to pull myself together when he's not staring at me with so much love I still don't yet feel I deserve. "I know you like untraditional, but I'd like to do it on our one-year anniversary. I want small and intimate. Maybe even just us." I don't want drama and yesterdays staring me in the face.

"I'd like that." He must feel the same.

"Okay. It's a date then."

"It's a date then," he repeats, breathy and sweet. "One I wouldn't miss on my life."

Later that night, we walk into Barrington's, a swanky bar just blocks away from our B and B. A chill runs the length of my spine from the bitter cold outside. I think the temp has dropped fifteen degrees since this afternoon. There are a few flakes of snow in the air and while I need to get back to the bakery, I wouldn't mind if we woke up to a foot of snow, stealing an extra day here. I'm in no rush to head back to Dusty Falls and everything that awaits us there. Spending uninterrupted time with Kael, away from it all—let's be brutally honest, away from Killian—is as if an enormous weight has been lifted from my chest.

I see nothing but Kael. As it should be.

"Oh, look, there's a nice secluded table in the back." A perfect place for slipping off a shoe and running my bare foot up Kael's thigh until his eyes dilate and hood. Until his cock gets so fucking hard, he makes me give him a hand job under the table. He refused to touch me earlier, making me shower alone. I'm still a little cross about that. He said, *"Anticipation heightens the senses, Swan. And I want every one of your senses strung tight as a bow by the time we get back to our room."* Well, I can string his senses into knots, too.

"Let's order a drink first," he whispers against my cheek. With a hand at the small of my back, Kael maneuvers us around to the far side of the long granite bar and smoothly orders. "I'll have a Babyface Nelson."

"A Babyface Nelson? What's that?" I ask, looking up at him. That sexy dimple of his pops when he simultaneously quirks the corner of his lip and winks.

The bartender nods and reaches for a bottle of Jack Daniels. My forehead scrunches. Kael doesn't even like Jack. But it doesn't come off the shelf. Instead, the bartender pulls it forward, like a lever or a switch, and the wall to our left, which is painted entirely black, slides open with a soft whisper.

"Thanks, man," Kael says.

"Oh my God. What is this?" I ask in wonder, staring at the open staircase in front of us.

Kael ushers me forward, my hand now trapped in his. When we walk through the open space it shuts behind, closing us in, muffling the noise. We're now on the landing of a dimly lit narrow wooden stairway. The steps are old and worn. Curved a little in the middle from so many years of use. A closed steel-gray door at the bottom traps us in.

"Where are we?" I whisper. It echoes loudly, sounding as if we've stepped right inside a tin can.

"The gateway to heaven," Kael smoothly answers.

I pivot and grab the lapels of his peacoat. Sliding to my tiptoes, I bat my eyes seductively. "You told me this morning that was between my beautiful thighs."

Storm clouds roll into his brown eyes, deepening them to an inky black. He steps into me. I step back. He steps into me again but I have nowhere to go because my back is now flush with the brick wall. Dropping his palms on either side of my head he presses his lower half fully into me. He's so damn hard. It takes my breath away.

"I want to fuck you so bad right now," he tells me. His tone is low and gravelly. Guttural. Yeah, guttural and sinful as hell.

"Here?" I'm panting. *Panting*.

Steely, determined dark pools of lust bore into mine. "Yes."

My body temp soars. I'm so damn hot and bothered right now I feel like I'm melting right into the wall. My eyes dart to the doors on either side of us. "Right here? In this stairwell?"

"Yes," his husky voice whispers with surety against the shell of my ear. My lids drift shut. My lips part on a gasp. One of his hands has slid down my outer thigh. Finding bare skin, he's now trailing it back up. Pretty soon he's going to discover the surprise I was saving for later. "Oh fuck, Swan," he growls long and low when he hits my bare, uncovered pussy. My bare, uncovered, *dripping* pussy.

Then I'm the one to curse when he pushes two greedy fingers inside me. And I hoarsely gasp his name when he starts fingering me with pure, focused dedication to my pleasure alone.

It feels so good all I can do is hold on for the ride.

I'm fully aware we are dangerously exposed. My dress is pulled up to my waist, my privates on full display as my husband finger fucks me in a public place. Anyone could walk through either door. At any moment. But that also heightens my need...deepens this primary element inside me to connect with him on every possible level.

"So wet," he rumbles as if in pain. "So ungodly wet, Mavs." God in heaven, I am. The sound of my flesh being worked is wild and decadent.

I snake a hand between us so I can grip his erection over his slacks. He groans and pulses twice in quick succession when my fingers wrap around his girth. I stroke him up and down. He swells more with each pass.

"I should have bent you over the bed and taken you in front of that floor-length mirror before we left," he grunts against my lax mouth.

"You should have," I manage to cobble together. I'm so lost in us, in the places he's pushing me, that I act without thinking. With my free hand, I undo the single tie on my side holding the two halves of my dress together. I tug the material apart, exposing my sheer black bra. It barely covers my beaded nipples.

"Holy shit, Swan."

Every nerve tingles with unimaginable sensitivity as he zeroes in on my breasts. The way he looks at me is electrifying. Like I'm the last meal he'll eat on earth so he's going to make the most of every single bite.

Never stopping his diabolical inner caress, Kael dips and clamps a protruding bud between his teeth. He strikes fast and hard over the thin fabric. I cry out, my painful pleasure reaching my ears in short waves. Then he sucks just as hard, wetting the cup.

My sex clenches, tightening so I feel every push and drag of his fingers against my walls. It's not enough. Nothing is enough.

Winding a leg around his opens me up farther to him. He takes advantage of my new position by adding a third digit. The second his thumb begins feathering my clit I start to quiver.

"Kael, God. I'm going to explode."

"And you're gonna make me ruin these pants if you keep that up." With every brush upward, I circle right under his sensitive glans. Good Lord, I wish my mouth was on him right now. "Maverick, fuck that feels good."

I feel drunk right now. High, free, heady. So damn brazen I want his cock driving me into the brick instead of his hand. Without his objection, I pop open the button on his slacks and drag his zipper halfway down. Suddenly the scrape of metal against concrete sounds right before laughter reaches our ears. We both freeze.

"Shit," Kael mutters.

My core feels empty when he quickly withdraws his fingers and wrenches my dress back together. But he doesn't move back. Instead, he grabs my face between his palms, wetness glazing over my cheek, and smashes his lips to mine. He kisses me with passion and longing and serious frustration. Feet pound against wood. Voices get closer. A few whistles are heard. Aimed at us, I'm sure. And *still*, Kael keeps kissing me. He only stops when we hear the secret door slide shut, leaving us alone once again.

Pressing our foreheads together, he grumbles, "I almost fucked you right now. Damn the consequences."

The air is charged, crackling. Beckoning me on bated breath to be wickedly bad.

"Do," I press him, breathlessly. *Jesus, what am I saying? Public sex?*

He angles back slightly, his gaze gripping mine. His ambers blaze hot. So hot my entire being is on fire. Wordlessly, he reaches his hand down. When I hear his zipper separate, I let my dress fall back open. I feel his cock, stiff and velvety, against my stomach only a second before he runs the thick crown through my wetness. He wraps a palm around the back of my thigh and winds it around his so my heel brushes his calf. The breath whooshes out of me when—eyes never leaving mine—he plunges inside in one vicious thrust.

"Oh, God."

My orgasm, which had waned with our interruption, barrels back. It's sharp, instantaneous. It takes me by such surprise, Kael has to slam his mouth to mine to swallow my keening wails.

He fucks me hard, almost callously. His hips slap, relentless and bruising, his pubic bones slamming against mine with each rough drive.

"Holy fuck, Mavs," he breathes, impaling me twice more before releasing on a long, broken stutter. Spent, his body goes slack against mine. His weight makes my shoulder blades dig into the grooves of the wall behind me. The weight feels good, though, so I don't push him back. We should move. We don't. "That was..."

"Yeah," I pant in agreement. My eyes are screwed shut. My skin beads with sweat. My heart's pounding against my ribs. The scent of sex loitering in the air is unmistakable. "That was."

"Don't use the restroom," he says, grunting. "I want my come sticking to your thighs." He pushes these dirty words into my ear. Holy mother, the things he says sometimes.

"That's kind of cavemanish," I tease as he sweetly but efficiently rewraps my dress. He even ties the bow nice and pretty before tucking himself back into his pants.

He leans back in and presses his lips gently to mine. "Guilty. You make me completely lose my head, Maverick. Always have."

I grin, all glowy. Positively overflowing with all the feels for him. "So, ah...where were you taking me, husband of mine, before you fucked me half to death in a secret stairwell?"

He expels a rush of air that washes over my face. It still smells like the mint he had after dinner. "I love hearing that, you know."

"What?" I reach up and run my finger along his strong jawline, loving the feel of trimmed stubble under the pad.

"Husband. I *love* being your husband, Maverick. I've always wanted that and there was a time when..." He stalls. Throws his gaze to the floor quickly. Returns it back to mine. The heat that was in them before has been replaced with some sort of ache. "There was a time when I thought maybe that wouldn't happen."

My smile drops and my breath catches in that little pocket at the back of my throat. Is that why every time he's inside me, it feels as if he's trying to brand not only my soul but my very spirit as well? Is he worried I'll change my mind and run to be with Killian instead, given the chance? *Would I?* I'd like to be able to say with 100 percent certainty the answer is no, but the honest to God's truth is...I can't be sure. Killian will always be wound around me in some way. Regardless of if I'm ever successful at severing that hold he has on me, his *imprint* will always be left behind. There's simply nothing I can do about that.

Time kinda slows down as we search each other's souls. What does he see? Does he see a woman who has changed over the past few months? Does he see a woman who has truly fallen *in* love with the man before her? Or does he see one who he thinks betrayed him with his brother of all people? That's what I feel when I look at him now. Even though Kael and I were not a thing until Killian and I were well over, I feel as though I've betrayed him somehow. I suppose I have in a way.

We both know it. We both think it. Neither of us will acknowledge it, though.

My heart beats double time. This is the part where we edge up to that ambiguous line. But do we cross it? Do we mention *his* name and pick that scab at long last or do we skirt around it once again?

I honestly don't know what to say, so I stay mute and just wait.

He leans in. Touches his lips lightly to my forehead. Then pulls back way too fast. "Come on," he says, reaching for my hand. "I wanted to show you a real live twenties speakeasy that's so exclusive you can't get in unless you know the right people."

Circle it is.

"Okay." As I flash a brief smile and set my palm in his, letting him lead me down the rickety stairs, I have to wonder about that circle, though. It keeps getting smaller and smaller and smaller. We've worn the edges smooth and thin.

They're fragile.

They're cracking.

Pretty soon there won't be anything left.

Then we'll have no choice but to enter the very center where hurt feelings lay buried beneath our feet, waiting to be unearthed like ghosts in a graveyard.

I've lost track of time.

How long have I been in this room? It's supposed to be a sanctuary but feels like a sinking ship in the middle of an ocean. Oxygen's precious and each shallow breath in will eventually be my last.

Has it been minutes? Centuries?

I don't know.

I'm not sure I care.

Several people have come in and out of the chapel. I watch them, silently. They sit or kneel. Some light a candle. Some don't. They whisper in prayer. Weep softly. Beg and barter for their loved ones. They don't think I hear them, or maybe they don't care. Maybe they think if we all band together in a show of unity, it will save at least one of our loved ones currently fighting for their lives.

But unless it's mine—unless it's *him*—I don't care.

Callous. Selfish and heartless. Say what you want about that thought. It doesn't make me a bad person. All it makes me is human.

I may not know how long I've been sitting here by the traditional marching of seconds and minutes, but it's been long enough to know the people who pass through this refuge fall into two camps.

Life or death.

Loss or hope.

Defiance or defeat.

I know which camp I'm in.

I am defiance. Defiance is me. If he dies, I'll know it. I'll *feel* our bond break in the very depths of my being. And right now, while my soul feels crushed, it doesn't feel dead. I know I will feel dry and barren if he leaves me here alone.

So while he fights, so do I. I fight for strength where I'm weak. I fight for hope to replace despair. I fight for us, because if he makes it through this, he will need me by his side more than ever before.

The soft whoosh of the door opening alerts me I'm no longer alone. I hope no one has found me. I can't stomach any of their faces right now. Not a one.

Out of the corner of my eye, I see a frail old woman shuffle past to the small altar in the front. She reaches out a shaky hand and shortly afterward, I hear the distinct friction of a match being lit. I think that tiny piece of wood will disintegrate before she gets the wick of the candle going, but she manages just fine. Once the votive burns, she pivots slowly and is taking a seat in the first pew when she spots me.

She straightens.

I square my shoulders.

We stare soundlessly.

I can read her pain.

I think maybe she can read mine, too.

A glint of a name badge pinned to her blouse catches the light. Volunteer probably. She's far too old to work here.

Suddenly my eyes burn and itch and blur. I try to stop them. It's hopeless. For some baffling reason, she's managed to trigger an avalanche of gut-wrenching loneliness I'm helpless to keep inside anymore.

Then she heads my way.

She's a stranger yet not. I feel drawn to her for some odd, unexplainable reason. She must feel the same because she sits and slides over until our thighs practically touch.

Still, she looks at me and I at her.

Without a word, she places her hand on top of mine. It's cool and clammy. I would feel her age by her hands alone, even if my sight didn't work.

Water zigzags down my cheeks. It drips down my throat, soaking into the neck of my shirt. I can hardly see her now through its endless stream, each big drop pushing the others out of the way to make room for the ones behind them.

She squeezes her fingers against mine. Her simple human touch sends this peace and calm throughout my soul. Then she rasps in a voice more solid than her age would lend, "I know it seems like it, dear, but you're not alone. You can let go. I've got you."

Then I lose it. Completely fucking lose it. He's said that to me so many times over the years that I feel as if it's him sitting here, talking to me, reassuring me through this apparition. Telling me to be strong, not to give up hope. That the time we've had together has been far too short and he's coming back for me.

Some people call it hooey, but I believe in divine intervention. I felt it when I stumbled across Old Man Riley, fated as we were to meet. I felt it when I was moments away from dying in that frigid lake at age eleven. I felt it when *he* watched over me all these years.

And with my head now resting on an old woman's shoulder, sobbing uncontrollably, I feel it now.

I feel *him* now.

I sink into that security he's always given me, refusing to believe there is any outcome other than a long life together. The one we've always imagined.

"I can't believe I let you talk me into this," I grumble, adjusting the strangulation device circling my neck—aka my tie. I suppose I should get used to it. As a lawyer, I've no doubt I'll be expected to don a suit and tie daily, although I'd much prefer jeans, a Henley, and my beat-up Chukkas.

"Oh stop your bitching." She pushes my hands away and huffs, taking over the pitiful job I'm doing of massacring this piece of thin, slippery material into some semblance of a knot.

"I mean it, Swan. How did you ever get me to agree to this ridiculous idea?" I know how. She batted those fucking eyelashes. One flutter. That's all it took. It wasn't even a flutter, really. It was just a...a *look*. She's the honey trap I fall for. Every. Fucking. Time. Without fail.

Mavs stops what she's doing and looks up at me. Her eyes are wide. Stunningly gorgeous. She's put on a touch of mascara and dressed her eyelids with a color that's relatively neutral, but whatever it is makes them shimmer just a bit. A swipe of shiny berry gloss coats her lips. And that's it. No other makeup cakes her face. Simple. Pure. So understated, yet so her. She's a complete oxymoron. Sultry, yet innocent. Sweet, yet so fucking wild it makes my head spin.

"I caught you at a weak moment?" she offers playfully.

"I'm always weak around you," I murmur, reaching up to wipe a dark splotch from her front tooth. I let my finger whisper across her cheek before I force it back to my side.

If I'm honest with myself, we both know why I'm here. Besides the fact she's impossible to deny, it's simple: to keep other guys out of her pants. And with the curve-hugging baby blue silk she's sporting, guys are gonna wanna crawl inside that hot spot and get a little taste. It's not their fault, though. It's *hers*. She's so damn beautiful it's like descending into your own personal madness because you know you can't have her. I know. I've been in my own personal hell for years with—and without—this woman. And the thing is...she's clueless about it all. Still.

"Are you sure I look okay?" she asks, shifting her attention to the cleavage hanging precariously out of that sinful dress. A stray chocolate curl slips down, down, down the valley of her tits and disappears inside the flimsy fabric. *Fucking fuck of all the fucks.* I wonder what she'd think if I threw a sweatshirt over her before we left.

She tries in vain to tug the two pieces closer together, but all she's succeeding at doing is plumping up her perky tits even more. In my head I groan, trying like hell to keep my erection under control. There will be a helluva a lot of chicken choking going on later in the little boys' room, that's for damn sure. It burns my insides knowing I'm not the only one fantasizing about Maverick DeSoto.

Unable to take any more, I grab her hands and shove them to her sides, holding fast. "Stop. You're...Christ, Mavs." I pull her into me and rest my forehead to hers. "Those high school chumps will have woodies for days remembering what you look like. You're every man's dream. Wet or dry," I finish on a whisper. What the fuck am I saying? Any dream involving Maverick will be wet. Filthy wet.

"Kael," she half laughs, half gasps.

"What, Swan? Just callin' it like it is."

Her head cocks back, that wide-eyed gaze cutting to me once again. Her expression is unreadable. She blinks those big green doe eyes several times before replying softly, "Thank you."

"Welcome," I croak. *God, if you're out there I think I'm gonna need a solid tonight, man. Please do not let me fuck things up with her by mauling her or vomiting how I'm hopelessly in love with her.* "We'd better go. We're already an hour late."

Her lips curl. Then she gasps that gasp that makes alarm bells go off for normal people, like something's life or death. Only with Mavs, it's that she's remembered something she wants to tell you. Usually unimportant. Scared the ever-living shit out of me the first few times she did that. And when she does it while I'm driving down the road, I think a deer's gonna jump out in front of us or her appendix just burst. She almost made us crash once with that sudden hitch she does.

"I almost forgot! Your corsage."

"Oh, hell no." I snag her hand just in time as she tries to flit away. "It's bad enough I'm going to your senior prom when I'm of legal drinking age. I am not—ah, ah, ah"—I place a finger against her open mouth, secretly relishing the pillowy feel—"no arguments. I am not wearing a fucking flower with that loose white shit in my lapel until I get married." I refused a tux, too, opting for a conventional black suit.

"But it's tradition," she whines.

"Don't care, babe. You want me to go with or not?"

The corners of her mouth turn down in a pout. Jesus H. Christ, do I want to kiss that off her, but I know better. I tried that once when she was in fifth grade. I was thirteen. She was ten. It was the one and only time I had my lips on hers. My head was floating in the clouds until the slap that resonated through the woods brought me hard and painfully back to earth. Then she bolted on me faster than a jackrabbit and I didn't see her again for three days. It took about a dozen times of apologizing before she'd talk to me again. She made me promise I'd never do it again.

I did.

I lied, though.

I *will* try again, but timing is everything. Getting out of the friend zone is tricky. Push at the wrong time, you lose your best friend for good. And I can't chance losing Mavs. Ever. I know now is the time to dig deep for patience, not a commitment. As much as I want it to be, with me off at college and starting law school and her leaving for college shortly, now is not the right time for us.

"Fine. Be that way," she says, crossing her arms.

"I will," I say, crossing my own, easily matching her stubborn.

She smiles. I smile.

She laughs. So do I.

All is good.

Ten minutes later we're done with pictures and are free to leave. Vivian even let us stand on the edge of her "sitting room" for a few. Mavs purposely tripped so she'd fall onto the pristine carpet. Her mom went wild.

Fucking Vivian and her precious rug. She had that damn rake out faster than I could blink, any thoughts of capturing her youngest daughter's last prom all but forgotten. It slays me that Maverick hangs on to the bottom rung of her mother's priority list. Vivian and Richard DeSoto are not *bad* parents, they just have other priorities that are not their children. When she's mine, I will worship her like the rare find she is.

"Come on." I snake my bigger fingers between her small ones and haul her toward the door. Only minutes later, we're strolling through the double doors of Saint Bernadette's High my hand possessively at the small of her back.

When we get to the gym, the party is in full swing. The dance floor is packed. People are milling on the outside edges, chatting in small groups. But already, heads are turning. Eyes bug. Tongues wag. Male minds spin with dirty thoughts of what lies beneath her delicious gown and how to get her out of it.

My eyes travel over her, my view from this height spectacular. But holy merciful God. *Where's that fucking favor I asked for earlier, cuz this ain't it.* Her nipples are like goddamn beacons, proudly beading against the fabric of that dick-strangling piece she's wearing. When she came down the stairs, balancing awkwardly in her fancy shoes, my cock swelled so painfully hard I had to button my suit jacket to conceal the evidence.

My teeth clench and my fingers tighten around her, tucking her closer to me. I have half a mind to throw my coat over her, only I think the buttons would hit right at chest level, drawing even more attention than she's already garnering. I catch a few horny assholes checking her out and they immediately shift their eyes away. Good. I have a feeling I'll have a scowl plastered on my face all night long.

"What's wrong?" she asks, all innocent and so fucking oblivious.

"Nothing," I grit. My jaw hurts already. "Let's get something to drink."

We weave our way through the crowd. My teeth clamp together as I hurl vicious unspoken warnings to all those swinging a stick within a hundred-yard radius. I think everyone's starting to get the message loud and fucking clear.

She is mine.

She will *always* be mine.

We stand there with our little plastic cups full of some god-awful sweet punch and take in the cheesily decorated gym. It seems so small and unimportant now than it did when we were trying to make it to boys' basketball regionals just four short years ago.

"You do this?" I ask, gesturing around to the gold, green, and purple balloons strung together to form an arch around the gym entrance. I spy a photo booth in the corner with various hats, boas, and other crap. My eyes travel over cutouts of masks taped to the wall then to the multicolored beads around her neck someone threw over her head on the way over here. They've also joined the boob party, hanging out right in that sweet spot between her mounds. Seems like no one can get enough of them.

Fuuuuuck.

It's going to be a long-ass night.

She gifts me with a withering look, making me chuckle. "Hell no, I didn't do this," she harrumphs. That's my girl.

"I'm surprised you wanted to come."

A bare, delicate shoulder lifts and drops. "MaryLou was relentless until I caved. It's pointless to fight her when she gets like that."

Said ankle biter waves at us from across the room. She and Larry are in line for the photo booth. I wouldn't be surprised if they were married with three kids by the time they're twenty-five. I'm thinking the married part is a novel idea. The kids? I want them, too, but there's no rush on that account. I need my fill of Mavs first.

Mavs takes a sip of her sugar water, trying to act all nonchalant like. "So...Killian's back, huh?"

And just like that, my heart sinks like a stone, taking my stomach with it. No...not a stone. A fucking five-ton boulder. The kind that gravity drags down mountains during avalanches. The kind that crushes, killing hopes and dreams, taking lives. Yeah...*that* kind.

"Yep. Moved back last week."

"Daddy said he's going to be working at DSC?"

That hopeful thread in her voice makes my skin tighten to the point of itching. I slide a finger between the collar of my shirt and my throat. I tug, loosening up the fucker so I can breathe. "Yep," I answer tightly.

Maverick's obsession with Killian has only seemed to grow instead of wane. And, dammit, so has his. Which is exactly why I'm here this summer, interning for DeSoto Construction. I want to be back in this town like I want to spend time in my jockstrap after a five-mile run, but Killian's move thwarted that. And Maverick's here until the fall when she starts college. And there is no fucking way I'm leaving the two of them alone, unguarded all summer long. Not gonna happen.

"Hey, Maverick," someone with a deep voice booms from behind. I spin around and come face-to-face with Bruce Chutney, otherwise known as One Nut Chut. Bruce comes from a long line of farmers and he made the ball-busting (literally) mistake of stepping over a PTO (power take-off) while it was running. Any farmer will tell you that's a big no-no. He's lucky he's not dead instead of just getting one nut chopped off in the incident when the leg of his jeans got caught in the rotator and sucked him in. Story goes, he held on for dear life for nearly three hours until his dad got worried and came to check on him.

"Hi Bruce," Mavs answers sweetly.

"You, uh...you wanna maybe, uh..." Chut's gaze sweeps to mine briefly, then back to Mavs as if I don't exist. As if I'm not here as her date. And why would he think I am? Everyone in town knows how tight we are. *As friends*. As just fucking friends. "Uh, dance with me later?" he finishes stuttering. Looks like dickhead lost more than his left nut in that accident. Like his ability to interact with the opposite sex without wetting his pants.

"Sorry," I pipe in just as Mavs is getting ready to respond. Probably accept. "Her dance card is full for the night."

A tiny gasp escapes from Mavs's throat when I yank her into me and wrap a strong arm around her waist. Then I feel her blaze lighting up the right side of my face as I continue to stare at One Nut, who hasn't quite gotten the clue yet.

Thank God I'm here tonight. They may be able to look, but I'll break their fucking fingers off if they even so much as think of touching. Not even a dance. She's mine. All night long. I don't get her to myself very often, so I'm going to make the most of it when I do.

"Oh, yeah. Uh, okay. Sure. I'll, uh...I'll see you around then." Christ, I almost feel sorry for the poor dude. *Almost*.

As soon as he's out of earshot, Mavs turns on me. "What the hell was that?"

"What?"

"*What?* 'Her dance card is full for the night.'" She drops her voice low, doing a horrible impression of me while air quoting what I just said.

"I don't sound like that," I tease, trying my damnedest not to swoop down and take her lips in a punishing kiss, showing every fucking asshole here that she is already spoken for. Showing *her* she's already spoken for. And not by Killian.

*Patience, Shepard.*

"You don't sound like what? Like a possessive, jealous boyfriend?"

My molars clamp together. Every word of that statement is true except the last. The one I want most. The title I fear I'll never have.

It's hard to keep my tone light when I'm seething inside, but I manage. "I was doing you a favor, Swan."

"A favor?" She doesn't ask as much as she challenges me to expand. So I do.

"Yeah, a favor. I could just envision it now." I wipe my hand across the empty space in front of us, conjuring up an image for her. "You dance with that poor schmuck and he'll fall in love with you." *True.* "He'll court you. Then you'll fall in love with him." *Like fucking hell.* "And soon, after the two of you are married," *over my dead, lifeless body,* "you'll find out not only did he lose one testicle in that accident, but the swimmers in the other are floating in a dead pool." *That part could be true.* "Aka, no little miniature One Nuts running around the farm."

As I paint this picture of what her life would be like with One Nut Chut, her smile grows wider and wider. By the end of my elaborate fairy tale, she's laughing so hard I see tears forming in the corners of her eyes.

"See? Favor."

"Yeah. I can see that." Still laughing.

Just then, Lifehouse's "You and Me" starts filtering through the speakers. I don't ask, I just drag Mavs to the dance floor and tuck her into me as I start swaying us to the music. She stiffens for only a second before relaxing, muscle by muscle, until she's pressed fully against me.

As I inhale her intoxicating scent, absorbing this gorgeous, wild, incredible creature into my body, I know One Nut is just the tip of the iceberg. There'll be a thousand One Nuts standing in line for a chance with her, one behind the other, popping up like fucking jacks-in-the-box.

I know she's going to college soon. I know she'll be subjected to other attempts. It sickens me she'll be invited to frat parties, may have her drinks spiked, may get taken advantage of and not because she's not smart but because she's so fucking alluring and magnetic. I also know I won't be able to do anything about that. I can only hope and pray she doesn't find someone else.

That thought sends ice-cold shards of panic firing through my veins and instead of stewing on my thoughts for a few minutes so I can talk myself off the ledge, I do something rash and stupid. Something I'll come to regret for years. Her words cut me in two, both haunting me and infuriating me every time I replayed them.

"Go out with me."

"What?" she asks lazily.

I stop the sway and lean back to capture her eyes. "Go out with me."

She stares at me blankly. Clearly confused.

"A date, Swan. Go out on a date with me. A real one."

Her brows tug inward. I swear she stops breathing. She opens her mouth once, her tongue getting ready to form words, but rethinks herself. Then she stomps all over me. "Kael, I...I can't." She looks genuinely sad. For me, I suppose.

"Why? Give me one good reason."

Cocking her head, she answers slowly as if I'm brain damaged, "Because we're friends."

"Friends go on dates. All the time. Friends even go on to fall in love and get married. And live happily ever after," I tack on idiotically.

"I can't," she almost whispers now. Jason Wade is still crooning in the background and right now if he were standing in front of me, I'd throat punch him. I think his sappy words and hypnotic melody softened me into believing I could sweet-talk her into being mine. I should know better. Nothing with this girl comes easy.

"That's not good enough." She tries to disengage from me. I refuse her. I tighten my arms and dig my fingers into her back. "Tell me why."

Her eyes look anywhere but mine. "I don't want to hurt you."

Every single muscle in my body tenses. From scalp to heel. That sick feeling I had earlier in the pit of my stomach at the mention of Killian's name gets worse. Far, far fucking worse.

"You won't," I rasp. *You will.* "Tell me," I gently coax her. I can't bear to look into her heart when she ruins this life I already have planned for us, so I set my cheek to hers and whisper again, "You can tell me anything, Mavs."

I feel her throat work to swallow. Her warm breath fans the lobe of my ear when she confesses softly, just as Lifehouse's last note is played, "I'm in love with someone else."

That hurt like a motherfucker. Not gonna even try to deny it. I feel as though a knife has just been lodged between my ribs, the tip piercing my heart. It sits there, burning hot as the flesh around it is branded with the agony her words inflict.

"Well," I finally push the heavily weighted word out, "I guess that's a reason."

"Kael," she starts, pressing her hands between us, trying to escape again.

But I hold on. I can't look her into her eyes just yet. I can't witness the pity I know I'll see skimming the top. "It's okay. I understand."

I want to ask who. I want to make her utter the name of the man who's always had that one piece of her I haven't. But I don't, because I don't want to hear my brother's name come out of her mouth again. So I hold her through another song, paste on a fucking plastic smile, and get through the rest of the dance in a haze of equal parts hurt and fury.

When I drop her off shortly after two in the morning, I have half a mind to drive straight to Killian's and beat him to a bloody pulp. We talked about Maverick once. Just once. It was when I was fourteen. I told him I loved her and that I wanted to marry her. I was staking my claim, even then. But so was he. His response after my declaration of ownership was simple and enigmatic: *"What if that's not what she wants?"* But it wasn't the words themselves that tipped me off because it was a fair question. It was *how* he said them. Possessive. Jealous. Determined.

When I was younger, I would have given my brother anything he wanted. I would have done anything to please him. *That's* how much I idolized him. But that day by the lake when Mavs had me mesmerized changed me. I realized there was someone else I wanted to worship more.

And if I thought for a single solitary second I could thrash the feelings he has for Maverick out of him, I'd have gone. I've have spent all night torturing the brother I used to exalt until I realized he was competition. But I know it's pointless. I think he'd fight for her as long and brutally as I would. She's worth it and we both know it. So instead, I drive the five hundred yards from the DeSoto driveway to my parents' house, where I'm staying for the summer. I dig through my box of CDs. I watch Lifehouse burn and melt into a globby puddle of plastic in the sink. I take my mom's shit the next day when she chastises me for ruining it.

Then I make a vow. I will not give her up. I will not give up on her, either. Maverick is all I've ever wanted and I can't just throw away that dream until my nightmare becomes reality. And as long as they're not together, I still stand a chance.

I give the dial a spin, watching one through ten whiz by in a blur of colors.

"Eight," Kael calls out when the plastic clicker thingy stops the disc from twirling. He's lounging on his side, head propped up in one palm, a cocktail dangling in the fingers of his other hand. He's been acting strange all week—distracted if I had to put a word to it. He says it's work, but I'm not so sure. I'd hoped a fun, relaxing game of Life would lighten him up. We used to play it all the time as kids. I'd whip his butt, although I think he really let me win most of the time. But I don't think it's working. It's our second round and he seems tenser than ever.

I dutifully move my yellow, six-passenger car eight blocks, counting them off out loud as I go. I moan about all the Life tiles I'm leaving behind on the way, seeing if I can get a rise out of him. Again, I fall flat. He's stoic, staring at the board, clearly lost in thought. My eight takes me past the "Get Married" space, but I have to stop to take a spouse. When I pluck a pink figure and put her shotgun, he doesn't even bat an eye.

Kael drops his glass to the floor and takes his turn. I got to take the college trek while Kael shot out of the gate with his career and is half a board ahead of me, his red car weighted down with a wife and three kids already. He covers the yellow space with his hunk of plastic, not even bothering to read it. I pop up and move it over, announcing, "Another boy." I wedge a blue figure into the one remaining empty slot. "I didn't realize we were having so many kids? We'd better get started."

At that, his eyes dart up to mine, gripping them with such intensity it steals a breath, maybe two. This is the first time he's been engaged in anything outside his own head in the last hour. He pushes to sit, scooting his glass over so the contents don't spill. "We haven't talked about that yet, you know."

Gulp.

"What? Kids?"

His head moves in an up-and-down motion. Slow and steady. I pluck at my baggy Old Navy tee suddenly feeling warm even though it's thirty degrees outside. "I mean, I know you want kids. I know *I* want kids. And I was on the money when I told you One Nut wouldn't give them to you."

I watch his face, watching for a smirk, thinking that's a horrible thing for him to say. Bruce Chutney has been married for five years now to Carrie Ann Miller, a sweet girl three years my junior. He comes from a big family. So does Carrie Ann. Farmers tend to breed big broods to help with the chores and leave their legacies to, but five years later they're in that big empty farmhouse on the south side of town all alone.

Then the corner of his mouth fires up, making his eyes dance. "You're terrible," I tell him, pushing his shoulder so hard he falls over. On his way down, he manages to grab ahold of me, taking me down with him. He pinches my sides, tickling me until I'm squealing like a stuck pig, begging him to stop. I feel wetness soaking into my yoga pants and realize we spilled his vodka gimlet in our tussle. By the time he lets up, I'm gasping for air. Mostly because 185 pounds is lying on top of my back, squishing my lungs.

"I heard they're pregnant," is thrown straight into my ear. My heart stops. Just stops right there in my chest cavity. I feel it beat its last beat. I'm sure of it. "Ran into Bruce at the bank the other day and he told me the good news."

*Oh fuck.* It starts again. Thumps so hard against my bones it hurts, taking a few pulses to get back into a normal rhythm. I let my forehead sink into the rug beneath me, chastising myself that I thought he was talking about Killian and Jilly. And that the news absolutely gutted me.

Why? Why after seven months of marriage can I not just let this go? Why do I have to care what they do, where they go, if they procreate or not? Why—fucking *why*—am I still hanging on to the notion of him by the hair of my chinny chin chin when I know beyond a shadow of a doubt I'm in love with the man currently crushing me?

My body flips and now Kael straddles me, gazing down with concern. "Did I hurt you?" he asks so sweetly it kills me.

My forehead scrunches up. "No. Why?" *Oh, I'm rubbing my chest. Right in the center. Trying to ease the dull ache that settled there.* I tell my brain to tell my hand to stop moving in little circles over my heart. My fingers slow, then finally stop.

"Did you hear what I said?"

"Uhhhh...yeah. That's great for them," I bumble.

"I thought so. He looked happy."

Is that what's the matter with Kael? Does he want kids and is afraid I won't? Is he afraid this is all some surreal alternate reality we've temporarily found ourselves in? Are we?

The smile on his face is almost sad. He bends over, putting all his weight on his forearms. His fingers tunnel in my hair, anchoring us as one. We're chest to chest. He touches his forehead to mine. He does that a lot. Like he can transfer the love he has into me through that one simple connection. Through osmosis. And the funny thing is...it feels like he does. I always feel calmer when he's touching me in some way. He's that gravitational pull that keeps me grounded in all things real and true.

I stroke his flank up and down in slow, calming motions. "What's wrong, baby?" I coax softly. I've asked the same question half a dozen times this week. I'm met with the same curt answer: "Work."

He breathes deep, his heavy exhale swirling across my face. It smells of cinnamon and vodka and a touch of fear. His body shakes a little and the confident man I'm always used to seems to have disappeared. His voice is so low I strain to hear him. "Are you happy, Maverick?"

Somehow his question doesn't take me by surprise. It's only a matter of time before we're going to need to have a frank and very hurtful discussion. Maybe that's one of the reasons Killian's ghost hangs over us. Because we both refuse to acknowledge it's there. Maybe if we unite, we can eradicate his hold over us for good.

"Very," I assure him simply, truthfully. Despite that lingering melancholy over Killian, I've settled into this life with Kael and am happier than ever. I'm starting to feel like an actual newlywed. Maybe seven months too late, but beggars can't be choosers.

"Because if you're not happy, if you've changed your mind and this isn't what you want—"

"Stop," I angrily cut him off. "This is exactly where I want to be. Right here with you."

"I sometimes feel like this isn't real, Swan."

"Kael," I mutter on a light cloud of regret. The tone of his voice is like a gunshot through the center of my heart. Wrapping my arms around him, I tug until he comes flush with me. He's heavy. It's hard to breathe. I don't care. And I don't even pretend I don't know what he's talking about. I'm tired of pretending. I infuse my voice with strength and confidence, meaning what I say. "We're real, Kael. We're real. More real than anything in my life." Truth.

"Sometimes, when I go to bed at night with you curled into me, I'm convinced I'll wake up and you'll have been this horribly fantastic dream. It eats at me all the time. I worry I'll open my eyes and you'll be gone."

Tears spring up. They quickly roll into my hair, except the one on my right side. That drop of salty moisture works its way around the plastered-together flesh of our cheeks. *I* have done this to him. To us. How do I fix this? What do I do?

"I won't be gone. Ever," I manage to say through the constriction in my chest, now for an entirely different reason. I squeeze him harder. Try to make him believe me. "I promise. I love you so much,

Kael." *I know I can't live without you.* "I know this is where I'm meant to be." I hope he understands what I'm *not* saying.

He breathes evenly at my ear, speaking quietly. "I want kids. I wanted to wait and just enjoy being husband and wife for a while but I've waited a lifetime for you, Mavs. I have this burning inside me to see your belly grow big with our baby, knowing together we created a life that's part you, part me, forever us."

After we married, it took me weeks to just take a full breath without panic. It was a lot like the stages of grief, letting Killian go and accepting my life with Kael. Denial, anger, nearly debilitating sorrow. Then I'd repeat them all in no particular order. Gradually, though, I've moved to acceptance. *More* than acceptance, in truth. I've come to realize in the arms of this selfless, amazing man is where I should have been all along. Of that, I'm convinced.

I know I've made a lot of progress since that day I walked down the aisle. I'm not perfect. Not sure I ever will be as my reaction tonight will attest. I didn't realize how far I'd come until this very second, though...until faced with the decision to bind us together forever with our combined DNA in a tiny human life we'll both be responsible for loving and raising. I can say nothing else but, "Okay."

Kael breaks my hold, drawing back to look inside me where he'll find certainty. Solemnness has been replaced with pure, unadulterated, flabbergasted joy. "Okay?"

I nod. More water falls, even though a smile breaks out on my face. He scoops the ones on the left side away with his thumb before doing the right. "Why are you crying, Swan?"

"They're happy tears," I whisper. And they are. Mostly. The ones not filled with remorse for planting and nurturing that kernel of doubt about us anyway.

"You really want to start trying?"

"I do." I really do.

"God, I love you, Maverick Shepard."

Smiling through watery eyes, I take his face in my hands and assure him in the strongest, most genuine voice I can muster, "I love you, Kael Shepard. *Believe* that, please."

Desire instantly smokes up his liquid amber pools, but flames behind the smolder make them glow brightly. It's mesmerizing and dizzying to know he wants me so much. Always.

Untangling one hand, he skates it slowly down my body, on the outside of my now aching breast. He teases around my nipple but it's just a tease because he keeps moving down my torso. He then slips it between us. Under the elastic of my pants. Between the silk of my panties and my naked flesh. Over my mound, through the wetness of my pussy.

"My God." My back arches off the floor when he pushes a lithe finger inside.

"I want to start right now."

I start to laugh but huff out a harsh gasp of air instead when he drags that wet finger to my puckered hole, circling it. "Kael," I beg, not sure what I'm even begging for but I don't stop begging anyway. "I'm...I'm on the pill."

"Then we practice," he offers on a husk. Watching me with raw hunger, he tugs my loungewear down my long legs. The clingy material catches on my feet. I start to laugh when he yanks and the fabric stretches with his long arms.

"Impatient?"

"Enthusiastic," he replies with that sexy smirk once he's finally rid me of them. Efficiently, he has my tee over my head and my bra unclasped. The last garment to join the pile is my nonfrilly underwear.

He sits back on his haunches, eyes raking leisurely over my nude form. I twist under his scrutiny, aching, feeling needy everywhere his gaze kisses along my flesh. Unable to take any more, I hold out my hand, palm up. "Come here."

His eyes come back to mine. They shine bright with happiness. That smirk morphs into a delicious smile. It takes over his whole being. Then it takes over mine.

In a flash, his clothes are gone, thrown haphazardly everywhere. Covering me with his rock-hard body, he kisses me until every nerve flares to life and every bone feels weak and sloshy. He pushes inside me with focused purpose until I cry out his name over and again. He makes love to me for hours on end, making my body sing, my soul soar, and my heart meld into one with his.

"I think we have this baby-making thing down pat," I tell him wearily in the dead of night as he holds me tight. Instead of going upstairs to bed, in Kael style, he insisted we make a fort and sleep here on the floor together. It was almost as if he *needed* that connection from our past, so I couldn't argue. I needed it, too.

"Mmm, I think we'd better keep at it so we don't lose focus." Warmth flashes through me where his lips find my temple.

"I'm game." I snuggle closer, feeling sated and fuzzy everywhere. "I'll be here when you wake up," I promise softly, placing a gentle kiss on the pec underneath my cheek.

His grip on me tightens. "I believe you."

"Good night, Kael."

"Night, Swan."

Instead of playing the *game* of Life—which we never finished by the way—shit's turning real and I am deliriously happy about it. My heart is bursting out of its seams. *We're going to make a baby. A. Baby.* And I'm not panicky or feeling sick in the pit of my stomach or wishing I was having this conversation with someone else.

That's when I know: instead of looking over my shoulder, watching my footsteps fade, wishing I could fossilize the memories that came with each impression, I'm truly putting one foot in front of the other, making new ones—impressions and memories that will pave my new life.

And I'm excited about it.

chapter TWENTY ONE

four months ago

*Maverick*

L ast year our family had a hell of a scare. And let me tell you,
there's nothing that brings broken factions of a family
together more than the dreaded word "cancer." No matter
how far apart you are in proximity or beliefs or morals, there are two
things that are guaranteed to rally a family: new life and the ending
of one.

During a routine Sunday family dinner, I noticed a bump on my
father's neck. It protruded from the left side and was barely visible to
the naked eye, but I'd always been fascinated with this particular
birthmark on his throat in the perfect shape of a horseshoe. He told
me when I was little it was his good luck charm, that he knew it
meant he was destined for great things. I used to wish I had one, too.

And this lump was right underneath that birthmark. It was large
enough that it distorted the shape just slightly, which was what drew
my attention. Apparently it had been there quite some time and my
father had been ignoring it. But I was relentless until he visited his
local physician, who sent him to a specialist in Des Moines, who,
after some initial tests that were inconclusive threw around words
like lymphoma and leukemia. After several weeks of poking, prodding, scans, and biopsies he was diagnosed with Hashimoto's
thyroiditis, an autoimmune disease that causes your body to turn on
itself, destroying your own thyroid. Some simple meds and frequent
tests to be sure they were working properly were all it took to get him
back to new.

Yet, here we are again. Back in the hospital. Pacing. Scared as
hell. But this time, it's far, far more serious than inflamed nodes. I bite

my nails. Bounce my leg. Tap my fingers until the pads are numb. I wait for word. Any word. Any news. *Anything.*

I hate hospitals. I hate the smell. The sterile, cold surroundings. The desolate feeling that overtakes your senses. The pain and suffering that permeates every part of you until you feel a dozen miles or showers or years won't wash it away.

A flash of color draws my attention away from chewing the skin raw on my thumb. *Killian.* In his red windbreaker. Busting through the emergency room doors in a rush.

He scans the room briefly before his concerned gaze lands on me. With three long strides, he eats up the distance between us and without even asking wraps his arms all the way around me. He holds me close. Strokes my hair. Whispers it's going to be okay.

"Any word yet?" he breathes.

I haven't been surrounded by Killian's broad body in over three years now. And it feels...foreign. Different than I thought it would after all this time. I'm used to Kael's lean frame. That little rasp he has in the back of his throat when he hums in my ear. I'm used to those extra two inches he has on Killian. How I click perfectly into the dips of his body.

"He's still in surgery," I mumble into Killian's chest. He releases me but holds my cheeks between his palms. His thumb lightly caresses my chin. My skin tingles there. My breathing picks up when I realize we're close. *Too* close. His breath drops in billowy clouds over my face as he glances between my eyes and lips. For a split second, I'm afraid he's going to kiss me. For just the hair of another, I feel as though I would let him.

Just that *one* brief, fleeting second.

Then it's gone. I'm pulling back, breaking his hold. His eyes shift, landing on my mother. He leaves my side—reluctantly, I can tell—to go to her, drawing her into a tender hold. She sniffles. I half wonder if it's fake, but the red of her eyes and the draw of her face tell me it's not. She loves my daddy in her own strange way.

"Where's Kael?" Killian asks as if suddenly realizing my husband isn't present. Thank the good Lord he's not after that blatant, inappropriate display of affection we just shared.

"Minneapolis," I reply absently.

As he did months ago, his brows draw in confusion and I add, "He's on his way. He'll be here soon."

Daddy was brought to the local Dusty Falls ER three hours ago with chest pain. This time, words like "massive heart attack," "unconscious," and "severe damage" were the phrases tossed around. They immediately transferred him to Des Moines, over an hour away. Mother and I piled into my Chevy Malibu, following the ambulance the seventy-nine miles to Mercy Hospital where they have some of the best cardiac specialists in all of Iowa.

A surgical team whisked him away and we've been waiting ever since.

"Have you talked to Jilly?"

The muscle in his jaw jumps a few times before he answers. "She's at the airport. She was able to get on an earlier flight. It leaves in an hour and a half."

I feel the muscles in my own jaw clench. Our father could be dead in an hour and a half. Apparently Jillian flew to Chicago for the day with some friends. *"To shop."* Oh yeah...that was said with loads of sarcasm. And God forbid she rents a fucking car and drives the five hours needed to be with her father who could possibly be dying. She'd be halfway home by now. That's what I would have done. Then I would have driven like a bat out of hell to get to his side.

My relationship with my parents is strange. Strained is probably a better descriptor. They're my parents and I love them regardless of their flaws or faults. They gave me life. They raised me well. They taught me morals and values and I never wanted for anything. They may not support a lot of my decisions; then again I don't necessarily support theirs, so I guess that's fair.

But there's something missing in our family dynamics and I've always had a hard time putting my finger on exactly what that is. It's not love. They love me. I'm pretty sure my daddy would lay down his life for me. My mother? She might, but I wouldn't bet my bakery on it. I guess maybe it's that they usually put themselves first. Their wants. Their desires. Their goals. Their friends. Their business. Their charities. We were always an afterthought.

At least that's how I felt. Jillian doesn't see things the same way I do, though. She was a suck-up as a child. Still is. I think that's why she has a better relationship with them than I do, particularly with my mother. She's a pleaser. She kowtowed to them where I rebelled. If they wanted her to go left, she would, happily. No questions asked. Me, though? I'd argue ten minutes on the prudence of taking that left. Why not right, straight, backward, forward, up, down, or sideways? Why *left*? It infuriated my mother. Daddy, on the other hand, thought it would make me business savvy.

And it has. Just not the business he wanted for me, which was to run DSC. When I was little, I imagined myself at the helm. We talked about it even. I'd visit Daddy in his big corner office, sitting behind his oversized desk in an oversized chair. He looked so important. Sounded so authoritative. He spoke; people reacted. I wanted *that*. Respect. Power.

But all that changed when Killian came back. Only he didn't come back for me—he came back for Jillian. For my father. For another life that didn't include me. And only a masochist would subject herself to working with her former lover turned brother-in-law daily. I'll never forget my conversation with Daddy the day I handed in my resignation. He gave me a hard time, challenging my choices, but eventually he acquiesced. He knew how hardheaded I can be when I want something. He taught me well.

Two weeks later, I walked out of DSC with a heavy heart but a weightless soul. I later told Daddy that the bakery had been a dream of mine for a long time when in fact, it was a spur-of-the-moment decision the second my hate-filled gaze landed on my sister's hand twined with Killian's.

"Hey." Said traitorous hand circles around the top of mine. Killian's fingers slip to my palm and squeeze. I don't pull away. I know...I'm still apparently far too weak when it comes to him. "You know the devil's probably kicking him out as we speak because of all the grief your father's giving him right now, don't you?"

I half snort, wiping off a waterfall of tears. "You're probably right," I lie.

Dread sits stiff like a gigantic rock in the pit of my gut. My father is going to die. I saw it in their faces back at the Dusty Falls ER. It was compassion. Sympathy. When they saw the pallor of his skin, they knew, as well as I, that we'd be planning a funeral in the next twenty-four hours.

"I'm not ready to lose him yet." My breath catches on a sob.

"I know," he offers softly. He understands the complicated relationship I have with my parents better than anyone except maybe Kael.

Sitting back, he brings me with him, throwing an arm over my shoulder. The couch we're on allows his thigh to be snug with mine. Under any normal circumstances, this would be acceptable: my brother-in-law comforting me platonically in a time of distress. But we aren't normal. And our past is anything but platonic. This is wrong. Letting him hold me tenderly. Slanting into him. Laying my head on his shoulder. Clasping one hand with his. But I need an anchor and right now, he's it.

"It's going to be okay, Small Fry."

I don't respond. I know he's just placating me. It's the fallback phrase used during crisis. What everyone wants to hear. What people say because there's nothing else to be said. So we fall quiet. We don't move, except for our breaths, which are now in sync with the other. I tense when he whispers, "I know this makes me an ass, Maverick, but fuck...it feels so good holding you in my arms again. No matter the circumstances."

Guilt sweeps over and through me, making my skin prick and my face flame. I take stock of how his fingers feel trailing lightly up and down my arm, of the unique smell of woods and Killian pressing into my nostrils, the texture of his bulk against my chest and realize I don't miss this as much as I thought I did. I crave everything Kael right now more than air. "Killian—" I make to pull away, but his grip tenses.

"Don't. Just a few more minutes. Please."

I can't. I can't do this to Kael after everything he's done for me. It's not fair. To him. To me. To any of us. I'm breaking away when I feel the heaviness of my husband's stare push me into the cushions. *Oh. Shit.* I can just imagine what we look like all twined around each other. I lift my eyes to find his scorchingly hateful glare not on me, but on his brother.

"Kael," I cry, jumping up and into his arms. They curl around me, but they're stiff and cold. The hug feels forced. It's soul destroying. I start to sob and they soften. Then they crush me to him. A palm cups my head and the other wraps snugly around my middle. I wind my legs around his waist and he carries me across the waiting room before sinking down in a chair, me still in his lap.

"What have they said," he asks brusquely, but I ignore him.

"It was nothing," I assure him. "I was crying. He was comforting me was all."

"I don't want to talk about Killian, Maverick. Tell me about your father."

I drag myself back enough to bore straight into his eyes. Twining my arms around his neck, I bury my fingers in his hair. "I love you. *You*, Kael. Please do not doubt that."

His lids look heavy as they fall slowly shut. He wets his lips before opening them back up again. Some of the ire has left, but I see it still simmering, hardening the outer edges of his irises to a dark chocolate. "Your father."

I swallow hard past that thick lump now sitting in the middle of my throat. He doesn't want to talk about what he saw? Fine. This isn't the time or place anyway. But I'm tired of dancing around him. We're going to have this conversation sooner rather than later. Then we're going to exorcise Killian once and for all.

"He had a massive heart attack. He's been unconscious since the ambulance picked him up at his office. They took him for surgery the second we pulled up here. It's not good, Kael. We didn't even get to say good-bye," I choke.

His face falls when he says quietly with sincerity, "I'm sorry, Swan."

Just then, I hear my mother's name called. I look over to see her, Killian at her side, standing in front of a salt-and-pepper-haired gentleman in green scrubs and a long white coat. His hands are stuffed in the pockets. His shoulders slumped. The weary doctor stands next to a man who can't be missed.

A chaplain.

*Oh God no.*

Then my mother cries out. It's a piercing noise I will never forget.

Her legs buckle.

Killian catches her.

My vision blurs.

A sob escapes from somewhere deep inside me.

My husband holds me together as life as I know it shatters around me.

*My father is gone.*

The next few days blow by in a blur of condolences, casseroles, and crying. Apparently my parents had their funerals all planned and paid for, so our decisions on music, burial plots, caskets, and even readings at the mass were minimal. Franklin Parrish, the funeral director at Parrish, Parrish, Winewsky & Billings Funeral Home was an old classmate of my father's. He took care of the smallest of details for us with compassion and empathy. I honestly don't know how you couldn't be emotionally broken dealing with death and grief day in and day out. It takes a special soul to help others through the very worst time of their lives while keeping yours intact.

Kael's been a rock. I couldn't have gotten through this without him. He's been with me every second of every day. Never leaves my side. I insisted on staying at my parents' house with my mother. He insisted on staying with me. She was distraught, not handling the death of the man she'd spent the last forty-three years with well at all. I wish she would have shown her love for him in life as much as she has in death.

But Kael took care of not only me, but my mother as if she were his own. He made sure she ate and got out of bed. He drove her to the funeral home. He helped pick out the suit my father would wear to his final resting place.

And me? He held me when I cried myself to sleep at night. He helped wash me this morning—the day we're saying our final good-byes to my father—when I fell into a puddle on the tiled floor of the shower and wept uncontrollably. He dressed me when all I could do was stare at that black sheath as though if I slipped it on, *I* was the one who would end up in the ground instead.

But I didn't. I made it through the car ride to the funeral home. I made it through mass at Saint Bernadette's. I made it through standing at the graveside and walking away on wobbly knees with the knowledge that as soon as everyone was gone, they would lower my father's remains into the ground and cover him with dirt.

Now I'm here, at the requisite luncheon where people trade stories about my father's life then move on with their own when they walk out the door. The chatter in this small space, which is bursting to capacity, is almost deafening. I want to be anywhere else. I want to rewind time to only days ago when Daddy and I shared a beer in my sunroom and I told him the barley pop story. He laughed. Then he asked me how my business was doing, for once not making a dig about my choices.

I think back to that conversation. It was nice. Easy. I felt connected to him more than I had since I was a child. My father wasn't an emotional man by any means, but he was filled with raw feeling when he told me, *"I love you, Tenderheart. More than you know. So does your mother. We just don't always show it very well."*

I've replayed that conversation—the last conversation we had—a hundred times in the past six days. It's almost as if he knew our time was up.

"How you doing, Mavricky?" I feel a hand on my shoulder and tilt my face up, grateful to get out of my own head for a while. The corner of my mouth tries to lift, but the muscles aren't cooperating.

"Why do we have fifteen Marshmallow Fluff salads and no lettuce ones? Daddy hated marshmallows."

MaryLou grabs the empty chair next to me, the feet scraping obscenely loud along the floor as she yanks it out. She plops down. Leans forward with her chin in a palm, asking, "Do you want a lettuce salad? Because if you do, I'll go whip you up the biggest, baddest, bestest lettuce salad on the planet."

Now that smile comes. Barely, but it's there. "You would, wouldn't you?"

"Damn straight."

I shove away the plate of food I've only pushed around instead of eaten. "I can't."

"I know." She grabs my hand and holds on. "I know."

I gaze over the crowd. There are so many people here; I think the whole town has shut down in mourning. I don't give two shits about most of them, present company excluded. Half of them are here just to be seen anyway. It's not as if Richard DeSoto was the easiest man to get along with. It wasn't just me.

My attention lands on Jillian across the room. Normally the center of attention, she's off in a corner by herself. She looks sad and lost and alone. She's pale. She's lost weight. Her clothes hang haphazardly from her thin, fragile bones. She's a hot mess. I wonder what's less than size 0. Negative 1 maybe? I'm so far away from that number I honestly don't have a clue.

"I kind of feel sorry for her," MaryLou surprisingly announces. MaryLou hates my sister with a passion and empathy is the last emotion she'd ever have for her. But right now, I think she needs it.

"Me too. She's taking it really hard." Jilly's been completely withdrawn from everyone since Daddy passed away. That in and of itself doesn't surprise me. Death either bonds or breaks a family. She's chosen to break. What does surprise me is how at arm's length she's keeping Killian. She's slept in her old bedroom down the hall from us. She refuses to let him stay. She refuses to talk to him when he calls or stops by. She didn't even want him to be by her side today, but he put his foot down and told her to stop acting like a spoiled fucking brat. Everyone handles grief in different ways I guess, but the whole thing is beyond bizarre.

"Have you seen Kael? I can't take any more of this fakery. I just want to go home, take a bath and drink a bottle of wine." Sleep in my own bed in the safety of my husband's arms. I'm completely drained of everything, including pleasantries. I think I'll find Killian first, though, and ask him to spend the night at Mother's. I don't care if Jilly protests. She's clearly in no shape to be taking care of anyone, herself included.

"I haven't. Want me to find him?"

"No." I push my swollen feet back into my black heels and heft my weary body up. "I need to move before I fuse with this plastic."

Her mouth turns down into a sad smile. "Call if you need anything?"

"You know it."

"Don't worry about the bakery, Mavs. I got it covered."

"Thanks," is all I can muster. We've been closed all week. MaryLou insisted we open tomorrow and that she'd take care of everything. I agreed knowing it's probably best. I have no idea when I'll be back, but it's not tomorrow.

I take off in search of my husband, leaving my best girl behind. I make a beeline to Arnie and Eilish, asking them to be sure my mother gets home. They readily agree. I find my mother. Tell her good-bye. Tell her I'll be over first thing in the morning.

It takes me fifteen more minutes to weave my way through the crowd because I keep getting stopped. I don't spot either Kael or Killian. A quick walk through the sanctuary shows it empty. I traipse the halls, even check the men's room. Nothing.

Pushing through the outer doors, the cool March air hits me square in the face. I take a moment to drag it in and clear my head. Then I scan the parking lot, noting a few people milling about, but see no sign of the Shepard boys. I'm just about to head back inside when Killian's deep, angry boom carries from around the corner. My hairs stand on end as I near the edge, shamelessly eavesdropping.

But just as I get to the brick corner, Kael flies around it and runs smack into me, almost knocking me over. He's breathing hard. His face is beet red. Eyes are bright and wild. He's clearly pissed.

"What's wrong?"

Grabbing me in a bear hold, he squeezes the air from me. "Nothing. I'm sorry I left you so long. You okay?"

My eyes lift over Kael's shoulder and latch right on to ones that remind me of long fall days when we used to rake piles of leaves and jump into them. "You're upset. I can tell." I'm not sure which Shepard brother I'm talking to right now. Killian is a replica of Kael. Can't they get along just one fucking day?

Kael's lips find my neck and he just presses them there, letting them remain while he breathes me in. Killian's eyes flare with unmistakable jealousy. "You ready to go?" he mumbles against me.

I just nod, my gaze not able to break with my past.

Kael releases me but immediately slides his hand in mine and starts walking toward the parking lot, not even acknowledging Killian.

We're a good twenty paces away when I remember. "Wait," I say, tearing away from his hold. I rush over to Killian and stop, probably too close. I feel my husband's eyes boring into us. Killian has to as well, but he doesn't yield to the temptation to gloat. "I need you to stay at the house tonight. Watch over Mother."

"You're going home?"

"Yes," I breathe lightly. "I need a break."

"You hanging in there?" he asks with such concern my eyes prick with tears. He raises his hand but drops it back down a second before it touches me. I shiver when a fingertip grazes my arm on the descent. I bite my lip to stop the burn stinging like a thousand suns behind my lids.

Nodding is all I can manage.

Killian looks down at his feet momentarily. "Okay. Sure. Anything else?"

I shake my head and am starting to turn away when I do something completely selfless. I turn back around and tell him, "Yes, there is one more thing."

"Anything. Name it."

Looking him in the eyes, I'm reminded of how much he still loves me. It's there and it's beautiful yet painful all at the same time. But death makes you reevaluate your own life. Your choices. Your future.

I know. I've been doing it for days, always coming back to the same conclusion: I am where I'm supposed to be. Then I take a deep breath and demand, "Take care of Jillian. She's a wreck."

That jaw tick is back. I can tell he was hoping for something different. "She's being stubborn."

"You're the King of Obstinate, Killian."

"If you're the Queen of Will, Maverick." My mouth twitches, causing the corner of his mouth to quirk and his dark eyes lighten somewhat. "Any more impossible tasks, Small Fry?"

"I'm sure I'll think of one or two. Give me a bit."

"I'm sure you will," he retorts smartly, fighting a smile.

I stand still for just a second longer before I say fuck it. We all lost a man we loved. Out of respect for Kael, I've worked hard to keep my distance from Killian since that day at the hospital, but he's family and I'm sure he's hurting in his own way. I lean in and quickly wrap my arms around him faster than I can blink. Before he even has time to return the hug, I'm stepping back, mumbling, "Thank you."

I watch his Adam's apple bob up and down. "Anything for you, Maverick." I don't let his raspy voice affect me.

With a quick smile, I retreat back to my husband. I throw my arms around his neck and hold tight, whispering in his ear that I want him to take me home and make love to me. Make me forget for just a little while that I have this hole inside me now, which will never be quite filled.

"Hey, Swan."

"Hi," she replies a little out of breath.

I pull myself onto a barstool and signal Candi for my usual. "You on your way?"

It's Thursday night. Our traditional night out for drinks and darts. One we'd started in summers past when we were both home from college.

And in the last few weeks, we've picked that tradition up again, because Maverick has moved back home. She graduated with honors from Iowa University four weeks ago. Started working for her father in a rather entry-level position, even when she told me she wasn't sure that's what she wanted to do.

I'm not sure I want her working for her father, either. Hell, I've been trying to find a way out of DSC myself, but I stayed. If there was a chance in hell Maverick was moving back to Dusty Falls after graduation, I was going to be here because this is our time. After all these years of waiting and pining away for her, it's *our* time.

Her education is behind her, her future bright and limitless. She's back within arm's reach. I can woo her, love her openly, date her, *marry* her. I intend to make her see that everything she needs has always been waiting patiently for her. Everything I've ever longed for is finally within my grasp.

But I know I need to slow my pace with her. It's been gut-wrenching to do, but it's my only option. Slow and steady gets the girl and that's what I aim to do. I want her to see that she can't live without me any more than I can without her. She loves me, yes, but she's not *in* love with me just yet, and I know it's because she hasn't given that side of us a chance.

So this summer is all about changing perspective and perception. I'm going to do my level best to alter how she sees me. How she sees *us*. Open her eyes so she understands we can be best friends *and* lovers *and* lifelong mates. I plan to not only get her but keep her and make her the happiest, most loved woman alive.

Just like every other summer, we've picked up right where we left off. I spend as much time with her as she'll allow, only now I've started dropping subtle hints. About us. About the future. About *more*. With the coy looks and fluttery eyes she's given me, I thought I'd actually been making progress, but then my gut started to burn.

I'm not the only one who thinks "it's time."

"Oh shoot. I'm sorry. I, ah...I can't tonight, Kael."

I clamp my teeth together. That burn starts to flame, fueled by the hot coals of suspicion stirring inside me.

Keeping my voice steady, I ask, "You mean you're already breaking with Thursday-night tradition? I was looking forward to an ass whooping." Actually I was just looking forward to spending time with her. I don't particularly like to lose but if it means I have Mavs by my side for a few hours, I'll gladly suffer defeat.

Her laugh feels forced. "I'm sorry. I just...something else came up. But next Thursday, I'll be there and it will be my pleasure to whoop your ass until you can't sit." She adds the last part quickly, trying to soothe me. It doesn't work. Normally I would laugh and tease her back, but instead, I want to press her. Ask her twenty questions until she spills what suddenly has her so busy. I'm afraid I already know the answer to all twenty of them. I settle for, "It's a date."

"I'm sorry, Kael." Now she sounds genuinely contrite.

"Hey, no big deal. I'll just call Killian. See if he wants to join me."

Oh yeah, I threw it. Laid the bait. I hope to fuck it rots right there on the ground.

"Oh, ah..." she sputters. "I'm sure he'd love that."

I smell the spoil already. I hate that I know Maverick so well. I know every inflection, every telltale tick, what each hitch of her breath means, except the one I want to know most intimately. I fear I may never learn that part of her just like I fear Killian will.

I'm utterly sick.

"Talk to you tomorrow?"

"Yeah. Love you. Sorry again."

"Love you, too, Mavs." So fucking much. *How can you not see that?*

I stare at the phone in my hands, the screen now black. I shouldn't do it, but I can't stop. I curse myself the entire time my fingers fly through my contacts. I hate myself when I tap his name.

He answers on the fourth ring. "If this is business, I'm afraid it will have to wait."

A corner of my mouth ticks up. It probably looks like a sneer. Fuck....it *is* one. "It's not business. I wanted to see if you're free for a drink."

"A drink?" He sounds surprised.

"Yeah, a drink. Complete with alcohol and everything. My treat."

"Tonight?"

It's true. Killian and I were once inseparable, but our relationship is strained from both ends. It's hard to hang on every word of the brother who also wants the same thing you do. The same woman, the same life, the same everything. He probably feels the same.

I bark a laugh that borders on sardonic. "Yeah, tonight. Why? Got plans? A hot date maybe?"

Bait laid once more. Only I know Killian. He won't pick it up. He's not that outwardly transparent. But I know my brother just as well as Mavs. Killian hasn't dated anyone in months. Except Maverick. I know this, not because of her, but because he tipped his own hand. The stick in his ass magically fell out and I *knew*...I knew it was because of Mavs. Because she has that effect on people. She's a flickering candle in their dark world. A living, breathing fantasy come to life.

"I can't tonight." Short. To the point. No elaboration. Very Killian-like.

"Maybe after you get done with whatever it is that has you tied up? I can wait." Killian has been the one pushing to get together more lately, so the fact he's turning me down is telling.

I swear I hear crickets chirping through the silence on the other end. Finally, "I'd love to, Kael, but tonight just doesn't work."

It's confirmed then. My worst nightmare has come to life. My gut is now engulfed in a wild inferno of jealousy. Images of them together tonight flip through my brain in agonizing slow motion.

"Some other time?"

"Yeah, sure," I manage to spit out. I stick my hand in my pocket, fingering my keys, and fight the urge to drive to her house, following them like some fucking lovestruck stalker. Even I can't stoop that low. Seeing them together that way would completely break me.

"I'll see you first thing in the morning to review the DeVries contract."

"Yep." I throw the phone on the bar top without a good-bye, disgusted with the way I'm feeling. Just as it stops bouncing, it rings again and for a brief moment, I hope it's Maverick saying she's changed her mind. I snag it, taking in the name on my screen. *Vanessa.* I punch ignore and throw it back down, harder this time, uncaring if it breaks.

Jesus fucking Christ, this is gutting me. I'm a twenty-five, almost twenty-six-year-old man. I'm certainly not pure, but I've limited the women in my life because of Mavs. Because all I can see in them is her.

There was a period of time when I kind of gave up on the notion of us, not believing it would ever come true. A quarter of a century is a long time to wait for anyone, so I started seeing Vanessa. I'm a man. I may be in love with a woman I can't have right now, but I'm not a fucking saint. Yet every time I was inside of Vanessa it became harder and harder until it almost became unbearable. Even though it was stupid, I felt as if I was betraying Maverick so I broke it off a few months ago.

Vanessa's been calling me ever since. She's relentless. Like a bloodthirsty piranha.

"You look like someone ran over your cat," Candi twangs as she sets a draw in front of me. I palm the cold mug and take a long drink, hoping it will cool the fire in my belly. Knowing it won't.

"The only good cat's a dead cat," I say as I slam the glass against the wood. Her horrified look shames me. I forgot Candi volunteers at the Humane Society and is part of a team that rescues abused animals. "Uh...I didn't mean that."

Her already thin lips press together. The line it makes reminds me of an Etch A Sketch.

"Sorry. Been a shit day. I love cats." I'm allergic, so I don't particularly care for cats, but I'm not heartless. Don't wish them dead either. "Better bring me another one of these. I'm gonna need it."

Nodding in understanding, she leaves me alone to wallow.

That incessant ring comes back. I just ignore it. It stops but starts back up immediately. In frustration, I power down my phone and finish my beer. I breathe deeply. Try to hold my sanity together, but that fucker is fraying big time.

My imagination starts running wild and rampant at what they'll do tonight.

Mavs will laugh that laugh she does that draws you in and keeps you spellbound. She'll throw her head back and expose that sleek neck that begs for your lips. Killian won't be able to resist. He's only a mere mortal, after all. A man that's driven by a base need to claim the woman he thinks belongs to him.

Fucking hell, I can't breathe.

I imagine him kissing her, stripping her blouse first, then her bra. I see the ripe nipple he takes in his mouth, moaning around it when her flavor bursts on his tongue. I imagine his fingers moving inside of her before he sheds the rest of her clothes until she's naked and trembling, begging him to ease that ache between her legs with his cock.

I imagine him doing everything I want to do.

The fog of denial starts to roll in. My gaze falls despondently to the tacky wood beneath my fingers, unable to physically stand anymore. Hope is stripped from my spirit, ribbon by bloody mother-fucking ribbon. A hundred thousand bees buzz around in my head and when it stops, desolation takes up residence inside me.

My brother knows how I feel about Maverick. How much I love her. But he loves her, too, doesn't he? That's what this is all about. He's as in love with her as I am, and he's as stubborn as I am when he goes after something he wants. She's not worth giving up. I know this. So does he.

And he's won.

This is the time I have to ask myself the hard questions. Can I stay here if they end up together? Do I get on my knees, flay myself, and beg her to choose me instead? Should I have pushed harder, faster, not waited so fucking long because I was afraid our friendship would turn awkward and I'd lose her for good? Can I live my life *with* Maverick DeSoto knowing we'll always be friends and nothing more? Can I live my life *without* her, feeling as if I've had a lung removed and will never breathe fully again? Hell, can I live without her, *period?*

I wish I had the answers. I simply don't.

Honestly, I don't know how long I sit there, my imaginary vision of them getting more realistic by the second. At some point, I feel wetness on my legs and realize it's me. I'm crying. Like a goddamned baby.

The glint of my phone in the low light snags my attention. Before I know what I'm doing I reach for it. It's turned on. My fingers are dialing and she answers on the first ring. I'm numb while we make plans to meet. I'm numb when I start the car and slowly back out of the gravel driveway behind the bar I'm parked in. I'm numb as I drive down the streets of Dusty Falls. I'm even numb as I drive into Vanessa later.

In fact, I remain numb for a good long time to come.

I'm in the kitchen checking on supper, humming along with Fifth Harmony's latest catchy tune. It was a busy day at the bakery and I'm glad I put supper in the slow cooker, otherwise it would have been a big ol' bowl of Cap'n Crunch's Oops! All Berries for each of us. Best. Invention. Ever, by the way. All berries? Brilliant.

I'm in an unusually up mood today. It's a good feeling after spending so much time being blue. It's been nearly two months since my father's death. We're all finding our new normal with a key piece of our lives now missing. It's hard, but we're marching on because what other choice do we have?

By unanimous vote, Killian took over running DSC. He tried telling me that spot was mine. It was what my father always wanted, but I don't belong there anymore. I love my bakery, my freedom, my new life. Besides, it's not in my blood like it is his or my father's. Regardless of what he said way back when he left to move to Florida, he's always wanted to make a name for himself at DSC. I think he secretly wanted to show my father he was worthy of his daughter. Of *me*. I always knew he was. I hope he feels that way now, even if it is too late.

My mother seems to improve daily. She's resumed a few of her club activities. She told me a couple of weeks ago she's now coleading the widow's support group at church. That seems to have given her purpose and a reason to get out of bed in the morning, so whatever works. I've spent more time with her over the past two months than I have in the last two years combined. She's softened and in her own way apologized for not being the best mother she could be. Promised to do better.

And Jillian? She's still distant and withdrawn. Her snark is all but gone. She's turned into a waif, just a shell of herself. I think she and Killian spend more time apart now than together. I've spent my entire life wishing Jillian were someone else and now that she is, I'm not sure I like it. I keep waiting for the sister I've loathed all this time to return with a vengeance and she just...doesn't. Surprisingly, I'm really starting to worry about her.

It's also been close to three months since Kael's and my conversation about having a baby. The joy of starting new life fell to the wayside at the reality of one lost. Kael and I haven't talked about it since. I went off the pill, though, and we haven't been using protection.

I have to admit I was torn when my monthly visitor showed up just a few days ago. I want this next step with Kael, I'm just not sure I'm ready for the joy of parenthood when I'm still mourning the loss of my own parent. I've decided if it happens, it happens. I'm not gonna stress.

As far as Kael and I, I'm not sure things could be better between us. He doesn't work as many hours. He's home for dinner by six or six thirty most nights. He's loving and attentive as always. But he also seems more focused on something. I can't quite put my finger on it, though. He's always been protective of me and the issues with my parents—issues that he took on as his—but I wonder if the death of my father has hit him harder than he'll admit.

Pushing sad thoughts away, I turn up the radio as loud as it will go, letting the beat of the music take me over. I find myself wiggling my ass and singing at the top of my lungs about being worth it.

My cell lights up, vibrating noisily against the granite. I spare it a glance, frowning at the name on the caller ID. I stop moving, panting slightly, and debate whether to answer it. I argue with myself as the vibration continues. I'm just reaching for it when Kael's voice brightly calls, "Hi," as he walks through the garage door. I abandon the call, letting it roll to voice mail and quickly reach over to turn down the radio's volume.

My *hi* comes out as a squeak when his arms coil around my waist. Warm lips skate along my throat and I'm reminded of the day he did that so long ago shortly after we were first married. I kinda wish I was making crème pâtissière instead of fishing out a pot roast from the roaster so he could smear the custard all over me again. Only this time, I'd think of no one but him as he ravenously licked it off. I'd feel only *his* fingers as they twisted my nipples and pumped inside me. Hear only *his* voice in my ear as he commanded me to come. Know only Kael as he brought me to the brink of orgasm and over it so hard I shook in the strength of his hold.

I take the lid off the cooker and breathe deeply, the scent of slow-roasted meat and veggies filling my senses. "You seem to be in a good mood," I say breathlessly as my lobe is captured between his teeth.

"I am," he whispers with it still in his grasp. His teeth lift, but his lips wrap around the flesh instead. Then his breath trickles over the coolness left behind, making me shiver. "Pot roast?"

His hold loosens enough so I can turn in his arms. I set down the slotted spoon and spin, twining my limbs around his neck. "You sound disappointed."

"Not at all. I love pot roast."

I cock my head, studying him. "But?"

His brows go up. "How do you know there's a but?"

"Because I've known you for twenty-six years, counselor. I know a stiff...solid"—I trail one hand down his back and grip his taut ass —"butt when I see one." We break out in laughter before he slants a scorching kiss on my lips.

"So, you're home early," I say, now a lot breathless and ready for dinner of a totally different sort.

But his eyes. They stop me short of sliding my hand around the front of his hip. Now that I'm looking straight into them, I see a little wariness.

"What's wrong?"

"Nothing's *wrong*, Swan."

"Then what's up? You have that wary, guarded look in your eyes like when you had to tell me they were canceling *Teen Angel*. What is it?"

A self-deprecating smile pops out. His elbows squeeze into my waist and I feel the lace of his fingers at my back. He's caging me in so I can't escape. "Sometimes I hate that you know me so well."

Red alert. My pulse skitters. There's definitely something going on. "No, you don't. You love it. Now spill. Is it something to do with DSC?"

"No, Maverick," he answers fast. Too fast. After a quick glance out the window, he draws in a deep breath and announces, "But there is something I wanted to tell you about, actually."

Under normal circumstances, I would bust out a smug grin and tease him but my senses are tingling like lit sparklers. The moment feels heavy, electric. He's nervous.

I keep my voice steady when I prod, "What is it?"

He holds my eyes. Holds them so tight it's as if we're magnets. Powerful and unbreakable. In literally one second, I'll wonder if we are.

"I got a job offer."

I just stare. Blink and stare and blink some more. *Job offer?* But he already has a job. "What do you mean, you got a job offer? You have a job, Kael. Here, in Dusty Falls. Working for my *father's* company." I gasp, a sudden thought hitting me. "Did Killian fire you?" Would he do that? Would he abuse his power that way?

Kael's nostrils flare out and a corner of his mouth tugs up, but it's nowhere in the same vicinity as a smile.

"Because if he did, I'll—"

"No, Swan. He did *not* fire me. And I don't need you to fight my battles," he tacks on rather bitterly.

I stiffen a little, trying not to let that needle me. "Well, then what happened? Why did you get a job offer? I don't understand."

And where? It's not as though there are a lot of places for an attorney to work in Dusty Falls.

He never looks away as he says evenly, "I accepted."

It takes my brain a few seconds to catch up to what he just said. I thought I heard him say *I accepted.* And when I realize he did, in fact, say those two words, the wind feels knocked straight from my lungs.

"You did *what?*" I force that question out on the last rasp of air I have left because I feel like I can't breathe right. I push him away with all the strength in me. He lets me, staggering back, undaunted. "How could you do that without consulting me first? DSC needs you, Kael. *Now* more than ever."

His jaw is set tight. His stare firm, digging into me with unchecked resolve. "They don't. Everyone is replaceable, including me."

Seconds ago, I was thinking Killian fired him. Now, my thoughts have swerved 180 degrees. "Killian will never accept your resignation."

His demeanor doesn't change a bit. "He already did."

*This is why he was calling only moments ago. It has to be.*

"How could you do this?" I breathe hotly.

Determination schools his features tight. He nods slightly when he tells me, "This is what's best for us, Swan."

"Best for *us?*" I parrot in utter disbelief and shock. Yes, shock. That must be what's making my limbs numb and my mind shut down. No. It's whirling. Whirling and spinning and reeling so fast my stomach revolts. I don't know how long we silently argue before I find my spine again. Then I straighten my back. Square my shoulders. Pick up my scattered thoughts from the floor, piecing them together in the only pattern that makes sense. "Best for us or best for *you?*"

Caramel eyes harden right before me. "*Us.* We need to get the fuck out of this town, Maverick, before it sucks us under and ruins us. Before it breaks us and everything we're trying to build together."

"Ruins us? What in the hell are you talking about, Kael?" My voice shrills more and more with each word I'm flinging. "Our lives are here. Our *livelihoods* are here. Our memories. Our histories. Our loyalties. Our families!"

He just stands still, stony and steadfast. "Exactly." As if that one word explains it all. And I suppose it does. One word sums up the reason he wants to abandon everything we've known, leaving our entire lives behind. One word that can be found hidden within each of the reasons I just gave.

*Killian.*

My blood boils hot. Hot and sweltering. Blisters are forming inside. Sweat dots my brow. "I can't believe you did this without consulting me."

His gaze slides over my rigid form. It lands on my curled hands, then my fixed jaw. "Because I knew you'd react like this."

"How the fuck am I supposed to react when you tell me you've been off making plans for our lives without me!" Then it hits me with the force of the sun at high noon on the equator. Why didn't I put two and two together sooner? Why didn't I push this when I had doubts about what he was doing? Doubts Killian planted. "Is this why you've been going to Minneapolis?"

*Please say no. Please say no. Please don't say yes...*

He doesn't even bother looking ashamed when he answers. "Yes."

My knees feel weak. They crumple a little but I catch myself with a hand on the counter. The other is pushing into Kael's chest as he tries to get to me. "Don't touch me," I mumble. He takes two steps away.

I feel utterly sick. He's kept this from me for months. We stare at each other, the air thickening with anger and hurt.

"Who is the job with?" I force the question through a tight throat. My flags are all flying high and blood red. I know who else is up in Minneapolis and I'm hoping beyond all hope he's not going to say what I think he is.

His hard swallow makes my skin prick. "Braham Construction."

"Oh my God. But that's..." Oh God, I can't...air...I'm gasping for it. "That's...*Kael*." That's DSC's biggest competitor in the Midwest.

I turn my back to him and drop my head, gripping that granite top so hard my fingers scream as loud as my mind. I close my eyes and strain to drag in long, slow lungfuls of patience and forgiveness. It's not fucking working. I feel unimaginably betrayed right now. Confused and so, so betrayed.

"How long have you been working on this?" I muster.

"A while."

*A while*—air quotes. It's been months. That's why he took me to Saint Paul. That's why he wanted to show me around. That's why he wanted me to love it. *Jesus Christ.* Yeah. I fucking said it. And it tastes as sour as vinegar in my mind as the ash of duplicity tastes in my mouth.

I whirl back around, my hair flopping wildly. I don't want to look at him right now but I have to see his face when I ask, "Were there ever any meetings with the National Guard?"

He looks a little hurt. I don't feel bad in the slightest. "Yes."

"How many?"

He hesitates only momentarily, eyes darting to the floor before coming back to mine. His sigh alone answers the question. "Just the one. It stalled just like I told you."

"Then why didn't Killian know?" I press.

His lips purse into a thin, angry line. *He's* angry? Well, fuck that. Again, not feeling bad.

"It was a favor for your father. They contacted him directly. They were interested in DSC, but your father didn't want to send Killian because he didn't want to taint the procurement process." When I remain silent he adds, "It was a back-of-the-napkin meeting, Mavs. I never mentioned it to Killian and I don't know if your father did. I didn't ask."

I absorb his explanation. When Kael lies, he always ends up wetting his lips. I'm not sure he's even aware of it, but his lips are as dry as a bone right now. I want to ask him why he didn't just tell me that from the beginning, only I already know.

"You lied to me," I say in a shaky voice.

"I didn't—"

"You fucking *did*," I yell. "Withholding this is the equivalent of lying. We are married, Kael. *Married* people are supposed to talk about big, life-changing things like this. Not hide them from each other."

His lips snarl in a way I've never seen before. "Really? Is that what we're supposed to do, Mavs? Because I have *things* I'd like to talk about, then."

My chest tightens. *Oh God.* This is it. The moment we've waited our whole lives for. The discussion that will rip us apart or unite us so we're unbreakable. I've wanted to go here dozens of times since we've been married and now that we're standing on the doorstep looking into that tarry pit of hurt, I just want to close the door and plaster over it for good.

But I can't.

Because *he* is the reason we are even here in the first place.

"Just say it," I push. I *dare*.

That distance I made sure was between us has now vanished. The tips of his shoes press against my bare toes. His chest grazes mine with each ragged inhale. His head is bowed down, his face close to mine. Swirling red-hot orbs of anger hold me hostage once again. When he speaks, his voice is thick and hoarse and guttural.

"Yeah. This is about *him*, Maverick. About the taboo subject we pretend doesn't exist between us, but he's always fucking there. Always between us. He's all that's *ever* been between us."

"Kael—"

He grabs my chin between his thumb and finger, pinching to make a point but not to hurt me. "You don't think I know he's held what's mine? Kissed what's mine? Loved what's mine? *Fucked* what's mine?" He runs his trembling free hand through his hair until the pieces stand on end. "You don't think I know you even named your fucking business after him?"

I open my mouth to deny it, but I can't. I did it as a backward fuck-you to Killian. In college, I read Taleb's book, *The Black Swan*, on outliers and unpredictable events. It was fascinating. Kael listened to me chatter about his theories of fourth quadrant empirical and statistical properties endlessly. So months later, when Killian's unimaginable, *unpredictable* betrayal occurred, I was full of spite and embarrassment and it seemed fitting. Now it just seems petty.

"Jesus fucking Christ, Maverick! I know everything and I still don't care. *That's* how much I love you. *That's* how wound around the very fucking center of my soul you are. It's the same place you'll be until I close my eyes and take my last breath. You are rooted in here"—he pounds his chest—"in the bowels of me so far I will never be rid of you. No matter how much I've tried. No matter how much I wanted to while I knew you were with him."

His voice cracks. He stops. Pants. Pins me with a look that devastates me but not more than his confession or the tears I now see gleaming. "While he was the sun that lit your world, you were the darkness that shadowed mine."

I suck in a sharp, painful breath. My soul feels crushed. Literally. Stomped on with a boot heel until it's nothing but one big black mass of self-disgust.

"Why?" I can't possibly fathom why he loves me. Why he married me. Why he gives two shits about someone who has done nothing but hurt him over and over, albeit unintentionally.

Why? Why? Why?

"Why what, Swan?" His voice is hoarse and aching, but there is no mistaking his affection. Still. Even now, after everything I've done to him, I couldn't find more love in his eyes if I tried.

"Why anything? Why are you here with me? Why do you want me? Why did you *marry* me?" *Please explain it to me, because I just don't get it. I don't deserve it. I never have.*

He simply shakes his head as if I'm the densest person on the planet. "Because I have enough love for the both of us. I always have."

That's it.

My knees give way. I fall unceremoniously into a heap on the floor and sob. I'm not quiet about it either. I wail. My body shakes with shame and heartbreak. With loathing that I haven't been what he needs.

Strong arms circle me. They lift and carry me. He settles me, holds me, comforts me. He loves and forgives me, petting my hair. Kissing my temple. Embracing me until my sobs slow to just occasional shudders. He brings a tissue to my nose, making me blow. His love for me is as deep and boundless as the clear blue sky.

"Do you remember that first time I followed you to Old Man Riley's lake?"

I nod, sure my voice box won't work. My entire being is weak and not just my muscles. My soul and heart are, too.

"I knew you knew." He chuckles. I like the feel of his body shaking under me.

"You were about as stealthy as a bear," I whisper back. My voice sounds like it's been rubbed with coarse sandpaper. I twist my fingers in his shirt, holding fast as if it's the only thing binding me to earth. It may be.

Kael slides two fingers under my chin and lifts. "I've been in love with you my whole life, Maverick. Even before I knew what love was. But that day..." He chokes up. The waterworks start fresh. "God, that day I watched you let the real Maverick DeSoto completely out and I thought...*She is all I want. She has to be mine. I want her to be mine.* That was the day I knew I'd never love another the way I already loved you."

Oh, the guilt. How it's eating me alive. Its sharp teeth clamp hard and fast. They're unyielding. He's loved me in that beautifully painful way I've loved Killian. It's nearly unbearable to hear him confess it.

His eyes search mine. For long seconds, he penetrates that place so far inside a person it's hard to let anyone find it, let alone into it. "We can't help who we love, Maverick," he tells me softly.

And this is the selfless man I know. He knows how I've felt about

Killian and he's telling me in his own words it's okay. But it's not. My love for his brother has been a burden he's had to carry alone all his life. I've loved the wrong man all along. Given all of me to someone I shouldn't have. It should have been Kael. Always Kael.

"I'm sorry."

A sad smile flashes across his lips. "No need to be sorry, Swan. But I'm done. I won't share you with him. Not anymore. If we have any chance of making it, we have to get the hell out of Dusty Falls. We have to make new memories in a place where I don't feel suffocated by those daily reminders that he still wants you."

He's right. Of course he is. Yet still...

"I know I went about this wrong, Maverick. I *know* that. I should have discussed it with you first. I should have given you that courtesy and for that, I am truly sorry. But I knew you'd need a push and it doesn't change the fact this is what we need. *Both* of us. I genuinely believe that." His strong hand circles my jaw, tilting it back up. "That being said, if you tell me this is a deal breaker for us, then I'll decline the offer. We'll stay here and I'll work tirelessly to make sure you only see me."

I can actually feel how hard that was for him to say. "You would do that for me?"

The smile that flashes across his face is quick and sorta sad. "I think we've established I would do anything for you, Swan."

I bite my lip, my emotions all over the damn place. I'm hurt, angry and as always, I feel immense shame. We're at another crossroads. One I drove us straight to with these underlying feelings I still have for his brother and that he still has for me. I don't know what to do. Which road do I choose? Both are equally scary.

"But what about my mother? She's still so fragile."

"She has the Illians." That draws a small smile from both of us. "And her friends, her community. She'll be just fine."

"What about the bakery?"

*Am I really considering this?*

"MaryLou can run it. Pay her a management fee. Hell, sell it to her. I know it's your baby, Maverick, and I don't want to sound callous, but you're brilliant and talented and strong-minded. You can open a bakery anywhere or do anything else you want."

Then he reaches into his pants pocket and pulls out a business card, handing it to me. I turn it over in my hands.

*Mia Banks-Cyrus, Owner*
*Greenbrier Pastries*

It's from the bakery we visited in Saint Paul.

"Where did you get this?" I ask.

"I remembered she said her partner was moving. I swung by when I was up there the day your father..." He pauses briefly. I bite my lip. "Anyway, she said she wants to find another partner. The right one. She remembered you and she's interested in talking to you. If you are, that is." The corners of his mouth turn down slightly when he adds, "It's your decision, Maverick. Do we stay or do we go?"

This is all so overwhelming it's hard to digest. Kael wants to move. Away. From everyone and everything. Start over again in a strange, *big* city.

But can I do that? He's given me so much and never asks anything of me in return. Never. Can I give him this one thing that clearly means so much to him? Can I truly leave my life behind? Leave our house? Our friends?

The bigger question, though, is can I leave *Killian*? That's the *only* question he's really asking me to answer.

And that answer this very second is: I don't know. I honestly do not know since the thought never crossed my mind. Maybe it did in passing but never seriously. And if I don't—if I *can't*—what does that mean for us?

"Wow."

"Yeah."

"Huh."

"I know."

"I'm...wow."

"You're not helping."

"I know, I know. Just...let me breathe it in for five seconds," she chastises. MaryLou pinches the bridge of her nose. Tweaks her eyes closed. Then snaps them open. The intensity slices into me. "I don't understand why you're hesitating, Maverick."

"What?" *This* is her advice? After "breathing it in" for all of five seconds? It killed me to say it but I told Kael last night I needed to think about this for a few days. He was disappointed, I could tell. God, it hurt to see his hurt. But he's had months to come to terms and I just got blindsided about twelve hours ago. Twelve hours with no sleep accompanied now by a raging headache. It still stings that he was sneaking around behind my back. Blatantly lying about why he was making trips out of town. In truth, it pains me he didn't trust me with this sooner. But I guess I kinda deserve that.

MaryLou powers around our work surface covered with white flour and dough chunks and grabs me by the shoulders. "Yeah, I mean he's right. You need to get out of this place."

"I don't—"

"Yeah, you don't. That's part of the problem, Maverick." That sigh coming out of her mouth is deep and thoughtful. Oh, and did I mention fucking irritating? Grabbing my hands, she drags me over to two plastic chairs lined against the wall. She shoves me in one and whips the other around so we're face-to-face, knee-to-knee.

"You've come a long way, Mavs. You have. You've finally found a way to let that asshole go and to make a life with Kael. And even with your dad's death, you're still bright and glowing and happier than I've seen you in...honestly...ever. I give you all the credit for that because only *you* can make you happy. But while you've put all that focus on Kael, Killian's still breathing in the background. And that breath is toxic, Mavs. It's fucking poison. It will slowly strangle you and you won't even know it because you can't see it and you can't smell it and you can't taste it until it's too late."

She pauses to drag in some air before starting again. "I don't know what Killian's story is and quite frankly, I don't give the fucks of a farmer's dozen. But there is one thing I do know."

MaryLou lowers her chin and raises her brows so her eyes stay glued to mine.

"What?" I say in a snarky tone, tired of her theatrics.

"He's biding his time until he can get you back."

I start shaking my head. I don't believe that's true. If Killian wanted me back, I wouldn't be sitting here discussing uprooting my entire existence and moving it for another man. I'd be married to him. "I don't—"

"Ah, ah, ah." She squishes her sticky finger into my lips, shutting me up.

"Hey!" I shove her dirty hand away and rub my mouth, frowning at the blackberry jam now smearing my chin.

"Again, that's your problem, Maverick. You always 'don't.' Do for once. *Do*," she emphasizes.

"Do," I repeat more to myself than her.

"Yeah. *Do*."

I stare at my lifelong friend who is telling me to pack up and move away from the only place I've known like it's just that simple.

And I suppose to MaryLou, it is. She always makes complicated deci-sions sound so rational and easy.

On the other hand, though, I think I always make them too hard.

"Quite the shindig," my mother states, her laugh tight. She's uncomfortable here. It's written all over her stiff posture and rigid spine. She's holding that glass of "house" wine in her hand with just the slightest hint of disgust. It hasn't escaped my notice she's not taken a sip, the quality far beneath her refined tastes. But hey...she's here and for that, I guess I should be grateful.

I let my gaze flow over the crowd at Peppy's. Kael rented out the place for the night and is paying for the entire party. Our last big hurrah before the move to Saint Paul next week.

"Yeah." I take a sip of my Jack and Coke, extra Jack. "Quite the shindig."

The last few weeks have been a whirlwind. For two days, after my talk with MaryLou, I pondered that one word of hers: *do*. Of anything, *that* one word hit me square in the chest. It hit and it stuck and I couldn't get rid of it. That one word started eating away at every excuse I had until they were nothing. Until it's as if they never existed and there was never any doubt at all.

I remembered how I felt freer than I had in forever that weekend Kael and I spent away from Dusty Falls. I recalled the peace that settled around me knowing we could walk the streets and just be us Kael and Maverick—a regular ol' married couple, instead of someone's brother or sister or daughter or shunned former lover.

Once I sorted through the betrayal I felt about Kael keeping his job hunt a secret, I knew the only decision I could make was to follow my husband. Why did I even doubt that? I *love* him. I want to have babies with him. I want a life with him and *only* him. But the most important thing is...I want him to be happy. Kael's waited patiently for me all this time and he deserves a life free of those goddamn chains Killian has cinched around him. And so do I.

After my epiphany, I wholeheartedly agreed to follow Kael wherever he wanted to go. Minnesota, Paris, London, The Maldives. I tried hard for the Maldives, trust me. Shoulder shrug. But the frigid winters of Minnesota it is.

"How is Kael doing?" my mom asks.

"Good. Yesterday was his last day at DSC. He starts his new job on Monday." To say he's been stressed would be an understatement. He's been working until ten or eleven every night. He promises me it won't be like that at Braham but I know how a new job works. It takes time to get up to speed, and time equates long days. But that's okay, too. I've been in contact with Mia several times and we're set to meet for cocktails on Tuesday night to discuss potential partnership in her bakery.

I've also discussed selling my baby, Cygne Noir Patisserie, to MaryLou. She's on the fence. She's nervous. I get it. I was nervous being a business owner myself. So for the time being, she's agreed to a raise to manage the day-to-day operations. We've posted an ad to hire someone to replace her. I'll eventually convince her buying it is her one and only option. I know Kael and I won't be back and I can't run a small business like that from afar.

"Any luck finding a place?"

"We have a few lined up to see next week." Until then, Braham is putting us up in the Ordway Suite at the Saint Paul Hotel, a stunning, upscale hotel that looks more like a castle on one side than a place to hang your hat at night. And the room? It's fantastical. I'll probably never want to leave.

"Are you excited?" I shuffle my attention from the throngs of people drinking and dancing and chatting to my mother. I look for derision or jealousy. I see none. I see only genuine concern for her daughter. And support of her decision.

"Nervous," I admit. Incredibly nervous. And while I know in my heart of hearts this is the right move for us, it still saddens me somewhat it's come to this. We're fleeing an entire life, shedding old skin, because of one person in five thousand. A needle in a haystack that keeps poking us no matter how much we wiggle around to dislodge it.

"I think it's the right decision, Maverick."

I'm almost stunned silent. I know it must be hard for her to see Kael leave her deceased husband's company. No matter what Kael's trying to lead me to believe, it's a great loss for DSC. "You do? Why?"

My mother, who has been avoiding eye contact with me during this whole conversation, connects her eyes to mine. In them, I see depth and years of experience waiting to be passed on to the next generation so we don't make the same mistakes. She smiles. It's soft and worldly and kind of motherly. Huh. "I know a lot of things, Maverick. And I know I've not done a good job of sharing them with you. But this...*this* I know is what you two need to bloom and grow into the couple you were always meant to be. Dad would have approved."

Shit. Those tears seem to be at the ready more and more lately. I blink them away, not wanting to bring the night down. "Thank you, Mom," is my husky response.

"Welcome, sweetie." Then she surprises me even more by giving me a hug. A real one. It's brief, but it includes full arms and body contact. Not a fake one with a double back pat and an inch between us.

When we break apart, a heavy arm swings around me, drawing me into an—eeeewwww—sweaty body. "Hey, sweet thang," a low voice rumbles in my ear.

"Hey J," I garble back, short of the air I need to talk properly because J Ton is crushing it from me.

"Where's your boy toy? We need him."

I groan. Karaoke time. "I don't know." In fact, I haven't seen Kael for quite some time.

The "Illians" arrived about an hour ago. Killian hovered over by the bar, ordering drink after drink. I tried to ignore him, I really did, but I felt his eyes all over me, like a thick film glazing my skin. I never did return his voice mail from the night Kael came home and upended my world. He's tried me countless times since. Even popped into the bakery, but Carol's now been schooled about Killian's surprise drop-ins. She told him I was "indisposed." He huffed and left.

But as I look around, not only do I not see Kael, I don't see the man we're both trying to escape. "Let me take a look around," I tell him. Then to my mother, "Be right back." I set down my nearly empty drink and take off through the crowd.

I push my way through the throngs and make it to the hallway leading to the restrooms. I stand on my tiptoes, giving me another inch, and scan the room. There are so many people here, it's like salmon swimming upstream. Everyone looks the same.

"Hey," I grab Leigh David, an old classmate of mine walking by. "Have you seen Kael...or Killian?" I add quickly. I have a feeling wherever Kael is I'll find Killian.

"Hey, Mavs. Congrats on the move. Sounds like a good gig."

"Yeah, yeah," I quickly agree. "Kael? Have you seen him?"

"Uh, yep. I think I saw him go out back with Killian." He hooks his thumb toward the emergency exit.

"Great." I pretend smile. "You having a good time?"

"Awesome. This is a great party."

Uhhhh...any *free* party is a great party. "Thanks," I say tritely, rushing toward the back door. I push it open, spilling into a back alley that's dimly lit.

The second I'm outside I hear them. Their voices stream from my left. They're heated, just shy of yelling. Exactly like the day of my father's burial. Their disembodied voices flow from around the corner.

It only takes about five steps before I've completely tuned them in. I push my back up against the wall, listening.

"It's over now. She needs to know," Killian growls.

"And what purpose would that serve?" Kael fires back.

I have to assume the "she" they're referring to is me. *Why is my heart racing, picking up pace while my ears strain to hear Killian's response?*

"She deserves the truth, Kael."

*What's over? What truth?*

"And what truth is that?" Kael parrots my thoughts.

"That this whole fucking thing was her father's doing!" he roars so loud my body vibrates.

Kael's laugh is sharp and short. "Her father's? No, Killian. It was *our* father's doing. And yours. Don't forget you wouldn't be here right now if you hadn't gotten Jillian pregnant in the first place. Richard may have pulled the trigger, but you loaded the gun, brother."

*What? Kael has to be mistaken.*

I expect Killian to deny it. Tell Kael he has no idea what he's talking about. Jillian was never pregnant with Killian's child. If she were she would have taken out an ad in the local paper to announce it.

He doesn't, though. He stays silent.

Suddenly my lungs feel weighted down with a metric ton of water.

*Jillian was pregnant? When?*

"Just what the fuck do you think she's going to do with all this now, Killian?" Kael contends vehemently. "Forgive us? We all have dirty hands here. You, me, Jillian, our parents. *Her* parents. For Christ's sake...Richard is dead! This shit is so far behind us, it would only hurt her at this point."

*What in the ever-living fuck is going on here?* I want to scream that I'm here, I'm here, I'm here! I want to charge around the corner and pound my fists into both of them until they stop talking in riddles and spill the secret it seems everyone knows but me.

Killian doesn't respond. For what seems like forever, all I hear are the sounds of cars driving by on Main Street, the occasional bois-terous drunken laugh, and the beat of my heart thudding so hard against my ribs I'm surprised they don't hear it, too. The silence we're all in screams at full volume. It's so loud I can hardly stand it.

I want to take another step, but I can't. My muscles are on lockdown. When Kael speaks his tenor drips with pure contempt. "You think if you tell her the truth you'll get her back? Don't you, you fucker?"

Killian's response is icy and even. "If you don't tell her, Kael, I swear to fucking God I will."

*Tell me? Tell me what? What, goddamn it? Just say it!*

I hear a scuffle. Shoes crunching against gravel. A thud, followed by the sound of breath heaving. "You're right about one thing. This *is* over. You do whatever the fuck you feel you have to do, Killian. I don't give a rat's naked ass. But you breathe a word about this to Maverick and *I* swear to fucking God, brother or not, I will ruin you. She's happy. She's finally fucking happy and you will *not* take that from her. You hear me?" Kael's voice is low and threatening, textured with menace.

"I'm already ruined. And you are not taking her from me." Killian's voice sounds husky...as if maybe his airway is being cut off.

This must be why Killian's been trying to reach me. I think back to his cryptic comments that day Kael was out of town so many months ago: *You think you want answers, but sometimes it's the truth that destroys, Small Fry, not the lies. I have tried protecting you my entire life and this...I'm sorry I couldn't protect you from this.*

When Kael responds to his brother, it's more of a growl than anything else. "She is *my* wife. Mine. Not yours. Get that through your thick skull, brother. And I can take her wherever the fuck I want."

"She should be *my* wife, not yours."

Catching air becomes nearly impossible. Heat crawls over every inch of my skin, pooling like liquid fire in the center of my chest.

My head is spinning. This is the first time since Killian stood in front of me with Jilly, announcing he was going to marry *her* instead of me, that he's admitted it should have always been me. Like we'd talked about. Like I always knew. Killian wanted *me* to be his wife, not Jillian.

Then why am I not? And what do our fathers have to do with any of this?

And other questions start creeping in, smothering out the ones before them. Equally important ones like: Is this move coincidental or strategically planned? Is it really about Kael and I starting a fresh life together or did Kael just want to get me out of town to keep some sort of sordid secret from me?

And the answers...they seem so fucking clear, it's as if I'm looking through a magnifying glass. Whatever it is Killian passionately wants me to know, Kael doesn't with equal fervor. Of course this was methodically planned. How could it not be? Kael all but just admitted it.

*We all have dirty hands here. You, me, Jillian, our parents. Her parents.*

I choke back a sob, stuffing my hand in my mouth.

What do I do? What the fuck am I supposed to do with this? I'm leaden, stuck in indecision. Turns out I don't have to decide. I cringe when a loud bellow floats from behind me. "Maverick, what are you doing out here?"

*Great fucking timing, Larry.*

"Shit," I hear Kael mutter. Seconds later, he appears from behind the brick, Killian on his heels. The rays from the lone streetlight hit them just right and I can make out every emotion they're wearing. Guilt, worry, and rage are written in the hard lines of their faces. We stand there staring at each other, my eyes bouncing back and forth between them. I ignore Larry when he brushes against my shoulder.

"Hey." Kael tries for lighthearted. Big fat fucking fail there. He takes a step toward me. I hold out my hand, palm facing him.

"What's going on?"

"Nothing," he answers evenly.

"Nothing? Really? *That's* your answer?" My blood pressure soars as my gaze shifts to Killian. He's working his jaw back and forth so hard he's probably wearing down the enamel on his teeth, but his gaze never wavers from mine. "What exactly is it time for me to know?" I ask him pointedly.

"Maverick—" Kael starts, but when I whip my attention back to him he shuts up quick.

Returning to Killian, I ask again. Almost beg, "Tell me, Killian. You owe me *that* much."

He hesitates, glancing over at Kael. "Everyone's out of sorts, Small Fry. It was nothing. Just a disagreement."

He's hedging his bets. Wondering how much I overheard. Well, fuck them both. I'm not leaving this spot, and neither are they until I get some goddamn answers.

"If that word—nothing—comes out of either of your mouths again, I swear to fucking God someone's going to get hurt," I say through gritted teeth. My fingers curl into my palms, the nails biting the thin skin.

"Uh, I think I'll just be going," I hear Larry worriedly say to my left. *Good call, Larry.* I don't bother responding. Neither does Kael or Killian. Then the three of us face off. I don't plan on moving a fucking inch until I get the truth.

Kael takes another subtle step toward me, his baritone voice smooth and coaxing. "Mavs..." He looks like he's ready to crack. Well so am I. I feel as if I'm going to split right down the middle.

"Please don't," I whisper. The dam I've been using to hold back fresh tears breaks and water gushes over its broken walls. "Don't lie to me. Not now. Please, Kael."

His face pales. Even in the low light I watch the blood drain out of it. Then his posture slumps. His head hangs. I think I even see his eyes glisten before he hides them from me. In fact, I know I do. When my attention shifts over to Killian, he just looks resigned. And sad. So very, very sad.

*The Black Swan Theory.*

According to Nassim Nicholas Taleb, a small number of Black Swan events explains almost everything in our world, from the success of ideas and religions to the dynamics of historical events, to elements of our own personal lives. Sit back and take stock of your own life. How many things went according to plan?

Life is unusual. Extreme events occur. They are unpredictable and impactful and our human brains work overtime trying to explain those phenomena away.

That's exactly what I'm trying to do this very second. Rationalize why I know the two men I love most in this world are about to shatter it to fucking shards.

It's right then that I knew Killian's betrayal in marrying my sister wasn't my Black Swan event. I thought it was, but it's not. It was simply a byproduct. It's this, right here. Whatever they've hidden from me is bigger than that. Far bigger and far, far reaching. So far reaching in fact, it was wholly unpredictable and its impact will be felt a lifetime.

By all of us.

chapter TWENTY SEVEN

three years and eleven months ago

*Kael*

**K**illian is back. Fucking Killian is back. Here. In Dusty Falls. At DSC. I watched him walk by my office. He didn't turn his head. Didn't stop and say hi. I didn't even know he was coming. But that's not a surprise. Killian and I aren't exactly tight anymore.

The fact that he's walking through the halls of DSC is not a good sign. He's been gone just over four months and if he's meeting with Richard DeSoto, it can only mean one thing.

He's coming back.

Fuck.

Fuck.

Fucking fuck.

If Richard hires him again, I'm outta here. I may not have Maverick. I may never have her. In fact, I realize now that's probably always been a pipe dream. Unrequited love and all. But I simply cannot stomach sitting day after torturous day watching the woman I love be with my brother. I can't know she's in his bed, wearing his ring, bearing his children. I just fucking can't.

She's curled around my every thought and feeling, so one would think I would have gone after her the second the sole of Killian's shoe hit the first step on that 747. Well, one would be wrong. He may have been out of her sight, but it was crystal clear he wasn't out of her mind.

In fact, I've been spending less and less time with her because I just can't stand to be around her anymore and not tell her how much her snubs are slowly killing me. I can't beg her to choose me when I know she wants him, but I also can't keep these feelings of desperate love I have for her inside me anymore. It's too fucking hard. And if I tell her, I lose her. Period. And I can't handle that either. I would sacrifice everything *I* want for *her* wants just to keep her in my life, because the view without her in it is unbearable, but with Killian back...

...that all changes.

Acid pushes its way up my throat. It tastes of hate and failure and loss. I look around my spacious office, taking in everything I've worked for the last two years. It's all meaningless. Accolades. Promotions. Money. There are a dozen DSCs out there and I can easily get picked up by any of them. Or by another company for that matter. I didn't return to my hometown to be Richard DeSoto's lap dog. That was the last goddamn thing I wanted. No. I came back to Dusty Falls for one reason and one reason only.

And now that reason is irrelevant. Lost to me forever.

I've known this for months—ever since Maverick moved back from college and started secretly seeing Killian. It's just taken me this long to accept it. It took seeing my brother again just now to shove that goddamn Dear John letter straight into my heart so I have no choice but to read the words I've been avoiding for years.

Maverick is in love with my brother. Not me.

It fucking kills me—decimates me—but I have to let her go. If Maverick wants Killian, why shouldn't she have him? If he makes her happy, who am I to step in between that? All I want—all I've *ever* wanted—is to see her happy. I hoped it would be with me, prayed it so many fucking times I've lost count. But if it's not, it's not. So be it. I will accept it like a man. Killian was right all those years ago. I'm apparently not what she wants. He is.

But I sure as Christ don't have to sit on the sidelines and have it shoved down my throat daily either. No...I'm fucking out of Dusty Falls. Tonight I'm polishing up my resume. I'll put a few feelers out and get on with my life. Hell, I may not even wait that long. I mentally calculate how much I have in savings. Probably enough to get by a few months.

Yeah. Yeah, it's the right thing. Tomorrow I'll give my two weeks to Richard; then I'm dust in the wind.

Mind made up and with lungs so taut I feel I might choke, I try turning my attention back to the contract in front of me. The words blur together. Just when I get them in focus, they blend again. In the very definition of insanity, I keep trying this exact same thing, but the end result is the same. The squawk of my phone a while later is a welcome reprieve from my futility. "Yeah?" I say blandly when I pick up the handset.

"Kael, I need you in my office."

"Now?" I ask, confusion drawing my features tight I'm sure.

"Now."

Richard hangs up before I respond. A short walk later I'm standing at his open door and the tension pouring from his cozy corner office is so thick it's stifling. It sticks to my suit, sitting as heavy as humidity. He rests behind his desk, a scowl on his face. Not surprisingly Killian sits stiffly in a guest chair. What does take me aback though is that our pops is in the other.

"What's up?" I ask, my gaze bobbing between the three of them.

He nods to the door. "Close it and have a seat. I need you to draw up some papers."

"Papers?" I practically snarl. *Of course, you fucking idiot. Employment papers. Well, Richard, this is my last task at DSC, because I've just decided I can't even stay here another day let alone another fourteen.*

Reeling my emotions in is like grappling with a twenty-five-pound bass. I manage, but barely. Doing as he asks, I shut the four of us in together and pull up a chair between my father and brother, careful to stay out of choking distance of Killian.

When I've sat, Richard looks to my father. "Arnie, do you want to explain or should I?"

Now I'm confused as all hell. What would Pops have to do with

Killian working here? All eyes fall to my father and now that I look closely, he's positively ashen. All his color is gone. His face is drawn. His eyes are broad and desolate. The hair on my arms stands on end.

This meeting isn't about Killian at all.

"Pops, what's wrong?"

"I, uh—" He stops and swallows so hard I hear it. He holds Richard's angry stare. Those two have been friends as long as I can remember; only they look anything but friendly right now. I look at Killian and his gaze is not on Pops but on the floor. His teeth are grinding together and he's gripping the arms of his chair so hard, the wood may crack. Whatever it is they need to tell me, it's big. It's bad. And I'm the last to know.

I reach over and take my father's hand. "Whatever it is, Pops, just say it. It's okay."

Killian snorts. I ignore him, focusing on Pops. Tears well in the eyes of the man I've looked up to my entire life. My role model. My teacher. My protector. My mentor and now my friend. But when he starts telling me why I'm sitting in Richard DeSoto's office being asked to draw up legal papers, I go into shock.

"I took something that wasn't mine to take," he starts.

"That's an understatement," Killian mumbles under his breath.

I slide my gaze to Killian then back to Pops. My father is about the most honest man I know. There's no way what he just said is true. "What do you mean you took something that wasn't yours to take? What?"

"He stole over twenty million dollars from DSC, that's what," Killian sneers when my father clams up.

"He *what*?" I stammer, not believing a word out of his mouth right now.

"Yeah, you know. Keeping up with the Joneses and all that shit," my brother growls.

"You're lying," I throw down, pushing up from my chair. "This is all some big mistake. A problem in accounting is all. We all know

Margie is completely incompetent." I start pacing, eyeing Killian who doesn't have a sympathetic fleck in his hard stare. Richard is an exact reflection of my brother and when my gaze finally lands back on my father, I see it's all true. Every goddamn word of it.

They aren't lying to me.

There isn't an accounting mistake.

My mind races over vacations, cars, clothes, the years of Catholic education and, as the CFO, the access my father had to cook the books any way he wanted.

Fuck.

Holy. Fuck.

"Pops," I croak, pleading for this not to be true.

"I'm sorry, son. I screwed up."

"You *screwed* up?" I spit.

Somehow, I find myself back in my chair, still staring at my father. I rewind the last few minutes. Replay them again. Repeat and repeat.

*Oh my fucking God.*

This is not happening. It's a nightmare. I'm about to wake up in a cold sweat, my heart pounding, my blood pumping fast and furious. But I don't. I remain glued to this spot, stuck in a living, breathing nightmare.

This is real. My father is a criminal. A white-collar *criminal*. Then a thought hits me. "You're going to go to jail. Fuck, you'll have *federal* charges brought against you."

We deal with government contracts. A huge chunk of our business is county, state, and federal contracts, which means he can be indicted under *federal* law. Penalties will be stiffer. They'll make an example out of him. This scandal will rock Dusty Falls. It will be national. It will be talked about on the nightly news and featured on shows like 20/20 and *Nightline* for years. Our family will be dragged through the mud. Our name ruined. My mother...*good God.* My sweet, innocent mother. This will destroy her.

And DeSoto Construction? Jesus Christ. This will sink the company Richard DeSoto has built on blood and sweat and the backs of this community. Not another government entity will hire him again. Ever. He'll be blackballed. Bankrupt within two years. Gossip will travel through generations, embellished with each new tell.

"No one is going to jail," Richard belts. "Outside of these four walls, no one will find out about this. Arnie is taking early retirement effective immediately. Health issues. Killian is returning to DSC and will work off your father's debt, plus interest. You'll draw up an employment contract for Killian. You will find a way to make sure that contract holds Killian's feet to the fire and stands up in court but doesn't disclose enough to land all of us in a goddamn prison cell for life."

I gape at Richard DeSoto, unable to believe my ears. "You want me to bury embezzlement? A *criminal* act?"

He doesn't respond, but his silence is all I need. Of course he does. He's thought through all the ramifications just as I have. This will not only ruin both our families, it will crush Dusty Falls, too. Countless people rely on DSC for their livelihoods and if he falls, Dusty Falls will become a virtual ghost town. My father stole twenty mil from him yet he's letting him off the hook, unscathed. But someone *is* paying the price, aren't they?

My brother.

"What are the terms?" Christ almighty, I can't even believe I'm asking this.

"The debt is paid in full when he's hit forty million in sales. So if that takes him two years or ten, well..."

"Forty million?" Twice the amount my father stole?

"It was Killian's offer to keep your father from spending the rest of his days rotting in a jail cell." Richard glances at Killian waiting for a response. Killian just nods.

What are the symptoms of shock exactly? Cold, clammy skin? Ragged breathing? Confusion, anxiety, nausea? Sweat running down your balls? Well, check, check, fucking check. Check all the damn boxes. I'm there.

"You agreed to this?" I finally ask my brother.

For the longest time, he just stares at me. He's not back here for Maverick at all. He's back because our father fucked over his employer and my older brother is bailing him out the only way he knows how. He wants to be back here about as much as I want him to be. I see that now.

I can't believe we've found ourselves in this situation. Never, in a million years, could I have predicted this. Neither could he.

"Yes. Draw up the papers, Kael."

"But—"

"Do it," he barks. Then his tone softens when he reaches out and clasps my wrist. "Please. Just do it."

For a few seconds, I'm taken back in time to when I idolized my older brother. He was smarter. Driven. Loyal. He bullied me as all older brothers do, but he also protected me and loved me fiercely. I miss that. I miss him. But with Maverick between us, we can never be the same again.

So I nod. Just nod, then choke, "Okay. I'll do it." Fuck, I am about to commit a crime myself. Jesus H. Christ. *I* could go to prison. Be disbarred. Spend years being some big dude's little bitch. I scrub my hands down my face, trying to absorb what it is I'm about to do. When I lift my eyes to my pops, he sees my internal struggle and I see his remorse. Right now, it's not nearly enough.

"There is just one more thing, Kael," Richard says as I'm numbly making my way toward the door.

I pivot but don't speak. I just wait for it.

"I need you to draw up a prenuptial agreement."

I practice corporate law. Contracts, securities, taxes, intellectual property rights, zoning. *Those* are things I'm familiar with. A lawyer with a family law background would be more acquainted with all issues marital. I studied it, of course, I had to, but I have no practical experience with it.

"A prenup? For who?"

"For Killian and my daughter..."

I swear I stop breathing. My lungs are not working. My body can't move. I'm having a hard time concentrating as my ears ring with denial. But then I'm saved at the same time I'm thrown off balance when he utters Jillian's name instead of Maverick's.

"Jillian?" I clarify. "Not..." I stop myself just in time. "*Jillian?*"

"Yes. Killian and Jillian are getting married." Richard beams. As if this is common knowledge we all should know and be thrilled about.

I snort, letting slip, "Since when?" And that question is directed smack at my brother. Now he knows I know. About Maverick. About their sordid affair. About his unintended betrayal.

"Jillian and Killian are expecting," Richard adds.

"Expecting? Expecting *what?*" I am seriously clueless here.

"Why a baby, of course."

"A baby?" I realize I'm repeating everything Richard is telling me, but god damn. I am in total disbelief over everything that's happened in the last ten minutes. When I try to meet Killian's eyes, this time, he looks away.

I am blown the fuck away right now. Killian cheated on Maverick with her sister? He's expecting a baby? *With Jillian?* And now he's going to *marry* her?

Fucking hell.

I have a thousand unnamed feelings rushing through my body right now. So many I can't catch them all, but the one I do latch on to as it spins by is fury. Hot, raging fury.

That cheating bastard. Regardless of whether I wanted to acknowledge it or not, Maverick is in love with Killian and he just threw her away like she didn't matter.

He cheated on her.

With. Her. Sister.

Mother. *Fucker.*

I walked down the hallway just minutes ago ready to let him have everything I've ever wanted because that's what *Maverick* wants.

And even though it isn't me, I want her to have everything her heart desires.

But he doesn't deserve her.

He obviously never has.

"Congratulations, Killian. That's the best news I've heard all day." That brings him back. And we hold each other's eyes for what feels like a full unbroken minute. His anger matches mine. "I'll get to work on those documents right away, Richard."

I walk out of that meeting, those muddled emotions now untwining. The rage is still raw and fiery. I want to shake my father. I want to demand he tell me just what the hell he thinks he was doing stealing from his best friend and why he's now making criminals out of all of us.

But more than anything I want to punch Killian's fucking face in because this will absolutely crush Maverick. The last thing I want is to see her hurt by anyone but especially by this. Betrayed by her lover and her own sister? Jesus Christ. I can't even fathom. No one deserves that.

Along with anger, though, I feel a whole host of other things.

Heartbreak.

Disbelief.

Grief.

Shame.

Gratitude.

But most of all...*hope*. Hope: A new breath. A fresh start. A prayer that was answered at the very moment I decided to throw in the towel.

Could this be a new chance for me? For us? With Killian no longer available, is it possible I can get her to see me as more than just her best friend?

I don't know, but I'm sure as hell gonna try because as much as this will crush her, I have been handed a gift and I am not squandering it. I'll be there to comfort Maverick, to get her through what

I'm sure will be the worst time of her life, but *hope* that my chance with her is not entirely lost is already ballooning up.

I'll give her time. Of course I'll give her all the time she needs to put her shattered heart back together, but then I'm going in. And I'm not going to give up until she's in the safety of both my arms and my heart.

I will never hurt her like Killian. Never.

chapter TWENTY EIGHT
five weeks ago

*Maverick*

I t's been two weeks since Kael left Dusty Falls to start his new
job. Two weeks apart. Two weeks of uncertainty, our future in
limbo. Two weeks, and I still have no idea what I'm going to do.

Caught red-handed, Kael and Killian stood in that shadowed
alleyway and divulged their whole sordid, un-fucking-believable
story. About the lies, the deceit, the illegal and immoral acts they both
participated in. In some sick way, I understand why they both did it,
but facts are facts.

And the facts are: Kael lied to me. He deceived me for years. He
confessed he knew about Killian and my sister all this time. Even
drew up a prenup. He *knew* how devastated I was about that
wedding, yet he still said nothing. I don't know how to forgive him for
that. All I've been doing is soul-searching, but there are no cut-and-
dry answers to be found. My trust is stripped. I don't know how to
tape it back together.

Everyone who is supposed to love me lied to me. Kael, Killian, my
father. Even Jillian. Killian confessed that Jilly also knew about the
embezzlement, so she lied, too. Even my mother was in on it. The
only innocent in this whole scandal is Eilish Shepard. Both Kael and
Killian assure me she doesn't know a thing. I believe them. They've
both risked jail time to protect their father. It's not a stretch to think
they'd go to the ends of the earth to do the same for their mother.

"Hey, did I interrupt?" I ask when she answers.

"Uh, no." MaryLou's heavy breathing on the other end is a dead
giveaway. The only exercise she gets is bedroom aerobics.

"Why'd you even answer the phone? Go back to making babies."

"I'm not—" *Crack.*

"Did he just slap your ass?"

"Knock it off," she yells in a loud whisper. Larry chuckles and MaryLou squeals.

"We'll talk in the morning," I tell her. I need to get off the phone before I hear moans or the hum of a vibe in the background.

I'm getting ready to hang up when she says, "Larry can wait. I'll be over in ten."

I sigh. Do I want her to leave her husband with blue balls? Self-ishly, yes. But I'm also not even sure why I'm calling. I'm talked out. I'm thought out. I'm all emotioned out. There's nothing left to do but make a decision. One I can't seem to make. The taste of betrayal is bitter and hard to get rid of.

I glance out my kitchen window, staring into the dark night. "Nah. I'm not even home. I'm driving around."

"You sure, Mavricky? We can meet somewhere."

"No. Forget it. See you in the morning."

"Okay. If you're sure?"

"I'm sure."

We hang up. I stand there for a few minutes, thinking that I should be in bed. It's close to ten and I have to be up at four in the morning. But the emptiness of this house and my heart is weighing on me so heavy, I feel as if I'm drowning under its oppression.

Scooping up my keys from the counter, I find myself in my car, driving purposefully through town. Then, parked in a familiar grassy place, I make a phone call and wait, while I reminisce on a night I have no business replaying, waiting for someone I have no business waiting for...

---

*"We shouldn't be here."*

*"This is exactly where we should be," I tell him quietly. We've*

been zigzagging around us too long. It's time. I scoot across the bench seat until you couldn't fit a piece of paper between us.

"Someone could see us."

"There's not another car in the whole park," I retort. "And besides, it's dark and we're so far back from the road no one will see."

"Maverick," he hisses when my hand goes to the growing bulge in his jeans. I grip it. I stroke it. I get wet between my legs and my mouth waters. I start to draw down the zipper, the metal teeth separating to reveal a cock so big it looks shrink-wrapped in his black briefs.

I don't look at him, instead keeping my attention focused on the prize begging to be released. I want to, though. I want to look into his eyes as I take his cock in my hand, in my mouth. I want to see them haze over with his want for me as he swells and explodes. But I don't. Because if I do, my fear is he'll stop this. And I'm tired of stopping. Tonight he's going to be mine. If I have my way, he'll be mine forever.

His breaths have picked up now. They're quick and shallow. His head thuds softly against his headrest. He's not stopping me, so I keep going. I slip my hand inside the elastic band of his underwear and boldly slide the briefs down over his hardness until it stands tall and proud.

"God," I mutter.

"Fuuuuck," he breathes at the same time when I wrap my fingers around him.

He's thick and huge and a heavy vein runs the length of his underside. I trace it from the base and his dick jumps in my hand. When I reach the tip that looks like the top of a mushroom, I swipe my thumb over the glistening bead of wetness leaking out.

"Maverick, Jesus Christ." His hand fists in my hair. He yanks my head back and slams his mouth onto mine. He shoves his tongue inside, sweeping in long, demanding strokes. He bites my bottom lip until it hurts so fucking good I'm moaning his name. He takes and takes, dominating me in the way I've always imagined. Then he holds me still, his savage eyes drilling into me. "Put my cock in your mouth."

*I want that. I do, but damn, I've waited nearly twenty-three years for him. For this.* "I want to feel you inside me."

"And I will be inside you, Small Fry, but I need to sink inside that mouth first. I've fantasized a thousand times over the years of you sucking me off. Don't make me beg."

*God. His confession. It dances all over my skin, chills joining the party. The side of my lip twitches in play.* "I think I might like to hear you beg for once."

*His eyes hold fast to mine and he whispers a simple plea I'll never, ever forget. I'll always remember the way his lips pressed together when he said it. I'll hear the gravelly, eager vibration of his voice when I drift off to sleep at night. And the way I feel everything he's feeling for me when he sincerely utters,* "Please," *will be branded on my soul for life.*

*He guides my head to his lap. His moves are slow and gentle and he keeps his hand wound around my hair as I grip him tighter in anticipation.*

*I don't tease. I go in with purpose. I wrap my lips around his girth and push my way downward until he's as far as I can take him. I drag back up, working my tongue against his velvety flesh. I do this over and over again, working him into a frenzy. Until I'm drawing those moans and entreaties from his lips I've been dying to hear my whole life. He stiffens. The muscles in his thighs harden. I know he's seconds from releasing down my throat when he uses my hair as leverage, yanking me off.*

"Wha—"

*A fiery kiss ashes that thought. His hands start tearing at my blouse. It's over my head. My bra is off. He's ravenous, sucking at my neck, my nipples, and down my quivering belly while he works my shorts and panties down my legs until I'm completely naked. He rids himself of his own shirt and has a condom rolled over his hard length before I can count to five. His own shorts are in a pool under his feet, along with his briefs, and then, with my back against the leather seat, he's hovering over me, gloriously bare. I run my hands all over him,* loving the feel of his muscles bunching and flexing as I pass over them. God in heaven, he's gorgeous.

"The first time I come with you, it will be together," he tells me passionately as he works his dick between my wet folds and starts to push inside.

This is happening. This is really happening.

"Oh shit, Killian." My eyes want to roll in my head as he works his way in. I want to weep with how fantastic he feels stretching my tight tissues until he fits as if we were made just for this. But I don't do either. We stay locked on each other, neither of us able to break away.

"Goddamn, you feel good. So good, Maverick. So wet, so tight. So...fuck." His voice is strained, contradicting his movements. He's slow and purposeful, lighting each nerve ending on fire as he inches in and out at a frustrating pace. I can tell he's holding back. I can tell because his body is shaking with the effort.

"Fuck me. Hard." I want him to let go. Take me. Possess me.

His dark gaze widens a second before he drives back in, his hips slapping roughly against mine, making me gasp and want more. But instead of moving he holds himself still. "I'm not fucking you, Maverick."

"But—"

Cupping my cheeks, he puts a thumb over my mouth. His sweet words make me cry. "I'm going to make love to you slowly, Small Fry. I've waited too long to take you like it's a meaningless act. This means more to me than you can possibly know. I'm going to worship your body, love your heart, own your soul, and make sure you remember this night for the rest of your life."

It's not possible to ever forget, I want to say. Instead, "I love you, Killian," breaks through along with a small sob. I've never felt as loved as I do right now. Or as happy.

He presses his lips to mine, kissing me as slow as he makes love to me. "I love you, Maverick. I have always loved you."

"You okay?" he asks, sliding inside my car. The door shuts with a resounding click and the moment it does, I feel his presence suck up the entire space in my small vehicle. My stomach flips over a couple of times. I begin to breathe a little harder.

"Yeah," I reply, now positively short on breath.

He stares, trying to figure out why I've called him. Why I asked him to come. Why we're *here*, of all places.

*What are you doing, Maverick?*

"I need some air."

I hop out, not bothering to see if he's followed. I walk around the front of my car and lean against the hood. It's still warm to the touch. It didn't take him long to get here. I listen to the crickets stroke their legs together, along with the smooth rush of the river not far away.

Killian steps beside me, careful to leave an appropriate amount of space, whatever that is. A state away may not even be appropriate enough.

"How's the new job?"

"I don't know. He's giving me space." We've texted a few times, but other than one short talk we had a few nights ago, which may have prompted me to come here tonight, I haven't talked to Kael since he left. I spent Saturday night at MaryLou's and waited to go home on Sunday until I knew Kael had left for the cities. I also haven't seen or spoken to Killian since that night.

"What am I doing here, Maverick?"

I don't know. I don't fucking know. "I didn't know who else to call."

His exhale is heavy as he reaches for my hand. His fingers curl over mine. They feel warm. Reassuring. I shouldn't let him touch me. I should be with Kael right now. In Saint Paul working things out between us. I should be anywhere but here. Secluded. In the dark of Harbor Park, alone with a man I still care too much about, in the exact same spot we consummated our relationship.

Stupidity at its finest, right here.

"MaryLou busy?"

"Yes," I answer quietly. She's fucking her husband Fifty-Shades style trying to get the little swimmers to latch on to her elusive eggs. She's probably inverted as we speak.

His question is expected and thick with anxiety. "How do I make things right between us, Small Fry?"

Hmm. I wish I knew.

From where we're perched, we have a perfect view of the Swinging Bridge, one of the oldest suspension bridges in Iowa. I spent a lot of time in this park. On that bridge. Most of my friends refused to cross it when they were little because the sway scared them. The more people on the bridge, the more sway. But not me. I craved the freedom I felt when I was swinging from side to side, even if it was subtle. Now as an adult, when I cross that bridge, it doesn't hold near the allure it used to when I was little. It seems small and functional, not imposing and potentially life ending.

"Do you remember when Kael and I jumped off suicide cliff?" Suicide cliff is just on the other side of the Swinging Bridge. It's the only way to get to the high cliffs that tower above the Keg River about forty feet.

Killian chuckles lowly. "Yeah, I remember."

He was livid. Threatened to take me over his knee and spank my ass red if I jumped. Little did he know that only fueled my fire. I was just thirteen at the time. Kael was sixteen. Killian eighteen. It was one of the last things I did with Killian before he left for college that August.

"You were so mad."

He's quiet for quite a few beats. His hand leaves mine as he crosses one arm over the other. "I still had nightmares of you drowning, Maverick. Of pushing air into your water-filled lungs. That horrifying shade of blue on your lips. Of how stiff your limbs were. Christ, if I had it my way, you'd never have even taken a bath again."

I laugh, but he doesn't. I turn my head to study his profile. He's dead serious. I never stopped to think about how my near death affected him. The gravity of that day hits me hard. "I'm sorry, Killian. I had no idea."

"Fuck, if Kael hadn't insisted we go that way, then..." He lets that little newsflash hang. I never, ever knew that. I didn't know how they stumbled across me that day. I'm stunned to learn that although Killian may have pulled me from the water, *Kael* was ultimately responsible for saving me. I wonder why he never mentioned it?

I'm stuck in that memory until Killian's comment brings me back to him, "You're always so fucking stubborn. About everything. But thank God you were. I'm convinced that's the only reason you didn't die that day."

I flash a smile, his backhanded compliment making my blood heat. "Like knows like I guess."

He fights a smile. He loses. When he slides his eyes my way, my breath catches. He's still as beautiful in the moonlight tonight as he was the night he told me he loved me. The night he made good on his promise and we shattered together. The same night he stole all of me, some parts of which he still has.

Suddenly I feel overwhelmingly sad.

"Will you tell me why?"

That panty-melting smile drops like it's hot. "Why what, Maverick?" He pretends he doesn't know what I'm asking, but he does.

I decide this is it. If he doesn't tell me this time, I'm not asking again. I'll go to my grave never understanding why a night of whispered promises ended up the broken mess it is today.

Maybe this is why I called. Maybe this is what I need so I can saw through the last vestiges of that cord. Maybe I need this before I can fix what's wrong with Kael and me. I decide, either way, tonight is my closure.

"Why did you cheat on me with Jillian? Why didn't you love me enough?"

His muscles tighten. His tongue darts out to wet his lips. He drags in a huge lungful air. He turns away from me to stare into the darkness ahead. It's the same thing he's done every time I've asked. I count the seconds as they go by until I get to 120.

Do you know how agonizingly long it can take 120 seconds to pass? Torturously, endlessly slow. So slow, in fact, you feel each crack in your heart as it keeps time with the ticks of the second hand.

Well...that's that.

Pursing my lips, I push myself from the car and start toward the driver's side but his low voice freezes me in place. "I didn't cheat on you, Maverick."

Then it fires me up. My laugh is cutting and nasty. I pivot back and practically fly into a rage, moving forward until I'm right in his face. "Is that so?"

He doesn't move a hair. "That's so."

"You're a fucking liar, Killian. Not only are you a cheater, you're a goddamn liar, too. I overheard you and Kael in the alleyway that night. I heard every fucking word." I stop and wipe a tear that had the audacity to wet my face.

"You don't know what you heard."

I shove him. Two hands on his chest pushing so hard he's falling backward. But in a flash, he rights himself and my wrists are shackled between us. He's squeezing so tight I wince.

"You got her pregnant." God *damn*, that hurt to say.

His chest rises and falls fast. His eyes are practically feral. "You don't know what you're talking about."

"You didn't deny it."

Silence.

"You didn't deny it," I repeat. In my mind, that went differently. I wanted it to be forceful, demanding. It came out weak and pathetic and all croaky instead.

"Maverick, please. Don't do this."

"Just say it." I feel his heart racing beneath the palm of my hand. "I loved you, Killian. I waited for you. I wanted to marry you. I thought you wanted the same things I did. The same life I did."

"I did," he tells me with an impassioned plea. It's so ripe with longing and truth, I almost believe him. "Fuck...I *still* do."

My head starts shaking. It's violent and jerky. I try to twist out of his hold before the bone-deep sorrow I feel inside unravels me. He only pulls me closer, tighter.

"Liar," I whisper hoarsely, my muscles starting to weaken and fail. "You're a liar. A goddamn liar," I mumble into his chest as I let my head drop. He wraps his arms around me and hangs on as I wet his shirt with my anguish.

"The baby wasn't mine, Maverick," he says softly into my hair as he places his lips to my crown. "I didn't have sex with Jillian."

"Then why?" I ask, numb all over. What he's saying makes no sense. Do I even care what the answer is now? It doesn't make any difference. "Why did you marry her?" I ask again anyway.

His chest expands deep a couple of times. "The baby was my father's."

I jerk back. He lets me lean away but he doesn't let me go. "What?"

"The baby was my father's," he says slower this time. So slow it sounds muddled.

Ohmygod. Oh my... "*What*—?"

"It's true."

Jillian was pregnant with Arnie's kid?

"Did he...did he..." Oh my God...*did he*—

"No, Maverick. If he'd have raped her, he'd be rotting in a concrete cell right now. I'd have made sure of it."

"Then it was consensual?" What the ever-loving fuck? Jillian was having an *affair* with Arnie Shepard? Mind. Completely. Blown.

"Yes," he grits through clenched teeth.

"Did you know?" I gasp sharply. "Is that why you went to Florida?"

"Fuck no, I didn't know. You think I would have let that continue under my nose?"

"No, I...of course not."

"I went to Florida for exactly the reasons I told you. I needed to be my own man, Maverick. Make my way without either of our fathers' interference. I was drowning here under them. I was doing well for myself there. One minute I was making plans for us and the next my whole fucking world was in ruins around me."

I roll this all around in my head. It's a jumbled mess and I'm still confused. "I don't understand, Killian. I don't understand why you didn't just let your father's due come to him? He stole from my father. He had an affair with a girl less than half his age. A girl who was like a daughter, for heaven's sake. Why were you protecting him?"

"Why do you think?"

I say the only thing that makes sense. "Eilish?"

He nods. "Fuck knows my father didn't deserve it, but I just couldn't do that to her, Small Fry. She had a fucked childhood and my pops was all she had. For better, for worse, he was it. He was her world."

I remember their story well. It was one Eilish told me often. How they met when Arnie studied abroad one summer in Ireland. She came from a poor family. Her dad was an abusive alcoholic. Her mother long gone. She worked three jobs trying to make ends meet but her father would drink and gamble it all away. Arnie strolled into a pub she waitressed at one night and according to them both, it was love at first sight. She told me many times over how he saved her from a life of destitution. They married six short weeks after meeting and when he returned to the states, he brought her with him. She was eighteen; he was twenty.

Killian straightens and drops his hold on me, pacing toward the river. I follow him. We stand on the bank looking down into the black waters below and I wait for him to be ready to tell me the whole story.

"Jillian called me in an absolute panic one night. Said she was in Pensacola and needed to see me. I picked her up and brought her back to my place. After a couple hours, she finally calmed down enough to tell me everything. Their affair had been brief. She regretted it. So did he. But then she missed her period and Richard found the pregnancy test because she was stupid enough to take it when she was at your parents' house." He stops and scrubs his face a few times with his hands. "She panicked. He demanded to know whose it was and she said the first person that popped into her mind."

"You," I mutter.

"Yeah, me. And you know, for all her flaws, your sister was not about to go against her beliefs and abort that baby. She was scared to death, but she wanted to keep it. I respected her for that, even if I was angry as fuck at what she did. At what *he* did."

I think about Jillian having to handle that situation virtually alone. I can imagine the pressure from my father to marry and not tarnish the DeSoto name with a bastard child. He was old-school. I can also imagine how backed into a corner she must have felt not wanting to displease our parents. I find myself feeling a smidge sorry for her, even if it was her own doing.

"Anyway, I told her we'd work something out, but that I wasn't marrying her because I loved you."

"You told her that?" I ask, my heart beating a little faster.

"Yes."

Empathy? Yeah...that was short-lived.

"A few days later, I get a call from Richard. They'd apparently been investigating my father for almost a year. He told me I had two choices: he would turn everything over to a federal prosecutor or I could come back to DSC, do the right thing by marrying Jillian, and he'd conveniently bury the evidence."

"My father blackmailed you?" I ask in utter disbelief, the bile in my stomach churning.

"He pressured me, let's put it that way." He turns fully toward me now, addressing me directly. "I could have said no, Maverick. I could have said no and watched everything unfold. Saw my father go to jail. DSC would have gone up in flames, the scandal too much for them to handle. I was so pissed at the position your father and Jillian put me in, I almost did. I almost called his bluff. But then I thought of the fallout. How it would impact innocent people, including you and my mother and I knew I could either carry the weight of all that chaos or suck it up and just make the whole fucking thing go away with some conditions of my own."

"Why didn't you just tell me all of this?"

"You don't know how many times I sat in front of your house at night wanting to bust down the door and do just that. But, fuck...I was committing a *crime*, Maverick. I couldn't drag you in on that."

My gaze falls. Reluctantly, I understand. I chew on my lip and push around the dirt pile underneath my feet. "Why didn't she rub it in my face?"

He knows I'm asking about the pregnancy. She certainly rubbed their marriage in my face every opportunity she got so there had to be a reason she didn't with the baby.

"I threatened not to go through with it. I needed time to think. I wanted to be the one to break it to you. I could never find the right words. Then..."

His eyes glisten in the moonlight. They're tears. It's not for Jillian, though, I know that.

"When did she miscarry?" This is the part I'm not getting. They were engaged six months before they married.

"Two and a half months before the wedding."

"Then why did you go through with it? The baby was the only reason you were marrying her, right?"

He waits for the light to go on. When it does, it's blinding. "You were stuck."

"Yep," he agrees. "The paperwork was already signed. If I didn't marry Jillian, it nullified my employment contract with DSC. If I divorced her before the terms of my contract were satisfied, it nullified it. The only way I could successfully leave both DSC and your sister was to hit that magic sales goal as fast as fucking possible."

A memory surfaces. One I need an answer to. "So that day in the kitchen at my parents you told me you were close. That's what you meant?"

I think he shuffles closer. I'm not sure. I know his voice drops. "Yes."

My feet move a couple inches forward. "Then what would you have done?" I ask lowly. The headlights of a car rounding the curve briefly illuminate us. We both stay quiet as it passes and keeps going.

"I would have been free to leave DSC."

"Would you have?"

He's close enough now, his hand lands on my hip. His thumb starts circling around my hipbone as he answers, "Yes."

"What about Jilly?" I rest a palm on the arm holding me.

His breath scatters over my face. It's warm and smells of rum. "I was going to divorce her. She knew this was temporary. She's always known."

"Does she love you?"

"Yes," he states matter-of-factly.

"So when my father died..."

"I already had divorce papers drawn up. Two days before his death I'd closed that deal. Richard knew I was leaving. So did Jilly."

My head is reeling right now. That explains her sudden behavior change. I wait for the empathy to return. It doesn't.

"And Kael?"

Killian's body tenses. He winds his other arm around me and draws me flush to him so I have to crane my neck. "What about him?" He sounds angry, just like Kael does when I mention Killian's name.

"Did he know you were divorcing Jilly and leaving DSC?"

*Please say no.*

"He did."

My heart sinks. It falls to the ground at my feet, bleeding the whole way down. The empty space in my chest hurts so fucking much I can hardly breathe. Kael was trying to get me away from Killian before this whole thing blew up. If he had his way, I'd never have known.

I almost don't want to ask, almost can't stomach a truth that could bleed me dry, but I need to know how far down everyone's deception goes. Including my husband's. "Did he know about the baby? That it wasn't yours?"

His lips thin out. His fingers flex against the small of my back and he briefly drags his gaze over my shoulder. With every second that passes the pins and needles I'm balanced on dig further into my skin. It's excruciating, the wait.

Was everything I thought I knew about my husband a lie? My entire body floods with relief when he answers, "No. No one outside of me, Jillian, and my father knew."

Killian focuses all his attention on me then. His eyes run over my face, his own softening as he studies me for so long my heart starts beating double time. Tucking an unruly lock of hair behind my ear, he cups my jaw in a tender hold. He thumbs my bottom lip and his breaths quicken, too. Love is absolutely pouring from him. It's breathtaking, piercing, and warm. Just like it used to be: unreserved and untainted with events that poisoned it.

"I want you, Maverick. I'm in love with you. I always have been and I want us to be together. I want to marry you and move the fuck away from here and forget these insufferable years apart ever happened."

He lowers his face to mine, giving me the time I need to turn if this isn't what I want.

God forgive me, I don't.

I close my eyes, let him slant his mouth over mine and kiss me for the first time in close to four years. When I lean into it instead of pulling away, he groans an unholy groan and takes my other cheek in his hand, too.

Then he's kissing me with the same passion and fever I remember. He picks me up and carries me back to my car, laying me on the hood. He wedges himself between my legs and attacks my lips, my face, my throat. He laces my collarbone with love bites while he runs his hands up my torso and cups my breasts through my thin tank top, cursing when he finds my nipples pebbled through my unpadded bra. My legs wrap around his waist and he rocks his erection into my center. He mumbles my name so many times I lose count. I'm lost to everything but him and this familiar feeling he's unearthed in me, never wanting it to end.

But then he stops. He leans his forehead to mine, works to catch his wind, and I'm reminded immediately of Kael. Of how he does this when his emotions overflow. Of how much *he* loves me. Of the fact I'm married and on the cusp of committing the most unforgivable sin possible.

Killian draws back, a pained look in the hard lines of his face. He weaves his fingers through my hair, drops a sweet kiss to my lips. "I know it's wrong of me to ask you this. I know it will hurt Kael, and I'm truly sorry for that, but not sorry enough, I guess. Stay with me, Maverick. Divorce him and be mine. I don't want one sordid night. I don't want to be a dirty secret. I want forever. With you." When I don't respond right away he quickly adds with a quirk of his mouth, "I'm not above begging, Small Fry."

The way he's adoring me makes me want to bawl. He wants me. He's never stopped. He wants to marry me and make all my dreams come true.

The conflict inside me is tumultuous and very fucking real. Either way, either decision I make, someone will end up hurt. He starts blurring under the moisture welling up. Everything I thought I wanted is looking me straight in the eye. It's tangible. I can reach out and grab it.

All I have to do is say yes.

"Please," he pleads thickly. "Please, Maverick. I don't want to live without you anymore."

His mouth finds mine again and I feel that kiss all the way through me. I wind my arms around his neck, canting my head to deepen our connection. One I've missed so much.

All I have to do is say yes.

## chapter TWENTY NINE
### four weeks and five days ago

*Maverick*

Introspection is hard. No one wants to acknowledge their failings, their true feelings. Wants versus desires. Right versus wrong. It's far easier most of the time to keep those thoughts dormant and safe where they lie. Especially when someone you love gets hurt at the end of it.

But *true* introspection—not just skimming the surface—is not only hard, it's excruciating. Going way under the black and slogging through the muck, through the good, the bad, the unpleasant, takes a lot of fortitude. Turning over those moss-covered rocks, even the ones you don't want to flip, is exhausting and gritty work.

Because what do we find when we dig that deep?

Answers, of course.

Answers to the questions we were asking all along.

And once we find them, we have to do something with them or what was the point of the entire gut-wrenching exercise to begin with?

I've spent the last two weeks digging and sifting through the sludge, remembering every little detail of my life with two incredible men I have always loved, just in very different ways.

Both Kael and Killian made mistakes. They kept secrets from me they shouldn't have. But I've forgiven them because they also both sacrificed so much at the same time. Killian sacrificed me, yes, but Kael sacrificed everything, including his pride, to be with me when he knew I was still in love with his brother. And that sacrifice can't be overlooked either. Neither can the one he made four nights ago.

I think back to the conversation Kael and I had a few nights ago at two in the morning. It was heavy and heartbreaking and he did something completely unexpected. Totally selfless, as usual. He gave me an out.

*"How long did you know?"*

*"Know what?"* he hedges.

*I sigh, tired of fucking games. Tired of lies, secrets, of being in the dark. Of beating around bushes with thorns that constantly make me bleed. "That Killian was divorcing Jillian."*

*The quiet eats at me. I want him to tell me he didn't know. That he wouldn't keep something like that a secret, but then part of me can't blame him either. He knows how Killian feels and telling me that Killian was going to be free of the drag that is my sister would have been like serving me up on a silver platter himself to his competition. I have to grudgingly admit I would have likely done the same thing if I were in his shoes.*

*"He told me the day he had the papers drawn up."* So two days before my father died.

*"Did you do it?"*

*He huffs a laugh. "No. He didn't even ask."*

*That makes me feel a tad better. I guess. Maybe not.*

*"Maverick..."* he starts, but then stops. Now the silence pushes us both down. It's thick and hot and stifling. I feel the same foreboding I did in Saint Paul all those months ago. And now that also makes sense.

*"I want you to know I'd do anything for you. I'll never love another woman but you, Swan, but if..."* He curses under his breath and that niggle in my stomach feels like knots twisting me up. When he speaks again, his voice is barely a whisper. *"I know you love him. I know you've never stopped. And if he's the one who makes you happy, if he's the one you want, then I'll understand."*

*My eyes well and burn. My heart just took a thousand-foot nose-dive. "You're..."* Oh my God. *"You're telling me to be with Killian?"* I ask in disbelief.

*His groan is filled with so much pain I feel it, even across the hundreds of miles that separate us. "Fuck no. I'm not telling you to be* with him because it shreds me to fucking pieces to think of it. What I'm telling you is if that's what you want, Maverick, then I will accept it. It'll burn like a motherfucker, but..."

"You just want me to be happy," I finish for him when he trails off.

"Yes," he chokes.

"No matter what?"

"No matter what, Swan." I'm silently sobbing as he continues, "Follow your heart, and if that leads you back to me, know that I will spend every one of my days smothering you with love, but if it leads to Killian..." He pauses to take a deep breath. "If it leads to him, then I know he will do the same."

---

*Follow my heart.*

My fingers drift over the ratty box in my hands. The one I've kept hidden with memories of old and a pulse I swear has never stopped beating. I trace the heart I drew on the top. I outline the *M loves K* in the center of it. I draw a nail along the arrow I drove straight through. I set it back down on the rock next to me.

Tipping my head back, I close my eyes, letting the heat of the sun drive into me. It feels good. Strengthening me for what needs to be done. I draw in a long breath and blow it out just as slow, delaying the inevitable.

My soul has been searched until it's raw.

I have my answers.

Now I have to do something with them.

Today is going to be both the hardest day of my life and the happiest one. I have to tell one man good-bye, crushing him, while I make the other the happiest man on earth when he finds out he's my forever.

It's true with every breath I've taken over the past twenty-six years I've tasted Killian Shepard. But with every heartbeat of mine, I've felt Kael's drumming in synch.

Opening my eyes, it's so bright I'm forced to squint as I let my gaze drift over water that sparkles with the sun's rays. I haven't been back here for a few years now, but it feels like coming home, even if it is different.

My swans are long gone and other than a few frogs croaking on the lily pads across the lake, the pond seems lifeless. But I know it's not. I know underneath the surface, it swarms with vitality. Life goes on, even if it changes. And while I know I'm about to change a man's life, a man I will always love, I truly believe his life will move on and he'll allow himself to change with it. He has the strength and resilience to do it.

Killian has given me time, just as Kael has. With this being the biggest decision of my life, it's time I've needed. Choosing between two incredible men who have both made me happy is not a decision to be made on the hood of a car in the dead of night.

But as I stare off into the distance, my heart's racing faster. She's known the answer all along. His presence has always surrounded me, even when I didn't think it did.

I stand, wipe the dirt sticking to my shorts, and leisurely make my way back through the woods. I walk straight to my car and get in, bypassing a trip inside to make pleasantries with either my mother or Jillian.

Once I really thought about it, it was easy to forgive Kael and Killian. They were protecting family. Mine should have done the same, especially Jillian. I'll forgive them both in time. But that clock's still ticking fast and loud and I need to wait for it slow and quiet before I'm ready. Through it all, they're family. The only one I have. At some point we'll talk and hash things out, but that day isn't today.

With singular focus, I drive through town, stopping restlessly at all the red lights. Finally I pull into Killian's driveway. Killing the engine, I sit there for a few moments, gathering my thoughts. As if in synch, the second I open my car door, his front door opens, too, and there Killian stands in all his manly glory.

He's so beautiful it hurts to look at him. Plaid board shorts hug his trim hips and thighs. A baby blue tee stretches across his broad shoulders. It drapes down his cut torso perfectly. He's all man, of that there is no dispute.

"You're here." The smile on his face ignites him brighter than the Northern Lights.

"I'm here."

Heart throbbing against my ribs, I make my way slowly up the sidewalk, up the stairs and slide easily into his arms the way I've done so many times before.

I bet and lost.

I kept an unforgivable secret from Maverick and I've lost her for good.

I knew what I was doing when I asked her to marry me. I knew she still loved my brother. I knew Killian and Jillian would eventually divorce. And if that happened, he would come for her. I just thought...*fuck*. I thought if I loved her hard enough, it wouldn't matter. That she'd choose me. Love me. *Want* me when the time came for her to decide. Because I always knew that day was coming. There was no way Killian was letting her go without a dogfight that ended up with one of us on the other side of despair.

Meet misery. That's me.

Being without her is sheer, utter fucking hell. Like a vital part of me has been cut out and the hole is gaping open, grief oozing from a wound that won't ever close. I reach out in my sleep and she's not there. My arms feel cold and empty, my life pointless. I wake in the morning and can barely force myself from the bed to my new job. I can't eat. I can't think. I can't function.

I can't anything.

I've been kicking my own ass daily for words that I forced out of the back of my throat with every ounce of power in me. But had I not...had I begged her to come back to me instead of cutting her free, I would never know if she was doing it out of obligation to our vows or because she truly loved me enough to *choose* me. It's the same reason I didn't circle her ankles and hang on for dear life the first time she chose Killian.

I want her to want me for *me*. Period.

There's nothing wrong with that, I suppose. I deserve it, even. But now...*now* I'm questioning if begging wasn't the way I should have gone instead. I may only have half of her, but half is better than nothing at all.

I shift around in my hotel bed, trying to get comfortable.

Impossible.

Every move sends shards of agony zinging through me. There aren't enough painkillers that can dull the pain of knowing she's with my brother.

Unable to deal with the reality that's become my life, I escape inside myself, immersing into a particularly salacious memory of our weekend in Minnesota when we were happy...

---

*"What exactly is it you plan to do with those?" she asks, nodding to the packet of Pop Rocks in my hand, her laugh husky and enthralling. It winds around my cock, tugging mercilessly.*

*"I told you, Swan, we're going to make our own explosion."*

*I climb up the bed, admiring the perfection of her luscious naked curves sprawled out for me. Jesus, she is ethereal. Most days I can't believe I have her. I pray nightly I can keep her.*

*I hope she forgives me for keeping this from her, but we have to get out of Dusty Falls if we're ever going to survive as a couple. My only hope is that when the time comes, she sees I'm doing this with the best of intentions, not subterfuge.*

*"Hey," her voice draws me back.*

*"Hey, what?"*

*"I was just wondering if you're going to actually take advantage of me or if you're going to stare off into space all night? I mean, you did promise to keep up with my book boyfriends earlier."*

*God, how I love this woman. I grin, latching my mouth to the inside of her thigh. She squawks when I bite a little too hard. "Defi-*

nitely take advantage. Although if you're that easy, I'm not really sure I'm taking advantage."

I laugh when she swats my shoulder, pretending to be mad. "I'm not easy."

"Don't worry, Swan, I like you easy." I spread her legs wide, groaning as I run a finger through her dripping slit. "But I love you like this," I gruff, inhaling her scent as though it's my lifeblood.

"Like what?" She squirms when I shove a single finger inside her, testing how tight she is for me. So fucking tight. My cock throbs with the need to have her wet heat glove me.

"Needy. Your body writhing," I reply. Ripping the bag of Pop Rocks open with my teeth, I dump a pile on my tongue, the tiny blue crystals starting their crackling party already. I watch her watch me, wondering what I'm going to do next. I think she already knows.

Dipping back down, I sweep her lips open with my fingers and set my tongue on her sensitive labia to the left of her clit. The rocks crackle and melt even faster. She whimpers and squirms at the sensation, but I wrap an arm around her hips and hold her still. "Tell me how it feels," I demand, dumping more in my mouth to assault the opposite side.

"I don't know...weird, I guess." She gasps when I go in again, moaning, "Kael, please."

This time, two fingers enter her and she cries out as I finger-fuck her, hell-bent on coaxing a quick orgasm out. Mavs is so damn responsive, she's already clenching around them.

"Please what?" With the candy now all gone, I suck her clit between my teeth before clamping down lightly.

She grabs a handful of hair and yanks upward as she sits and gets nose to nose with me. "Please everything."

That hits me in the very center of my chest. I love her so much I ache. Never losing my rhythm, I now start feathering that small knot that bends her to my will. In just moments, she shatters and before she's had a chance to come off that high, I lift her and plunge her onto my straining cock, declaring as I fuck us both into oblivion, "I'll give you anything you want, Mavs. Just ask. All you have to do is ask."

I awake abruptly, working to slow the race of my heart. I want to dive back into another memory of her, a place I don't want to leave, a place I now want to live in permanently, but something woke me.

I blink into the darkness listening for sounds out of place when I hear it.

Slow, even breaths to my right.

And then I feel them, too. Washing over my arm. Diving into my very soul.

*It can't be.*

I lay still for several seconds wondering if my imagination is in overdrive or if she's really here, beside me. I almost want to drift back off so I can keep feeling the trueness of the moment but I have to know. Is it me or is it possible she's real?

Gathering courage I don't have, I manage to twist my head on my pillow, praying the whole way.

It's then that I start to weep like a fucking baby.

Maverick is curled up beside me, fast asleep. Her hands are tucked under her face. Her eyelids flutter slightly with her dreams. She looks peaceful and happy and so fucking gorgeous I lose it, sobbing harder.

What does this mean? Has she come back to me? Or has she come to officially ask me for a divorce? Fucking hell. At this point, I don't want to know. I can't stomach the answer.

I sit up just to take her in, but either the movement or the hitches of my breath stir her. Then her dark eyes are blinking open. The second the fog of sleep clears, she's up and in my arms. Clinging to my neck. Sobbing into my cheek. Cutting off my air supply.

And then I know.

She's come back to me.

"I'm sorry," I tell her over and over.

"Me too," she replies for each apology I give.

"God, I love you, Maverick. Tell me you're staying." I sound needy and pathetic. Countless fucks couldn't be given. I *am* needy and pathetic. I'm a twisted mess of raw emotion right now. My body is trembling, but my soul is finally at peace. It's a weird combination to experience at the same time.

"I'm staying. I'm staying," she keeps repeating until our air is caught and our quaking subsides.

I don't want to let her out of my arms, but I need to see her face when I ask her this, so I sit back against the headboard and pull her astride my lap.

"Why?"

Jesus, I have to know why she chose me over a man she's loved her entire life. The one I practically pushed into her arms the other night. I wanted her to choose me, yes, but I am in complete shock right now that she did.

Her face is just as tearstained as I imagine mine is, but that smile. God damn. That breathtaking smile she gives me puts me under every single time. "I know you want me to say something profound and romantic—"

I cut her off. "I don't need lyrics or romance, Swan. I just need to know that you're mine. Forever. Just the two of us and no one else."

"I am. I choose you." She stops to inhale and I know I'm not gonna like what she has to say, but I know I'll listen. I owe her that much. My suspicion is confirmed when her eyes drop fast to my lap. When they rise back up, my fingers curl around her hips, reminding her that she just committed to being mine. Or maybe it's to remind me because I know the next words out of her mouth will hurt.

"I love Killian. I'm not going to deny that." *Fuck, that hurt like a mother.* "But I realized that love all by itself isn't enough." The warmth of her hands covering my face is pure bliss and so damn needed right now or I may crumble. "And this last year I also realized there are different kinds of love. There's the dreamy kind you always thought you wanted and then there's the steady one you never understood but the second you let yourself feel it...it's nothing like you could have imagined in your wildest dreams."

Maverick dips down and fastens her lips to mine. I want to ravage her. Throw her on her back and make love to her until we're both rippling with emotion we can't keep inside. But this is her time. I want her to have it. There's more she needs to say. I feel it and I need all the words.

"I love you, Kael. There just is no me without you. There never has been," she whispers against my wet mouth. "I realized that the one person who has always, without fail, been there for me is you. And the thought of not having that—of not having you beside me every day—killed something inside of me."

*Is this happening? Am I really holding on to her, listening to her profess words I've always wanted her to say but never thought she would?*

"You choose me?"

She smiles. It's bright and stirs my cock something fierce.

"When I thought about it, there was no choice, really."

Her face blurs when she leans in. Warm lips skim my cheek and, fuck, I can't help but roll my pelvis slightly when her core lines up with me perfectly.

"I want a crazy man who melts me with songs of love and who will watch *North by Northwest* with me a hundred times even though I know he hates it."

Now she's moved on to my jaw, nipping lightly as she spills. She has to feel me rock hard underneath her. I want her to.

"I want to make pillow forts until we're too old and decrepit to get ourselves off the floor. I want to find a new Tastie's to walk to on Saturday mornings. I want to have sex in roadside bathrooms and talk about nothing and everything with the man I know I can't live a day without because I've never *been* without him until just recently. And I was miserable, Kael."

I groan when she pulls back, but I'm so mesmerized by the love shining like stars from her eyes that I can't move. Or breathe. I can hardly even think when she draws a finger down the side of my cheek. I don't realize it's wet again until I feel the cool moisture smear. The soft curve of her mouth is about the only thing grounding me to earth.

"I thought Killian's love defined me, but your love changed me forever. I'm so sorry it took me so long to figure that out."

*Oh hell...that was pretty profound and romantic.*

I can't stand the space between us any longer. I band my arms around her and hang on for dear fucking life. So does she.

My Maverick.

My swan.

My wife.

---

Mavs and I were apart for exactly sixteen days, twelve hours, and seven minutes. I know this because I couldn't stop counting those fuckers off as my life blurred by without her. Then, exactly sixteen days, twelve hours, and eight minutes later, she was in my arms.

I've called in sick the last two days—something I've never done. We haven't left the hotel room. We've slept the days away and talked the nights through until our throats were sore. She told me everything. Some of it shocking. Some of it not.

The fact that Killian asked her to leave me for him? Not shocking.

The fact that she chose me? Quite frankly...I'm still trying to take that one in.

The fact that she kissed him in Harbor Park? Hurtful, but not shocking. I think in a way she needed "The End" to be written so she could close that book forever.

But the revelation that Arnie Shepard fathered Jillian's baby? Like a Taser hit me full force in the nutsack. I did not see that one coming. I have to hand it to Killian; he sacrificed a lot—no, he sacrificed *everything*—to save a man who didn't deserve it. But I understand why he did it.

Honestly, I'd like to think if I were in his shoes I'd have made the same decision, the same sacrifice. But I'm not sure I would have. He selflessly gave Maverick up. He had to know he was risking losing her forever, yet he did it anyway. And I know what a gut punch it feels like to know she's not yours. We've walked in each other's shoes too many times to count over the years, so regardless of the fact he tried to steal her out from under my nose, I will always have a certain measure of respect for him.

Maverick sighs against me, snuggling closer, mumbling something in her sleep. She's exhausted after I spent the last three hours gorging on her. Her knee grazes my dick and he immediately starts flying at half-mast. I want to wake her and go another couple rounds, my need for her rabid after being parted for so long.

But I need some shut-eye myself. Tomorrow's a full day. I'm taking the rest of the week off. Uncool after just a couple weeks on the job, but Gaylen insisted  very pointedly—I was to be with my wife for the rest of the week and stop pretending to have the fucking flu.

I've developed quite a camaraderie with my new boss, who has been wooing me away from DSC for months. We became friends after meeting in the bar at a conference two years ago. I eventually confided in him about my situation with Maverick and Killian. He was the one to make me see leaving Dusty Falls was my one and only option to save my marriage. Otherwise, I'm not sure I would have considered it knowing how it would upset Maverick. There are a lot of good memories in our childhood town, but the bad were starting to overshadow them. I started to see he was right.

When it became clear Killian wasn't going to let her go after he divorced Jillian, I had to get us out of there. It was the one selfish move I've made in my lifetime, but I would do it over and over again. It wasn't to keep secrets from Mavs, it was to keep *her*. I'm only glad she forgave me for not trusting her to talk it through instead of just springing it on her. All I can say is that I was a man blinded—literally blinded—by love for a woman. She has affected my sight in every conceivable and inconceivable way.

So tomorrow we go house hunting and start planning our new life in Minnesota. Together. And nothing or no one will take her from me again.

I'm falling. It's so black I can't see a thing as I fall past nothing and everything.

I fall...

...and fall...

...and keep falling, knowing any second now I'm going to hit bottom.

But I don't. I just keep tumbling.

I'm lost. So very lost.

So alone and so lost.

*Why am I so alone?*

I hear my name. *"Maverick."* I don't know where it's coming from. I hear it again. It's urgent, demanding. *"Maverick."* I open my eyes wider. Try to see who's calling me but it's no use, so I close them again and just wait for the end to come.

Then I'm being shaken. A sting flares up on my cheek, slowly drawing me out of the horror I thought my life had become.

"Maverick!"

I blink my eyes open, realizing I'd been dreaming. It seemed so real. *Felt* so real. The features twelve inches from mine gradually come into focus and I see the sweet face of the only person I want to.

"MaryLou," I sob, remembering where I am and why I'm sitting in a darkened chapel. "You're here." I pop up and throw my arms around her. "You're here, you're here," I keep repeating.

"I'm here," she keeps saying back. Then she pries me off. It takes great effort because I'm holding on to her like I haven't held on to anything before. Grabbing me firmly by my arms, she gets right in my face. Makes sure I'm paying attention.

"He's alive, Maverick. He pulled through surgery."

Instantaneous sobs rack me. "He's alive?"

"He's alive!"

"He's alive," I repeat. Denial and elation battle fiercely. Is my mind playing sick tricks? Am I still dreaming?

"Yes. He's in recovery and they're moving him to ICU. They said the next couple of days are critical, but the bullets miraculously missed all his vital organs. He's alive. He's going to make it. I know it."

"He's alive," I mumble. Then my body reacts. I'm up off that pew. I vaguely realize the old woman is gone, but I don't care. I push through the chapel doors. I sprint down the halls. I will the elevator to rise faster, all the while chanting under my breath...

"He's alive."

"He's alive."

"He's alive."

I place a protective hand over my belly and whisper to the tiny life growing inside me. The one I just found out about this morning and whisper, "Daddy's alive."

Every fucking part of me aches. Burns like a motherfucker on fire.

My head.

My skin.

The tips of my fingers and the backs of my knees.

My goddamn heart feels as though it's working overtime to get me from one minute to the next.

My eyelids have to be made from sandpaper. I can't get any relief.

"Kael," a familiar voice calls softly.

God, *that voice.* That hauntingly beautiful fucking voice. My skin burns where a hand now rests on my shoulder, gently stroking down my arm before starting over again. It's her touch. I'd recognize it anywhere. Even my dreams morph to cruelty, emulating my waking hours.

"Kael, please open your eyes," she coaxes.

No. I can't do it. I won't open my eyes to watch her fade away like so many times before. A distant, incessant beep tries to peel back another layer of my fantasy, plunging me once again into a horrific reality. The one without Maverick. I hang on to my make-believe world just a little longer. I shift. I think I moan. There's rustling and then warmth rushes through my veins, numbing me from the inside out.

*Yes. I want to stay here with her.*

"Kael, please." Her voice cracks like she's still here. As if she still cares. "I need to know you're real and alive and with us."

"Maverick," I moan.

"Yes." She sounds excited. That small hand now circles my own and squeezes. Skin-on-skin contact. I sigh in absolute fucking heaven. "I'm here. Please open your eyes."

"You're not real," I tell her plainly, my vision still blissfully dark.

Then I feel her breath ghost over my face a second before her lips land on mine. They move gingerly and slow. Barely touching me, but they're so pillowy and supple and feel so goddamn real I choke out a sob.

And open my eyes.

Timeless, red-rimmed emerald ones stare back at me. They're wide and scared. I try to blink her away, but her red, splotchy face isn't fading. It's only blurring. I attempt to lift my hand, needing to touch her, to wipe away the unhappiness I see rushing down it. Jesus, I need to make sure she's not a figment of my imagination, but my hand is heavy and not responding.

"You're here," I breathe. It's a question.

Her mouth turns up, but it's fleeting. "I'm here. I'm here. How are you feeling?"

How am I feeling? How the fuck am I feeling? *Elated.* My wife is here.

That beeping noise gets louder. Antiseptic suddenly pierces my nostrils. The coldness of the air starts infiltrating my skin. I don't want to look away from her beautiful face. The second I do I just know she'll be gone. But this foreboding feeling crashes over me like a rogue wave I can't stop.

It's sticky and skin prickling. It's *fear*. I recognize its icy claws right before they sink deep. Only this time it's not because I've lost Maverick. I haven't. I remember that now. She came back to me. It's because of the rapid gunfire and ear-piercing screams of terror that still linger in my ears.

Holy fuck.

I was shot.

Shot in my place of work by the man we'd just fired three hours earlier for sexual harassment of another employee. The same one we'd come to learn had three complaints filed against him in three different states. I was barely a month on the job at Braham when utter fucking hell broke loose.

I don't know how many times hot lead was pumped into my body but I know it was more than once. The agony I felt before I collapsed was beyond excruciating. But the sorrow at knowing I would never set eyes again on Maverick was debilitating.

I'm alive, though. I don't know how many others are sharing my fortune. I find I can't think about that now. About the hows or the whys of surviving. Staring at my gorgeous wife, all I revel in is that I am here. Maverick is by my side and God spared my life so I could see her again. He answered my prayers as I let the pain take me under, thinking I was sucking in my last breath.

I start to cry, which makes Maverick cry harder.

"It's okay, Kael." She lays her head lightly on my shoulder, careful not to jostle me. The pain sits there, slithering under my skin, just waiting for the morphine to wear off. But I ignore it, focusing all my attention and effort on my sobbing wife.

"I'm alive."

Her body shakes as she repeats, "You're alive. You're alive."

I'm fucking *alive*.

My wife is by my side...and I am alive.

That's the last thought on my mind as I let whatever they shot into my veins drag me under once again.

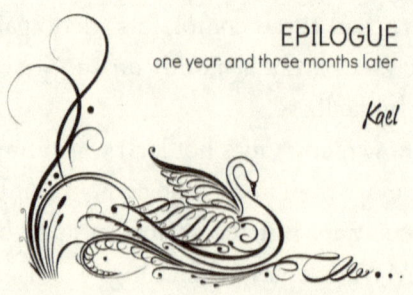

It's back.

That horrible, panicky feeling that twists my insides to knots. The void slinks over me and I feel helpless to stop it. I'm hovering on the cusp of something that is bigger than me when I'm vaguely aware of the bed dipping. Of the sheets sliding down my thighs. Of fingers climbing their way back up. But when that tiny hand circles my steely erection and those sweet lips wrap around the tip and suck, my eyes fly open and snag the most mesmerizing sea-colored pools that exist. They're alight with unconditional love, glassy with unmistakable lust.

Then I know I've been dreaming. Again. My perpetual nightmare starring those unbearable few weeks when I thought my life was over. Both literally and figuratively.

"Morning," she whispers, swirling her tongue through my slit before taking me back in.

"Oh, fuck, yes." I palm her head and squeeze the base of my dick with the other hand, willing my seed to stay put for a few minutes so I can bask in the unholy pleasure that's her mouth.

I fight the natural instinct to close my eyes, needing to soak in a moment I wasn't sure I would have again.

Ever since I've come back from the brink of death, I've been loath to let her out of my sight, even in sleep. Getting gunned down in the workplace by a madman tends to have a profound impact on one's life. But I daresay it wasn't even in the same ballpark as the thought of losing the love of my life to someone else.

Quite frankly, I'd rather *be* dead if that had happened. And I know I'm lucky to have survived three gunshot wounds. Four people didn't make it out that day when an ex-employee lost his shit and unloaded over two hundred and fifty rounds into the offices of Braham Construction before taking his own life.

Only days before our one-year anniversary, just when I thought I had everything, I almost lost it all.

The slight twist of my balls brings me back from less pleasant thoughts to her. And to the fact I'm going to blow in about five seconds, tops. I scoop my hands under her arms and drag her up my body until I have her positioned just right. "Ride me, Swan."

Her green orbs are this glazed, half-lidded mess of sexy. She is utterly bewitching when she is turned on. "But I want you to come in my mouth." She's breathless as she obeys my command and her pussy swallows my length whole, making my eyes roll. *Sweet, merciful Jesus. Thank you for her.*

Grasping her nape, I draw her to my mouth. "Not this time. I went six weeks without you wrapped around my dick, Maverick. I'm going to be inside you every chance I get."

Oh, yeah, I'm grinning like a son-of-a-bitch about now and it's not because I'm insanely happy when I'm buried between my wife's snug walls. I am, but that's not why.

I'm a dad.

Avery Jameson Shepard, born June 3.

"I'm going to come," my wife announces in my ear just as our little girl starts fussing in the background.

I take over now; shifting so I can hit her smack in the spot I know drives her wild. "Good. Let's come together."

"Oh God, Kael." Her pants, moans, and erotic hitches are my undoing. I release violently, hoping she's with me, praying I didn't leave bruises on her fair skin where I gripped her like a vise.

As I catch my breath, my gaze travels over to the framed selfie of us in the Casey's bathroom so long ago now. We are flushed from sex and grinning like fools. Mavs has two thumbs up and this gleam in her eye I've come to know very well. Sated bliss. The picture sits on my nightstand, a constant reminder of how very much I love this crazy, impulsive woman.

"Christ, how I love you, Swan," I tell her softly, stroking her now damp hair from her forehead.

She sighs. It's contented and happy. "So much you want to marry me again?"

"Yeah, about that…"

She pops up, still straddling my softening dick, her mouth gaping open. Laughing, I grab her face, and, with my thumbs hooked under her chin, shut it. "I do believe I told you I would renew my vows with you every single day for the rest of my life."

That earns me a double-wide smile. "You did."

"And that my life has *always* been pledged to you."

"You said that too." I did not just mistake the sultry tone her voice took on. I start thickening back up as her hips begin their seductive, alluring roll, but a glance at the clock shows we don't have time for another round as much as I wish otherwise.

Kissing her swiftly, I scoot us to the edge of the bed and stand up, dropping her from my lap. I turn her and swat her ass, guiding her toward the bathroom. I know that whine of Avery's. We have less than four minutes before she's full-fledged wailing.

"Up and at 'em, Swan. We need to shower and get Avery ready so we're not late."

How is it possible that one extra bundle of ten pounds has doubled the time it takes to get out the door?

Maverick tries to dart from my hold to get our daughter, but I usher her into the shower instead. "She'll be fine for a couple of minutes. Let me wash you."

She reluctantly gives in, but I make her enjoy our short time alone. It's harder to come by these days, but I'm not complaining. When we emerge from the spray, Avery is out-and-out wailing and my cell starts ringing. We look at each other and just smile, overjoyed to be living a crazy, stressful life.

"I'll get Avery. You need to get ready," I tell her with a peck to her plump lips.

"She's probably hungry."

The phone stops, but Avery's cry has now turned shrill and angry. "Then I'll stall for time while you dry your hair."

"Good luck." She laughs. "I'll be fast." Watching her wrap a towel around her luscious curves, even more pronounced with Avery's birth, makes me sad. She swats me and tells me to go. I run to get our baby girl, trying unsuccessfully to calm her. Finally I give up. On my way to Maverick, I freeze in the doorway of our bedroom.

Maverick has her back to me, talking low. Her head shifts my way due to Avery's fussiness. My cell is pressed to her ear, and by the look on her face, I know exactly who she's talking to.

"I appreciate that, Killian. I know Kael will, too."

She pauses, listening to my brother on the other end. A sad sorta smile tilts her lips. Like the giving man he is, Killian graciously accepted Maverick's decision. Even tries to stay in touch once in a while. Especially on special days, like today. But I know it's hard for him. How can it not be? He doesn't have the woman he's longed for his whole life. Someone else does.

"Thank you. It means a lot that you called." Another pause. "Yes, she's hungry. Do you want to talk to Kael?" She eyes me while waiting for his response. "Okay. Bye," she says softly.

Surprisingly, she hands me the phone. We swap and she quietly exits with Avery, who has calmed substantially now she knows she's going to be latched to Maverick's breast in a few seconds. "Hey, man. How are you?"

"Busy. Putting in lots of hours." My brother's voice sounds tight and strained. It always does when we talk nowadays.

"I bet. Heard DSC won the O'Hare project."

"Yeah. Quite a coup."

Small talk blows. "So..."

"Yeah, so, I just wanted to tell you I'm thinking about you and Maverick today and...that I'm happy for you both."

I don't say anything for a second or two. He's a bigger man than I could have ever been in this situation. No fucking way could I have called with my congrats. "Thanks, Killian."

"Well..."

Yeah, our conversations are still stilted and awkward. I cut him free. "Hey, I gotta run. We're gonna be late. We'll talk soon?"

"Sure. Sounds good."

I hang up and only dawdle for a few beats before swinging into action. Dressing. Packing. Burping. Codling. Changing. Diapering. I move with an efficiency I've mastered over the past couple months, but even so, it takes us over an hour and a half before we're all three buckled in the car. We're ten minutes late, but we're getting better at juggling a newborn and ourselves.

Half an hour later, we pull up outside the church. Avery's sleeping soundly in her car seat with a full belly and a clean romper, after spitting up all over the dress Mavs had bought just for today. "Should we do this?" I ask.

"Hell yes."

She's absolutely beaming. God, I'm one lucky man.

We collect our daughter and quickly make our way inside the Cathedral of Saint Paul. Another thing a near-death experience tends to do? Deepens your faith. I had a lot of shit to deal with after the shooting. Mavs had a lot going on with not only losing her father but discovering all of our betrayals and taking care of me for months while I slowly recovered.

The last year has been both the best, yet probably the worst, of my life. I married the woman of my dreams. Then I almost lost her. I saw the edge of death and witnessed the miracle of life. I moved, started a new job, and started job number three after I recovered from my injuries. Mavs sold her business to MaryLou and is now a full-time mom in the first home we bought together.

It's been a lot of shit to deal with. But Father Reddick has helped us through it and we've grown close. And because of that, he's agreed to do a special rededication ceremony and let us just speak our hearts freely. He knows all that we've been through. Well...most of it anyway.

"Ready?"

"We're ready," I tell him.

Father R. eagerly takes the car seat from my hands. I throw him a look not to wake Avery. He only winks, walking away. I hear him cooing at her. I just shake my head.

Our hands locked together, we make our way through the huge, barren church. This is so different from the last time we pledged our lives in front of hundreds of family and friends. That day still lives in my memory. How she took my very breath away.

---

*Hand to the good man himself, when Maverick walked down the aisle on her father's arm I cried. Tears of pure joy and gratitude sprang into my eyes and I've not been able to get rid of them since. I've been standing here with her at my side thinking I am the luckiest son-of-a-bitch in the world. She is a vision, yes. That was a given, but I am marrying Maverick DeSoto. I know she's nervous, uncertain even. I'm not a fucking idiot to know her heart's not 100 percent into this, that it's still broken over Killian, but I have so much love inside, I know it's going to be enough for both of us.*

*Father Tiegs's booming voice commands us to turn to each other and hold hands. I can't spin fast enough.*

*"Kael Shepard and Maverick DeSoto, have you come here freely and without reservation to give yourselves to each other in marriage?"*

*I know I have. It makes me ache to think Mavs hasn't, yet we answer in unison, "We have."*

*"Will you honor each other as man and wife for the rest of your lives?"*

*I will not only honor her. I'll worship her, revere her, make sure she wants for nothing. "We will."*

*"Will you accept children lovingly from God and bring them up according to the law of Christ and his Church?"*

*She hesitates. It's slight but it's there. I start to answer, "We will." She's a half second behind.*

*"Since it is your intention to enter into marriage, join your right hands, and declare your consent before God and his Church."*

*I look to Father Tiegs. He nods indicating it's time to speak the words I've memorized. I take half a step into Mavs, gaze deeply into her eyes, and repeat the bland Catholic vows, but there's so much more I want to say. I want to tell her there's nothing I won't do to make her happy for the rest of her days. I want to tell her no one can possibly love her with the depth I do. I wish I could get her to understand she's not making a mistake by becoming my wife because there is nothing in my life I will treasure more than her.*

*She repeats the same vows, but while she says the words, I know her thoughts are far away. I bury that hopeless feeling in the depths of my mind. She is mine now; that's all that matters.*

---

That day, she may have pledged her life to me, but today she'll pledge her love. Today I have it all.

We stop in front of the altar. Father R. putzes around a bit before he comes to stand in front of us. Avery is tucked safely on the floor at our feet, still snoozing away. Luckily.

There are exactly four people in attendance outside of our priest.

Mavs.

Me.

Avery.

And our unborn child.

We found out yesterday Mavs is pregnant again. We are both over the moon. I know it's soon after Avery, but we want a big family and there's no reason to wait. If anything, life has taught us you need to take what you want by the horns with all the gusto inside you. Our time here is fleeting.

I feel lucky every single day Maverick forgave me and came back to me, though I know it took her a while to work through it. So it's not to hurt anyone's feelings or to leave them out, but it felt right that the day we rededicate ourselves to each other is just for us and our children.

Father R. says a few prayers and blessings. Then it's our turn to speak from the heart.

Taking both her hands in mine, I start. "Maverick...I don't even know where to begin." She's already tearing up. So am I. "I want to say I always knew we'd end up at this very moment with so much love for each other it's hard to contain, but I admit I lost hope along the way a few times." That makes her breath hitch on a sob. I keep going, though.

"I could stand here and repeat those words—I love you—until I have no voice left, but in the end, they're just words. What's far more important are my actions to show you that every single moment of every single day you're my everything. My sun and moon. My light and darkness. My one true love. I'll make sure you never regret choosing me, Swan."

The makeup she worked so hard to put on is streaked. Her eyes are red. Mascara is pooled under her lower lashes. She's a mess. And she is the loveliest creature I have ever seen.

After a few deep breaths, she tells me what I wanted to hear two years ago. Today isn't the exact date of our anniversary but I kinda like it that way. Now we have two special days to celebrate.

Mavs rubs her lips together a few times before exhaling with her mouth framed into a cute little circle. Then she starts.

"When I think of you, Kael, I've always had this easy, comfortable feeling." Her voice cracks. Her eyes well again. Neither of us will make it through this without splotchy faces and snotty noses. "You've always been beside me. Caring for me, protecting me, loving me. Quietly erecting our life for us so it was ready when I was. You never gave up even when you should have. I—" She stops to take a few deep breaths. When she sinks her top teeth into her lower lip, I squeeze her hands, encourage her to continue with a soft smile. She returns it and my heart flips.

"I didn't make it easy on you, but you hung in there and you will never know how grateful I am for your perseverance or how happy you make me every single day. We've had a lot of milestones already, but milestones don't make a life; it's all the little things in between that bridge the gap from one monumental event to the next. You've given me a thousand little things, Kael, and I know because of those we are unbreakable and everlasting." Then she shrugs before her last words break me in the best possible way a man can be broken. "I followed my heart and it led me back to you."

She stops talking and it may be fair to say she's not the only one who's a hot mess.

Father R. clears his throat. Good. At least I'm not the only pussy here. He holds out his hands and our wedding bands shine under the light streaming through the stained-glass windows. A few moments later, with them slipped firmly back in place where they will forever stay, I kiss her. Too long and probably far too inappropriate for a church setting, but fuck it. I didn't get this chance the first time I married her. I'm not wasting my second one.

Mavs and I have fought through a lot of obstacles to get to this point—even each other. *Especially* each other, I think. Hard doesn't even begin to scratch the surface of what it took to get us here. But I know with my wife's hand in mine and my daughter in the other as we head back home to celebrate in our own private way, every second of that fight was worth it. I will not take a single second of the time I have left on this earth with her for granted.

Not one.

**Want more of Killian, Maverick and Kael...**

# OTHER

**Want more Black Swan Affair?**

Well, you're in luck! I have a FREE prequel to Black Swan Affair called *Everything*, available ONLY to my newsletter subscribers. And as a bonus, the prequel is told from Killian's POV! You can subscribe to my newsletter here: https://goo.gl/MxHvHg

Also, if you're wondering about Killian's HEA, you'll definitely want to make sure you're signed up for my newsletter, as his story, *Thin White Lies,* will be releasing sometime in 2023. You can keep up on all the news, including release dates, and special access to sneak peaks and bonus scenes only through my newsletter.

**Are you a signed paperback lover?**

Want your own signed copy of **Black Swan Affair** or any of my other published works? You can order one by going to my website at klkreig.com (read directions on international shipping in the form). I also offer signed bookplates on my website if you already own your paperback copy but want it signed.

**Need a place to talk Black Swan Affair?**

This is an emotional book! If you want a place to discuss it with other Black Swan Affair survivors, join my Black Swan Affair Spoiler group on Facebook.

## PLEASE NO SPOILERS!

I know it's hard not to post publicly when you feel passionate about a story, but I ask that you PLEASE do NOT post spoilers about the ending of Black Swan Affair because, quite frankly, the biggest part of the journey is not knowing who Maverick ends up with. THANK YOU for letting other readers experience what you did just did!

## Last But Not Least...

For audiobook lovers, you can find Black Swan Affair on Audible. Also look for many other of my titles to be released on audiobook in 2023!

## I LIED...

Do you like alpha, millionaire, second chance romances with dirty talk and hairpin twists that give you all the feels? Yah? In that case, keep reading for an excerpt from *Forsaking Gray,* the first in my Colloway Brothers series, which is FREE on Kindle Unlimited.

# EXCERPT: FORSAKING GRAY

**Prologue**

Five years earlier...

## Livia

"Do you, Peter, take this woman, Livia, to be your lawfully wedded wife? To have and to hold from this day forward, for better, for worse, for richer, for poorer, in sickness and in health, to love and to cherish, till death us do part?"

"I do," he responds. Smugly.

"Do you, Livia, take this man, Peter, to be your lawfully wedded husband? To have and to hold...."

Every little girl dreams of her wedding day. That magical moment when you pledge your undying love to the man who makes your heart beat a little faster, who makes your panties a little wetter and who you think will make the most handsome salt-and-pepper-haired ninety year old ever to walk the earth. Your father will walk you down the aisle, arm in arm, in a wedding dress so beautiful, your childish vision couldn't do it justice and he'll struggle to hold back the tears of both happiness at giving you away and sadness that you're no longer his little girl.

Every young woman dreams of the honeymoon that will quickly follow. Will he whisk me away to Paris, where we'll live on wine and cheese and each other for two weeks solid? Or will we fly to a secluded island, sit on the beach, soak in the sun and drink pina coladas that our private butler delivers every hour on the hour? Or maybe we'll decide to cruise the Mediterranean, visiting exotic stops such as Istanbul or Rome or Santorini. But at the end of the day, it really doesn't matter where you go, because you'll be together.

And every girl, young or old, dreams of being married to a man who worships the ground she walks on, puts her on a pedestal and would give his life for hers without thought or hesitation.

I was every girl. Except, instead of the fancy wedding, complete with tears of joy, I'm standing in a courthouse in front of a justice of the peace with tears of heartbreak welling in my eyes. Instead of the elaborate gown, complete with a long, beaded train that I picked out with my sister and my best friends, I'm wearing a simple black sheath and matching pumps, which fit my somber mood perfectly. And instead of marrying the man who I love to the depths of my very soul, who will love and cherish me all the days of our lives, I'm marrying a monster...

"You may now kiss the bride."

...who will make the next one thousand two hundred and twelve days of my existence a living nightmare from which I cannot wake.

### Chapter 1

#### LIVIA

I see him across the room. I'm utterly breathless.

My heart races.

My stomach flutters.

My soul disintegrates into a pile of scattered ashes once again.

I'm a complete fucking mess. No muscle will obey my command to move, even my eyelids. They refuse to take away his image for even a second.

*Why is he here?*

I shouldn't be taking this risk. I shouldn't be openly ogling him, but I can't look away. Holy mother of perfection...he's everything I remember and more. As breathtaking as the very first time I laid eyes on him. He's every woman's fantasy, probably men too. I see other women watching him and I want to scratch their eyes out. Some blatantly stare, as I do. Some sneak sly glances so their spouses or dates won't notice.

Foolish.

Of course their dates notice a textbook male specimen such as him in the room. All other men are busy pissing in a circle around their women to ward him away.

As if sensing my weighty stare, his eyes lock with mine. Neither of us move.

The woman dripping off his arm, hanging on his every word, seems oblivious to our connection. Every sound fades away as we stare into each other's eyes from across the ballroom. Eyes I'm all too familiar with but haven't seen in what seems like a lifetime. Eyes that haunt me.

God, I miss him with a raw ache that intensifies daily.

"Wow, look at that fine piece of ass. He's fuckable," whispers one of my best friends, Kamryn, following my stare.

*The best of my life.*

He starts across the room in my direction, his date all but forgotten as he leaves her in his dust. She's calling after him, but he simply waves his hand in dismissal, not bothering to look back. His angry eyes never leave mine, his full lips drawn in a tight thin line.

*Oh shit.* Time to go.

"Kam, I'm not really feeling well, sweetie. I'll call you in the morning after my interview." I'm frantic to escape. I turn to leave, heels clicking as I quickly walk toward the exit. Kamryn practically runs to keep up.

"Let me call my driver for you, hon."

I call over my shoulder as I race toward my escape. "No, no. It's fine. There are plenty of cabs out front. I'll just hop in one and be home in no time. Really, it's fine."

Her grip is like an iron fist around my arm as she maneuvers me back to face her. Kam frowned, clearly not believing the blatant lie I threw her way. Whatever. Over her shoulder I estimate he's just fifty feet from where we now stand and moving at a clipped pace. As if by divine intervention, he's stopped by a buxom blond whose nipples are ready to fall out of her slutty dress any second. One deep breath and pop, they're free. He shakes her off, heading in my direction once again. Can't blame her for trying.

*Crap Livia. Get. Out. Now.*

"I think I may be sick, Kam. I'd really like to get home before I lose those little shrimp thingies I just ate." Not so much of a lie this time. My stomach *is* doing somersaults.

I turn and flee. I hear Kam call after me, but keep going this time. Making it to the safety of a cab before *he* reaches me is paramount.

Damn Kam and her insistence that I wear her four-inch Louboutin heels. So what if the fire engine red is a perfect complement to my also borrowed black leather strapless sheath. The shoes are still half a size too small and pinch my feet, making a hasty escape nearly impossible.

I should ditch the damn things like Cinderella. I bet she didn't even 'lose' her glass slipper. She was no doubt trying to escape this supposed Prince Charming because he was an arrogant asshole, and it fell off in her urgency to get away. In traditional antifeminism fashion, a man weaved an elegant story about how much better a girl's life would be with a boy in it. He would swoop in and save her from her persecuted life and they would live happily ever after.

Bullshit. All of it.

There is no happily ever after. Not for me anyway. That childish fantasy was ruthlessly shattered over five years ago.

I make it out of the ballroom, down the stairs and have the front hotel door halfway open when a strong hand clamps down on my shoulder, effectively stopping my forward movement. An electric current runs through my body and I feel him everywhere. His hand may as well be between my legs for all my body cares.

*Damn you Louboutin and your impractical shoes.*

"Hello Livia," a deep sensual voice drawls behind me. His voice and touch combined almost make my knees buckle. After all these years, he still has the same effect on all of my senses like the day we met. He sounds the same, albeit a bit more grown up. And a *lot* more sexy.

Jesus, I don't think I can do this.

*You can do this Livia.*

*You* have *to do this.*

*Be cold.*

*Be unaffected.*

*Lie.*

I take a deep breath, will the tears back, and steel myself before turning to face him.

"Hello Gray. Fancy seeing you here." *Holy...breathe, Livia, breathe.* I am almost taken aback by how utterly gorgeous he is. He had been stunning across the room and he was always beautiful, but up close he's like a golden angel sent directly from heaven—or hell— to tempt me. His face is no longer boyish, but all man, complete with the sexiest scruffy whiskers I have ever seen. This is more than a five o'clock shadow, but not quite a full beard. I'm a sucker for scruff. Especially on Gray, but he's never worn it like this. It's downright sinful.

Double damn.

"What are you doing here Livvy?" *Livvy.* I haven't heard that name in over five years. It sounds so damn good I want to weep.

*Dig deep, Livia...maintain the façade you've perfected so very well.*

"I came for the same reason you probably did, the animals." Bravo for me. I sounded very confident...and very *stupid*. My internal head is shaking at me sadly.

He says nothing, remaining stoically silent, his eyes searching mine for the truth.

Subject change, before he asks too many more questions, for which I'll have to build lie on top of lie. I've told so many lies I need a cheat sheet to keep track of them all. "So, why are you in Chicago?"

His penetrating gaze makes me even more nervous than I already am, and I start to squirm. I never intended to run into anyone I knew here, let alone him. I would have never let Kam talk me into this stupid fundraiser otherwise.

*Shit. Shit. Shit.* This is so not good.

"I took over my father's company, and we moved the headquarters from Detroit to Chicago last year."

He lives here? In Chicago? My mind is spinning. I'm trying to process the fact that my ex-fiancé lives in the same city as I do, and that he took over his father's company already. I didn't remember Frank being that old. I shouldn't be engaging him in conversation, but I can't help but ask, "Did he retire?"

"No. He died." I gasp and my heart sinks.

"God, I'm sorry Gray, I had no idea. Your dad was a wonderful man." He was like a father to me, more so than my own, who'd essentially sold me to save his own life. I loved that family. They were like my own until they weren't anymore.

"Of course not, Livvy. How could you possibly when you fucking disappeared over five years ago, without a trace, without a call, without a forwarding goddamn phone number?" His retort was ripe with barbs, and it stung in the way it was meant to. I deserved some of his ire yes, but not all of it.

Gray has no clue the living nightmare I've endured. What I had done for my family or for him. And it would stay that way. I have to get away from him before I do something stupid, like spill my guts. He is my past, and as much as it deeply pains me, he has to stay that way. Too much has happened in the last five years that I simply can't overcome. I am damaged goods now, and Gray would never want me if he knew the truth. I need to get the hell out of here before I break down. I can't keep the tears back much longer.

"I have to go. It was nice to see you again, Gray." I need to get out of here before I throw myself at him and beg for his forgiveness. Because even though I don't quite deserve it, a small part of me desperately craves it. Gray is my first love. The only man I will ever love. And that young, naive woman now buried deep inside me will hold tightly to the memory of her first love with her last dying breath. It's all that has gotten me through the worst days of my life.

And it's all I have left.

I spin to leave when a strong hand pulls me back once again. Every time this man puts his hands on me, I bend to his will, and right now I feel like a torch has been set to my bones and they are far too pliable. My eyes flit between it and his ever so handsome face. He gets the gist and lets go.

Although his voice has softened, his annoyance clearly rings loud when uttering his next words. "How can I get ahold of you, angel? I'd like to have dinner. Catch up."

My heart skips a beat. I haven't heard that endearment in so long, I have to blink back the tears threatening to fall. I *want* to agree. I nearly do. But then common sense slams back into my frontal lobe at a hundred miles per hour. If I spend time with Gray, he'll pepper me with questions. Questions he has *every* right to have answered. But those are answers I won't give. I can't. He can never know.

Gone is the young, naïve, rosy-colored glasses woman he fell in love with. Gone is the carefree, idealistic woman he'd asked to be his wife. What stands in her place, instead, is a cynical, horribly used and hopeless one. Shattered beyond all repair.

"I can't," I whisper. Then I do turn and flee. Luckily, there are several cabs waiting out front and I hop in the first one, yelling at him just to drive. As I turn around, I see Gray standing on the sidewalk, breathing hard, watching me drive away. Deja vu cuts me like a sharp knife and I begin to sob silently. These are the first tears I've allowed myself to shed in four and a half years.

Once again, I am leaving the only man to ever make my stomach flutter and my heart race. The man who pursued me relentlessly for that first date by returning for six straight nights to the pizzeria I worked at until I said yes. The man I'd dreamed of having children with. Growing old with. The only man I have, and ever will love.

All because of *him*. Always because of *him*. As with every day for the past five years, I curse the day Peter Wilder set foot into my life. And I curse my father for bringing him there.

### Chapter 2

## LIVIA

"Right this way ma'am," the petite, slightly overweight receptionist directs, as we walk the short distance to a small, but very nice, conference room. "You're rather early, so it will be a while before Mr. Nichols is ready to see you. Help yourself to water or soda in the fridge over there while you wait."

"Thank you," I murmur.

Yes, I am a good thirty-five minutes early. Without a car, you have to follow the train schedule. I pass on the drink. I'd already stopped at a Starbucks across the street from the tall downtown office building and had a double shot espresso hazelnut macchiato. I am buzzing from the copious amounts of caffeine I'd just ingested.

But the caffeine is an absolute requirement. I had been up half the night unable to stop thinking about Gray. Seeing him had been like picking an old scab. Now you have to treat it, disinfect it and bandage it again because it's bleeding. If you ignore it, blood leaks everywhere, leaving behind stains you can't get out. I can't afford any more stains. I already have too many.

I look out the window and wonder how, out of all the cities in the world, could we possibly be *living* in the same one? I'd moved to Chicago because no one knew me here, it is big and I could get lost in the millions of people.

So is it karma or fate that I'd ran into my former fiancé at an event that I should have never been at in the first place? If Kam's date hadn't bailed at the last minute, I never would have been there, and I'm not yet sure if I'm grateful or regretful that I was. It'd been crushing to see him with another woman, to see that he's moved on. But it was nice to add a new recollection of him to my well-used memory banks. My memories of him were all that got me through some very dark, very rough times.

Walking away from him last night flooded my heart with nearly unbearable pain, and I'd spent a good hour sobbing into my pillow, wallowing in self-pity. And that was a deep, black pit I couldn't allow myself to fall into again because God knows, I would *not* make it back to the top this time.

During the little sleep I did manage to get, it was as tortured as my consciousness. I dreamed of Gray, as I often did, but this was different. It seemed so very real, and I'd dreamed of Gray now versus the Gray I remembered. Of his scruff tickling the inside of my thigh before his mouth latched onto my aching sex. Of the way his thick fingers stretched me, readying me for his heavy cock. Of the way he'd grab my hair and use it as leverage while he pumped ruthlessly into me from behind until I shattered around him, screaming his name. But this was rougher. Raw. Fast and hard.

And I loved every minute of it. I only wish it were real.

When I woke, I was so achy and needy I exploded after just a few swirls on my soaking clit, and I was still in agony. Both physically and emotionally. That was a very bad place to be. I breathe through the familiar sadness that always shrouds me, willing it away.

Gray would surely not like the sad, cynical woman I've become underneath my crusty outer shell. Hell, *I* don't like her either. I know that façade slipped a little when I saw him last night. For a fleeting minute, I felt like the old Livvy that he'd known and loved. And I know he'd seen it.

I feel off kilter after seeing him. I need to call Dr. Howard and make an urgent appointment because my regularly scheduled one isn't until next week. I need to talk to someone, and she's only one of two people that know my entire story. The other I haven't seen since he helped me escape two years ago.

For the first year I lived in Chicago, I saw Dr. Howard three times a week, gradually weaning down to just every other week now. I'm a far cry from where I was when I stepped foot into this city for the very first time and there's no doubt I wouldn't be where I am today, both mentally and emotionally, without her. But I feel thrown for a giant loop after last night and I'm floundering. A balloon let loose in the gusty winds, unclear on where I'll end up.

"Ms. Kingsley?"

"Ah, yes, sorry." I wonder how long the fair-haired receptionist has been calling my name.

"Mr. Nichols will see you now."

"Yes, thank you." I glance at the clock on the wall as I exit the room.

8:55 a.m.

I have effectively wasted an entire half hour daydreaming instead of preparing for the job I so desperately need. And to what end? The past is what it is. It can't be changed or altered. *Or forgotten.*

I've been free of Peter Wilder for over two years now. I need to stay in the here and now and put on my best game face. I have my lies all neatly in order. Lies no one can really verify, but would garner me the sympathy I need to land the job all the same. The fact that Kamryn knows someone high up here will probably help too.

I smooth out my borrowed black pencil skirt and straighten the blood red sheer, long-sleeved shirt that I've paired with my own red camisole underneath. The outfit is complemented with three-inch black peep toe shoes and some light jewelry. It's edgy, but not slutty. If I do get the job, Addy graciously said I could borrow her clothes anytime until I can afford some nice ones of my own, since my wardrobe is made up almost entirely of Goodwill hand-me-downs. She is really a great roommate and friend.

Blondie shows me to the elevator, inserts a special card key, and instructs me to take the polished glass lift to the twenty-sixth floor where I will wait in the reception area until Connie, Mr. Nichols' current admin, collects me.

"Good luck," she whispers as the doors shut. I do my best to give her a genuine smile, but it's difficult with the butterflies churning in my stomach. All too soon the elevator doors open. Quickly spotting a few chairs off to the left, I sit and scan the area.

Typical layout, with cubicles and offices lining the wall, a glass display case on the far wall houses the many awards HMT Enterprises has received. I know one of them is for an employee-friendly environment.

In preparation for today, I've done a lot of research about HMT Enterprises. They have quite a few technology patents and recently expanded into the residential space. Their main business, however, seems to be very high end, very sophisticated and very expensive commercial security systems.

Wesley Nichols, whom I'll be interviewing with, has been with the company for three years, quickly climbing his way up the corporate ladder. HMT is a privately-owned company, and I like that about them. They only have to answer to their board, not Wall Street. I'd read enough to know they are a very fair, very employee-friendly company to work for and offer a lot of free on-site benefits, such as a fitness center, a café and dry cleaning services.

With money being as tight as it is, free is good. Hopefully, I can land this job and I won't be so strapped. Maybe I can even think about going back to school to finish my education degree and I can eventually do what I've always dreamed of doing. Teach. It sure would be nice to fulfill one of the many dreams I had once upon a time.

A movement in my peripheral catches my attention. A very beautiful, very tall and very pregnant young woman is heading my way. "Ms. Kingsley, I'm Connie."

"Pleased to meet you," I say, rising from my plush chair.

As we walk—well, I walk, Connie waddles—down several long hallways, she chatters my ear off as if we're old friends. I like her instantly.

"As you can tell, I'm ready to pop any minute. My due date is in three weeks, but it could really be any day now, so we need to get my replacement hired ASAP. I'm going to be a stay-at-home mom since I just can't bear to leave my baby boy with anyone else. I told Wes to get on the stick earlier, but he dragged his feet, as usual. If you do get the job, you'll really have to stay on top of him. Deadlines, meetings, calendars, lunch. All that stuff. I like him, but he's pulled in so many directions and really is a bit of a scatterbrain, but he's a good boss. You'll like him too, I think."

We stop at a closed office door and Connie takes a big gulp of air, replenishing her lungs from her long tirade. "We're here."

She knocks and after a deep male voice gives her permission to enter, she opens the door and walks in, looking over her shoulder to ensure I'm following. The comforting smile she offers me eases my tension a bit.

My nerves must be visible. It took me several agonizing days to make my decision to apply for this position and finally get up the nerve to go to the DMV and get an official state ID. I've spent most of the last two years trying to keep a low profile, taking on relatively menial jobs where they didn't check your background or care that you didn't have a driver's license, but I'm tired of living paycheck to paycheck. So much time has passed that I feel it should be safe now to have a real job.

"Wes, this is your nine o'clock interview, Livia Kingsley."

A very handsome, thirty-something looking man stands and walks around the front of his desk holding his hand out to mine, which I take. "Ms. Kingsley, pleased to meet you."

"Pleased to meet you too, Mr. Nichols."

Glancing at Connie, he says, "Thanks, Connie. Now go get off your feet and take it easy."

"Gladly. Good luck," she murmurs excitedly as she walks by, closing the door behind her.

"Take a seat." Mr. Nichols gestures as he rounds his desk, sitting in his fancy leather, rolling desk chair. "Now, where did I put your resume?" he mumbles scanning his desk, which is in complete disarray with papers scattered everywhere. Connie may have understated the situation. It appears that Wesley Nichols is very disorganized. As Vice President of Research and Development, I'm not sure how he can afford to be.

"Here," I offer, handing over another copy I'd brought with me.

"Thank you." He smiles. "Point for you already."

I study him while he studies my resume. He really is quite handsome, with wavy light brown locks and long lashes framing his dark blue eyes. He's wearing smart-looking dark-framed glasses that make him look older than he probably is. His trim, athletic build makes it obvious he takes good care of himself. I also notice he's not wearing a wedding ring. Too bad he doesn't stir a thing down south. No one does anymore. I wish I could just move on and let a man fuck my brains out, but I can't. The only man that's stirred those feelings is a man I can never have again.

After a few quiet minutes of reviewing my skills and experience, which he had clearly *not* done before our meeting, he raises his eyes to mine. In a very unexpected and unprofessional move, he rakes them over my body, stopping too long on the swell of my breasts, which are clearly visible through the scant blouse. Suddenly I wish I'd worn something a little less...sheer.

"So, Livia...may I call you Livia?" I nod, and he continues. "There seems to be quite a gap in work experience here. Three years, to be exact. I don't see where you were attending college during that time period either."

It wasn't really a question, but a statement that demanded an answer nonetheless. One I'd been fully expecting.

"Yes, Mr. Nichols. I had to take some time off work. My father was diagnosed with pancreatic cancer and we didn't have the means to really afford home health or hospice care, so I had to quit my job to take care of him."

Number one rule when weaving your precarious web of lies... always sprinkle as much of the truth with it as possible. My father *had* gotten pancreatic cancer and we *couldn't* afford any care because he'd spent every penny he earned gambling, but that had been after I'd married Peter Wilder. I hadn't quit my job to take care of my father; instead I'd been sold to pay a debt to the mobster that my father owed hundreds of thousands of dollars to and couldn't pay, except with one of his daughters. Alyse, my younger sister, had been saddled with caring for our poor excuse of a father as he died a slow, painful death. For her sake, I'm glad he's gone. But if I had it my way, he'd still be alive, suffering, which is the least he deserves for the torture he put me through.

"I'm so sorry, Livia. I hope he's better."

"No, he passed last year." Also true. *And his selfish soul is rotting six feet under where he belongs.* My shrink would be none too happy to hear me think like that, but I can't help the way I feel. No amount of therapy will ever allow me to let go of my hatred for him and what his actions did to our family and so many others.

A sympathetic smile turns his mouth. "I'm very sorry for your loss. I lost my mother six years ago to lung cancer, so I can empathize."

"It gets better each day," I reply, trying to inject a little sadness into my voice when that's the last thing I feel.

A half hour later, I'm being escorted out of Wes's office—he insisted I call him Wes—with his hand at the small of my back, and I am told he'll be in touch shortly. The interview went well. I was sure I'd gotten the job, even though I didn't have much executive assistant experience. It helped that I could start right away. Dundee's, where I currently waitress, didn't need much notice. It wouldn't be a hardship to replace me.

An hour later, I walk into my quiet apartment and strip out of the borrowed attire, returning it to Addy's closet. I call Dr. Howard's office. Luckily she had a cancellation and can get me in tomorrow afternoon.

I have to work the late shift starting at five, and it wasn't quite noon, so I throw on a pair of sweats and crawl back into bed, hoping to get at least a couple hours of shut eye before I have to get ready.

Snuggling under the covers, I try to clear my thoughts of Gray, of Peter, of my father, of my fucked up life. Like every single day for the past five years, I try *not* to remember that I should be happily married to Gray Colloway and teaching third graders. I try *not* to imagine how beautiful our children would look with Gray's piercing hazel eyes and my dark hair and full lips. I repeat Dr. Howard's words: *One day at a time.* I try *not* to fall into that empty pit of lonely, murky, desolate despair when life hands you a shit deal and you're helpless to change it.

Instead, I try to be strong as sleep's fingers pull at my consciousness. Only I know my dreams will once again be filled with what could have been but will never be.

*Happiness.*

I'd thrown that chance away when I gave myself to the devil to save my sister from the same fate.

## Chapter 3

### Gray

"What the hell is up with you, man?" Asher asks.

*Plenty.*

"Nothing," I grumble.

Apparently not listening to a word I've said, he continues, "Bullshit. You haven't been acting like yourself for weeks. I've had to repeat myself three times already, and the Board of Director's meeting is in just two weeks. Did you even hear what I told you about a possible accounting discrepancy in the CFC business?"

"No, sorry. Go on."

Sighing and scratching my stubbly chin, I lean back in my chair and stare at my younger brother, Ash. He starts talking again, but I'm unable to focus, my attention elsewhere entirely. I watch his mouth move, but don't hear the words.

When our father, Frank Colloway, died several years ago, I took over his consulting business, which we now call Colloway Financial Consultants, CFC for short. Asher and Connelly, my younger twin brothers by a year, followed in my footsteps, both graduating with an undergrad and MBA in business and, together, we not only run my father's successful financial consulting business, we have substantially expanded it in a very short period of time. CFC was the initial company, but we've purchased two more in the last three years.

Asher is now CEO of CFC and Conn took over as CEO of Wynn Consulting, a Human Resources consulting firm that we acquired last year. A new security company we bought six months ago rounds out our three current companies under GRASCO Holdings, where I now act as Chairman of the Board.

At just thirty years old, there was no doubt I was young for my position, but there was also no one as driven to succeed as I am. I threw myself into my career, sometimes working eighteen hours a day, only to get up early the next day and do it all over again. One of the reasons I offered as many of the on-site amenities to my employees as I did is because I needed them. I eat, breathe and sleep this company, and I expect my employees to do the same. If you give them everything they need at work, free food, free gym, free dry cleaning, free on-site clinic, then they work harder and longer and are more loyal. It's a win-win for all, really.

In some strange way, I owe my success to Livia Kingsley. After the woman I loved more than life itself crushed my soul by disappearing the day after I proposed, never to hear from her again, I threw myself into my father's company and climbed the ladder quickly.

When my father died of a heart attack three years ago, the board easily named me CEO.

But my brother isn't wrong for questioning me. Ever since I laid eyes on Livia Kingsley two weeks ago at the Shedd Aquarium fundraiser, I've been a fucking emotional mess. She is all I can think about and it *is* affecting my attention at work. Truth be told, she has never been far from my thoughts and, in part, the reason I work as hard as I do is to eradicate her from my brain. And most of the time it works...until I lay in bed at night.

I went through all the gut-wrenching stages of grief and loss when she up and left me. At first, I simply didn't believe it was true. I repeatedly called her cell, her father, her sister, her friends, her work. I was relentless. Livvy loved me, she'd agreed to be my wife, there was no way she would simply desert me the very next day with no explanation. The note she left said she'd be back soon. She wasn't.

It didn't take me long to move onto anger, and fuck, was I ever. I told myself that if I ever saw her face again, I wouldn't be responsible for the vile and cruel things that would involuntarily spew forth. I was a sleeping volcano, seething with fury and rage and hate just below the surface and it was actively seeking an outlet.

I eventually hired a private detective to see if he could turn her up because I'd convinced myself something must have happened to her. I was sincerely worried about her safety, and I didn't believe the bullshit her father was trying to cram down my throat about her leaving of her own accord, that she'd changed her mind about marrying me. But it was like she was a fucking ghost. She was gone, with absolutely no trace. I constantly scanned the obits, convinced I would come across her name because the only way she would possibly leave me was through death.

After a bout of brief depression where I drank everything and fucked anyone I could get my hands on in a desperate, but failed, attempt to forget, I finally moved onto acceptance. That was, by far, the hardest part. I had to finally accept that it was *me*. That *I* wasn't good enough for Livvy, and she thought her only recourse was to flee. That was a very bitter, and ego-bruising pill to swallow.

"For the love of Christ, come find me when you get your head out of your ass," Ash complains as he slams my office door.

I ignore his outburst, turning my chair toward the glass windows that overlook the Chicago Loop, lost in thoughts of my angel. Every day of the past five years without Livvy in my life has been bleak and dark. The pain has lessened, but only marginally.

Over the past few years, I've tried not to think of the days that I was once happy. But since I saw Livvy a couple weeks ago, I've done nothing else *but* remember. As I stare out into the crystal blue sky, I let myself drift back to the first time I saw her.

*Conn, Ash and I walk into Rocky's, in my opinion one of the best pizza joints in Detroit. We're all home from college for the holidays and I'm happy to spend some time with them.*

*We're shown to a table and take a seat, looking over the menus that the hostess left with us, but I already know what I want. It's the same thing I get every single time I come here. Deep-dish pepperoni with black olives and green peppers. I may not be creative, but I certainly know what I like.*

*I hear her laugh first. It's deep and sensual and enthralls me like a siren's song. I look around to find the source that's stirring my dick. When my eyes settle on a waitress two tables down that I've never seen here before, I feel this strange buzzing in my chest. My God in heaven, she's stunning and I can only see her profile.*

*Then she leaves their table, turning our way. My breath catches and my dick hardens painfully when our eyes connect. This magnificent green-eyed, chocolate haired beauty is a siren and I will gladly follow her to the depths of the ocean, even if that means my certain death.*

*I'm not one of those guys that believes in love at first sight, but I guess even I can be proven wrong. There is something special about this creature. I don't know her name, I don't know her age, I don't know her hopes and dreams, I don't know if she's already spoken for,* but I do know this. I want to. I have to know every single thing about her. I've dated a lot of women. Fucked a lot of women. But I have never felt like this about any of them without even a word uttered between us.

Her steps slow briefly as she heads our way and I know she's also feeling the heat that's running hot between us right now. I feel like my skin is on fire and if anyone touches me, they'll get scorched.

My brothers quiet, following my gaze until the curvaceous vixen stops right in front of me. Her eyes leave mine and land on my brother Conn and my temper flares. Conn could charm the panties off of a woman with a simple scan of her body and a crook of his finger. I don't want her looking at my brothers. I only want her eyes on me.

"Hi. I'm Livia and I'll be taking care of you boys tonight. Can I start you with a round of beers, maybe?"

I can't help but notice she's avoiding all eye contact with me now as I continue to stare. I hear Conn and Ash talking, but I have no idea what they're saying or what the question was because I'm stuck back on her name. Livia. Sounds like the perfect name for my wife.

She walks away without another word in my direction and I follow her with my eyes until she rounds a corner and I can't see her anymore.

"Careful there, lover boy. You're going to scare her away if you keep looking at her like you want to eat her," Ash says while laughing.

"I do." I don't laugh, because I'm dead serious. I want to consume her.

Livia spends the rest of the evening trying to ignore me, but much to my brothers' chagrin, I ask her out repeatedly. And she repeatedly, but politely, declines. I know when a woman is playing hard-to-get, but Livvy isn't just playing. She is hard-to-get, which only makes me try harder.

What she doesn't understand though is that she snared my soul the second she stared into my eyes. If I didn't think she was interested, I would leave it alone, but I know she is. I see it with every shy stolen *glance. I see it in the flush of her skin. I see it in the flutter of her pulse when she's standing next to me.*

*I want her. Desperately. And my desperation makes me relentless.*

I smile remembering my feeble attempts to impress Livvy that first night backfired when I boasted that I would be finishing my undergrad in business at MIT that spring and would be applying at Wharton for my MBA. She told me I was arrogant and 'accidentally' spilled a glass of water on my lap when she was clearing the table, to which she barely apologized. My brothers laughed their asses off and told me I was losing my touch.

I was. She had me so flustered that night, so completely infatuated, that I was acting like a sixteen-year old trying to ask a girl out for the first time. It was embarrassing.

That evening, I left her a tip that was double the price of our meal, which I paid for the next night when I returned and asked for a seat in her area.

*When she sees me, she stops dead in her tracks for a moment or two, a slight blush creeping adoringly up her neck. She is not as unaffected by me as she'd like me to believe. Her mouth lied, but her eyes and body did not. And I would absolutely use that to my advantage.*

"I don't need your charity," she says caustically as she approaches my table.

*I can have any girl I want. I am young, smart, good-looking and rich, and someday destined to take over my father's business, along with my two brothers. But I don't want just anyone. I want her. I want this girl beyond any rational reason and I will not let up until I have her. In my bed and in my life.*

"It's a good thing I'm not a charitable person, then," *I reply, drinking in her essence as if it's the only thing keeping me alive. I'd gone twenty-four hours without looking into her mesmerizing eyes and I was starved for her. How I would go back to Massachusetts for my final semester after the holidays were over, I didn't have a clue.*

"Go out with me," *I state plainly.*

"Are you really that conceited or are you just stupid? I thought MIT was a college for smart people?"

I laugh, shaking my head. My God, I love her wit. "I'm that confident."

"I already told you I didn't want to go out with you," she huffs, but once again I call bullshit.

"I don't give up that easily, Livvy."

Anger causes her face to redden. "My name is Livia. Not Livvy."

"Tomorrow night. Just one date." My voice remains stoic and calm, but inside I am begging.

"I have to work tomorrow night."

"Then the night after that."

"Sorry. I have to work every night for the next six nights. Some of us need to make a living."

The rest of the meal she conducts her obligatory waitressing duties, asking if I'd like another beer, asking if I'm ready for the check, but refuses to make any more small talk or answer my question about when she would be free.

But she'd unknowingly given me a piece of information, which she'd regret the rest of the week. She'd given me her schedule. And it didn't matter how much pizza I had to eat or how many parties I had to miss, my ass would be planted in her section every night until she relented.

Every day I came in she softened a little more, gave up a little more information about herself and when she saw me there on the sixth night, I knew I finally had her.

"Aren't you getting sick of pizza yet?" she sighs, a small smile turning her gorgeous lips. Lips I desperately wanted wrapped around my cock.

"To tell you the truth, I'm really starting to fucking hate it," I tease, drawing a laugh from her. I will never forget it. My very first laugh.

"Then why do you keep coming back?"

"You."

*She looks at me thoughtfully, like she's trying to work out a puzzle. "What are you really after, Gray?" she sighs.*

*Wow. A smile, a laugh and the use of my name. I got a triple tonight. I'm hoping for a homerun and a "yes" to going out with me would get me there.*

*"You," I tell her sincerely.*

*She shakes her head. "You're a good-looking guy. You could have anyone you want. Why me?"*

*I'm a little taken aback at that question and her lack of confidence in herself. I try for humor but she just cocks a brow at my joke. "You think I'm good-looking?"*

*I try again, going with the blatant truth this time. "Why not you, Livvy? I find you extremely attractive, but there's something more about you, unique, different. And I have this visceral need to figure it out. There's white hot chemistry between us and I know you feel it too."*

*She hesitates before answering. "You're going back to school soon."*

*Excuses, excuses. "What are you really afraid of, angel?"*

*Her gaze drops momentarily to the floor before sweeping back up to mine. "We're very different, you and I."*

*If she means social status, I couldn't give a fuck. I don't care that I'm going to MIT and she's going to a community college. I don't care that she's a waitress and I'm being positioned to run a multi-million dollar company. I don't care about her address or the clothes she has on her back or what kind of fucking car she drives. I don't care about any of that. I care about her, but I can't tell her that without sounding like some crazy asshole that's just trying to get into her pants.*

*"I've heard opposites attract," I say instead.*

*She smiles and chuckles lightly, eyeing me shyly. "I don't sleep with a guy on the first date, so if that's what you're after then you might as well not come back."*

*I smile back. "Good. Neither do I." That's a lie, but I find that even if she wanted to end our first night together in bed, I'm not sure I would. It would demean the evening and her and I want far more from her than just sex. She just doesn't know it yet.*

*"Okay," she says quietly.*

*"Okay? Okay you'll go on a date with me?"*

*Her lips curl. "You've worked pretty hard for it so I guess I'll throw you a bone."*

*I lean back in my booth and grin. She stands there for long seconds smiling back at me before pulling out her little notepad and writing on it. She rips off the paper, handing it to me. Glancing down I see it's a phone number.*

*"This real?" I ask, shaking it in the air.*

*She laughs. God I'm already addicted to it. To her. "Yes. It's real. Well, ah, I guess I should get back to work."*

*"Okay. I'm going to call you later."*

*She nods and turns to leave, taking care of her other stations. For the next hour I watch her work, barely touching my pizza, barely drinking the beer sitting in front of me, because I can barely take my eyes from her. Whenever she catches me, she beams and it makes my heart soar.*

*Later when she brings me the check, I finally ask her what I've been dying to know all night. "So, ah...what date do you sleep with a guy on, then?"*

*Smiling, she answers, "I guess you'll know if you get there."*

After finally convincing Livvy to go on a date with me, the rest, as they say, is history. We clicked, like I knew we would, and spent every free minute together until I had to return to school three weeks later. I loved school, but being away from Livvy was excruciating and the last few months dragged by slowly. We talked and skyped daily. I came home as much as I could and she came to see me when her class and work scheduled allowed, although that was infrequent because she couldn't afford the plane tickets and was too prideful to let me pay. I hated it, but loved her all the more for it at the same time.

That's one of things that I ended up loving about Livia the most. She was extremely proud. Her mother left her when she was young.

Her father was a gambling addict and they had to struggle for everything they had. She was a born fighter. Livia worked hard to put herself through school because all she ever wanted to be was a teacher. I wonder if she's doing that now. Teaching somewhere. I hope so. She was always suited for that calling.

Once I moved back to Detroit that May, Livia and I were inseparable. We spent most nights at my apartment, because she still lived at home with her father and younger sister. I remember feeling insanely jealous when she insisted on sleeping at home, because I wanted her always with me where she belonged. But I also understood her need to spend time with Alyse, her younger sister, because her father did a piss poor job taking care of her.

Livia was the first serious relationship I ever had and I haven't had a serious relationship with any woman since because I am not whole and I never will be. I can't offer something of myself that isn't available. I am irreversibly damaged, a part of me dead and gone with her. I've done my fair share of dating recently—if you want to call it that—but with each slide between a woman's legs, I can still only imagine Livvy. I have base needs to sate, but I don't want the women I fuck. The only thing I really want is *her*.

When I felt the weight of a stare across the ballroom, the hair on the back of my neck prickled, and when our eyes connected, my breath stopped. She was alive. And seeing her in that tight, short black dress and those red fuck-me shoes gave me an instant hard-on.

Throughout the years, I'd often imagined I've seen Livvy. At a bar, at a restaurant, walking down the street. But it was never her. Having no choice, I left my date, Lena, in the dust and chased after her to see if *this* Livvy was real, but she ran. Just like she'd done so many years before. And once again, I was ruined.

The day after the fundraiser, I tried unsuccessfully to find her. If she has a phone number, it's unlisted. I've been struggling ever since on what my next step will be. I have this gut-wrenching, burning, instinctive need to find her. Now that I've seen her again, now that I know she's alive, I will not let Livia Kingsley off the hook that easily.

She owes me some fucking answers and I aim to get them. I don't know if she's living in the city, but when I told her I had moved to Chicago, she could not hide her surprise, so I have to believe she's here. Somewhere.

And since I can't find her on my own, I'm doing the only thing I can.

Bonnie, my admin's nasally voice, rang through the speaker. "Mr. Colloway, I'm sorry to bother you, but a Burt Jaffrey is on line one. He insists it's important."

"It's fine, Bonnie. I'll take it." Pressing the flashing light, I answer the call I'd been anxiously waiting for. "Burt, I have a job for you."

"Of course, Mr. Colloway."

"I need you to find a woman. Livia Kingsley. She doesn't appear to have a listed phone number and I can't find any type of account on social media. No Facebook, no Twitter, no LinkedIn accounts, but I do believe she's living in Chicago, or the burbs somewhere."

"Any other pertinent information?"

I relay her description, date of birth and give Burt Livvy's father's address as I last knew it.

As I place the phone back into the receiver, Bonnie's voice fills my office yet again. "Mr. Colloway, Ms. Ramsey's on line two."

Christ, I am in no mood to deal with Lena today. Or *ever*. Sensing I've been pulling away, she's been a stage five clinger these past two weeks, and it's time to cut her loose. I should have never have taken her to the fundraiser after she'd casually mentioned going to her parents for the holidays, which are still *months* away yet, but I loathe attending those events alone.

But I do with Lena what I've done with every other woman since Livvy. I use her. Judge me if you want, but she's just a warm body and a tight pussy, nothing else. I'm not serious about her in the slightest and it appears she's starting to hear the Wedding March, so it's time. Lena's just another stand-in for the woman that my mind pathetically won't let go.

They all are.

"Tell Ms. Ramsey that I'm busy for the remainder of the day. In fact, tell her I'll be out of the country on business for the next week."

"Of course, Mr. Colloway." Gotta love Bonnie. She does whatever I ask. No questions.

I don't really know what I'll do when I finally find Livvy. Because I *will* find her. I'll use every resource at my now extensive disposal to do so. I've pined after her memory for years and seeing her now, healthy and alive, my anger and hurt came back with renewed vengeance.

So when I sit down across from Livvy and force her to tell me why she left, will I finally be able to forgive her and get the closure I long for? Or will I strip her down and fuck her raw, like the visceral need inside clawed at me to do?

I despise myself for wanting her so much. Despite the fact that she ripped the beating heart out of my chest, after seeing her again... fucking her until she screams for me is all I can think about. All I want with a desperation that borders on obsession.

So...maybe I'll do both. Maybe I'll fuck her one more time so I can finally forget about the woman who ruined me so long ago. Maybe then I can finally stop seeing her face in every other woman I take.

Then I can walk away. *Will* walk away. My heart will remain unscathed because it's already dead. Mangled beyond all repair. *By her.*

But even as I think it, I know I can't do it. I know I'm lying to myself.

*Fuck her?* Absolutely.

*Walk away from her?* Not a hot chance in hell.

I already know that once I find her again, no matter the reason, I can't walk away from the one woman who, whether she knows it or not, whether she *wants* me or not, still owns every part of me. Regardless of why she left, regardless of the pain she's caused me, and regardless of if she's over me...I am *not* over her.

And I never will be.